MOONSHINE

PHANTOM QUEEN DIARIES BOOK 11

SHAYNE SILVERS
CAMERON O'CONNELL

ARGENTO
PUBLISHING

CONTENTS

Shayne Silvers & Cameron O'Connell

Moonshine

The Phantom Queen Diaries Book 11

A TempleVerse Series

ISBN 13: 978-1-947709-39-3

SHAYNE AND CAMERON

Shayne Silvers, here.

Cameron O'Connell is one helluva writer, and he's worked tire-lessly to merge a story into the Temple Verse that would provide a different and unique *voice*, but a complementary *tone* to my other novels. *SOME* people might say I'm hard to work with. But certainly, Cameron would never...

Hey! Pipe down over there, author monkey! Get back to your writing cave and finish the next Phantom Queen Novel!

Ahem. Now, where was I?

This is book II in the Phantom Queen Diaries, which is a series that ties into the existing TempleVerse with Nate Temple and Callie Penrose. This series could also be read independently if one so chose. Then again, you, the reader, will get SO much more out of my existing books (and this series) by reading them all in tandem.

But that's not up to us. It's up to you, the reader.

You tell us...

WITCHES AND WEREWOLVES AND REDNECKS, OH MY!

After surviving one Hell of a journey, Quinn MacKenna—black magic arms dealer turned demigoddess—was really looking forward to spending some quality time with friends. And maybe a beer. Unfortunately time is the only thing Quinn *doesn't* have, and all her friends are either missing, in hiding, or imprisoned—including her favorite bartender. Then again, after being gone a year and six months without sending so much as a postcard, what should she expect?

With the world having literally spun out of control since she last stepped foot in the mortal realm, Quinn finds herself wandering Boston, penniless and without a home. To make matters worse, it seems a very powerful, very mysterious someone has overthrown the powers that be and set something Wild loose in her city. Something determined to Hunt down every last soul Quinn cares about.

Unless she turns herself in before the next full moon.

Facing a decision she cannot afford to make and a deadline she cannot afford to miss, Quinn has no choice but to leave Boston in someone else's capable hands. Fortunately, if her adventures have taught her nothing else, it's that she can't do everything herself.

Which is why—when a pack of Missouri werewolves lead her to question the motives of a white witch—Quinn looks for an enchanting solution.

In the end, Quinn will be called upon to weigh the needs of her city against her own. But first, she will have to tap into a power she does not understand, reunite with some exceptionally Sick acquaintances, start a witch-hunt, and stop a massacre. And all before the next full moon—unless she wants to owe a certain goddess a debt that could take an eternity to repay.

Turns out being immortal isn't as much fun as Quinn thought it would be. But then, nobody ever said moonlighting as a deity would be easy—though they probably should have mentioned the tremendous sacrifices she'd be asked to make.

Like having to wear a freaking dress.

~

~

FOLLOW and LIKE:
    Shayne's FACEBOOK PAGE
    Cameron's FACEBOOK PAGE

We try our best to respond to all messages, so don't hesitate to drop us a line. Not interacting with readers is the biggest travesty that most authors can make. Let us fix that.

CHAPTER 1

I knew a philosophical drunk once who offered nuggets of what he called wisdom after tossing back his fourth cocktail, oblivious to the nuances of relevance or reception. Occasionally, that meant bastardizing dead celebrities like John Lennon or Oscar Wilde —insisting life was what happened when you were busy making plans, or that real friends stab you in the front. Usually it was more like listening to a grown man slur his way through a small batch of Hallmark cards. During one of his less inspired rants, he told me that home was a place you grew up wanting to leave and grew old wanting to get back to. It was a tidy, trite platitude that had stuck in my craw for years, if only because it lacked perspective. After all, shouldn't that depend on what you were leaving behind—not to mention what you'd be going home to?

Take me, for instance: the last two times I'd left Boston, I'd done so of my own free will—first trading in a grey winter's morning for a balmy Scottish coast, then again for a cottage made of candy in a storybook realm where gravity was negotiable, colors had a smell, and children were considered edible until proven otherwise. And yet, in neither instance had I thought to be gone for particularly long, or at least no longer than I had to be. Despite everything, Boston had always been my refuge, my sanctuary from a mad and callous world.

Indeed, I knew Boston so well it was like it belonged to me and me alone—as if the entire city was my sandbox and everyone else played in it at my leisure. Of course, a large part of that could be attributed to the hubris that comes with living anywhere long enough to call it home. But the rest was bloody well earned—a bevy of hard-won insights that I'd accumulated over decades. When I was younger, that meant knowing which venues had the laxest security, or which highways to avoid during rush hour, or which happy hours to take advantage of. In time, it meant knowing which logos to wear and when, which neighborhoods were heavily patrolled and why, and even which lowlifes to contact and how. For years now, I felt I knew Boston *better* than the back of my hand because the term "skin deep" simply didn't apply; I could trace the city's bones. Hell, I could map its very veins.

Or at least I used to be able to.

Unfortunately, without a watch to account for hopping between such obscenely different time zones over a span that I'd barely been able to track, it seemed my late arrival had bypassed fashionable and gone straight to dickish. Metaphorically speaking, I wasn't the girl showing up as the appetizers hit the table so much as the girl banging on the door of a dark, empty restaurant begging to be let in. Actually, it was worse than that; I was the shellshocked girl gaping at the newly erected bowling alley where the restaurant used to be.

Because that's what happens when you're gone for eighteen freaking months.

A year and a half, that's how long I'd been away—a fact I'd discovered perhaps an hour after Charon, the boatman of the river Styx, dropped me off along an abandoned stretch of dock outside Boston Harbor just after sunrise. Of course, the hoary bastard was long gone by then; he'd zipped away in the fancy, magical ship I'd procured for him in exchange for the ride and my contraband goods, saluting me with a beer as though he knew precisely what fresh hell awaited me. But then, I supposed he *was* the expert.

Still, I'd have to pick a bone with him later.

On that note, do you have any idea what all gets taken away from you when you've been essentially missing for a year and six months —especially if you have no immediate family to speak of? Spoiler alert: it's shit you'll want back. Like your apartment, for example, or all your worldly possessions, or your freaking *life*. I had to admit, though, none of that bothered me as much as the fact that the Tobin Bridge had finally been fixed, or that they'd added two new metro stops to the orange line, or that we'd lost several dynastic football players to bullshit free agency. Basically, the fact that my city had somehow survived my absence.

Of course, you know what they say about reality.

She can be a real bitch, sometimes.

Take my choice of accessories, for example. In the afterlife, toting around a spear with enough juice to redefine a landscape would have earned me some respect. In Boston, it was far more likely to earn me a deadly weapons charge. Mercifully, I'd had enough wherewithal to shove Areadbhar into the collapsible guitar gig bag I'd stolen from under the nose of a leering store clerk not long after arriving. Not my proudest moment, obviously, but I could handle a little shame. Getting stopped by Boston PD for walking around with a glorified javelin in hand and not a single form of identification on me? Not so much.

In hindsight, of course, I should have known better than to pop back into the mortal realm without an ID, not to mention at least one working credit card. But then, after surviving the combined perils of the Otherworld, the Fae realm, the Eighth Sea, and the godsdamned afterlife, it hadn't occurred to me to worry about anything as insignificant as money or credentials. After all, I was Quinn MacKenna, part-time goddess, full-time badass—rightful wearer of Brynhildr's legendary Valkyrie armor, wielder of the mighty and terrible Areadbhar, and defender of the not-so-innocent.

Who needed your freaking driver's license when you could take out a city block on a whim?

The short answer? My bank. My mortgage lender. My cell phone provider. The storage facility holding all my shit hostage, the new owner of my beloved apartment, *and* the unfamiliar building manager who threatened to call the cops on me for losing my shit on said owner. In essence, the list included anyone who'd never actually met or talked to me before...and even that was beginning to feel generous.

In the end, without a phone and with increasingly limited options, I'd begun a pilgrimage from one local haunt to another in search of familiar faces. First, I'd thought to visit Christoff, my long-time friend and bartender, at his popular pop-up bar. Once there, I figured I could at least beg for a drink to take the edge off and maybe even enough money to see me through the next few days. Unfortunately, I found the bar closed indefinitely for renovations. I'd briefly considered going by his house, but—assuming he was even home— the Russian werebear lived out in the suburbs and was therefore too far to reach on foot before dusk. Besides, he had two cubs at home; unsupervised, my nocturnal neighbor was a liability I was loath to force on anyone, much less a single father and his children.

Indeed, with that contingency in mind, I'd tried a trendy boutique next; the witches who owned it were survivors by nature and owed me a favor. Plus, they'd been in the process of refurbishing their magical supply shop when I'd disappeared, including an upstairs living space I could potentially take advantage of. Unfortunately, when I arrived the storefront remained only half-finished, the murky glass of its unpainted basement door dominated by a single sheet of pink paper I didn't need to read to know what it heralded.

For a long moment, I'd lingered outside, fretting over the fate of Camila and her brother, Max—the brujo I'd helped rescue from the clutches of a mad scientist back in Helheim—before rebuking myself for wasting precious time. Even if the Velez siblings *were* in some kind of financial trouble, it wasn't like I could do anything about it. If I wanted to help them, my best bet was to get up to speed and back on my feet as quickly as inhumanly possible.

Which, of course, was what had brought me here—to quite possibly the last place on Earth anyone would want to approach like a beggar with their hand out. Why? Because some hosts are better than others, for one thing, and because some favors cost a hell of a lot more depending on to whom they are owed. And so I lingered on a familiar stoop, shifting from one foot to the other as I studied the nameplate which represented my last hope in the world of finding a legitimate place to sleep that wasn't a park bench or one of the shelters downtown—assuming my inner goddess would even let that happen, or that the volunteers at the shelter would sign off on a homeless redhead in designer threads carrying a bejeweled spear that occasionally followed me about like a poltergeist.

After parsing through every alternative option—and with a very heavy sigh—I knocked on the door of the law office of *Hansel, Hansel, and Gretel.* I held my breath, wary of any Faeling shenanigans that might ensue. As a front for the Faerie Chancery, this quaint, unassuming townhome tended to ward off even the most ardent of evangelists and savviest of sales folk.

Of course, there was being cautious, and then there was being prepared.

Before I could knock a second time, the door swung open and a hand the size of a baseball mitt latched onto my sleeve, yanking me into the office's gloomy interior hard enough to pull my damned arm nearly out of its socket. Frustratingly, the Valkyrie armor I'd retrieved from Charon—locked in its current, far more casual state until I said otherwise—did nothing to ease the painful sensation. Sadly, I'd had to forego the armor's substantial fringe benefits in order to avoid walking around Boston looking like I'd robbed the Renaissance Faire.

"Fee-fi-fo-fum, I smell the blood of an Irishman. No, wait, that's not right..." The voice was deep and inhuman, so gravelly it might as well have come from a talking rock. It was also achingly familiar. Three gurgling sniffs sounded before I could say as much, however, each inhale like the crank of a diesel engine. "A woman. An Irish woman. Fee-fi-fo-fum, I smell the blood of—"

"Paul?" I interrupted, squinting to make out my old friend's hulking shape in the dim, windowless room. "Paul, is that ye?"

"Who asks my name?"

"It's me, Quinn!"

"Quinn?" Paul fumbled about in the dark, sending at least two urns crashing to the floor, followed by what sounded eerily like a brass gong being struck so hard it shattered in two. The noise was both deafening and cringeworthy. By the time Paul finally found a candle and lit it, my eyes had already adjusted enough to see the bridge troll in all his hairy, hulking glory.

Standing several feet taller than me and as broad through the shoulders as I was long, Paul was one of the very few Faeling friends I had here in Boston who made me feel tiny. Of course, at six feet without so much as a kitten heel to prop me up, being dwarfed by anyone was a rather rare occurrence. Once, I'd have given anything to be smaller. More petite. The sort of girl who could scan a room full of men without having to clock the ones whose heads cleared the fray. The sort of girl who could tolerate sitting in the backseat of a cramped car or could fly coach without wanting to stab everyone in sight. These days, however, I appreciated the perks more than I despised the drawbacks. There were merits in having a longer reach, after all—not to mention being able to intimidate people without speaking.

In that respect, Paul was a master.

The bridge troll stared down at me with his filmy, jaundiced eyes, his protruding tusks gyrating as though he were chewing bubblegum, looming like a terrifying statue made of sinew and green skin. Unfortunately, I wasn't able to read his expression; most trolls were notoriously dim-witted, mercantile creatures who had trouble expressing themselves outside the context of tax collection, and Paul was hardly an exception. His understanding of the world was frustratingly child-like. When he lost, he got angry. When he won, he became insufferable. And, when you refused to pay his toll, he had a habit of bashing away at whatever happened to be nearby.

Like a brand-new car, for example.

That was how we'd met. Since then, he'd become the sort of companion every girl can appreciate: a bestial shadow capable of unimaginable violence if provoked. In fact, back when I was first starting out on my own as an antiquities dealer and working out of some of Boston's less gentrified neighborhoods, I used to have him follow me around at night as a precaution. I could still recall how his musk saturated the air in those days; I called it the world's most effective rape repellant. In time, we became something like friends. It was Paul who first told me of the Chancery, long before I could coax the truth out of Ryan—my only other Faeling acquaintance at the time. The bridge troll had confided a great deal to me over the years, going so far as to describe an alien world. A world I'd ached to know more about.

"What's wrong?" I asked, breaking the silence. "Kelpie got your tongue?"

A gasp of surprise sounded over my shoulder before Paul could answer, and I turned to find the infamous Gretel of storybook fame ogling me from across the room. The German woman was dressed in a flimsy nightie that made her look impossibly waifish and more than a little frail; with her long grey hair and puckered skin, I'd have put the fairytale heroine north of seventy if I didn't already know she had to be hundreds of years older than that.

"Surprised to see me?" I asked, grinning like a madwoman to be greeted by yet another familiar face, even if that face did belong to the Chancery's chief litigator.

"Well, yes, I—" she began, her face pale in the lamplight.

"Oy! Guess what?" I interjected, cheerily. "I stayed in that old gingerbread house of yours not too long ago. Well, not yours, obviously. The one where ye murdered that witch. The creepy place with all the candy and chains." I shook my head at the memory. "Hated every minute of it. Smelled like roasted marshmallows and barbecue."

"You stayed in the...but that isn't...I mean..."

"What's wrong?" I asked, cocking an eyebrow. "Look, I know I've been gone for a while...hell, a long while. But ye look like you've seen a freakin' ghost."

"You are a ghost," Paul interjected.

"Do I look like a ghost?"

Paul squinted at me, then turned to Gretel for support.

"My experience with ghosts is limited," Gretel admitted. "But I believe she is a living creature. A doppelganger, perhaps. Or a changeling. One can never be certain."

"What the hell are ye two on about?" I asked, more amused by their take than anything. "It's me, Quinn MacKenna! Paul, you're seriously tellin' me ye don't recognize me?"

"Quinn?"

This time my name was whispered, not barked. The bridge troll reached out a hand big enough to squeeze around my entire waist and brushed his fingers against my hair, my fiery tresses flowing over his knuckles. I let him, marveling at how long my hair had gotten since I'd last thought to cut it; I'd been too busy to notice until now. Paul hunkered down and shoved his massive face in close, sniffing at me like a dog. He drew back, flashed me a toothy grin that would have scared the shit out of me had I never seen it before, and roared.

"Quinn is alive!"

The bridge troll picked me up by the waist and crushed me to his chest, squeezing with enough force to make a chiropractor wince. I wheezed out a command to put me down, but he ignored it and began swinging me about the room as though we were dancing. Eventually, he slowed and loosened his grip enough so that I could pat him on his bulky shoulder.

"Glad to see ye, too, big fella. Now, what's this about me bein' alive?"

"Ah, well..." Gretel coughed into her fist, her face tight with concern and perhaps a small measure of fear. "I'm sorry to be the one to tell you this, Ms. MacKenna, but you are supposed to be dead."

CHAPTER 2

Though my experience was admittedly limited, I'd always assumed the difference between filing a missing person's report and a death certificate was the presence of a corpse —or at the very least an extremely suggestive crime scene. You know, like a carpet stained with more blood than anyone could survive losing or a charred skeleton among the wreckage of a smoldering car. Without one or more of these things, I'd have thought people like me were far more likely to be labeled Missing in Action than Dead on Arrival—our names splashed across milk cartons, not chiseled in stone. And yet, here we were, discussing my existence as though it were up for debate.

"As I told ye before," I said through gritted teeth, my patience wearing thinner with every fruitless exchange, "the rumors of me death have been greatly exaggerated."

I took a sip of the earthy tea Gretel had brewed before we "retired" to her office—her word, not mine. For some reason, her use of the expression made me want to curl up and take a nap in the leather armchair she'd offered. Or perhaps the dim lighting was to blame; I could hardly make out a single book title on the shelves that lined the walls. Gretel blamed the gloomy interior on a recent aversion to light—something to do with headaches—but there was a caginess to her explanation, a slight hitch in her body language, that suggested there was more to it. Still, I didn't pry; given how long I'd gone without makeup, I could appreciate a little mood lighting.

"Yes, that much is obvious, Ms. MacKenna," Gretel replied, halfheartedly. The old bird slid her dainty glasses up the bridge of her nose, still perusing the folder with my name scribbled across the top. Fortunately, she appeared far less gaunt now that she'd thrown on a plush robe and slippers—thereby completing her Ebenezer Scrooge ensemble just in time to start spewing negativity everywhere she went.

"Then why d'ye keep insistin' otherwise?"

"Because I have it on good authority that you were sighted on the other side, including confirmation from multiple witnesses. It's all right here."

I settled back in my chair and eyed the manila folder, struck by the sheer amount of paperwork it contained. And not just paperwork, either. I'd spotted what looked like a surveillance photo tucked away amongst the detritus. In it, I was crossing the street in an outfit I hadn't worn since returning from my brief stint in New York City, my hair infested with butterfly clips, the crimped ends descending onto my shrug sweater like crinkle paper at my very own pity party.

"What else does me file say?"

"Nothing that would surprise you." Gretel snapped the folder shut as though that didn't send a directly contradictory message, the wrinkled corners of her mouth crinkling in a disapproving scowl. "We like to document the activities of our members and their associates, that's all."

"I remember," I replied, recalling the intelligence gathering role that Robin—a Redcap I'd befriended some time ago—had played when we first met. Of course, that still didn't explain the potential blackmail material Gretel had in her possession. "Just how long has the Chancery been keepin' tabs on me, exactly?"

Gretel's scowl deepened.

"I saw the photo."

"Ah." Gretel reopened the file, found the picture, and sighed. "This photograph isn't what it seems."

"Then what is it? Because it looks like the Chancery has been spyin' on me for over a decade and change."

"In a manner of speaking, I suppose that's correct. But it's not what you think. Please, allow me to explain."

I gave her the go ahead with a gesture.

"As I am certain you'll recall, the Huntress once made it her mission to look after you, per an arrangement with your mother. Unfortunately, she had other obligations when you were growing up which made doing so far more difficult than she'd anticipated. Eventually, she enlisted those of us she felt she could trust to keep an eye on you from a distance. Hence the photograph. There's also the occasional unflattering report card. Oh, and the expulsion letter from your school principal. Is it true you went after your math teacher with a club?"

"Please," I scoffed. "It was a yardstick, and he deserved it. Now, quit tryin' to change the subject."

"Very well. In any case, it wasn't long afterwards that the Huntress told us to stop. At the time, I thought she'd either fulfilled her bargain, or she'd given up. Later, I realized it was because she wanted you off the Chancery's radar. And it worked, too, for a time. Which is why the majority of what's here are simply secondhand accounts of your exploits. News articles, security footage, and witness statements, mostly."

"News articles?"

"Auction sales. Missing or stolen items. A certain New York City bridge under construction after..." Gretel turned a page in the file and cocked an eyebrow, "an 'unprecedented' climate event. Anything we could link to you, either directly or indirectly, is here."

This was all news to me, and I let it show on my face. Not the bit about Scathach—more commonly known as the Huntress—

shielding me from the Chancery's numerous intrigues; I'd known about that for some time now. But the notion that the Faerie Chancery had been busy cataloguing my failures and achievements felt too much like finding out I'd been spied on in the shower or photographed in my underwear. Did either Scathach or Robin know that the file existed? And where the hell were those two? I'd expected to be reunited with them by now—especially once they realized I'd come to them for help.

"Who were the statements taken from?" I asked half-heartedly in an effort to keep the conversation going while I gathered my thoughts.

"Which ones?"

"All of 'em? I'm not sure what they say."

"Let's see..." Gretel began flipping through the folder's contents. "Here's one. Looks like a brief description of what happened in the forest outside Ipswich, taken from a tribe of local dryads. And another from a Russian *mavka*. Seems you were seen cutting the line of an establishment with direct connections to the Sanguine Council. And of course, we have multiple records of the incident during our Highland Games. Your sudden disappearance caused quite a stir."

"I'll bet it did."

"We investigated, of course," Gretel assured me. "But our agents found no concrete evidence of foul play."

"Should've looked harder," I grumbled before waving that away; there was no sense getting into what had happened to me immediately after my abduction. First of all, I didn't owe Gretel an explanation for my disappearance any more than I did for what had gone down between myself and the witches of Ipswich, or why I'd sought out an unsanctioned audience with the Master of Moscow. Secondly, her little dossier made me want to hoard what few secrets I had left—if only to maintain a mere semblance of privacy. "That's water under an otherworldly bridge."

"Pardon?"

"Nevermind." I took a deep breath, "So, accordin' to your file there, I'm dead. I don't suppose ye would care to tell me who I have to blame for the mixup?"

"I'm sorry, Ms. MacKenna. That is privileged information."

"Meanin' ye have eyes and pointed ears in the underworld, as well," I replied, thoughtfully. "I didn't realize the Chancery's reach extended quite that far."

Gretel's polite smile remained fixed, unwavering.

"I'll admit I did cross over," I confessed. "But that was more of an...out of body experience than an actual death. I was goin' after Ryan. Ryan O'Rye."

"You say that like I should know who that is."

Now, it was my turn to frown.

"He used to be a Chancery member, before he returned to Fae and became the Winter Queen's latest Jack Frost."

"Oh right, yes, that terrible business with the Faenappers. I apologize. My memory is not quite what it once was."

I cocked an eyebrow, surprised by the admission; Gretel had been the Chancery's chief litigator for decades, perhaps even centuries. Memory lapses weren't something an individual in her position suffered from, let alone admitted to. Of course, it was also possible she'd simply blocked it out. The "business" Gretel was referring to had been especially gruesome, including an investigation into the disappearance of Faelings who'd left behind limbs and bodily fluid like gory breadcrumbs. In the end, the whole mess had led me north on a literal witch-hunt that had ended only when Max, myself, and the Faelings who had survived their captivity escaped the clutches of those responsible—namely Ryan and Doctor Victor Frankenstein.

Both had died at my hands recently.

"Ms. MacKenna?"

"Aye?" I perked up, realizing I'd tuned her out. "Sorry, what was that ye were sayin'?"

"I asked if your so-called experience was a pleasant one, but there's no need to get into all that. I can see by your face that it was not." Gretel peeled away her glasses and stared at me, weighing me with her gaze. Her crystal blue eyes sat in a nest of wrinkled flesh, and I realized she looked perhaps a decade older than she had when we first met.

On a hunch, I reached out with my senses, channeling that alien part of me which had ascribed sensations to gods and scents to giants. It was harder to do here in the mortal realm than it had been on Circe's island, but I'd been practicing; I knew it had something to do with peering beyond the veil, that to master it meant peeling away layers of reality. I leaned forward in my chair and tried to see past Gretel. To see *through* her. In seconds, a peculiar smell rode the air. Something smoky, like the scent of a burning candle wick. I felt dry leaves under my fingertips, brushing my skin like wadded paper set to ignite. The combination of the two sent a shiver up my spine.

"Is everythin' alright?" I asked.

Gretel's smile wilted, replaced by the same distressed expression she'd worn when she first saw me. "A great deal has changed since you left, you know."

"That's why I'm here," I admitted. "I need information."

"Just information? Or shelter? You have an air of homelessness about you."

"Do I?" I glanced down at myself, then at the sagging guitar case propped against the arm of my chair. "Is it the strugglin' musician accessory?"

"Not entirely," Gretel replied, her lips twitching in the ghost of a smile. "Mostly it's intuition. You could not have been in town long, and yet you have come here of all places. What else would bring you to the Chancery's door so soon?"

"Maybe I just wanted to see some of me friends."

"If that were true, you would be visiting the Soviet expat whose bar you used to frequent, or perhaps the federal agent you grew up with."

My eyebrows shot up of their own volition at the mention of Jimmy Collins—an FBI agent and former flame who'd joined up with a task force dedicated to investigating cases that defied human limitations. I hadn't expected Gretel to make that particular connection, but I supposed I shouldn't have been surprised; if they'd had eyes on me for as long as all that, they'd have evidence linking me to the man.

Assuming you could even call him that, anymore.

After being brought back to life with the help of a god—long story—Jimmy had become something other than human. Not long after, he'd joined up with the Sickos, many of whom were plagued with similar circumstances. Unfortunately, thinking about that ragtag group of misfits reminded me of the clock that had started ticking the second I stepped foot in the mortal realm, of the deal I'd made with a goddess. One month. That's how long I had to find Hilde, the Valkyrie on loan to the Sicko squad, before I was forced to serve the Norse goddess, Freya, in her stead.

"Ms. MacKenna?"

"Ye know," I replied, rising out of the mire of my own thoughts, "Robin always praised your information network, but I'm startin' to t'ink they just had a really capable spymaster."

Gretel bowed her head.

"Anyway," I continued, "you're right. There are others I could turn to. But this is really more of a two birds situation. While I could certainly use a place to stay, I'm also dealin' with some...growin' pains that the Fae may be best equipped to handle."

"Growing pains?"

"Let's just say I've got more power than I know what to do with and could really use some advice. I assumed the Chancery's got some ancient geezers among its members, which means it's at least possible someone here has had experience with this sort of t'ing. Plus, without your help, I could cause a bit of a stir here in Boston without meanin' to."

"How big of a stir?"

"Depends," I replied, shrugging. "The last time it got out of control, I started a bar fight in Valhalla. And that's assumin' I ever really have it under control, which is a bit of a stretch."

"And you know how we feel about exposure," Gretel added, eyes narrowed. "This is beginning to sound more like blackmail than a request."

"Consider it a request with teeth. Look, I've bargained with the Fae before. In my experience, the only way to get what ye want from 'em is to make sure they feel like they're gettin' the better end of the deal. I'm askin' for sanctuary, but the Chancery should know it's in their best interest to grant it. How ye spin that decision when ye pass it up the chain is up to ye, but it *is* the right one."

"I see," Gretel replied, steepling her fingers. "Well, Ms. MacKenna, I would be glad to aid you in any way I can. I still owe you a personal debt for agreeing to save the missing Fae. But I am afraid the answer to your request to stay with us is no."

"No?" I spluttered. "What d'ye mean, 'no'?"

"I mean we are not in the business of providing sanctuary for fugitives, Ms. MacKenna, no matter who they are or what they've done for our organization in the past. We are a small community and taking you in would put us at considerable risk."

"A fugitive? From whom?" I gripped the leather armchair until it squeaked, outraged by the thought of being turned away. "And what the hell d'ye mean 'considerable risk'?"

"Please keep your voice down," Gretel hissed, glancing nervously past my shoulder as though she expected some vengeful god to appear at any moment and smite us both for exchanging blasphemous one-liners.

"Tell me why, and maybe I will."

"Because we would not want anyone getting curious and checking on us, that's why. As things stand, you are absurdly fortunate Paul was the one who found you knocking on our door. Anyone else, and we would not be having this conversation."

"And why is that?"

"Because almost anyone else would have contacted the Adjudicators first thing. Paul, however, remains loyal to you, as do several others who feel they owe you their lives."

"The Adjudicators?" I shook my head to clear it, frustrated to note that every answer Gretel gave only spawned more questions. "Why would lettin' Scathach and Robin know I'm back be a problem?"

"It wouldn't, assuming they were still in charge."

"Wait, what the fuck does that mean?"

Gretel searched my face as if gauging my reaction, unwound her fingers, and sighed. "I did tell you a lot has changed in your absence. Tensions are especially high, right now. Indeed—"

"Hold on, please. None of this is makin' any sense. Who the hell is in charge, if not those two?" A thought occurred to me. "Don't tell me Morgause and Sir Bred returned?"

"Sadly, no. We still have no word from either of the Arthurians. Not since they left for Fae, at least. No, the two individuals currently appointed are named Albi and Liam. I believe you've met the former."

Gretel made a disgusted noise in the back of her throat, but I was too busy trying to sort through the implications of what she'd told me to comment—though truthfully I felt the same way; Albi was a sleazy, morally bankrupt loan shark who just so happened to look like a clean-cut version of the demented bunny-man from *Donnie Darko*. Faeling or not, I knew a thug when I met one. Fortunately, Gretel must not have needed to hear me say it out loud to know my thoughts.

"I must confess I, too, never imagined I would witness the day when a Pooka and a Gancanagh were responsible for maintaining order," Gretel admitted, eyes downcast.

I swallowed, disturbed by the idea of Albi doling out punishments—because that's what the Adjudicators were all about; as representatives of a decidedly antiquated form of justice, the Adjudicators didn't so much rule the Chancery as police it. They weren't exactly the jury, but they were the judge and executioner. And with Albi on the bench, I had a feeling corruption was at an all-time high.

"But then," Gretel went on, tilting her head, "I suppose they are merely figureheads answering to a higher authority."

"And whose authority would that be?"

"A being unlike any I have ever encountered," Gretel replied, scrutinizing my face as though my expression might betray me, somehow. "She calls herself Catha, and she's very, very interested in you."

"In me?"

"Indeed, even after we passed along our latest report, she adamantly refused to accept you were dead. It was she who chased off Scathach and imprisoned both Robin and his supporters. She who appointed such unfit replacements. You see, that is why I cannot help you, Ms. MacKenna. The truth is that this city is no longer the Chancery's to supervise. Boston belongs to her, and her alone."

CHAPTER 3

Roughly around noon, I found myself crouched outside a bodega watching a dark-skinned Latina woman hand over a roll of cash to an uncommonly tall, absurdly broad-shouldered man wearing a hooded jacket that hid his face. In exchange, the woman received a mason jar filled with a thick, inky liquid that reminded me vaguely of tar. She casually slipped the container into her purse, but I had no doubt something sketchy was taking place; nothing prosaic was ever bought with a wad of bills in a dingy dime store in the heart of Mattapan. Of course, the woman I was spying on wasn't exactly ordinary, herself, so I supposed I shouldn't have been surprised.

But she, at least, might be willing to help me.

Gretel, on the other hand, had proven far less amenable; while we'd spoken for a good long stretch following her initial revelations, she'd still refused my request for sanctuary. Worse, she hadn't been able to answer my most pressing questions—like who this Catha person actually was, where she'd come from, or what her motives were.

Apparently, Catha cultivated an air of mystery around herself so thick that not even Gretel's spies had been able to peer through it.

Indeed, according to the Chancery's litigator, Boston's self-appointed overlord came and went as she pleased without warning, subject only to her own whims—which included the curious obsession with yours truly.

"She refuses to explain her actions, or her decrees," Gretel had gone on to say. "Queries of any sort are either met with silence, or worse, violence."

She subsequently had informed me that Robin had been overthrown in a bloodless coup only to end up beaten and jailed for sedition a few days later. Unfortunately, that was as much as Gretel had been able to tell me about the Redcap; where he'd been taken, or what they'd done to him since, was anyone's guess.

"Catha expects us all to submit to her will and embrace subservient roles. And most have done just that."

"But why?" I had asked. "What hold could she possibly have on ye?"

"On me? Nothing. My brothers and I are more like...independent contractors. We're Fae-touched, but ultimately human. All but a few of the Fae exiles, however, submitted immediately. She has a power over them that neither I nor they can explain."

"That is strange," I acknowledged, wondering how the hell that was possible. Perhaps Catha was an agent of the Faeling royals? Or some outsider with the ability to manipulate the Fae to their own ends? Whichever, Catha should never have been able to waltz right in and take over without inciting a full-on power struggle. "Wait, what about Scathach? I can't imagine her rollin' over without puttin' up one hell of a fight."

"I would have said so, too. But no, the Huntress ran mere hours after Catha arrived. Before she left, she told me she couldn't risk what would happen with 'her' here. It was my understanding at the time that she and Catha had a prior relationship of some kind. But beyond that, she refused to say. And you? Do you have any idea who Catha might be? Some specter from the Huntress' past, perhaps?"

"I have no idea," I admitted, utterly thrown by the idea that my former mentor would leave the Chancery—not to mention Robin—

to the mercy of some foreign invader. "Of course, I wouldn't say I knew Scathach all that well. She likes her secrets more than most. What I do know is that she's been around a long, long time. From what I've been able to glean, she's dealt with all sorts of sketchy people. Mercenaries, pirates, monster hunters, St. Louis natives...ye name it. Catha could be any one of the above, or none at all."

"Ah, well that is a shame."

"Aye, sorry." I bit my lip, thinking furiously. "But wait, ye said there were others who resisted? Exiles who weren't under Catha's spell, or whatever it may be."

"Yes. Many of them sided with Robin and were similarly apprehended. Those who continue to reject Catha's authority, but either did not or could not fight, have gone...underground."

"Does it get more underground than this place?" I asked. I cocked an eyebrow, finding it hard to believe anywhere was more clandestine than an unassuming business front which stood guard over subterranean tunnels, ornate bathhouses, a freaking speakeasy, and who knew what else. "Are ye tellin' me there are more of these in town?"

"There are other safe houses in the older neighborhoods, yes. Not as expansive or well-stocked as this one, admittedly, but the first generation of Fae exiles were practical creatures. They built many such shelters when this city was young in the unlikely event mortals ever discovered their existence. Assuming they haven't been compromised, those hideouts should provide adequate shelter."

"Ye t'ink it's possible they've been rounded up already," I noted, catching her defeatist tone.

"No, but..."

"Ye t'ink someone will talk, eventually."

"Despite my best efforts, the Chancery is an organization founded on principles of fear. Fear of exposure, fear of isolation, fear of exclusion. They were driven from their homes to a world that promised them nothing but pain and discomfort. Contrary to popular myth, the Fae are not social creatures by nature. They band together to wage war or to celebrate, but they largely disdain civilization. The Chancery as a concept was a concession made under unforgiving circumstances. You saw this for yourself, as I recall, when you prompted us to appoint the Huntress and the Redcap."

"Without someone to answer to, your members were goin' out of control," I recalled. "But I'm not sure whether that answers me question."

"The short answer is yes; I believe someone will talk. Someone hoping to curry favor or to avoid punishment, or perhaps even out of spite or malicious intent. There is no way to know for sure the reason why. The only question that matters is when."

Part of me considered reaching across the desk to pat the old broad on the shoulder, if only to give her some momentary comfort. But the way she kept switching between collective pronouns made me wonder where her motivations lay—whether she was working for the new regime or rooting for the old. If the former, then she was committing treason of a sort simply by talking to me. After all, if this Catha really was in charge and she wanted me that badly, I was a sitting duck.

"To be clear, which side of the fence are ye on?"

"Pardon?"

"I'm askin' where your allegiances lie."

"I think that should be obvious. I'm a lawyer, which means I am on no one's side. Alternatively, I am on everyone's side." Gretel's eyes twinkled with amusement for a moment so brief I thought I might have imagined it. "It's all about the argument, you see. A case could be made that it would be best for me—especially in the short term—to hand you over to this Catha creature. On the other hand, behaving like you were never here also has merit. There are some among the exiles, like Paul, who would be very upset to learn you were taken. It could result in further, more violent action on their part."

That made me frown. "D'ye actually believe this will all be solved peacefully?"

"It is not my belief, no. But it is my hope."

"Hope isn't the most reliable commodity," I countered. "Personally, I prefer leverage."

"As do I, but sometimes hope is all we have. Especially once one's position of strength has eroded." Gretel glanced at the clock on the wall and sighed. "Loathe as I am to admit it, very few of my people report to me anymore. Catha has...requisitioned them in her search for you and those few who continue to speak out against her. Which is why I'm afraid I must ask you to leave, and preferably before one of her lackeys discovers us."

Gretel gestured for us to rise.

"Hold on," I protested as I rose and hoisted the gig bag over one shoulder, still miffed at the thought of being turned out despite Gretel's seemingly legitimate reasons for doing so. "Ye never said what Catha wants from me."

"I confess I have no clue what she wants from any of us, beyond compliance. But I cannot imagine it would end well for us if she were to learn the Chancery harbored you for any length of time. Catha is exceedingly prone to violence, and her temperament is not what I would call even-keeled."

"So, ye aren't goin' to tell her I stopped by?" I asked, suspiciously. "Once I'm gone, I mean?"

"Of course not. It would hardly be in my own self-interest to admit I allowed you to come and go unmolested. Besides, I owe you a debt for what you did for us in a time of need. You may consider this conversation, as well as my silence, a balancing of the scales."

"Gee, t'anks," I replied, rolling my eyes for good measure. "Tell ye what though, next time I agree to help ye, I'll be sure to stipulate what currencies I do and don't accept. Like favors the Chancery can't refuse no matter the circumstances, for example."

"It is not that simple," Gretel admonished as we stepped out into the hallway. "I cannot risk jeopardizing my role here. As the sole remaining voice of reason, I am the Chancery's last line of defense should Catha decide to take a more...active leadership role. If she were to declare war on the human race, for example."

"Jesus, would she do that?"

"If provoked? Perhaps."

"What about your brothers?" I asked as we passed a familiar office door. "Shouldn't they be here?"

Gretel hesitated, stalling in the middle of the hallway. "Hansel the Younger has been away for some time now. He was looking into one of his pet projects with the help of an assistant. I've sent word for him to stay away for his own safety. Hansel the Elder is, I expect, sharing a cell with Robin."

"He what, now?"

"My brother may have wronged you in the past, Ms. MacKenna, but he has always been an advocate for this institution. He has put his whole life into it, and more besides."

"How much more?" I asked, suspiciously.

"Hansel is bound to the Chancery, as I am. Our well-being hinges upon its existence. That is why I am as you see me," Gretel admitted, smiling sadly as she ran her hand down the front of her robe, showcasing her aging frame. "Without him by my side, the burden is mine alone to bear. And, as a result, I require a great deal of rest."

I caught the barest whiff of a burning candle as she spoke—the mild sensation of dry leaves brushing against my skin—and realized I'd sensed her waning power. She was fading. Without intervention, I suspected Gretel would burn through her reserves until there was nothing left but ash.

"Are ye dyin'?"

"Death is an inevitability. But no, I am not sick, if that's what you mean. Merely paying the price for a deal made a long, long time ago. Now, come, before we are discovered."

I trailed behind the old lady as we approached the door, wary of stepping on her robe or having to catch her mid-faint; despite her assurances, I knew now what it cost her to soldier on. I felt a stab of pity for the woman; while it was true she hadn't been extremely helpful, Gretel had done a great deal more than others might have in her place. It didn't make us friends, or even allies, but that didn't stop me from hoping she'd recover when this was all over.

"What d'ye t'ink I should do?" I asked, breaking the subsequent silence moments before we hit the door. "About Catha, I mean."

"As I see it, you have the same options that the former Adjudicators had," Gretel replied, thoughtfully. "You may either run so that you might live to fight another day as the Huntress did, or you may follow in the Redcap's footsteps and oppose this invader.

"Except Robin's little sit-in failed, and I'm no pacifist."

"So?"

"So, what if takin' on Catha means violence? Isn't that somethin' ye hope to avoid?"

"Despite what idealists have to say on the subject, I believe violence is always a solution. I also feel it is often the messiest and least satisfactory option among many others." Gretel laid a skeletal hand on my shoulder as we reached the door. "I truly wish things were different, and that I could offer you a place here. But I am afraid I cannot in good conscience pay you what you are owed with the lives of those I would be endangering. Selfishly, I must admit I hope you will find a way to return things to the way they were without resorting to bloodshed, for all our sakes."

"I'd prefer that, as well."

Gretel hesitated before writing a note on a pad she pulled from the pocket of her robe, which she then tore it out and passed to me. "Presuming you intend to try, of course, I believe you will need allies. If you hurry, you might find one there."

It was the advice and scribbled address that had eventually led me to this corner store—arriving just in time to spot a familiar face through the murky glass. Unfortunately, the face wasn't that of an ally, but of an old acquaintance I'd avoided ever since I bargained away her freedom so Max and I could go after Frankenstein's monster.

Short and well-built, Detective Maria Machado wore plainclothes —a pair of dark denim jeans and red blouse emblazoned with floral designs that accentuated her tan skin and dark brown hair. Despite how long it had been since I'd seen her, she looked younger in the brighter colors. More herself, somehow.

As I watched, the detective slapped the dealer on his broad shoulder, slipped on a navy windbreaker, and headed for the door. I crouched lower, willing Maria to ignore me so I could follow and see what she was up to. Maybe then I could corner her; Maria and I had never been what you would call close even before I'd gone AWOL for eighteen months, which meant I might need some leverage if I wanted her help—like finding out whether or not what she'd just done was legal, for example.

Once I was sure she hadn't spotted me, I broke away from my hiding place, trailing far enough behind that I could duck out of sight behind another building should she turn around for whatever reason. I also adjusted my outfit using the *seiðr* magic I'd learned in the Norse afterlife, employing the transformative properties that Nevermore—the name I'd chosen for the armor I'd bargained for in exchange for tracking down Hilde—possessed. The effect was immediate; within seconds my spring attire included a baggy university hoodie and a nondescript ball cap. I adjusted the cap, donned the hood, and tweaked my gait to that of a dogged, plodding march.

Stealth Quinn, activated.

Regrettably, I managed to follow the detective for only two blocks before I lost her. At first, I couldn't believe my eyes; Maria hadn't slipped between buildings or stepped out of sight. Instead, she'd vanished into thin air so abruptly that even a couple passing on the opposite end of the street noticed; they began talking animatedly amongst themselves, gesturing with such exuberance it was as though they'd seen a world class magician pull a tiger out of a hat or reattach a limb. Personally, I wasn't so much impressed as I was ticked off.

How the hell had Maria pulled that off in broad daylight? And, more importantly, where had she gone? I muttered an obscenity under my breath and began scanning the street only to feel the sagging bulk of my gig bag yanked sideways, followed by the press of what felt like a muzzle against my spine.

"Don't move," an accented voice snarled just behind my ear, "or I'll have no choice but to kill you."

CHAPTER 4

I froze out of reflex, hands raised to show I wasn't armed, and yet the barrel dug deeper into the base of my spine as though I'd done something I shouldn't have. It hurt enough that—for a brief moment—I considered taking the risk and confronting my unknown assailant. I was a goddess, after all. What was a gun to a deity? Unfortunately, I hadn't yet tested the limits of immortality, and being able to survive being shot in the back wasn't the same as being able to walk away from it. An eternity was an awful long time to live without full use of one's legs.

"I didn't move, damnit," I hissed through gritted teeth. When the gunman didn't reply, I sighed. "What d'ye want, then? I don't have any money."

"I do not care about that. I want to know why you were following Detective Machado."

I stilled a second time, my heart racing. The speaker's voice, no longer laced with threat, was achingly familiar. I desperately wanted to turn, to find the face that went with it, but I couldn't risk it. Not yet. Not until I knew for sure that it wouldn't leave me paralyzed from the waist down—or worse.

"Max," I said, his name falling like a prayer from my lips, "is that ye?"

"How is it you know my name?"

The brujo's accent grew stronger with anger, slurring the hard consonants so that every word became somehow both sibilant and sinister. But there was a subtler emotion beneath all that rage. Fear. Max—for whatever reason—was afraid. But of what? Or of whom?

"Max, it's me. It's Quinn."

"Who?"

"Quinn. Quinn MacKenna."

"Am I supposed to know who that is?"

For a moment, we stood in complete silence while the wheels in my head churned. At first, I asked myself whether I'd mistaken Max's voice for someone else's. But he'd already responded to the name, so my guess had been the correct one. Plus, he was asking about Maria —a mutual friend. Hell, now that I thought about it, Max was witch enough to have made her vanish before my very eyes. But that still didn't explain why he was pretending not to know me. Were we being watched? Or had I really been gone so long that he'd forgotten all about me? I found myself hoping it was the former; no one hopes their absence will make the heart grow dimmer.

"Answer me."

Max jabbed me with the muzzle a second time, generating a wince and a curse. Which told me—assuming he wasn't faking it for someone else's benefit—that he wasn't going to pull any punches. Fine, then.

Neither would I.

"Do that again, and I swear I'll take that gun from ye and break it over your head."

"You are in no position to threaten me. Now, I will ask you one more time, what do you want with Maria? Who do you work for?"

"Jesus, Max, cut the act, would ye?" When Max said nothing, I cursed a second time. "I was followin' Maria to see what she was up to. I wanted her help."

"Her help with what?"

"Trackin' ye and Camila down, for starters."

The gun withdrew, only to be repositioned—this time against the back of my head. I heard the hammer cock and felt the first stirrings of true fear; immortal or not, I wasn't eager to find out how it felt to take a bullet to the brain. What's worse, as armed threats went, putting a loaded gun to someone's head was essentially playing one's trump card. From that point on, you were promising your victim a guaranteed death, pure and simple. Which begged the question, what on earth was Max thinking?

"Max, what the—"

"Why are you hunting my sister and me?"

"Huntin'?! I'm not huntin' either of ye! I stopped by your shop and saw the eviction notice. I thought I might be able to help. Or at least make sure ye both were alright."

"Did we know each other? From before?" The pressure against my skull eased incrementally. "My sister says I have forgotten things. That I slept too long, and that there was...damage."

The coma. I fought not to shiver in alarm, worried it would spook Max. But something must have given me away, because suddenly his hand was yanking back my hood and snatching at my ball cap. He tore it free, sending my hair flying across my face—thick tendrils that tickled my cheeks and covered my eyes. Still, I hardly noticed; I was too busy thinking about what Max had said. About the possibility that he'd suffered brain damage from the coma I'd gone to Hell and back to wake him from. Was it possible? Could he really have forgotten me? I cleared my throat but found a lump waiting for me and had to do it again.

"We knew each other," I managed. "Not as well as I would have liked, perhaps. But aye, we were..."

"Friends?"

"Somethin' like that."

What we'd been—or hadn't been—was still up for debate. From the moment we met, a thread of attraction had bound us to each other, and the constant threat of danger had only intensified those feelings. Then, in the wake of our initial run-in with Frankenstein and his Faeling monster, I'd discovered that Max and I had forged a bond of sorts—a circuit of energy that coursed through us like a two-way battery. A symbiotic link which had sent Max into a coma shortly after I left the mortal realm. Of course, where that link originated and what it meant for us remained a mystery.

In Helheim, for instance, our metaphysical connection had worked to our advantage; Max had snapped out of his fugue state the instant we touched, giving us the opportunity we needed to fight for our afterlives. And yet there had been an addictive quality to the experience, a constant underlying craving that sat like an itch beneath my skin, that I could neither explain nor truly appreciate even after returning from my sojourn in Hell. I preferred simpler addictions—the kind you could satisfy all on your own.

At the time, Frankenstein had intimated the two of us were somehow cursed. That Max and I weren't so much tethered as shackled. The mad scientist had also called the brujo my familiar—a title bestowed upon a witch's servant, or pet. Unfortunately, there was very little familiar about Max; aside from our mutual attraction and despite our frequent brushes with death, I realized I barely knew the man.

And now it seemed he didn't know me, at all.

"Why didn't you greet Maria when she first left the store, if you knew her?" Max demanded. "Why hide your face and follow?"

"Can I turn around?"

"No. Not until I am sure you are not lying to me."

"I wanted to wait and see what she did with that jar she got from the guy..." I groaned inwardly, realizing at last who the hooded man had been. "From ye. The jar ye gave her."

"Why not just ask her directly?"

"Because I've been...away." I shook my head, aware how guilty I sounded. "Look, the truth is I wanted to see what she'd do because I need to ask her a favor and I want her to say yes. If I caught her doin' somethin' she was embarrassed about, I figured she'd be more willin'."

Max grunted. "How did you know where to find her?"

"Pardon?"

"You could have simply called Maria and asked for her help. But instead you came here, and you followed her. You could not have known what she was doing or with whom, and yet you came. This does not seem like a plausible story." The muzzle brushed the back of my head again. "So, how did you know she was here?"

"Someone told me," I confessed, making a mental note not to underestimate Max's intelligence in the future. "A mutual acquaintance gave me the address."

"Please, I am tired of the lies. Just tell me the truth."

"Ye can't handle the truth!" I spat, screwing up my face to improve the admittedly terrible impression.

"Is that really your best Jack Nicholson?"

"I do a better Demi," I admitted, "but her lines aren't as good in that one, and quotin' *G.I. Jane* would probably get me shot on principle. Besides, ye told me once that *A Few Good Men* was one of your favorite movies. Somethin' about lovin' Aaron Sorkin's dialogue. Figured it would ease the tension."

"When did I tell you that?"

"On a..." I grimaced, wishing I had a less loaded term for what had been our first, and last, official outing. "We were on a date."

"A date? So, not just friends."

"It was complicated."

"Turn around, slowly. But do not do anything foolish."

I did as the brujo asked, though my shoulders were beginning to burn from the effort of holding my arms up for so long. At first, I could hardly make out anything beyond the curtain of my own hair, but then a calloused hand brushed my bangs back to reveal the man who held me at gunpoint.

Maximiliano Velez towered over me. Part of that was his height—he'd always stood several inches taller than me—but mostly it was sheer size; though baggy around the middle, the hoodie Max wore hugged his shoulders and chest like a second skin, the fabric straining to contain the breadth of him. Which meant not only had he gained the weight back that he'd lost while in the coma, but he'd actually gotten bigger, somehow. Oddly, however, that wasn't the change I cared about most.

"What'd ye do to your hair?" I asked, breathlessly.

Max's expression betrayed nothing, leaving me to study a face that was so achingly masculine it was almost painful to look at. I started with his lips. Large and softer than they looked, they turned what would have been a hulking jawline and sweeping cheekbones into something gentler, something you could actually touch without fear it would cut you. His eyes were next. A shade of brown so dark they seemed to melt into the depths of his pitch black pupils, they looked uncertain, uneasy. But it was the absence of the dark locks which had once spilled across his forehead and along the nape of his neck that drew my eye; he'd shaved it to the scalp—the result so severe that I might not have immediately recognized him had we passed on the street.

"It did not feel like me, anymore," Max replied, shrugging. "Plus, it's getting hot. This is easier."

I don't know what I would have said to that, or even what I would have done about the gun still pointed at my chest, because—at that precise moment—something happened. A shift in temperature, perhaps, or an odd scent wafting through the air. Either way, Max and I both turned to look, caught by surprise as a mass of hooded figures materialized out of thin air and began shambling towards us from the far end of the block. There were at least a dozen, spread across the street in a straight line as though no car would dare mow them down.

"*Mierda*!" Max spat.

"What's wrong? Who are they?"

"The slaugh."

"Seriously?" I squinted, trying to find the faces hidden behind the shadows of their cowls. According to legend, the slaugh was another name for the spirits of the restless dead called by Fae magic to join a soul-snatching chase—what some people called the Wild Hunt. But, as far as I knew, the Hunt hadn't ridden out from Fae in centuries. If they had, I doubted even mankind's ability to shove their heads in the sand could prevent them from acknowledging their existence.

Nothing screams we are not alone like spotting a horde of other-worldly creatures as they carouse past your window in the wee hours of the night looking to shoplift some souls.

"I thought there'd be more of 'em," I admitted.

"There are."

I shivered at the brujo's ominous tone. "What do they want?"

"Not what," Max corrected as he backed towards the opposite end of the street, scanning the sky as though there were more threats approaching from above. "Who. They want me."

"Why?"

The brujo gave me a long, considering look even as the hooded figures drew closer, their approach accompanied by the sounds of clawed feet scraping along the pavement. I met his weighing gaze with one of my own, trying to decide how much of the man I'd known was still in there. I felt a sudden urge to reach out and touch his face, to trace my fingers along the stubble that rode his cheeks. I wanted him to know me if nothing else—to remember our time together. To recall what we'd survived, and how. But what happened if that reignited our bond, somehow? Was I prepared to take that chance? Was he?

"I really hope you are what you say you are, Quinn MacKenna," Max said before I could make my decision. "Because we are out of time."

"Time to do what, exactly?"

"To talk," Max said as he shoved his gun into the waistband of his pants, his expression rueful. "I wish I could explain. But, if you really were my friend, then you will know to trust me when I say that if we stay out in the open like this, we will not stand a chance. Not against them all. Which means we have to run. Now."

CHAPTER 5

We ran together, moving as quickly as our loping strides would allow. Max took the lead as if he hadn't put a gun to my head only minutes before, weaving across a quiet street and bolting through an abandoned alleyway coated in posters and propaganda describing some sort of once-in-a-lifetime lunar event. Several minutes and at least a dozen blocks later, it finally occurred to me that we'd seen not a single soul since the appearance of those hooded figures—an improbability that bordered on the impossible.

"Where the hell is everyone?" I asked as we cut across a neighborhood park, angling towards a jungle gym.

"It is the flavor of their magic," Max explained, his own breathing only slightly labored. "Whenever they are near, even ordinary people sense it and stay away."

"Does that mean they're close by?" A quick glance over one shoulder assured me that no one followed. "We left the others behind a while back."

"Those were night hags. They do not move as quickly as the others."

"Night hags?" I made it a question, but I already knew what they were from some of the more horrifying stories my Aunt Dez had told me as I was growing up; she'd told me all about the Fae who stood at the foot of the bed of bad children when they slept, waiting to catch the dreamer's soul in bags sewn from multi-colored flesh. In fact, Dez had once tormented me and my mouthy teenage girlfriends by throwing a blanket over herself and standing over us after an impromptu slumber party, her face made up to look as hideous as possible until someone woke up, saw her, and started screaming. Dez thought it was hilarious.

I didn't have many sleepovers after that.

"*Sí*. They are dangerous if they get close, but they do not care for daylight. I am more worried about the Hobs. If the night hags are here, the goblins won't be far behind."

"Hobs? As in hobgoblins?" I shook my head as we passed the playground and headed for the tree line that bordered the south side of the park, struggling to make sense of what was really going on. "But they wouldn't be part of the slaugh, and neither would the night hags. If anythin', they'd be with the Chancery."

Max halted so suddenly that I had to skid to a stop not to leave him behind. I gulped down air, wishing I'd have thought to change into my armor before we'd fled. If I had, I wouldn't have needed to put nearly so much effort into keeping up with the brujo. Of course, then I'd have to explain why I suddenly looked like I was going to slay a dragon, and we didn't have that kind of time.

"What's wrong?" I asked.

"You know about the Chancery?" Max ignored my question, his hand disappearing behind his back. "Are you connected to them?"

"Define 'connected'."

"Did you come to take me in?" The brujo's eyes widened before I could respond as if another thought had just occurred to him. "You planned to follow Maria to the safehouse. To find out where the others are hiding."

"I have no idea what you're talkin' about," I admitted, truthfully. "But I t'ink we have more important t'ings to worry about."

I pointed, and the brujo tracked the gesture until he saw what I'd seen; across the park came dozens of what looked like children, but were most certainly not—because, last I checked, children didn't have muddy green skin and razor-sharp teeth or wield weapons fashioned from carved bone. And yet, there was something admittedly childlike in the way they moved; unlike the goblins I'd encountered in Fae, the hobgoblins were diminutive and awkward, their proportions disrupted by swollen joints and mossy patches of viridescent body hair.

"*Mierda!*"

"Ye must really like that word," I quipped.

"Stay away from me," Max hissed. The brujo drew his gun and fired haphazardly into the sea of incoming goblins, seemingly oblivious to the fact that we were in a public park. Or perhaps he simply didn't care.

"Are ye talkin' to me, or to the Hobs?"

"You! The Chancery cannot be trusted, which means neither can you!"

I fought the urge to roll my eyes as the brujo continued firing. A few of the hobgoblins fell away clutching at their sides or their legs, but there were simply too many. Max must have realized the same thing; he emptied his clip, cursed, and took off towards the trees. I did the same, acutely aware of the incoming wave of hobgoblins on our heels. They were close enough that I could make out their gleeful shrieks and the eerie pitter-patter of their bare feet in the grass.

"What are you doing?" Max asked, glancing over his shoulder. "I said stay away from me!"

"I can't help it if you're runnin' in the same direction as me." I sighed, swung the gig bag off my shoulder, and hunted for the zipper as we ran.

"I mean it!"

"Hold that thought." I turned on my heel and pried the bag open. Within, Areadbhar thrummed. I withdrew her, marveling at the terrible beauty of the legendary weapon. The spear—listed as one of the Four Jewels of the Tuatha de Danann and adorned with a light-sucking devourer that had once belonged to a Norse giant—glowed with power.

Behind me, Max gasped.

"*Dios mío...*"

"Areadbhar," I whispered, brushing my free hand along the shaft. I felt her quiver with anticipation—with her desire to be unleashed. For hers was the power to slay armies, the desire to spill blood. "Sick 'em, girl."

Areadbhar leapt from my hand, soared high into the air, and then came swooping down upon the Hobs like a vicious bird of prey. Where she descended, the hobgoblins broke ranks, their charge completely disrupted by the threat of her biting blade. Their war cries quickly became screams.

"But no killin'!" I shouted through cupped hands.

"No killing? So, you *are* with them."

I turned to meet Max's accusatory gaze and sighed, forced to raise my voice to be heard over the howling Hobs as they scrambled over one another to escape Areadbhar's assault. "I am not *with* the Chancery. If I were, I'd have at least some idea what the slaugh is doin' here in the mortal realm, not to mention why they are attackin' us in broad daylight. Look, the truth is I have no idea what I've stumbled into. But until that changes, I don't plan on killin' anyone. Not if I can avoid it."

Of course, that wasn't the whole truth. The reality of the situation was that—no matter the context—the Fae were my people. My mother was a goddess of the Tuatha De Danann, which meant I was descended from the original rulers of Fae. And with that lineage, came certain responsibilities—obligations the old me would have avoided at all costs. But that was before. Before I'd traveled to the Otherworld and had become someone who knew what it meant to be part of a tribe. Before I'd stood toe to toe with the current rulers of Fae and found them capricious and shortsighted. Before I'd thought to ask myself what I could be if I was willing to forsake my independence, if it meant keeping everyone I cared about safe.

"Can you prove to me you are not allied with them?"

"I don't need to prove I'm not on their side," I answered, stepping close enough to see the individual beads of sweat splattered across his forehead and pooling in the groove above his upper lip. The sounds of the retreating hobgoblins had grown faint. "I just need to prove that I am on yours."

I held out my hand.

"What does that mean?"

"It means touch me," I replied, firm in my newfound resolve. The simple truth was that Max and I simply couldn't go on like this, not with the threats we faced. The brujo needed to know he could trust me, and I needed his help navigating this strange new world I'd found waiting for me. If that meant reestablishing the preternatural connection and binding us together once more, then so be it. I could live with the consequences of a metaphysical addiction. What I couldn't live with was cowardice getting in the way.

"What will happen if I do as you ask?"

"Somethin' magical, probably."

The brujo's eyebrows shot up in surprise.

"Max!"

The call brought both of us round. A familiar figure stepped out from the shadows of the distant tree line, waving at the brujo with her free hand, holding a gun aimed in my general direction with the other. Max shuffled backwards like a man caught by a jealous spouse, eyeing my outstretched palm as though it were some sort of poisonous snake. That is until the newcomer lowered her gun and shouted a second time.

"Jesus, MacKenna!" Detective Maria Machado exclaimed. "Is that you?"

CHAPTER 6

It seemed the cavalry had finally arrived...if by cavalry one meant a tiny Hispanic woman with a loaded gun and an absurd number of open-ended questions that I couldn't easily answer while on the run. Questions like "where have you been?" or "why didn't you tell anyone you were back?" or "where on earth did you get that freaking spear?" Max, on the other hand, had fallen silent the instant we linked up with the inquisitive detective; the brujo kept looking sidelong at me as we bustled down the street as if he couldn't decide what to make of me now that he knew I'd told him the truth.

"Where are we goin'?" I asked, hoping to distract Maria before she blew a gasket. There was also something about her behavior which made me want to avoid answering her questions—something I couldn't quite put my finger on. In fact, it wasn't until she turned back to me with a reassuring smile that I realized what bothered me: she was being nice. Maria was rarely nice, and never to me. In fact, until this moment, I would have said her bristling, barely cordial tolerance of yours truly was as dependable as the rise and fall of the sun; if we made it a whole day without whaling on each other or her pointing a gun at me, I considered it a win.

"Somewhere we can talk," she replied, patting my shoulder. "Somewhere they won't come after us."

I glanced down at the spot she'd touched, baffled by the casual contact, but didn't argue. I was too busy trying to decide whether the detective had spent the last year and a half in mandated therapy, or if body-snatching aliens had begun replacing bitches all across the planet. Unfortunately, I didn't get a chance to ask which because at that precise moment a dark mass of hooded figures emerged from an alleyway on the other side of the street. The night hags began drifting towards us like encroaching shadows, their ragged cloaks twisting in a brisk wind that didn't exist. I couldn't see their faces beneath their cowls, and yet I could sense their malicious intent coming at us like a noxious fog bank.

"There! Get to the precinct!" Maria cried, pointing to red brick low-rise nestled between two office buildings. An American flag hung limp above the doorway and empty squad cars lined the curb. There wasn't a single officer in sight.

We did as Maria suggested, bolting for the entrance as the night hags waded into the middle of the street, trailing behind us like specters. None of us looked back, though part of me considered confronting the bizarre apparitions. Not to pick a fight, necessarily, but to at least find out what the slaugh were after. Honestly—between what Gretel told me and being hunted through the streets of Boston—I was beginning to feel like I'd gotten swept up into something far messier than I'd realized. Everything was moving too fast; I needed time to think.

I needed answers.

"You can't bring that in," Maria insisted as we hit the sidewalk outside the precinct, gesturing to the spear I held clenched in my right hand.

"Oh..." I fought to control my crestfallen expression. Maria was right, there was no way I was walking into a police station armed with a seven-foot spear without drawing all sorts of unwanted attention and quite possibly getting arrested for my trouble. Of course, I wasn't the only armed individual in our little threesome. "What about Max's gun?"

"Right. Good call." Maria held out her hand and Max passed over his pistol. The detective quickly slid it into a shoulder holster opposite her own and adjusted her windbreaker to minimize the bulges, which suggested it had been her gun to begin with. Once finished, the two of them looked at me expectantly, though Max's gaze quickly shifted to the encroaching hags at our back.

"We should hurry."

"Areadbhar," I whispered. I shut my eyes and pinned the wood to my mouth, visualizing what I wanted. "Would ye be so kind as to stay out of sight and wait for me nearby?"

I felt a rush of energy run the length of her shaft, leaving me momentarily breathless as it reached my lips. The sensation quickly faded as the spear pulled away and soared into the sky. And yet, even as she vanished from sight beyond the rooftops, I knew with a fierce certainty that I could call, and she would return to my hand in a blaze of violent glory.

Suck it, Thor.

"You coming?" Max asked, beckoning with the hand that wasn't holding the precinct's door open. Realizing Maria had gone ahead without me, I hurried past the brujo with a mumbled thanks, casting one last look over my shoulder as I went, expecting to see a veritable horde of hooded figures at our backs.

Except the night hags had, ominously, vanished.

"Hurry!"

I hesitated, then, but ultimately responded to the urgency in Max's voice and stepped into the lobby. Within seconds, it felt as though I'd woken from a muted dream; the floor squeaked beneath the shoes of uniformed officers bustling to and fro, elevators dinged as doors whizzed open and closed, and the room overflowed with the general hubbub of casual conversation. I let out a breath I hadn't even known I was holding, suddenly aware of how truly discomfiting it had been to wander the empty streets of Boston—to see the city I loved turned into some sort of ghost town. How *had* the slaugh pulled that off, anyway? Was it magic, or something intrinsic in their natures, that repulsed even ordinary people?

"Oy," I said, tapping a cop on the shoulder. "D'ye notice anythin' keepin' ye from steppin' outside, just now?"

"Excuse me?"

"Quinn!" Maria called, beckoning me from within a nearby elevator. "What are you doing?"

"Nevermind," I muttered, slipping past the baffled officer. "Hold your horses! I'm comin'!"

We took the elevator to the fourth floor but didn't speak; a handful of uniforms had joined the three of us, making it impossible to discuss what had just happened without drawing unwanted attention. Once we stepped off, however, I quickly realized Maria had a plan; the detective marched right up to a young, sandy-haired cop sitting behind a nearby desk as though she owned the place.

"Something I can do for you, ma'am?" The uniform smiled up at Maria, though the warmth never quite reached his eyes. Inwardly, I tacked on a few years to the cop's total; officers under twenty were typically too green to hide what they thought about you. His assessment of us was quick and thorough—a mere flick of eyes from one to the next, though his gaze lingered on Max the longest. But then I supposed I couldn't blame him; Max was *big*. Big in the way that made some men feel small, or even weak, by comparison. What's more, his features were both vaguely exotic and absurdly handsome —hair or no hair—which probably alienated the rest. In fact, I'd have put even money on the fact that Max was the kind of guy who *had* to smile, who *had* to be charming, or else be mistaken for an arrogant jerk.

"Detective Machado, C-11," Maria said, flashing her badge. "I need an empty holding cell."

"Sorry, detective, but could you repeat that?"

"A holding cell. Empty."

"And what exactly do you need a cell for? Or should I say, who?" The officer glanced from me to Max and back again, his expression clouding. "Neither of these two are wearing cuffs, Detective."

"Handcuffs weren't necessary," Maria replied, leaning in so as not to be overheard by the other uniforms milling about. "The redhead is a criminal informant. I need to talk to her in private, but it needs to look like she's being held. Hence, empty cell."

Realization dawned on the officer's face. "You don't want to show your hand by taking her back to your department. Got it. Let me clear this with my Lieutenant."

I waited until the officer was out of earshot before peppering Maria with questions, but the detective insisted I keep my mouth shut until we were alone. Max, meanwhile, kept searching our faces as though the two of us were conspiring together, somehow. In the end, I did what Maria asked; it wasn't like I could afford to throw a tantrum in the middle of the police station.

"Quinn," Maria whispered under her breath, "let me see your phone. I need to make a call, and mine's dead."

"I don't have a phone. Not anymore."

Maria gave me a look.

"It's a long story."

"Follow me, Detective," the uniform interrupted as he slipped between us, momentarily shielding me from Maria's dubious stare.

Two floors, a couple minutes, and several hallways later, the officer waved us through into a tidy little room dominated by a half dozen cells spanning the length of the far wall. It seemed we were in luck; they'd released their last suspect earlier that day, which meant we had all the privacy we could want. The officer was clearly skeptical; he eyed me up and down, clearly wondering what I'd done to end up in Maria's pocket. Was I the ex-girlfriend of some low-level mobster? An escort with a shady clientele? Or maybe a socialite turned junkie with friends in high places?

If only he knew.

Then our gazes met, and suddenly I saw myself through his eyes: improbably long-legged, my top half hidden beneath an unseasonably warm hoodie, my mane of red hair so tousled from running that it framed my pale face. My cheeks were flushed and dusted with the faintest of freckles. It was like looking in a mirror, except the mirror roamed, focusing on bits and pieces of me I would never have thought to focus on. Like my knees. Who looked at a girl's knees? Still, I knew somehow that he liked what he saw. Except maybe the height; he'd probably never dated anyone taller than he was who wasn't wearing heels. But then it didn't matter if I was attractive; I was a criminal, and he was a cop, and there were some lines you simply shouldn't cross.

That thought, I realized, wasn't mine.

I'd already crossed that line with Jimmy a long time ago, and besides, I wasn't a criminal. Not until I got caught, anyway. As soon as I realized whose thought it had been, however, the bizarre connection between the officer and me snapped—bursting like a bubble of chewing gum. Maria cleared her throat, and I saw Max and her staring at me like I'd done something horribly inappropriate.

And maybe I had.

"Ah, right," the officer said, his cheeks on fire as he headed towards the door. "I'll leave you all to it."

"Nice meetin' ye, officer," I said, without quite knowing why I said it. When he looked back, I flashed him a knowing smile and mimed shooting him with my finger like some sort of crazy person.

"Knock it off," Maria barked at me. "Thanks for bringing us down here, Officer O'Malley."

"O'Malley?" I asked, startled.

"Yeah, why?"

"Oh, nothin'," I said, hastily, as Maria leveled another glare at me. "Thanks again for helpin' us out."

"Anytime." Officer O'Malley flushed a second time before facing Maria, though I noticed he seemed awful intent on studying the floor. "LT says you have an hour."

"That'll work."

O'Malley opened his mouth like he wanted to say something else, but ultimately clamped it shut, turned on his heel, and fled. I watched him go until he turned the corner and disappeared out of sight, distantly aware that Max and Maria were giving me that disapproving look, again.

"What in the world was that?" Maria hissed.

"Sorry?"

"Whatever just happened between you and O'Malley."

"Oh, that." I shrugged as though it were nothing. "The man has a little crush, that's all."

"I could see that. I meant the magic! What spell was that? It was almost like your aura swallowed his for a second, which should be impossible."

I blinked owlishly. Had Maria really just said the word "aura" out loud? I could hardly believe it; for almost as long as I'd known her, the detective had refused to acknowledge the things that went bump in the night, preferring to double down on her faith and ignore any evidence that contradicted her puritanical world view.

"I felt it, too," Max added. The brujo clutched at himself as though he were cold and wore a troubled expression. But it wasn't jealousy which tugged at his lips so much as nausea; his naturally tan skin appeared sallow beneath the fluorescent fixtures overhead.

"Wait, you did?" Maria asked, nearly bouncing with uncharacteristic excitement. "Max, that's great!"

"Is it?"

The two of them exchanged looks I couldn't decipher—one troubled, the other sad. But, when neither of them seemed inclined to explain further, I began to think about what Maria had said. *Had* I done a spell? I doubted it; after discovering I had nothing resembling a formal education in magical theory, Circe had taken it upon herself to give me a primer of sorts for the duration of my convalescence, which meant I knew for a fact that spells were inherently ritualistic magic. For most practitioners, casting one meant completing a series of predetermined tasks. Of course, there were exceptions—people with genetic predispositions that caused them to levitate or breathe fire or what have you. And then there were those prodigies with so much juice pumping through their veins that they tended to disregard the rituals completely.

Nate Temple, anyone?

What had happened with O'Malley, on the other hand, fell into a different category altogether. Spells were governed by intent; you couldn't stumble upon one like finding five dollars on the side of the road. So, not a spell. Unfortunately, that meant it was more than likely the other thing. The thing the Witch of Aeaea had warned me to watch out for before I left.

O'Malley. Of course it would be an O'Malley.

"We can talk about it, later, Max," Maria was insisting by the time I shook off the thought that followed. "Right now, we have something else to take care of."

"About that," I said, "why'd ye bring us down here, anyway? Couldn't we have talked in the lobby?"

"Maybe. But the lobby doesn't have cells."

Before I could ask what that had to do with anything, Maria pivoted and shoved me as hard as she could. Caught completely off guard, I stumbled, flailing, only to trip over my own feet and collapse to the floor. My hands skid painfully over the concrete, though admittedly my knees took the worst of it; they hit the ground with an audible crack that sent shockwaves up my legs. I groaned, though I was too damned shocked to be properly angry.

That is until the cell door clinked shut behind me.

"Now, then," Maria said, leering down at me through a gap in the steel bars, "I think it's about time we have a little chat."

CHAPTER 7

My palms left bloody smears on the wall as I clambered to my feet, and my knees were already beginning to bruise. Unfortunately, pity seemed in short supply; Max wouldn't meet my gaze, and Maria tracked my every move with a level of hostility people typically reserve for someone who kicks dogs or shakes babies. Trouble was, even at our most fractious, Maria had never directed that look at me before. Hell, she'd have punched me in the face before it came to that. Which meant something else was going on, something I didn't understand.

Once I realized that, I took a deep, calming breath. After all, there was no point getting defensive until I knew what I was defending. If I wanted Maria to explain herself and let me out, I needed to make things better—not worse.

"What's this about?"

"Answer my question, and I'll consider answering yours. Who are you, really? And don't bother lying to me. You show up at the same time as the slaugh, you can't account for a year and a half absence, and you have no phone. You can't possibly expect us to believe your story."

I groaned, realizing too late that Maria's seemingly innocuous questions had actually been tests; she'd been busy poking holes in my story from the start. "Dammit, Maria, it's me. It's Quinn."

"Quinn MacKenna," she deadpanned.

"Aye. How many Quinn's d'ye know?"

Maria studied my face like I was a puzzle she couldn't piece together, but the contempt continued to tug at her bottom lip. "I don't believe you."

"Of course ye don't. Dammit, I knew ye hadn't changed!" I snapped, frustrated I hadn't poked at Maria's rosy demeanor when I'd had the chance. "Look, it's true, I was avoidin' your questions earlier. But that wasn't because I had no answers. A lot happened after I left, is all. More than ye could possibly believe."

"Well, that's convenient. For you, I mean."

"What d'ye want me to say? That I got pulled into another world? That I've spent the last year and a half jumpin' from one realm to another, puttin' out fires? D'ye have any idea how crazy it would all sound?"

"What I want is for you to tell me the truth. And I don't care how long that takes. See, I already know how your kind feels about metal." Maria rapped a knuckle against the nearest bar until it sung. "These bars may not be pure iron, but we both know you won't be able to break out on your own."

"Hold on, ye t'ink I'm one of the Fae?"

"Now, you might be thinking Officer O'Malley will come back for you," Maria continued, ignoring me. "But trust me, that isn't going to happen. If you fail to cooperate, I'll cast a spell to stop anyone from finding you in here. They will never open this door, and you'll rot in here until you fade away to nothing."

"Wow," I said, almost as impressed by Maria's bad cop routine as I was by the accuracy of her information. She'd clearly done her homework. Still, in all the years I'd known her, I'd never have thought Maria would threaten me with a spell—not while she was armed. "Why not just shoot me?"

"I want answers. If I kill you, I won't get any."

"Very practical."

"Please," Max interjected, sounding tired, "just tell us what the slaugh's mistress wants from us. If you do, I promise I—"

"No swearing!" Maria nudged him. "You know better than to make a deal with one of them."

Irritation flitted across the brujo's face, but he refrained from saying anything more. I, meanwhile, struggled to make sense of what I'd just heard. So, not only had Maria erroneously labeled me a Faeling, but now Max was under the impression that I worked for whomever held the slaugh's leash. The question was, how could I convince them otherwise?

Max was out; the brujo wouldn't have recognized me walking down the street. Which left Maria—one of the most stubborn, pigheaded women I'd ever met. A woman who, more than once, had jeopardized her career rather than see me get what I wanted. A woman who had refused to believe anything I said even *before* I went AWOL for eighteen months.

Of course, *there* was an idea.

I turned to the detective. "The truth is, ye and I don't like each other. We never have. I can only guess why that is. Maybe it's because ye had a t'ing for Jimmy and saw me as a threat, or maybe it's because you're a by-the-book bitch who holds grudges way too long. I don't know, and I don't care. What I do know is that in all the years we've known each other, I never managed to fool ye. Not once. Ye could always tell when I was hidin' somethin', even if ye weren't sure what it was. Hell, I'm pretty sure ye knew I had a crush on Jimmy before I did." I waved that away, sighing. "Point is, ye had me number from the start. So tell me, Detective Machado, d'ye honestly believe I'm lyin' to ye, now?"

"Yes, I do," Maria replied. But then a flash of uncertainty flickered across the detective's face, so brief I thought I might have imagined it.

"Why not do that spell Camila showed you?" Max asked. "To be sure."

"Because it gives me a headache."

Max gave her an eloquent look. The detective sighed, raised both hands, and used them to form a triangle in front of her face—creating a three-sided window for her right eye.

"Well? What d'ye see?" I asked, apprehensively.

"I don't see anything," she admitted. "Which means either you really are Quinn, or your glamour is just that good."

"Is it really that hard to believe?"

"Yes, it is. See, a good friend of hers, Robin Redcap, told us Quinn was dead." Maria lowered her hands and planted them in fists at her sides. "He insisted she was seen on the other side, that there was proof. It devastated him, and he got himself in all sorts of trouble because of it. So yeah, I'm skeptical."

I experienced an abrupt stab of guilt at the thought of Robin grieving over me—painfully aware that I could have done more to establish contact and perhaps prevented this. I could have sent word before leaving Fae for the Titan Realm, for instance, or asked Circe to pass along a message on my behalf before diving spirit first into the Underworld. Only I hadn't. I hadn't because they would have expected me to listen to their opinions, even though mine was all that mattered.

"Well, Robin was wrong. Not about me bein' on the other side. That happened." I lowered my eyes, forced to acknowledge the probability that everyone I cared about assumed I was dead. "It's a long story. But I went there to get Max back. When I found out about the coma he was in, I realized—"

"It was your fault?" Maria accused.

"That's not—"

"So, she's the one?" Max interjected. "The one who stole my magic?"

"Wait, I did what, now?"

"If she is who she says she is, then yes," the detective replied, scowling at me like an overprotective mother meeting her son's girlfriend for the first time.

I shook my head. "I didn't steal anythin' of his, I swear."

"Then explain how Max has managed to forget only two things

since he woke up. You, and how to do magic. Nothing we teach him sticks."

I held a hand up for silence as I processed this latest wrinkle; it had been awhile since I was last accused of robbing someone of their metaphysical gifts. Honestly, I'd assumed Max's memory loss was a result of being essentially brain dead for so long, but what if there was another explanation?

"Max was there," I said, at last. "In the Underworld. I found him."

"You did?"

"Well, technically we found each other. But he knew who I was and helped me escape. We saved each other. Anyway, I was there when he started to wake up. I even heard Camila. She was tellin' the doctor off and refusin' to leave the room." I shook my head, caught in the memory of Max's lips pressed to my own in a farewell kiss. "I told him to go ahead without me."

A glance in the brujo's general direction confirmed my suspicions; Max stared into the middle distance with a wretched expression splattered across his face. Maria must have noticed, as well, because she reached out to him almost instantly. Max jerked away from her touch like he'd been zapped.

"I thought it was a dream," he admitted, shuddering. "A nightmare, really. Victor was there. The things he did...the things he made me do..."

"He'll never hurt ye or anyone else, ever again," I swore vehemently, sounding far less sympathetic than I would have liked. "Frankenstein is dead."

Max choked out a laugh, though it sounded more like a sob. "You do not understand. He cannot die."

"I took his soul," I declared, my voice laced with so much bitterness I almost didn't recognize it. "I swear to ye that Victor Frankenstein will never steal another body. He'll never see another sunrise or smell another flower. He will never torment ye, or anyone else. I swear it by the screamin' stone and the arm that sings, by the black pot and the bright blade."

As I finished the strangely worded vow, the overhead lights flickered and a tension within me I hadn't noticed eased—spilling down my spine until I felt loose and oddly pliant. By the time the lights came back on, however, both Max and Maria were staring at me with wide, startled eyes.

"Now *that* was a spell," Maria said, breathlessly.

Max nodded, then turned to his companion. "If what she says is true..."

"It means Camila can actually go through with her plan," Maria finished for him. "We need to tell her. She'll want to start making arrangements as soon as possible."

"It will still be risky."

"She won't care."

"No," Max admitted, sighing. "She will not."

I held up a hand. "Sorry, what risky plan are we talkin' about, exactly?"

"No, I'm sorry," Maria said. "You may not be lying about Franken-stein, but I still don't trust you. Quinn or not, you've been gone a long time, and I have no idea whose side you're on. Which means, until we figure that out, I think it's best you stay here."

"Stay here? For how long?" I asked, more outraged than alarmed.

"That depends on what Camila says. She'll know what to do with you."

"If Victor is truly gone," Max chimed in, "then you will have her gratitude. Our gratitude."

"No offense, but I'd rather have the key to this cell."

"Just keep quiet until we come back," Maria insisted. "Do that, and I'll think about letting you out."

"Oh? And what makes ye t'ink this cell can even hold me, Detec-tive?" I purred, splaying my arms wide in challenge. I waited, daring her to dismiss the perceptible difference between the bright-eyed, foul-mouthed girl she'd encountered so many years ago and the jaded thing I'd become. I let her see how little the threat of incarcera-tion frightened me. How little anything frightened me, anymore.

And why should it?

Since leaving Boston, I'd lost my mind in a foreign land, had a lover murdered before my very eyes, and watched the lingering remnants of my mother's spirit fade away to nothing. I'd been reborn, first as a warrior and again as a goddess. I'd sailed across monster-riddled seas, fought alongside giants, and backtalked Titans. I'd survived a drinking contest with the boatman of the River Styx, started a bar fight in Valhalla, and leveled Atlantis. Oh, and let's not forget I'd slit my best friend's throat rather than watch him turn into a monster. I'd done all that and more—trading away what innocence I had left, not to mention a year and a half of my life, for the power it took to look Maria in the eye without so much as a flicker of fear.

"Nice try," Maria said as she herded Max towards the door with one hand and waved back at me with the other. "Try to behave while we're gone."

"Oy, Maria. Oy! Ye better get back here and unlock this door, Machado! I mean it!"

They were already gone.

CHAPTER 8

The steel bars of my prison were a whole lot sturdier than I'd have preferred, but I was glad to discover they didn't affect me the way they had in the past; at one point, the merest touch of steel against my bare skin had chafed like gritty sandpaper, while iron in its purest form had seared my flesh as though I'd shoved it against the glowing coil of a burning stove. I took it as a sign that my aversion to iron—an affliction felt to some degree by all with Faeling blood—had lessened since becoming a goddess. That, or I'd developed an immunity while on one of my many adventures. Unfortunately, there was no way to be sure either way, and no one to ask. Circe had helped me fill in a lot of gaps, but she was Greek from the tips of her sandy toes to the top of her sun-bleached hair. Her pantheon had inspired epic poems, architectural marvels, and the spread of civilization. Mine, meanwhile, found their way into fairy tales and were blamed for meteorological phenomena like moonless nights and dense fog.

I know, I know...first Otherworld problems.

But still.

I paced the tiny cell, stalking its perimeter while I debated what to do. On the one hand, I could play along, remain behind bars, and hope Maria kept her word. On the other, I could break out and end this little farce, consequences be damned. Not so long ago, it wouldn't have even been up for debate. I'd have changed into my Valkyrie armor, torn the cell door off its hinges, and put Maria in her place—by force, if necessary. Hell, even if unnecessary. But at what cost? I needed Maria to trust me, not fear me.

I sighed, walked to the corner of my cell, and leaned against the wall, letting my head rest against the cool stone. For the first time in a long time, I let my mind dwell on trivial things—like how long it had been since I last had a hot shower instead of a cold bath, or brushed my teeth with something other than a twig. I thought about how much I missed having nothing pressing to do. No lessons, no chores, no unwanted contact with the outside world, and certainly no quests.

And yet, there were some things I could have done without. Like all the ambient noise; for example, even within the confines of a concrete cell, I found the incessant buzz of the fluorescent lights and the gurgling rush of water gushing through the pipes almost unbearably oppressive. I'd simply grown too used to the sound of the surf lapping along a beach, to the beat of waves against the hull of a ship, to the crisp, pregnant silence of a valley cloaked in snow. Which is probably why I noticed the clatter of approaching footsteps across the tile floor long before their owner appeared.

"Come to let me out, Machado?"

Except it wasn't Maria who walked through the door.

It was a man, though unlike any man I'd ever seen before. Truth be told, I struggled to describe him; I got the faintest impression of someone tall and athletic, someone graceful and kempt, but that was as much as my brain could process. Stranger still, after I stepped away from the corner to see him better, all I found was a dark shape silhouetted in shards of light, like a saintly figure pulled directly from a stained-glass window. As I watched, colors arced across his body, shimmering in vibrant arcs like sunlight across the iridescent scales of a dragonfly, leaving me speechless with wonder. When at last he spoke, his lips and tongue shone red like ripe strawberries.

"Quinn MacKenna."

He said my name like a prayer. I shivered, feeling as though someone had walked over my grave, aware of my body in a way that I hadn't been in since I was a teenager; every inch of my skin tingled with need and an involuntary groan escaped my lips. Indeed, the abrupt desire to be touched hit me like a physical blow, turning my legs to jelly so that I collapsed against the door of my cell.

The instant I wrapped my hands around the steel bars, however, the need receded. I still craved the sensation of someone's flesh pressed against my own, but I could think. I could get angry.

"What are ye doin' to me?" I demanded through clenched teeth.

The dazzling being gazed upon me with eyes of every color. As I straightened, they eased from a bright blue sky to the darkest ocean hues, from honey brown to pitch black, from emerald to moss. The effect should have been disorienting, but it wasn't; every shade was lovely in its own way. Heart-wrenching, even.

"I am liberating you," he replied, and I could hear the power in his voice. "Do you not wish to be free?"

"I can get out anytime I want. So get the hell away from me."

"I do not speak of this cage. I speak of you. Of what you deny yourself."

"What are ye?"

"I am whatever you want me to be, Quinn."

I both heard and saw his power reach out to me this time. It washed over me in a wave of multi-colored light, clinging as it passed. And yet, the effect was minimal compared to what he'd done before; goosebumps pebbled along my arms as though I'd been licked by a cool breeze on a hot day, but I could tolerate it. I glared through the bars.

"Knock that shit off."

"Quinn, please, you look so uncomfortable. Step away from the door. Let me help you."

The door. I wound my hands tighter around the steel bars, gripped them until the metal creaked and my knuckles went white. Within moments, the nimbus around the stranger began to dim until all that remained was a faint glow. His eyes ended up stuck somewhere between green and grey, leaving them murky and unremarkable as they implored me to do what he wanted.

"Quinn, just let go."

"Not goin' to happen," I snarled. "Now, what manner of Faelin' are ye?"

"I have no idea what you mean."

"Don't play dumb, we both know why your magic isn't workin'." I shook the bars until they sang, and grinned like a madwoman. "Pretty stupid, comin' at me in a room full of metal. Who sent ye? And why?"

The Faeling sighed. "He said you would be difficult."

"He?"

"Oh, well," the Faeling said, holding a set of metal keys pinched between his fingers the way you might a stinking diaper. "It's as my father used to say: if you can't seduce them, kill them."

"Come again?"

The Faeling didn't reply. Instead, he fiddled with the keys until he found the one he wanted, then strode toward and shoved it into the lock of my cell door. When it refused to turn, he drew back and fetched another, clearly irritated.

"Humans and their ridiculous mechanisms," he muttered as he tried the next key.

I considered taking a swipe at the bastard, but the moment I eased my grip on the bars his glow intensified and his eyes began to swirl again. Which meant my options were limited; I could either lash out and risk being put under his spell, or hope it took him long enough to find the right key for help to arrive. Unfortunately, I found neither choice appealing.

"Help! Somebody help me!" I shouted, jangling the door. "Maria! Max!"

I continued to scream their names, but no one came, not even as the Faeling cried out triumphantly in Gaelic and the lock finally disengaged. Thinking he'd won, he tried to yank open the door, but I wasn't about to let that happen; I dug in my heels and pulled with everything I had, yelling until my poor throat felt raw.

Within seconds, however, a pitiable howl joined mine; the Faeling's hands sizzled where they touched the metal bars, and his ethe-real glow was completely doused. In its place stood a tall, lithe creature with uncommonly large eyes, milky skin, and hair so curly it framed his entire face like a helmet. Objectively, his was a lovely, effeminate face—the sort that, in repose, attracts artists and poets obsessed with innocence and youth. Or it would have, were it not for the hateful expression smeared across it.

"Stop struggling and let me kill you!" he hissed through crooked teeth and pale lips.

"Fat fuckin' chance."

"You are making this much harder than it has to be."

"Killin' me, ye mean? D'ye even hear yourself when ye talk?"

The Faeling opened his mouth to speak, but another voice cut through the din of our struggle so that we both froze like children caught chucking rotten fruit through the neighborhood bully's bedroom window on a bet.

Trust me, he'd deserved it.

"Quinn!"

This time my name was spoken not like a prayer, but like an invo-cation; I shivered as the sound of it reverberated throughout the room like a peal of thunder. As one, the Faeling and I stared at the hulking figure who charged into the room, panting with exertion. Unfortu-nately, the Faeling rallied first.

"Maximiliano Velez," he said, releasing the door. "I am so glad you have come."

Max staggered as if struck, his worried expression drifting towards confusion as he looked from me to my would-be assassin and back again.

"Please, you have to help," the Faeling pleaded, perfectly mimic-king a woman's voice. "Stop her before she hurts us both. That is why you came."

Too late, I realized what the Faeling was trying to do; if Max fell under his spell and took his side before reinforcements arrived, I would definitely be in a tight spot. And his plan might have worked, too, if the Fae bastard had been raised properly.

"Max, come here and—"

That was as far as the Faeling got before I rammed the whole freaking door—which he'd neglected to lock up after himself—into his sorry ass. The edge caught the bastard unaware and collided with his skull, sending him sprawling with a gash across his scalp. Thinking to run and get us both to safety, I snatched Max's hand and bolted for the gaping doorway.

Only Max would not budge.

I swore and wheeled, prepared to break whatever hold the Faeling had on him...but it wasn't the Faeling's influence which sent tongues of flame dancing along his skin like little bursts of lightning. It wasn't his magic that had the brujo's eyes blazing like gold discs in a face carved from an inferno. It was mine.

No, I thought.

It was ours.

"Quinn MacKenna," Max murmured, drawing my hand to his mouth, his smile so lascivious my heart rate spiked. "I remember you."

"Right," I replied, breathlessly. "Well, it's about time."

"What are you?"

The question came from the Faeling who knelt at our feet, one arm strewn over his eyes as though *we* were the bright and shining ones. Except it wasn't awe I saw in his face, or even lust—it was fear. And he wasn't looking at Max.

He was looking at me.

CHAPTER 9

Maria found us some ten minutes later, the mesmerizing Faeling nowhere in sight; the would-be assassin had fled through an impromptu portal before I could interrogate him. Unfortunately, he'd left pieces of his peculiar brand of magic behind; we'd discovered tattered remnants of his spells hanging from the rafters like transparent spiderwebs, the strands snatching at us whenever we moved. The euphoric aftermath never lasted more than a moment, but—after the third time I nearly collapsed from a sudden onslaught of unexpected pleasure—I'd decided we ought to get rid of it before some poor beat cop ended up in a puddle on the floor, jonesing for a cigarette.

So we'd started setting shit on fire.

As one does.

Max was busy tracing a wall with a hand encased in flame, burning away all evidence of the mysterious Faeling's power. I'd gone a more prosaic route and opted for the lighter Max had offered me. The result was pretty much the same no matter which of us did the deed, however: each thread went up in a harmless shower of sparks. Still, I supposed I couldn't blame Maria for reacting poorly; the two of us probably looked like an advertisement for Pyromaniacs Anonymous.

"What in Christ's name is going on here? Freeze, now!"

I turned, saw Maria had her gun out and pointed at me for the second time in half as many days, and snapped the lighter shut before she could put a bullet in me for attempted arson. Max, on the other hand, kept right on walking—forcing the detective to switch targets.

"Max?" Maria lowered her gun almost immediately. "Are you doing *magic*?!"

"Don't be silly," I replied. "I simply set his hand on fire and dared him not to cry about it."

"You did what?!"

"She is teasing you, Maria," Max interjected without sparing either of us a look. "The truth is it was a bet. If I clear the whole room without shedding a single tear, Quinn owes me a date."

"Liar, liar, hand on fire," I said, rolling my eyes. "Anyway, shouldn't ye be almost finished by now? The sooner we get out of here, the better."

At the back of the room, a strand ignited with a pop and hiss.

"*Si.* All done."

As if on cue, a cry sounded from further down the hallway. On its heels came another, followed by gritty gurgles of masculine laughter. Cops. The three of us exchanged hurried glances; we were about to have company, and the whole damn room smelled like butane. Maria holstered her gun, but not before pointing at Max and me in turn.

"One of you *will* fill me in on what happened here. I mean it." The detective beckoned us over. "If anyone asks, you're with me. Otherwise, keep to yourselves and try to look harmless."

Max nudged me with his elbow. "You heard the detective, be sure to keep your hands to yourself."

"Very funny, Casacoma."

"Are you two about done?" Maria barked.

"Ask Captain Spanish, he started it."

Max chuckled. "*Si*, Maria, we are done. Get us out of here, *por favor.*"

In the end, I managed to keep my hands to myself, and we managed to leave the precinct without anyone the wiser—though I suspected that was largely because O'Malley's shift had ended and no one else seemed to know or care what we were up to. Once outside, Maria called a cab, which gave Max and me more than enough time to summarize what had happened with the Faeling intruder while I waited for Areadbhar to return. It also allowed me to ask a few questions of my own.

"How d'ye know I was in trouble, anyway, Max?"

"I didn't. Camila sent me to ask you a question, but *el hada* used his magic to prevent me from reaching you. At first, I thought I had missed a turn and gotten lost, but then I heard you screaming and broke the enchantment."

"What d'ye call him?"

"*El hada*," Max reiterated. "It is our word for his kind. For what you call the Fae."

"Ah." I sighed, disappointed. "I was hopin' ye knew what he was. I don't suppose you've encountered anythin' like him in the past?"

Max thought about it. "There are creatures with similar power, but few who would dare attack in broad daylight in the middle of a police station. Seduction magic is an art honed in darkness and best reserved for a willing victim. For a creature to ignore such things, it would have to be either very powerful, or at least powerfully motivated."

I found myself staring up into the brujo's dark eyes, surprised by the eloquence of his response and remembered that I was talking to a practitioner who had accumulated at least two decades of experience that I lacked. At that precise moment, it occurred to me that I'd put Max in a box without meaning to. That, between the rampant flirtation and our mutual attraction, I'd been playing in the shallow end of a much deeper pool.

"Is something wrong?" Max asked.

"Uh, no. Sorry." I cleared my throat. "So, what was it that Camila wanted to know?"

"It doesn't matter now," Maria cut in, frostily.

"Why not?"

"Because," Max replied, "there can no longer be any doubt you are who you say you are."

"And why's that? Not that I'm complainin', but for a minute there I was sure I'd have to submit blood before you'd believe me."

"That will not be necessary," Max insisted, cutting off whatever Maria had been about to say. In the sullen silence that followed, a cab painted in candy-cane colors swerved through two lanes of traffic and pulled up to the curb some thirty feet ahead of us.

"And why won't it be necessary?"

"Because this." The brujo gestured from himself to me and back again. "Because us."

"Enough chitter-chatter," Maria snapped, her agitation palpable. "Come on, the meter's running."

"What's her problem?" I whispered out of the side of my mouth as soon as the detective was out of earshot, though I had to admit part of me was relieved to have Maria acting like her old, bitchy self.

"She blames you for many things, most of which she knows is not your fault. Deep down, however, I believe she sees you for what you really are and resents you for it."

"And what am I?" I asked, fully prepared for a lewd comment, or maybe some good old-fashioned ribbing.

"You are revered," Max replied, somberly. "And Maria is, in her heart, a very romantic woman who cannot tell the difference between love and adoration. The rest is just an excuse to validate how she feels."

I gaped at the brujo. "Since when d'ye get so insightful?"

"I am what I have always been, and more," Max replied, cryptically.

Maria poked her head out of the cab's rear window. "Hey! What's the hold up?!"

"Go on ahead, I'll be right there," I assured Max.

The brujo did as I asked, sauntering off while I ducked into the shadows of a nearby alley. Pedestrians wandered past on opposite sides in loose throngs, but I figured few were paying close enough attention to see Areadbhar come flying to my hand—and fewer still who would have believed what they saw. The moment she reached my outstretched hand, I sighed with relief, feeling whole in a way I hadn't since sending her away.

"We really need to find a way to keep ye hidden," I murmured, softly.

Areadbhar vibrated so violently in response that it made my teeth chatter. Startled, I let go of her shaft. At first, she seemed content to buck from side to side. But then, so suddenly I could only watch in horror, the devourer on her blade began swallowing the rest of her; the jewel consumed her like some gaping maw. Within seconds, all that remained was a glimmering stone hovering in mid-air. I found it almost hot to the touch.

"Areadbhar?"

The stone pulsed in recognition against my fingers.

"D'ye do this for me?"

The stone grew hotter, which I took to mean yes.

"But I'll still be able to call on ye, like before? When I need ye, I mean?"

Hotter, still.

Feeling remarkably relieved to have at least one thing go my way today, I grinned, pocketed the stone, and raced to join the others before the rising cost of Maria's fare gave her a legitimate reason to kill me.

CHAPTER 10

The driver, a middle-aged Italian man, whipped us through the streets as though the conventional rules of the road were open to interpretation, earning a series of startled grunts from Max and disapproving scowls from the detective. Personally, I was glad for the distraction; it was reassuring to see Maria pissed at someone other than me, for once. Unfortunately, the constant breakneck turns meant all our legs and shoulders routinely occupied the same space.

A tinny voice warbled out of the cabbie's radio talking about some lunar event taking place in a couple weeks—something about a supermoon. The announcer squawked with excitement, urging New Englanders to mark their calendars. Apparently, this was the closest the celestial body would be to Earth this century, making it the largest moon we were likely to see in our lifetime.

"Dependin' on the lifetime," I muttered under my breath. Max shot me a questioning look, but I waved him off as though I hadn't said anything; I wasn't ready to confide in anyone just yet. Not until I knew whether immortality was truly in the cards for me. Of course, that didn't stop Maria from noting the exchange.

"What happened to your spear?" she asked, irritably.

"Oh, she's around."

"Where did you get something like that, anyway?"

"Atlantis," I replied, matter-of-factly, as I patted the slight bulge in my pocket. "I like to t'ink of her as a souvenir."

Maria merely rolled her eyes. "Fine, don't tell me."

I shrugged. There was no need to defend myself; it made no difference what Maria did or didn't believe. Besides, I had a feeling my extended absence would come up again, and that I'd have some explaining to do when it did. So, until then, I'd save my breath.

The cabbie pulled onto the narrow streets of Boston's North End some ten minutes later, forced to slow to a crawl to avoid clipping inattentive pedestrians. The meter continued to tick until at last he found an empty stretch of sidewalk and jerked the wheel. Once parked, Maria fetched a money clip from her jacket, counted out the total on the screen, and handed it over.

"What, no tip?"

"Oh, you wanted a tip? I can give you a tip." Maria wedged herself between the gap in the seats so she could look the driver in the eye. "Here's my tip: obey the speed limits, stop at red lights, and use your turn signal, or I'll call your boss and have you fired."

"Whatever, lady. Just get the fuck out of my cab."

"That's detective to you, Mr. Russo," Maria said, sweetly, as she raised her phone to snap a picture of the man's Taxi license. "I'm in a bit of a hurry today, but don't worry, I'll be sure to check in on you in case you need any more tips. Unless you'd rather get together where I work?"

The cabbie grunted, clearly unimpressed. "Alright, you've made your point, detective. Now, are you done busting my balls? Some of us have a job to do."

I stifled a laugh as I stepped out onto the sidewalk, made room for Max to join me, and surveyed our surroundings. As Boston's oldest district, the North End practically oozed kitschy charm; dominated by red brick tenements and cracked cobblestone streets, it was the sort of place that saw more foot traffic than actual traffic. During the day, that meant shopping and business lunches. At night, it meant drunken happy hours and raucous pub crawls. And yet, for some inexplicable reason, the particular stretch of road where we stood was all but abandoned—not unlike the park during our run-in with the slaugh.

"What a mook," Maria muttered as the cabbie peeled off. "Come on, we better hurry inside, just in case."

"In case what?"

"In case we were followed."

"Is that likely?" I asked, casting furtive glances left and right.

Max shrugged. "It can be tough to tell, these days. Not everyone is as bad at tailing people as you are."

I opened my mouth to say something snarky, but my companions were already on the move. Maria took the lead, headed directly for what appeared to be a solid brick wall running between two buildings. Before I could ask what she thought she was doing, however, the detective slapped a hand against the wall's surface and mumbled something under her breath which sounded an awful lot like a nursery rhyme.

The air changed.

Thick with moisture and pregnant with energy, it felt like we'd stepped into a storm cloud; my hair hung heavy down my back while those on my arms stood straight up. And then, as suddenly as it had arrived, it dispersed. I let out a breath I didn't even realize I'd been holding as cracks began to spread outward from Maria's hand. They began small, at first—thin and arcing like forked tongues of lightning. Within seconds, however, the cracks became chasms as whole chunks of stone shattered and collapsed in a pile at Maria's feet. Dust swirled into the air like fog. And yet, there was no grit to speak of, nothing to irritate the nose or eyes.

"How did she do that?" I asked Max.

"You mean disperse the glamour? It is easy enough to do if you have the key."

Feeling foolish not to have seen through the illusion, I watched in fascination as the pile of rubble shimmered, wavering like a mirage to reveal a three-story building where the wall had once stood. Maria's hand lay on the door—a door that opened almost immediately, the creak of its hinges followed by a familiar, high-pitched voice.

"Lady Quinn!"

A pixie no bigger than my hand flung herself at me through the gap, her wings fluttering with such frequency that they made a buzzing sound somewhere between a bee and a dragonfly. I shied away in surprise, but that didn't save me from the diminutive Faeling's assault; Petal took hold of my finger and spun around it with all the grace of a Vegas stripper, squealing with glee.

"You two know each other, I take it?" Maria asked, cocking one of her painted-on eyebrows.

"Ye could say that," I replied, unable to hide my sudden confusion. "What are ye doin' here, Petal?"

"I should go on ahead," Max interjected, patting my shoulder. "*Mi hermana* will have questions."

Maria was instantly hot on his heels. "I'll go with you."

"The Huntress swore you'd come," Petal said, ignoring both my question and the others' departures. Her face was much as I remembered it—as expressive and rosy-cheeked as it had been beneath the Scottish sky on the day I was abducted. And yet there was a haunted look in her eyes I hadn't seen since I'd freed her from Frankenstein's prison, what felt like a lifetime ago.

"Scathach did? When was that?"

"Before she left. She knew what was coming, and that she could not hope to stop it."

"What was comin'? D'ye mean Catha, or the slaugh?"

Petal smiled at me in a way that could have meant anything, or nothing. "The others will be very pleased to see you've made it back. We were all very worried."

"Others? What d'ye mean, 'others'?"

"Everyone's inside. Come on, they'll be glad to see you, and they could really use the encouragement."

"Hold on. I still don't understand what—"

"There's something's different about you," Petal interjected, tilting her chin so that she could scan the length of my face. The pixie leapt from my finger and hovered, her wings beating furiously. "Have you come to save us, again, Lady Quinn?"

"Save ye?"

"Nevermind." Petal waved that away. "Come and say hello to the other refugees."

I blinked owlishly, realizing at last that the detective had brought me to one of the safehouses that Gretel had mentioned in her office. Was that why she'd sent me to find Max? If so, I owed the litigator a bouquet of flowers. Of course, it also raised a horde of new questions —like what Max and Camila were doing hiding out with a bunch of Faeling refugees, for example, or how Maria had gotten involved.

"Fine, but afterwards I want some answers," I replied, unwilling to drop the subject. "Who else is here, anyway?"

The answer surprised me. Faces, both familiar and unfamiliar, crowded an entrance hall that reminded me of an alleyway you might stumble upon in the oldest of the European cities; high stone walls bordered either side of a narrow path, their brick facades cluttered with doors and windows from which dozens of Faelings had emerged. Some I knew by name, others by sight. Ennis, a one-armed ogre with a face that looked far crueler than he actually was, loomed over a small tribe of shifty-eyed goblins. A Kelpie I'd once interrogated leaned out over a windowsill; the majority of her fishy parts hidden in shadow. Pixies flitted about above my head, occasionally alighting on clotheslines which hung across the gap. In the end, however, it was the sky that stole my attention; it surged and roiled with every color of a sunrise—blushing pinks and molten golds intermingling with pastel blues and fiery reds.

"Do you like what we did with the place?" Petal asked, her voice so close to my ear I nearly swatted at her out of reflex. She giggled and settled on my shoulder, kicking her little legs back and forth like a child on a swing.

"How d'ye manage all this?" I asked, gesturing helplessly at everything.

"Much of it was here before we arrived. Grammarie, unlike glamour, does not fade with time. This place was fashioned when Boston was ruled by Puritans, back when our magic was strong, and iron was scarce."

I did a little mental arithmetic and realized Petal was talking about events some three hundred years prior. The way she said it made me wonder just how old the pixie was—and what all she'd seen. For a brief moment, I considered taking her aside and telling the pixie what all I'd been through; perhaps she could offer me the clarity I was looking for. Sadly, there wasn't time.

"What is everyone doing out here?"

A voice cut through the din, and the gathered crowd parted like the sea—their myriad shapes peeling away in a kaleidoscope of color until there stood a single, solitary figure standing at the far end of the alleyway: Camila Velez. The bruja looked haggard, even hollow-eyed, as she took stock of her surroundings. And yet, I couldn't help but notice the Faelings straighten beneath the weight of her gaze.

It was clear who was in charge.

"You all know it is not safe for everyone to be out like this," Camila said, her accent somehow more sibilant than her brother's. "I am sure *Senorita* MacKenna appreciates the gesture, but now you must go back to your homes."

As one, the Faelings ducked their heads and dispersed like a defeated mob, though a few made sure to offer a friendly wave or fleeting smile before departing. Still, it put me in a grim mood.

"She is right to send them away," Petal whispered into my ear. "But also wrong."

"Why'd she do it?"

"We draw too much attention when we come together. It makes us easier to find. But if we must stay hidden away, then we are bound to fade."

"How long has it been?"

Petal's laughter chimed like a bell beside my ear.

"What's so funny?" I asked, mindful of Camila's stare from across the way.

"It's nothing. You mortals ask such silly questions sometimes, that's all."

"Aye, we mortals," I echoed, drily. "So, now what?"

"Now we find out whether Camila trusts you, or not."

"What's that supposed to—"

Camila beckoned us forward, turned on her heel, and began walking towards a door at the far end of the alleyway—an iron door, unless I was mistaken.

"Guess she's decided," Petal said before leaping from my shoulder in pursuit of the bruja, zipping away before I could ask which way the scales had tipped.

CHAPTER 11

The iron door had already shut behind the other two by the time I caught up and was far heavier than I expected. Though it took a while, I managed to open the thick metal slab in six-inch increments, its hinges squealing so violently in protest that the screech of metal followed me into the next room like chthonic theme music. And yet, no one turned to greet me when I entered, or even to bitch about the noise. Instead, I found a slew of figures squaring off in the middle of the room, fighting for elbow room as they squabbled.

"There are no guarantees it will work," Max was saying, his sultry baritone laced with uncertainty. "Harnessing that much power is one thing, but focusing it in such a way..."

"The spell will work," Camila countered, projecting confidence. "It has to. We won't have another chance like this in a hundred years."

"Perhaps. Perhaps not. There are other ways, Camila. Safer ways."

"And I have tried most of them, already. You were not yourself, or you would know that."

Max looked away.

"*Mi hermano,*" Camila said as she reached for his cheek and brought his chin back around, "this is not your call to make. It will not be you doing the spell. Saving him is my responsibility. I did not ask for anyone's help. I did not ask for any of this."

At this point, Camila turned away and caught me staring. Though unshed tears threatened her mascara, the bruja appeared much the same as the day we first met—a dark-haired gypsy whose beauty would only ripen with time. Of course, the old Camila would have let the tears fall and collapsed insensate in her brother's arms. This Camila, I sensed, would not.

"I am sorry for making you wait. We have had a lot to discuss, thanks to your news. Is it true? About Victor, I mean. Is he truly gone, for good?"

"He is. Truly."

Camila smiled, and that singular act smoothed away so many lines that she appeared a decade younger at least. I smiled back, genuinely pleased to discover not everything I'd put myself through was in vain.

"Please sit, and we will talk shortly," she insisted, pointing to a stool sitting in the corner of the room.

I opened my mouth to crack a joke about me and corners, then closed it; now probably wasn't the best time. Instead, I did as the bruja requested and let the others get back to their heated discussion while I took the opportunity to survey my latest surroundings.

The room itself was dimly lit, sparsely decorated, and horribly cramped; the ceiling was so low I could reach out and press my palm flat against its surface, while a pair of wall sconces gave it all the ambience of a cheap bordello. Worse, there were no windows, and the air was stale. Between that and an iron door which very few Faelings could feasibly open, the entire thing felt very much like a bunker to me. A safe room sitting smack dab in the middle of a Faeling safe house like a lockbox within a vault.

Question was, what were they guarding?

And how much was it worth?

The argument I'd been successfully ignoring grew even louder the moment Maria weighed in; the detective sided with Camila, though she sounded less than thrilled about it. Unfortunately, I was still struggling to put the pieces together. Camila was clearly in charge, and apparently intended to cast a potentially hazardous spell —though why and what it had to do with this "Hex Moon" remained a total mystery.

"See," Camila was saying, "Maria understands that I am only doing what is necessary. I cannot do this forever. The Fae need one of their own to guide them."

"So this has nothing to do with getting Robin back by any means necessary?" Max asked.

"And so what if it does?"

"Robin made his stand, Camila. It is not your responsibility to save him or the Fae. Walk away."

"Enough. Robin was there for me when you were not." Camila held up a placating hand. "I do not blame you, and I am glad your memories have returned, but that does not give you the right to dismiss my feelings towards Robin, or his people. I will not leave him at the mercy of that creature, nor will I forsake the Fae who followed him."

"This is not like you," Max said, his voice strained. "We do not fight battles we cannot win, *mi hermana*. It is not and never has been our way. We run, and we live."

Camila's expression softened. "What you are talking about is not living. Life is not about the fights you run from, but having something to fight for. I have found mine. Perhaps it is time you found yours."

Max looked away.

"That still doesn't answer the bigger question," Maria interjected. "Say the spell works and we find out where they're all being held, then what?"

An altogether new, vaguely pompous voice sounded from the shadows in response to the detective's question. "Then, you and the...treasonous misfits orchestrate a prison break."

Despite how long it'd been since we spoke, I recognized that voice almost immediately—though I certainly hadn't expected to hear it in this particular room. The speaker padded forward into the light, standing several inches taller than I remembered in a designer suit tailored to accommodate narrow shoulders, a barreled chest, and overlong arms.

"What are ye doin' here?" I asked, wondering how on earth I'd missed the Pooka when I first arrived.

Albi sought me out with his electric yellow eyes, the furry tips of his foot-long ears brushing the ceiling as they twitched—reacting to sounds none of us could hear. I must have looked as stunned to see him as I felt, because he spoke again without ever taking his eyes off me.

"She knows about me."

Those four words echoed throughout the room like a gunshot, and nearly everyone whirled on me as though I'd been hit, their expressions running the gamut from curiosity to alarm. Only Petal, who fluttered about on the far side of the room, seemed unperturbed; the pixie waved.

"Why are ye lot lookin' at me like that?" I asked.

"You've spoken with someone in my organization," Albi accused. "Who was it?"

"What's he on about?" I asked, turning to the others for help.

"Answer the question, Quinn," Camila replied.

I fought to control my face, realizing too late that I should have simply kept my mouth shut and played dumb until I could see the whole picture—until I knew what Albi was doing here, and why. Instead, I'd run my finger across the wet canvass and left behind a smear too big to be ignored.

"Fine," I said, shrugging. "But I have no idea what Albi is talkin' about. I've been gone a long time. What would I want with a bookie?"

"Not that organization," Albi snapped. "The Chancery. Who was it? Who told you I was in charge?"

"Who says I talked to anyone?"

"You did, the second you saw me. I expected some surprise, and maybe a little disgust. But what I got instead was pure shock."

"Aye, well, I had no idea they'd stoop to work with someone like ye, that's all."

That wasn't strictly a lie, which meant I was finally able to pour some real conviction into my voice. That's the funny thing about lying: those who do it best manage to believe everything they say...until they don't. Sadly, I hadn't gotten there, quite yet.

"No," Albi drawled, "you are hiding something. Protecting someone. You knew the instant you laid eyes on me that I should not be here. Someone has told you I took over for Robin Redcap, and that is —as the mortals like to say—privileged information."

"Did anyone follow you here?" Camila interjected, looking fiercer than I'd ever seen her as she turned from me to her brother.

"Not that I saw. But you must trust me in this, Camila. Quinn is no spy."

"So you have said. Repeatedly. But now I am beginning to wonder if your memories have returned, or if someone has given you new ones."

"Are you accusing me of not knowing my own mind?"

"Don't get sidetracked," Albi snapped, baring fangs. "This is bigger than you two and your petty sibling squabbles. Don't you see? If this gets back to the Chancery, it could ruin everything. Now, I want an answer. Who have you spoken to?"

Despite the brutal intensity of their combined attention, I never wavered; Gretel wasn't exactly a friend, but she'd done me a favor by not turning me in, not to mention passing along Max's whereabouts. Without knowing what Albi intended to do with the information, there was simply no way I was going to give her up.

"I can't—" I began.

"It was Gretel," Petal supplied, cheerily.

The others swung around a second time.

"How can you be so sure?" Albi asked.

"Because, I was the one who told her where Max and Maria were planning to meet, today. Which is how Lady Quinn knew where to find them."

"You told her what?!" Camila asked, aghast.

"You may not trust her," Petal replied, petulantly, "but Gretel has always done what's best for us. Since Robin and her elder brother were taken, she's gone out of her way to save us from the slaugh.

Sometimes that means knowing where you all are, so she can make sure the slaugh end up somewhere you are not."

"Except today, they found us," Maria hissed.

Petal rolled her eyes. "Yes, but whose fault was that? Or did some other idiot cast a clumsy illusion spell and send it out into the city?"

Maria blushed and muttered something under her breath I didn't catch.

"Of course it was clumsy. It bled so much magic a noseless, eyeless child could have tracked it. And the slaugh are not children. They are Fae's finest, most determined hunters. The only reason we have not yet been found is that the Huntsman remains in Fae and this city reeks of iron. And even then, while you all sit here with your bickering and your plotting, they draw closer."

"Does that mean you would be willing to strike a deal?" Albi asked in the silence that followed, pointedly ignoring the guilty expressions on display throughout the room.

"Albi!" Camila chastised. "She does not—"

"I am not a mortal child to be so easily swayed," the Pooka replied. "If the pixie cannot prove what she says is true, then our arrangement has come to an end."

Camila's shoulders slumped, and I got the sense that Albi had asked for something far more serious than it sounded. Before I could inquire further, however, Petal drifted forward into the center of the room. She spun in a slow circle.

"My wings if I lie," she said once she faced the Pooka. "Your loyalty to Lady Quinn if I do not."

A collective gasp went up from those around me.

Albi's smile was lecherous. "For how long?"

"Until the sun replaces the Hex Moon in the mortal sky."

"Hah. Until the witching hour on the night of the Hex Moon."

"Very well. The deal is struck."

"The deal is struck," Albi echoed.

Several seconds passed, after which the Pooka scratched manically at the coarse fur of his cheeks with a clawed hand the way a dog might. "Well, that is a shame. I'd have loved to pluck your wings, little flower."

Petal stuck out her tongue in reply.

"Can someone fill me in on what just happened?" I asked, raising my hand.

"Petal vouched for you," Albi replied, sounding terribly bored. "If she'd have been wrong, either knowingly or unknowingly, she'd have been stripped of her wings. Instead, I am on your side...for now."

"And I'm supposed to trust ye? Just like that?"

Albi shrugged. "That's how our contracts work. Once the terms are set, there is no way to break them."

"So, if we were to strike a deal, you'd have no choice but to stand by whatever ye said?"

Albi opened his mouth to reply, but Petal cut him off almost immediately. "Our contracts are binding," she said. "But those we make with mortals are not. Not anymore."

"Which means they were, though, once?" I clarified.

"Long ago, yes. Manlings had more honor, then. Their vows meant something. But that time has passed." Petal tilted her head. "I'm surprised you have not heard any of this before."

"It never came up," I admitted. "But then, I haven't exactly stopped to smell the wildflowers. There's a lot about Fae culture I'm still strugglin' to understand."

"That's alright. You are doing very well, so far. For a mortal."

"For a mortal, huh?" I coughed a laugh into my hand. "Aye, well, I suppose it can't be any harder than figurin' out what made the Otherworld turn."

A sudden cry snapped my head up; Petal had dipped a few inches, her skin so pale it was like someone had flipped a switch and extinguished the light beneath her skin. Albi, meanwhile, looked as though I'd socked him in the gut.

"Did we mishear you, or did you really say something about the Otherworld, just now?" the Pooka managed in a throaty rumble, his haughtiness all but forgotten.

"Where d'ye t'ink I've been all this time? Well, besides the Underworld, I mean. And the Titan Realm. And Fae, briefly." I waved both hands. "Look, it's a long story."

Petal came at me like a high fastball, stopping just in time to hover mere inches from my face, her eyes brimming with tears. She clutched her hands together at her chest as though it hurt. And maybe it did; I had no idea what was plaguing her, or Albi.

"Tell us everything," Petal said.

"Please," Albi added, uncharacteristically.

"Well alright, since ye asked so nicely...but ye lot should probably get comfortable. This is goin' to take a while."

CHAPTER 12

To their credit, no one interrupted me with a barrage of questions, though I suspected that was largely because no one knew where to begin. What sort of follow-ups do you ask someone who rode a Faeling hound bareback, or swan-dived off a floating island, or survived being carted around in the maw of a mythical sea monster? What clarifications would have possibly made any of it seem less fabricated? Frankly, it all sounded completely ridiculous—even to me, and I was there for every absurd second of it.

And yet, I could see they believed me—though perhaps not at first. My description of the Otherworld as a deathless realm locked in an eternal power struggle between codependent nations, complete with fugue-inducing edibles, made Fae seem downright pedestrian by comparison. At least there, change was possible. But by the time I made it to the cosmic hallway and my mother's final farewell, I noticed even Maria was hanging on my every word. From then on, they oohed and ahhed over each leg of my journey, though some anecdotes earned stronger reactions than others. My mention of the infamous Witch of Aeaea, for example, left all three practitioners in the room wide-eyed and open-mouthed. Similarly, the tale of my haphazard ascension to godhood—not to mention the schizophrenic episodes that came with it—earned an exchange of troubled looks. And yet, it was only once I began to talk about venturing to the Underworld to retrieve Max and save Ryan that anyone cut me off.

"I won't listen to this," Maria said, waving her hands about as if shooing away a horde of stinging insects. "I can't."

"But Maria..." Camila moved to take her friend's arm, but the detective pulled away.

"No, Camila." Maria took a deep breath. "Look, I've seen enough to know that there are some things the Bible left out. The Fae, the pagan gods, these other realms she's been going on about...fine. But if she really went to Hell, I don't want to hear about it."

"It wasn't Hell," I corrected. "At least, not the Hell you're thinkin' of. From what I saw, there were several afterlives all sort of sittin' next to each other like boroughs."

"I don't believe that," Maria said, shaking her head. "Heaven is Heaven, and Hell is Hell. That's just what I believe. You should finish your story without me. Someone can always fill me in, later, if needed. Besides, I still have a job to do, don't I, Camila? Assuming everything is going ahead as planned."

She and Camila shared a meaningful look.

"Your guy delivered?" Camila asked.

"Yes. He's getting curious, but he flipped the dragon's blood."

"Wait," I interjected, "that's what was in the jar Max handed over?"

The two women glared at me in disapproval, but I wasn't about to back down this time; I had friends who were dragons. Well, were-dragons. And they were more acquaintances, really. Okay, one-time drinking buddies. But the notion that Camila was trading in dragon's blood made my stomach queasy all the same.

"Well?" I urged.

"It was," Camila replied. "Why?"

"How d'ye get the blood?"

"How do you think? I bought it. Max and I used to own a magical paraphernalia shop before the hospital bills bankrupted us. But that does not mean I lost my supply chain."

Jesus. Hospital bills and bankruptcy? I hadn't even stopped to consider how much it must have cost. For a moment, I considered letting this one go. Whether I meant for it to happen or not, the brujo's coma was my fault, which meant I had no room to throw stones. And yet, I couldn't; guilt should make you want to speak up, not shut up.

"What I want to know is how it's sourced," I confessed.

Camila raised both eyebrows. "You are concerned for the dragons?"

"Why d'ye say that like it's such a huge surprise?"

"I am sorry. I did not mean for it to come out that way. It is just...you do not seem like the same person I met two years ago. *Sí*, I realize you have been through much. But such things tend to make people harder. Meaner. And you were already those things."

"Is that supposed to be an insult, or a compliment?"

"Perhaps both. But, to answer your question, I get all my supplies through a white witch network. Everything they procure is ethically sourced."

Maria coughed into her hand.

"Right," Camila continued, "feel free to go, Maria. But think about using someone else for the rest. Maybe several people. We want to avoid any suspicion."

"I'll do that." The detective looked as though she were going to add something else, but ultimately headed for the exit. Unfortunately, the bulky iron door proved even harder to push open than it had to pull; I watched Maria struggle for a very satisfying handful of seconds before adding my weight to the endeavor.

"Thanks," Maria muttered as we finally shoved the door open.

"Don't mention it. Although, if ye really are grateful, could ye possibly do me a favor?"

"What kind of favor?"

I bent down so as not to be easily overheard. "I need to find out where the Sickos are. Ye know, the FBI unit that Jimmy is assigned—"

"I know who they are. Why on earth would you want to know that?"

I opened my mouth to respond but realized the truth was too complicated to get into, especially considering Maria had no interest in hearing about my afterlife. So, I did what any responsible woman with a hidden agenda would do in my situation: I lied.

"I heard a rumor while I was away and wanted to check on 'em, that's all."

"I don't believe you. But it doesn't matter. I don't know where they are. Jimmy and I aren't as close as we used to be, not since he got married."

"Jimmy got married?" I asked, so startled I nearly shouted it. I could suddenly feel everyone's eyes on us, but I didn't care; I was too busy trying to decide how I felt about the fact that my childhood friend and former lover had gotten hitched. Sadly, this wasn't the time. "Nevermind. That's not important, right now. Could ye maybe put out some feelers and let me know? Ye know I wouldn't ask if it wasn't serious."

"Alright, fine. I'll text Camila if I find anything out."

"Great. I appreciate it."

Maria started to slip past me, then hesitated. "Look...I'm sorry I threw you in a cell and almost got you killed. Camila's right. You have changed. I don't know that I believe a word of your inner goddess crap, but you aren't the spoiled bitch I used to know."

"Good t'ing ye didn't shoot me, then," I teased.

"There's always next time," Maria replied before ducking out the door.

I wasn't sure how much of that was a joke and how much a threat.

"I still think you are making a mistake," Max was saying when I turned back around, speaking loudly enough to be heard over the piercing squeal of the door as it ground shut. "There have to be other, safer ways—"

"We are done having this conversation," Camila snapped.

"Can I ask what ye two are fightin' about?" I ventured, raising a hand for good measure. "I know it has to do with breakin' Robin out. And somethin' called a Hex Moon. But honestly, I had a hard time followin' it all. Also, I have some questions of me own. Like what are the slaugh doin' in Boston, and what do we know about this Catha person? And what was that t'ing that attacked us back at the precinct?"

"Wait, don't you want to finish your story, first?" Petal asked.

"There's not much more to tell," I lied, eager to stop reliving one traumatic event after another like I was in some form of voluntary exposure therapy. "Let's see...I found Max. Frankenstein found us. Max killed him, or so I thought. Max got called back to his body, and I went after Ryan." I stopped to clear my throat. "Frankenstein tried to take control of Ryan's body, and Ryan fought it, but he couldn't win. So, in the end, I did what I had to do."

Silence greeted my account, for which I was thankful; I wasn't ready to talk about what had happened in Atlantis. Of course, that meant I'd left out all sorts of other details—such as meeting Hades, or starting a brawl in Valhalla, or having a heart-to-heart with Nate's parents. For some reason, that thought compelled me to reach into my pocket, past Areadbhar, and wrap my hand around the strange object the Temples had bestowed upon me before I returned to Aeaea. Thanks to Circe, I knew now what it was—though why it had been given to me in particular remained a mystery.

After all, I wasn't royalty.

"I am truly sorry for your loss," Max said, snapping me back to the present moment.

The others mumbled similar sentiments.

"I appreciate that, t'anks."

"Ryan did much for our kind before his exile was lifted," Albi added, sounding oddly thoughtful as he turned to the only other Faeling in the room. "He was an exceptional liaison, always looking out for those who could not walk about unnoticed, especially those who had trouble adapting to life here. We will see he is remembered for such things, and not what he became."

Petal ducked her head. "Seconded."

For some reason, the Pooka's unexpected kindness rankled. It felt wrong somehow that there were others out there who might grieve Ryan's loss. Others he might have called friends. And yet, I knew I was being unfair; there was at least one other person who deserved to mourn him at least as much as I did.

"Christoff," I blurted. "How is Christoff? And his kids, how are they?"

"I wondered when you would ask," Camila replied, lightly. "They are safe. Before Robin was taken, he sent word to Christoff and the other independents who call Boston home. I believe most left the city. Last I heard, Christoff and his cubs were on vacation, though I have no idea why they chose Alaska of all places."

"Christoff has friends there," I said, grinning. Truthfully, I had no idea whether Christoff had gone to stay with the Alaskan werebears or not. I certainly hoped so. Their leader, Armor, was an honorable sort who could be depended on to offer sanctuary. And then there was Starlight—a drug-addled teddy bear whose foresight bordered on prophetic. If anyone could keep Christoff and his kids out of harm's way, it would be them.

"Well, you can never have too many of those." Camila gestured to Albi. "You should go, too. Your mistress may get suspicious if you are gone too long."

"She doesn't notice much, these days," Albi replied. "Though it pains me to admit it, Liam has proven himself a useful distraction. She seems far less volatile whenever he's around."

"Why do I know that name?" I asked. "Liam, I mean?"

"He's what you might call my other half," the Pooka explained. "The Gancanagh who Catha elected to replace the Huntress. He is what the mortals once called a love-talker. A seducer of Manlings."

Max and I exchanged glances.

"And what does a love-talker look like?" I asked.

"To a Manling? Like every beautiful thing they've ever seen or desired. Before they began wearing iron, mortals used to fall at the Gancanagh's feet and writhe like snakes as they passed. Or so it once was. This realm has made less of us all. Now, you would have a hard time telling him apart from an elf." Albi narrowed his eyes until they were little more than slits hovering amidst pitch black fur. "Why?"

"Because it is possible he is the one who attacked us at the precinct," Max answered.

"Except he didn't look like an elf. Not at first. He was bathed in light. And his voice..." I drifted off, shuddering. "If it weren't for the steel bars between us, I t'ink he could've cut me to ribbons, and I would have died beggin' him to kiss me."

"That's impossible," Albi replied.

"You all have been saying that a lot," Camila accused. "First when Catha came, then when the slaugh followed, and now when we find out your 'other half' came for my brother."

"Actually, I do not believe he was after me," Max said. "He wanted to kill Quinn. In hindsight, I think it is possible the slaugh were after her, and not us."

"Catha is looking for her," Albi noted. "She has refused to say why. But I do know she wants Lady Quinn alive, which means she would not have called on the slaugh. They are not accustomed to leaving their prey alive."

"The slaugh left, actually," I recalled, thinking back. "The night hags were gone before I went into the precinct. I didn't know why, although it felt weird at the time."

"The night hags don't retreat unless they are ordered to do so. But I was with Catha this morning. She gave no such commands."

"And was Liam with ye, this mornin'?"

"Of course, he...no. No, he asked to be excused. I'd forgotten..." Albi's ears drooped incrementally. "He never came back. And I didn't notice."

"So, is it possible Liam was holdin' the slaugh's leash?"

"No," Albi replied, though doubt had begun to creep into his voice. "He doesn't have that kind of power. None of us do."

"Except you said it yourself," Camila interjected. "Liam has distracted your mistress and escaped your notice. Only, what if it is more than that? What if he has seduced her, and bespelled you?"

"I do not see how," Albi replied, though doubt had begun to creep into his voice. "It would take more power than a Gancanagh possesses, even in Fae. Much more."

"What makes ye say that?" I asked.

"Bespelling Manlings is one thing. It is in our nature. What we were meant for, you might say. The ability to sway our own kind, however, is an uncommon one. But to seduce a being like Catha with nothing more than glamour..."

"What is she, really? Ye all talk about her like she's some sort of monster, except the Chancery has monsters of its own. So, what could possibly scare the creatures that go bump in the night?"

"That I cannot say."

"Why not?"

Albi shook his head.

"We made a deal to keep her identity a secret," Petal replied, chiming in for the first time in a while. "Every member of the Chancery is bound by it. Even those who fled."

"We have learned a few things, despite that," Camila added, though she sounded quite bitter. "We know she is more a force of nature than a person. We know that, since she arrived, the whole city has become more violent. There have been more accidents. Deaths. Whatever she is, her power seems unstable. Which is why Robin opposed her, and why we have no choice but to stop her."

Petal clapped her hands together. "Except now we have you, Lady Quinn. Which means we stand a much better chance!"

"Me? Why me?"

"Because you were meant to lead us. Albi has already pledged himself to you, and the others will undoubtedly follow suit. They know what you did for us. And once they find out who you really are, what you really are, they will stand with you."

"Petal—" Camila began.

"I know you have done what you could for us, Camila," Petal interrupted, "but Lady Quinn is descended from the Tuatha Dé. She journeyed to the Otherworld and drank from its waters. She has to do this."

Camila stiffened.

"I can't do that, Petal," I said, firmly.

"But you must."

"Look, I've only been here for a little over half a day, and most of that has been spent playin' catch-up. I can't just waltz into this mess and start barkin' orders. I could get ye all caught, or even killed. Camila, on the other hand, has an actual plan. Plus, she's kept ye lot safe so far. I say ye give her the support she deserves."

"Please, stop," Camila snapped. "I do not need your pity, Quinn. If the Fae would prefer to follow you, that is their right. I can find Robin on my own."

Max reached for his sister. "Camila, do not—"

"No. If they believe she can save them, so be it. She put an end to Victor, after all, so maybe they are right to rely on her. We both know I never could have done that." Camila wrung her hands together, her expression haunted. "I just want to find Robin."

"Well, it's a moot point, either way," I said, loud enough to quell the others before they could voice their opinions on the matter. "I'm not stayin' in Boston. I have somethin' else I have to do."

"Something more important than saving your people?" Camila stared at me like I was some sort of diseased creature thrashing about in the middle of the room. "What kind of coward are you?"

"Camila!" Max cried.

"That's alright, Max," I said, sounding a great deal calmer than I felt. "I t'ink we were about done here, anyway. I'll see meself out."

CHAPTER 13

Several entreaties and one relocation later, I found myself sitting alone in one of the tenements that lined the alleyway. The apartment should have been cramped, but wasn't; I lounged against the arm of a sectional at the far end of a lavish living room, sipping water from a glass one of the Fae had procured when my throat started to ache from all the yelling. A grandfather clock stood along a wall next to an empty fireplace, lulling me to sleep with its rhythmic ticking—so much so that I almost didn't notice the door to the street creak open. Petal floated in, her gossamer wings fluttering at her back. To my chagrin, Camila followed, shutting the door firmly behind her.

"Did they really send ye to mediate?" I asked Petal. "Or d'ye draw the short straw?"

"Manlings rarely draw straws anymore, you know," Petal remarked. "I've always found it odd, the way their expressions survive long after their bodies wither and die. Their history, too. Our kind neglects such things. The past is not dead. Not for us."

"Our kind?" I made it a question. "Does that mean ye believe I'm one of ye?"

Petal drifted over and settled on the opposite arm of the couch.

Camila, meanwhile, kept her back pressed to the door as if afraid to move further into the room. I supposed I couldn't blame her; she and I hadn't exactly been civil to each other after I'd tried to leave. Indeed, we'd quickly found that "coward" was a mild insult by our standards.

"I believe you are no longer human," Petal replied, drawing my attention back to the conversation at hand. "But neither are you Fae. Perhaps you never were. Though whether you have truly ascended or not...that I cannot say."

"What's that mean, exactly?"

"It means the Tuatha Dé Danann were never our gods," she explained. "The Fae have no gods. We do not worship, or revere. We simply are. We do not crave subjugation the way Manlings do."

"That's not exactly true, though. What about King Oberon? And the Queens?"

Petal waved that away. "They are not monarchs, and they do not rule us. They are more like...symbols. They embody what it means to be Fae, and the realm itself makes them what they are."

"That sounds a little too convenient, if ye ask me," I noted, reflecting on my largely unpleasant interactions with the Faeling royals. "The Winter Queen definitely has her own agenda. And the same goes for Oberon."

"You think like that because you were raised here. But tell me, have you ever seen either of them do anything that was not ultimately in the best interests of our people?"

I thought about that for a moment. "They've done a lot of harm. To your people, and to mine."

"I said they are the embodiment of Fae. That does not make them infallible. It does not even make them right. But our kind doesn't care about what's right or what's wrong. We care about what is and what isn't."

Like animals, I thought but didn't say.

"Alright, fine," I said, instead. "But don't expect me to be okay with that."

"That is exactly what I expect."

"Come again?"

"You need to understand us, Lady Quinn. And no one but an exile who has spent centuries among the Manlings could help you do that as you are, now. In fact, it is possible that is why you were raised here."

"Pardon?"

"Did it never occur to you that Boston was an odd choice on your mother's part? If she wanted you hidden, she could have chosen some small, magicless town. On the other hand, had she wanted you to take her place, she could have stayed in Ireland, or sent you to Fae."

"No, she left Ireland because it was dangerous..." But even as I said it, I knew how ridiculous that sounded. My mother wouldn't have fled her home out of fear. "Wait, she came with Aunt Dez. They wanted to get away from their old lives, that's all."

"Perhaps. But it is curious that she came here, of all places. And that then she struck a deal with the Huntress to keep you safe, even while stripping you of your power."

"What's your point?"

"I do not have one. I was simply thinking out loud." Petal shrugged. "The Tuatha Dé Danann always were an indecipherable race."

Another thought occurred to me, suddenly. "Wait, if the Fae don't have rulers, why d'ye give the Tuatha Dé titles? Why call me Lady Quinn?"

"Because you earned it, as they earned theirs."

"Aye, but how, exactly?"

"If you want to know that, you will have to ask one of them."

"Any chance ye know where I can find one?"

Petal opened her mouth to reply, then shut it with a grimace.

"Petal?"

The pixie shook her head, clearly frustrated. "I never met any of the Tuatha Dé, personally. It is said they retreated into their mounds not long before the Old Ones vanished, and departed soon after. Most of what I've told you is known to all of us, but rarely spoken of."

"That didn't exactly answer me question."

"I know."

"So, what you're sayin' is you've told me everythin' ye can tell me."

"Yes, though I could help you find your answers...provided you agree to stay and help us."

"Help me, how?"

"The Otherworld," Petal supplied. "It borders this realm as well as Fae. There are passages, long forgotten passages, should you wish to return and seek your answers among those who might know more. And, if you agree to stay until this is over, I can show you where they are."

"I'm sorry, Petal. I can't. Not now, anyway."

"Why not? Have we done something to upset you? Name the offense, and I will see it dealt with."

"It's not like that." I shot a glance at Camila, who at least had the grace to look away. "I made a promise when I was in the Underworld in exchange for something I needed at the time. A promise to find someone and escort that person back home. If I fail, I'll end up a servant. Forever."

"You should have said so in the first place!" Petal admonished, her skin strobing with light. "You made a deal. Of course you must honor it."

"I didn't know what I'd be comin' back to when I made it," I explained, guiltily. "I didn't know so much time would have passed, or that Robin would be in trouble, or that anyone would need me. If I had, I might have done things differently. I really am sorry."

"Nonsense. You did what you thought best, and now you must do as you swore you would," Petal replied, vehemently. "To be forsworn is a fate worse than death, trust me."

"You could have led with the apology," Camila muttered from the other side of the room, her voice just loud enough to be overheard.

"I shouldn't have had to," I snapped. "What's your problem, anyway? I backed ye up because ye had a plan, and I didn't. It had nothin' to do with pity. Ye were the one who let your ego get in the way and made it personal."

"You are damn right, I made it personal." Camila strode into the room, seemingly oblivious to my glare. "And yes, my ego was bruised.

Did you know that after Robin was taken, the Fae here panicked? A few even began to fade, while the rest talked about surrendering. They had all but given up."

"Is that true?" Petal asked, sounding startled.

"Wait, weren't ye here?" I asked.

"I hadn't left the court, yet," the pixie explained. "It wasn't until after Robin was taken that I realized what was really going on. You have to understand, almost none of us ever actually saw Catha. At first, we were sure the Huntress would return with reinforcements and chase her off. But when no one came for Robin, I knew that would not happen."

"They were scared," Camila continued. "Robin was taken. My brother was not himself. There was no one for them to turn to, no one to protect them..."

"So ye stepped in. And did a good job of it, from what I can tell." I shot Petal a look. "The Fae here respect ye, and now I know why. Ye put yourself between 'em and Catha."

"They do look to you for guidance," Petal acknowledged, taking my cue. "I admit I was wrong to dismiss you as I did. All I can say in my defense is you seem very reluctant to lead."

"I am." Camila faced us both. "This responsibility is a huge burden. But it was Robin's burden, and I love him. His people are my people. The thought that they did not feel the same..."

"Hurt," I finished for her.

Camila crossed both arms over her stomach and nodded.

"We are not used to Manlings caring for us so selflessly," Petal said, dipping her chin. "Please, forgive my earlier assumption."

"Consider it water under the bridge," Camila replied. "And Quinn...I apologize for what I said earlier. It was unfair and untrue. You are anything but a coward. And the rest of what I said—"

"Already forgiven. And ye should know I'm sorry for what happened with Max. I swear I didn't know we were linked when I left, or I'd have returned a lot sooner."

"I realize that, now. I blamed you, at first. But I know better than most that magic is like that, sometimes. That it often forges bonds none of us can explain. I only wish I better understood what it is that links you two. I worry it may happen again."

"It will not."

Both of us turned to look at Petal.

"What was that?" I asked.

"I suppose I meant it should not," the pixie clarified. "Unless Lady Quinn hops from one realm to another, again."

"How can ye be so sure?"

"The link between Max and Lady Quinn...it's as plain as the second sun which overlooks King Oberon's forest."

"Go on," I urged.

"He has been possessed."

"He what?!" Camila exclaimed.

"Possessed by what, exactly?" I asked, waving off the bruja before she got too hysterical.

"By a Salamander."

"And what's a Salamander?"

"They are what you might call an elemental. They are not indigenous to this world. Max has one, here." Petal tapped her chest. "It is curled around his heart, keeping him warm. Keeping him alive."

"And how the hell did it get there?" I asked, perturbed by the revelation. A glance in Camila's direction showed a similar reaction splashed across her face.

"You put it there," Petal replied as though that were obvious. "You obviously called the spirit and...oh, you did not mean to, did you?"

I shook my head, my mouth uncommonly dry.

"That is...unfortunate."

"Why? Is it hurting him?" Camila asked. "And why can we not see it?"

"Salamanders live between realms. They are from a different age. But no, the Salamander would never harm him so long as its master does not will it."

"Its master? Do you mean Quinn?"

"Yes."

"Hold on, I still don't understand," I admitted. "Max went into a coma when I got pulled into the Otherworld. Wouldn't that be considered harm?"

Petal shrugged. "The Salamander likely tried to follow you. Your touch feeds and comforts it, and its power calls to yours. I am no expert, but I believe if you were a witch, the Salamander would be very much like a familiar."

"*Dios mío*," Camila groaned, her face going pale.

I, meanwhile, settled back into my seat and began massaging my temples; the notion that Max was tied to me through an elemental spirit named after a lizard was mere seconds away from giving me a migraine. Still, at least it explained what was going on between us—though not what we could do about it.

"D'ye know how we remove it?" I asked.

"Remove it?" Petal echoed.

"Aye. Or exorcise it. Ye know, draw the Salamander out of Max so he won't be bound to me anymore."

"You cannot do that!" Camila shrieked. "Promise me you will not do that."

"Alright, I promise. But can someone tell me why not?"

"Because Max would die." Petal hesitated for a moment before realizing Camila was in no condition to elaborate. "The Salamander is all that keeps his heart beating. Max should be dead. At one point, he was dead. When you called the Salamander, Lady Quinn, you didn't so much save his life as take possession of it."

Suddenly, I felt like I was going to be sick.

"I have to find my brother," Camila said, heading for the door. "I have to tell him."

"Wait," I called, fighting against a cresting wave of panic. Camila was wrong; deep down, I was a coward. Sure, I could storm a burning building or leap off a freaking cliff, but courage wasn't about doing things that scared everyone else. It was about doing the things that scared you. And, in my case, that meant acknowledging I'd condemned a man I liked but didn't love to stay by my side in perpetuity.

"What is it?" Camila hesitated.

"I know ye have to tell him, and that Max has every right to know. But please, don't let him t'ink I did this on purpose."

Camila's face softened. "Very well."

"Oh, and before ye go," I added, "could ye check your phone and see if Maria texted?"

"Maria?" Camila fetched her phone from her back pocket. "Why do I have a text that says Branson, Missouri? What's in Missouri?"

For a long moment, all I could do was gape at her in disbelief. Frankly, I had no idea where Branson was in relation to St. Louis or Kansas City, but the sheer coincidence was crazy; the Sickos were holed up in the one state I'd sworn to avoid for ages. Distantly, I wondered whether Callie Penrose or Nate Temple had anything to do with what the Sickos were investigating. Part of me hoped not.

I doubted either of them would forgive me for popping by without calling, first.

And I was definitely popping by.

"Quinn, what's in Missouri?"

"The person I have to find," I explained, thinking furiously. "Can ye tell me what the plan is to save Robin really quick? Just the broad strokes."

"Later," Camila insisted. "I want to talk to Max."

"All I need to know is if it's happenin' soon. I have to start makin' plans of me own, but I want to help however I can."

"And don't forget Lady Quinn has Albi's allegiance," Petal added, helpfully.

"*Bueno.*" Camila sighed, but her hand fell away from the door-knob. "I cannot get into the details right now, but we will not be doing anything until the night of the Hex Moon."

"When is that?"

"Nine days from now."

Nine days. When weighed against the eight-week deadline Freya had given me, it seemed right around the corner. The trouble was I knew deep down that there would always be something—maybe not a freaking coup, but something—to preoccupy me. That I'd be tempted to solve every emerging crisis whether I was needed or not until, eventually, it was Freya's deal that was right around the corner. And that, unfortunately, was not a risk I was willing to take.

"And what's a Hex Moon, exactly?"

"It is what we witches call a supermoon. You may or may not know this, but a great many spells are tied to the position of celestial bodies. The closer the moon is, for example, the greater our power. Witches will often use this to practice spells that they would never have attempted, otherwise."

"The consequences of which are sometimes disastrous," Petal noted, eyeing the bruja. "Earthquakes being the most common."

Camila waved that away. "The work of amateurs. The spell I intend to cast is much more elegant, and the preparations are all but complete."

"Wait, so you're goin' to cast a spell to save Robin?"

"More than that," Camila said, grinning like a madwoman all of a sudden. "I am going to cast a spell to save the entire city."

CHAPTER 14

Over the course of the next ten minutes, I learned that the particular spell Camila had in mind was designed to lure every Faeling in the city to a single, predetermined location. It had seemed implausible at first, but Camila had assured me the spell was actually rather fundamental provided you had the right bait and enough juice to broadcast across miles and miles of terrain. It was only when I asked where she'd be broadcasting from, however, that the bruja clammed up; that bit was apparently need to know. Still, I knew enough about spell work to know what Camila was proposing would require tons of preparation and channel enormous power, which meant it was dangerous—especially for the caster.

"*Muy* dangerous," Max explained, his expression clouded. The brujo paced the room, his long legs making it difficult to get more than a few steps in before having to turn around again. He'd shown up unannounced after speaking to his sister, interrupting the call I'd been about to make on a borrowed cell phone. Which was frustrating, considering I'd waited until I was alone to bother.

"What sort of bait is she usin', exactly? And where is she lurin' 'em? Camila wouldn't say."

"She will not tell me, either," Max confessed. "She walked me through her entire plan, once, but it sounded like gibberish to me at the time. It was shortly thereafter that they determined I could no longer use magic."

"Were ye upset?"

"Frustrated, not upset." Max ran a calloused hand over the fine hairs on his scalp. "I was not a particularly gifted practitioner, so it never became my identity. Camila was always the better, more clever bruja. It came naturally to her in ways it never did to me. But, after Salem, that began to change. I came to see how elementary my understanding was. Not long after, I could make spells work that I had never even dreamed of trying. Eventually, I could take one look at any spell and see how to improve it. Even Camila's."

"I take it she wasn't happy for ye?"

"It is hard to think yourself the best at something your whole life, only to wake up one day and find that belief shattered. It created resentment between us. And when I woke from my coma without magic, I believe a part of her was relieved. Now that my magic has returned, however, I can tell she does not wish to include me in her plans. She is worried I will point out its flaws, or perhaps even take over."

"And would ye?"

Max grunted. "I do not know. She loves the Redcap, and I do not begrudge her that. He is not even so bad for one of the *el hada*. When I fell into the coma, I remember being glad Camila had someone to support her. I knew Robin would protect her with his life. It was comforting, then."

"Because ye didn't t'ink she'd end up doin' the same for him," I suggested, empathizing. "Bit unfair of ye, though."

"She is family. He is not."

"Somehow I doubt Camila sees it that way."

"I am not sure Camila knows what she does or does not see, right now." Max stopped pacing and faced me with his arms folded across his densely muscled chest. "Love blinds us all."

I shifted beneath the sudden intensity in Max's eyes, aware of how it lingered on my face before trailing down the rest of my body. It wasn't a polite look. And yet, it wasn't suggestive, either. More...appreciative, than anything. All in all, it was a good look.

"So, I take it Camila told ye? About the whole Salamander t'ing?"

Max simply nodded.

"I feel like I should apologize," I admitted.

"Camila says you did not do it on purpose. Is that true?"

"It is. I had no idea what I was doin' at the time. All I knew was that I didn't want ye to die. What happened after that was sort of...instinctive."

"Then there is nothing to forgive. With magic, even wild magic, intention matters. I expect the Salamander would not have heeded your call, otherwise. Besides, it has not turned out so badly. We are both alive. Quite possibly immortal."

"Immortal?"

"Goddess." Max pointed to me, then to himself. "Latest *Dragonheart* protagonist."

I cocked an eyebrow and fended off a smile. "Is that so?"

"I have a foreign creature wrapped around my heart to keep it warm and beating. It was either *Dragonheart* or *The Faculty*."

"Wouldn't that make me Sean Connery?"

"You said it, not me," Max quipped.

I wanted to laugh, but the realization that Max might have a point made the whole situation far less humorous than I'd have liked. Was it possible the brujo was right? Could the fire elemental keep him alive, indefinitely? And, if so, did that mean we'd be stuck together forever? I shuddered at the possibility.

"Are you cold?"

"Seriously, doesn't this worry ye?" I asked, gesturing back and forth between us. "The bond, I mean, and this t'ing between us."

"This thing?" Max echoed.

"Ye know, this insane attraction..." I clamped my mouth shut, my cheeks burning. Jesus, what if he didn't feel it? Too late, I realized that I'd never thought to ask if he craved my touch the way I did his.

"Your face," Max said, grinning. "Of course I feel it. But I felt this way about you before, when we first met, so it is hard for me to know how much is metaphysical and how much is simply...physical."

The way the brujo said that last word sent a flare of sizzling anticipation through me, and it seemed I wasn't the only one; the barest embers danced along his exposed skin, writhing along the swells of his body. Out of curiosity, I closed my eyes and expanded my other senses the way I had with Gretel earlier that morning. The instant I did, however, it was as though dozens of tiny needles were pressing against every square inch of me. It wasn't painful but wasn't entirely pleasant either—as if my brain couldn't make up its mind whether to enjoy what was happening or loathe it. Regardless, I couldn't place the sensation. The powerful scent riding the air, however, was much more familiar. Tobacco. Not the stale odor of club clothes saturated in cigarette smoke, but the spicy, full-bodied bouquet of smoldering Corojo leaves.

Unable to handle the skin-prickling sensation any longer, I opened my eyes. And that's when I saw it for myself: the Salamander. The elemental didn't curl around so much as clutch at Max's heart, its reptilian body wound around the organ's bulbous mass, its clawed hands and feet snared along the various valves like some infernal gargoyle welded to a cathedral spire. When at last I got to its head, I found the Salamander staring at me with blazing white eyes nestled in a face that glowed like heat-treated metal. An absurdly long tongue of pure flame wriggled out from its scaled lips, and then—I would have sworn—it winked at me.

"Quinn?"

I forced myself to stop staring at the creature before it did anything I would regret—like come leaping out of Max's chest in some perverse rendition of *Alien*. Instead, I took a few deep breaths and let my pulse return to normal.

"Sorry," I said, breathily, "what was it ye were sayin'?"

"I was asking you when you were planning to leave," Max replied, sounding concerned. "Are you alright?"

"I'm fine. And as soon as possible, actually. Your sister tells me I have a little over a week before this Hex Moon hits, and I'd really like to be back before it does."

"You think you will be able to make it to Branson and back that fast?"

"Camila told ye I was goin' to Branson?"

"Petal told me. Though she did not say why."

"It's a business trip. Sort of. I have to track down an old friend and pass along a message. Worse, I'm on the clock. Which means the sooner I get it done, the sooner I can get back here." I waved the phone. "I was going to see about rentin' a car, provided I can sort t'ings out with me bank. And track down me license."

"That sounds like it could take a while."

"Aye," I admitted, sighing. "I'd prefer to fly, but without a passport that's a non-starter. Besides, I'm a bit of a nightmare to be around once the sun sets. Even with the sleepin' potion Circe gave me, I'd be puttin' too many people at risk."

Max paused for a second, then headed for the door, beckoning. "Follow me but leave Camila's phone. I do not think you will need it."

"Huh?"

"Hurry up."

"Max, I'm sorry, but I really need to get this mess sorted. I can't just go off—"

Except Max was already through the door. He'd left it open, which meant I was able to make out a couple of Faeling bystanders peering from the windows across the street. I wavered for perhaps a solid minute before cursing and clambering to my feet. Then, for reasons I couldn't entirely articulate, I tossed the cell phone on the couch and went after the brujo.

At first, the alleyway seemed deserted. Overhead, the pastel sky continued to spin and whirl like some glorious art installation. But then I caught the sound of footsteps and saw Max's broad shoulders at the far end of the street. I jogged after him, waving.

"Oy! Slow down!"

"This way!" he called.

"What is it ye want to show me, exactly?"

Max turned a corner without answering, disappearing into a shadowed recess I hadn't noticed when I first walked down the alley. By the time I caught up to him on the other side of that dark corridor, however, there was no need for a reply: I had my answer.

It was a Jeep. Thick-bodied with matte black fixtures and a burnt orange paint job, the sporty four-door Wrangler sat in the middle of the enclosure on bulky rubber tires that poked out from the under-carriage and went up to my knees. A fifth was mounted on the back beneath a hard-plastic cover rimmed in stainless steel. All in all, she was a beauty. How they'd managed to park her here, of course, was a mystery—though hardly the biggest I'd encountered today.

"So, what do you think?" Max asked, his voice cutting through the stunned silence. A set of keys dangled from his hand. "Road trip?"

"Are messin' with me, right now?" I gaped at him. "Is this even your Jeep?"

"*Sí*, she is mine." Max walked around to the passenger side, manually unlocked the door, and held it open. "I bought her outright with cash, so the bank never came to collect. Hop in."

"Hold on, ye meant now?"

"You said you were in a hurry. The sooner we leave, the sooner we can return. Besides, this will make things easier for Camila. No matter what she has done for them, the Fae will always choose to follow one of their own if given a choice. With you gone, they will have no reason to question her judgment. And with me gone, she will have no reason to question her own."

I shuffled from side to side, more than a little hesitant to jump at Max's generous offer. Honestly, I'd intended to make the journey alone; letting someone crash my reunion seemed like an unnecessary complication. Still, the brujo's logic was sound.

"Tell me, when d'ye get so smart?" I asked.

Max barked a laugh.

"I'm bein' serious."

"Are you saying you thought I was just a pretty face?"

"That's not what I meant," I countered, smirking. "Smart was the wrong word. Insightful would be a better term for it. I mean, first ye talk to me about Maria like you're her therapist, and now you're hittin' me with incisive reasons to leave town that I hadn't even considered, yet."

The laughter in Max's eyes died away, leaving them cool and calculating. "Remember when I told you about how I could see spells?"

"Aye. Ye said ye knew how they worked."

"I can do that with people, too. It is not as precise, but I can sometimes pick up on what they are feeling. It is intuitive, I think. Like a seventh sense."

"Ye mean a sixth sense?"

"That I have, already. It is what makes me a brujo."

I waited to see if Max was messing with me, but—deep down—I could see that he wasn't. Of course, it was also clear he wasn't entirely comfortable with the fact that he'd died and come back as a human barometer; the brujo had turned to study the car's interior rather than meet my gaze. In a way, he and I shared that discomfort. It seemed I was constantly evolving, and rarely by choice. Perhaps that's why, rather than delaying further, I walked over and slipped into the passenger seat.

"You'll have to drive," I insisted as he went to shut the door.

"It is my Jeep," he replied. "I was planning to drive, anyway."

"I meant you'll have to drive through the night. Can ye handle that? The sun sets in a couple hours, and I have to be passed out when it does."

Max's brow furrowed in confusion.

"Sleep," I explained. "It's all that keeps me inner goddess from makin' a guest appearance, and I have no idea how she'll react to this strange new world."

"Should I be worried?"

"No, not if I take this." I fetched a slim tube fashioned from carved bone from the inner lining of my jacket. "Circe made it for me. Tastes awful, but it's plenty potent. So long as ye drive safe and be sure not to wake me up in the middle of the night, it shouldn't be a problem. Once the sun is up, I'll take over. We can do it in shifts."

"Tell me, how would you have done this on your own, exactly?"

"With great difficulty," I acknowledged, cagily.

"Uh huh," the brujo drawled. "Buckle up."

CHAPTER 15

Most dreams are fragmented things brimming with implausibilities that, for reasons we cannot explain upon waking, make perfect sense within the context of the dream. Absurdities like having a clock for a pillow or kissing a stranger with your best friend's face or being you and also not you, simultaneously. Dreams are strange, occasionally senseless, and often hazy.

Except, of course, when they are none of those things.

This dream was like that. It was vibrant and linear and so real it felt like I'd stepped over a threshold into yet another realm. Except I hadn't, because I couldn't move; I stood rooted at the base of a hill so steep it nearly blotted out the sky. Beyond, pale light pulsed against storm clouds that roiled and churned at alarming speeds. I could see figures among them—shapes that could have been women, or men, or even animals. A few had sinister aspects, their edges jagged and forked. Others were little more than formless silhouettes, as if they couldn't decide what they wanted to be. Each and every one of them, however, had one thing in common: they were waiting for something, or someone.

Tension rode the very air.

The instant I recognized that feeling, I realized I was not alone. Someone stood beside me—a presence, only. Though I couldn't turn to look, I experienced a distinct impression of familiarity. A sense that I knew this person, whoever he was. Knew him well enough, in fact, to picture what I would see if I turned.

He'd be a young man, about my height, his body hidden beneath a scarlet cloak that emphasized the russet undertones in honey blonde hair which would have been shoulder-length had it not been so coarse. Instead, it rippled outwards to form a mane around a pale, angular face dusted with freckles and dimpled at both cheeks. Though I recalled them best of all his features, his eyes came last: pale green and rimmed in gold, they were so like our mother's that it sometimes hurt to see them in someone else's face.

My brother spoke, and still I couldn't turn.

"The stone must scream for you."

A hand drifted into view. His hand—delicate and long-fingered—pointing to the hill. No, not to the hill, I realized, but to the rock formation which stood on top of it. I squinted until I could make out the exact shape of the tor; thick slabs of cragged stone emerged to form a crude throne garlanded in thick vines and patches of moss. Except, the longer I stared at it, the more I realized there was nothing crude about it. Instead, it struck me that this ancient seat was, in many ways, what a throne should look like. What all thrones aspire to be. Indeed, the sight of it stirred something within me—a wistfulness I'd never before experienced. And, with it, a sense of profound loss.

That delicate hand settled on my shoulder and squeezed as though its owner understood what I was feeling. Then, so gently I didn't even realize it was happening at first, he turned me until I could see his face.

Or what was left of it.

I stifled a scream at the sight of his hairless scalp and the grisly bone peeking out from beneath his rotting cheeks. His eye sockets gaped like empty pits, staring at nothing. He was dead—not undead, but truly dead. I wasn't certain how I knew that, but I did.

His voice when he spoke again was a ghost's voice, haunting me with its fervor...not to mention the fact that the lipless mouth never moved. "The stone must scream for you. Or all is lost, and I died for nothing."

CHAPTER 16

I woke with my pulse in my throat and Max's head in my lap. The brujo stirred but somehow slept right through both my harried breathing and the incessant creaking of the leather seat. Frankly, I couldn't tell you how long it was before I was able to think past the fear. All I knew for certain was that, by the time I could, the sun was cresting between distant hills steeped in shadow and wreathed in fog—a panorama only partially obscured by the condensation on the windshield. By comparison, the view from the rear window was much clearer; majestic evergreens hemmed the two-lane highway we'd pulled off of, the road snaking across the rolling countryside like a ribbon of stone.

In a way, it felt like I'd woken to a landscape as alien to me as the one I'd encountered in my dream; when I'd crawled into the backseat to crash just before sunset, we'd been surrounded by Connecticut's lush vegetation—a stark contrast to this much more temperate climate. Which of course begged the question: where were we?

Part of me considered waking Max and asking, but another part relished the silence. It gave me time to think and replay the dream in my head before I forgot it all. Of course, it quickly became apparent that wasn't going to happen; I could recall the whole thing as though it had been seared into my mind—the hill, the figures in the clouds, the throne of stone. And, of course, the dead man's face.

My brother's face.

Well, not *my* brother, obviously. But the brother of whomever I'd been in the dream. I shuddered, wishing I knew whether what I'd seen was real or a byproduct of Circe's potion. She had warned me about its potency, even going so far as to say no ordinary human could wake from it. Problem was, it hadn't felt like the sort of lucid dreams you can get on painkillers. It'd felt, well...prophetic.

"The stone must scream..." I muttered under my breath, trying to pry meaning from the senseless phrase.

Max twitched, awoken by the sound of another car blasting by us. He groaned as he sat up, one hand pressed to the small of his back, clearly pained after having passed out at such an awkward angle. I could sympathize; my neck and shoulders ached, plus it seemed my right leg had fallen asleep where the brujo's head had been. Pins and needles began dancing up my thigh as I unclipped my seatbelt and adjusted my weight.

"How far d'ye get before ye had to stop?" I asked through clenched teeth as I reached over the seat to snag a plastic water bottle from the cup holder. My mouth was uncomfortably dry—another unfortunate side effect of Circe's sleeping potion, I gathered.

"Branson should be seven miles that way, give or take," Max replied, groggily.

"How is that even possible? It's been, what, twelve hours since I passed out?" I gaped at the brujo. "Wait, I didn't sleep through two whole nights, did I?!"

Max grunted a laugh. "No, just the one night."

"Then that makes no sense. How did we get here so fast? It should've taken most of today, even without ye stoppin'."

"You did say you were in a hurry."

"I was! I mean, I am. But that still doesn't explain *how* this happened."

"You may not know this about me, but I have always had a thing for fast cars." Max let his head fall back and closed his eyes as though he planned to go back to sleep. "When I was a *niño*, I used to sneak out of our *abuela's* house on Friday nights and go with my cousin to watch the street races that took place on the outskirts of town. Have you ever been to Florida? Well, one thing you notice as soon as you get there is how flat it is. Most people do not know it, but Florida is actually the flattest state in the country."

"What's that got to—"

"There are whole swathes of Florida," Max interrupted, "where there are no palm trees, or golf courses, or beachfront apartments. There, the horizon is sometimes so empty it feels like you are standing on an ocean made of grass. And that is where the street racers meet, because the flatter the terrain, the straighter the road. And the straighter the road, the faster you can drive."

"Oh?" I found myself drawn in by the anecdote, dimly aware that I'd learned more about Max in the last few minutes than I'd found out in all the time I'd known him. "And what does any of that have to do with how we got here hours ahead of schedule?"

"When I finally got together enough money to buy a car," Max continued as though I hadn't spoken, "I itched to do what I had seen those street racers do. I wanted to peel out and press the accelerator down until the frame shook. But the roads on the east coast are winding, and traffic is never light. So, instead, I bought this Jeep."

"So, I guess I'm goin' to hear this story whether I like it or not, huh?" I muttered.

"At first, I will admit I was disappointed. Not so much about the Jeep as what it represented: that neither of us were going to be able to go home anytime soon. Camila must have noticed, though, because she quickly came up with a clever solution. A few of them, actually. She modified a displacement spell to straighten the roads as I drove them, as well as a compulsion spell to repel the other drivers. Oh, and a hex to remain invisible to cameras and radar, so the police cannot ticket us."

"Seriously?" I asked, astounded at his sister's creative use of magic. But then, he'd told me how gifted his sister was from the beginning.

"*Sí*. If you look closely enough, you can still see her spell work in the paint."

I twisted in my seat to look back through the rear window, hoping to find evidence of Camila's handiwork on the trunk. Instead, it seemed I was just in time to watch a squad car creep up behind us; the cop inside flicked on his lights with a tell-tale whoop whoop that made Max jump.

"What was that ye said about invisibility?" I drawled.

"It only works when we are moving."

"Well, I don't know about ye, but that sure seems like a design flaw right about now."

"Shame you were not there to say so at the time," Max replied, sarcastically. "Maybe then we could have avoided this."

Unfortunately, the rap of a knuckle against the rear window interrupted whatever exceedingly witty retort I might have come up with. Max and I held up our hands to show we weren't armed, but that was as far as either of us could get; neither window would roll down with the engine off, and no one in their right mind hops out of their car after being pulled over.

The cop bent over at the waist and peered at us through the glass like we were some sort of zoological exhibit. Then again, maybe we were: a man and a woman in the backseat of a vehicle on the side of the road in the wee hours of the morning almost guaranteed a spectacle. Fortunately for us, we had all our clothes on—a fact which seemed to surprise the officer. His bushy eyebrows climbed towards a receding hairline that matched his protruding gut, misshapen nose, and greying mustache.

"You two screwing, or sleeping?" the officer barked, his voice twangy and an octave higher than I'd expected it to be.

"Sleeping," Max called back.

The cop nodded absentmindedly before peering up and down

the road. "You know there's a whole town along the way. Lots of hotels. A few motels, too."

"I was too tired," Max confessed, ignoring the implication. "I did not want to risk causing an accident, so I pulled over. It was a long overnight drive."

"Yeah, I see the plates. Massachusetts. That's a lot of ground to cover." The cop's eyes flicked to my face. "Couldn't you have taken over for him?"

"Took a sleepin' pill," I explained.

"Right. Well, I'll tell you what. Let me check your licenses and registration. Then I'll let you be on your way."

"I have my license, but my registration is up front," Max explained. "Can I get it?"

The cop narrowed his eyes but nodded, stepping clear of the door with a hand resting on the pistol he wore at his hip. "Keep your hands where I can see them at all times, alright? You too, miss."

"Aye, sir." I wiggled my fingers for emphasis.

Once in the driver's seat, Max handed over the requisite documents. The officer thumbed through the contents, then gave the brujo's license a good looking over. He handed it all back, and frankly, I thought that would be the end of it until the cop spoke to me.

"Alright, ma'am. Your turn."

"Me turn for what?"

"Your license." The cop gestured for me to hand it over. "Let me see it."

"Oh," I replied, feeling foolish for not having realized what he'd wanted sooner. "I don't have one. Or rather, I lost it."

"You lost it?" His fingers curled into a meaty fist. "And when was that?"

"What's it matter to ye? I wasn't even drivin' the car."

"It matters because I say it matters. Fact is, we've had some trouble around these parts over the past couple weeks, so when I find two people who ain't from around here, it makes me suspicious. And when one of those two refuses to show identification, it makes me more suspicious."

"Officer, I—" Max began.

"No, sir, I wasn't talking to you. I'm talking with the young lady, here. She was about to tell me a very plausible story about when and how she lost her license."

I opened my mouth, closed it, and opened it again without a single word spilling out. Deep down, I knew I should have lied—a stolen purse, or a drunken night out, or even claiming I'd left it at home by mistake would have sufficed. But I couldn't think fast enough—arguably the worst side effect of the potion.

"Well?"

"Wait..." I began replaying what he'd said on a loop in my head. "D'ye say you've been havin' trouble? How much trouble are we talkin' about, exactly?"

"That's none of your business."

I decided to take a shot in the dark. "Ye don't happen to know Special Agent Leo Jeffries, by chance?"

"Excuse me?"

"He's an FBI agent. Hispanic guy, average height, tan. Probably north of fifty, though you'd never know it."

"What does that have to do with your license?"

"So, ye do know who I'm talkin' about, then. D'ye work for him?"

"I work *with* Jeffries, not for him," the cop clarified, coolly. He made a face that I recognized well: he knew the Sickos. Only cops who'd met them could look that perturbed. "Anyway, what's he got to do with you?"

"He's why we're here," I lied, realizing I'd have to pull some shit out of thin air if we wanted to get this guy off our case long enough to find Hilde and the others. "Leo asked us to come. He wants our help."

"You're not Feds."

"No, of course not. We're more like consultants, actually. I helped with the Boston murders, if Leo has mentioned those at all."

"He hasn't. But in a city that big, I'd wager murders are pretty common."

"Not these ones. These were serial killin's that started on the west coast and ended in Boston. Real ugly stuff."

"Christ, you're talking about the Christmas Carol Killer, aren't you?" The officer shook his head so violently it made *my* neck hurt. "They kept it out of the news, but cops talk. I didn't know Jeffries worked that one, or that they had a civilian on that case."

"They brought me in late," I explained. "I'm from Boston. Pretty sure they wanted some fresh eyes, that's all."

Funnily enough, that was largely true. What I left out was that the serial killer Leo and his people had been after—the one responsible for dozens of deaths linked to the English Christmas jingle—had been a Faeling who went by the name Jack Frost. Oh, and that I was the one who shot and killed him. But then, cops tend to frown on that sort of thing, and I was playing nice.

"So, what's your area of expertise?"

"Huh?"

"You said you were consultants," the officer clarified. "What is it you two do?"

"Antiquities," I replied, without thinking.

"Like antiques?"

I bristled at his tone. "Like artifacts. Relics with cultural significance. Old weapons most coroners wouldn't recognize. You'd be surprised how often that sort of t'ing comes up."

"Uh huh. And what about you?" he asked Max.

"I work at an occult shop."

For some reason, that seemed to mollify the officer; a tension I hadn't noticed left his body in a rush. He sighed and scratched idly at a patch of razor burn. "Guess you two will be headed to the crime scene, then."

"Is that where Leo is?" I asked. "We rushed down here, so he wouldn't be expectin' us just yet."

"Yeah, well, I'm not sure what Jeffries has told you, and I wouldn't want to give anything away in case it's your fresh eyes he's looking for..." The officer let that hang in the air for a moment before continuing, "But if you're here to help clear this mess up, I'd be happy to play escort. None of us have seen anything like this. Branson isn't as small as some people think. We have trouble with drug trafficking.

Mostly opiates, maybe some meth. But mass murders? People dumping bodies all over the Ozarks like trash? Not a chance."

I fought to keep a straight face, pretending I knew exactly what the officer was referring to. "We'd really appreciated that, Officer..."

"It's Deputy. Deputy Holt. But you can call me Holt."

"Holt," I echoed, nodding. "I'm Quinn. This is Max."

"Pleasure's all mine," Deputy Holt grunted. "You good to follow me, son?"

"*Sí.* I mean, yes, sir."

The deputy waved that off. "I took enough Spanish in high school to know that much. Try not to get lost. I'll go slow, but the roads out here are a real pain in the ass."

"I will do my best."

The deputy slapped the door of the Jeep, turned, and headed back to his patrol car without saying another word. I let out a long sigh and settled into the backseat, aware of Max's eyes on me through the rear-view mirror.

"What?" I asked.

"Why are we following a policeman to a crime scene? And did he say mass murders?"

"Aye..." I put my seatbelt back on while I decided how much to tell Max about who we were meeting and why. "So, the friend I'm here to see is sort of on loan to a branch of the FBI that investigates supernatural crimes. I mean, the other cops don't know that's what they do, obviously. But that's sort of the point."

"Uh huh..." Max looked like he had a dozen questions, but eventually settled on a practical one. "Does your friend know you are coming?"

"Not exactly. I kind of need her to quit her job and return home with me so I don't get deported back to the Norse realm to serve as a glorified foot soldier for the rest of time."

"That," Max said as he cranked the engine, "sounds easier said than done."

"Aye, it does," I admitted after hearing it out loud. "Good t'ing I'm so persuasive."

Max snorted a laugh.

"What's so funny?"

"*Nada,*" he replied as we pulled out after the deputy. "Nothing at all."

CHAPTER 17

Max pulled in behind the deputy, parking along the opposite side of the road from an additional squad car and one of those fuel efficient, cookie-cutter rentals. The ridge beyond appeared to be a steep climb, though it was hard to tell for sure with such dense forest blanketing damn near everything in sight. To be honest, I was surprised; I'd expected a flatter, browner Missouri, and said as much.

"Yeah, you'll find that, too," Holt said as we hiked that ridge several minutes later, angling towards a crime scene which was at least a mile out by his reckoning. "The Ozarks ain't like that, though. This area here's called the Springfield Plateau. Over that way, you have the Boston Mountains, which extend from Oklahoma to Arkansas."

I watched the deputy's finger as it worked from right to left, impressed by his sense of direction. "D'ye say Boston Mountains?"

"I did," Holt replied, puffing a bit as we ascended, his eyes scanning the rocky, overgrown terrain ahead as though afraid he might lose his footing. "Way back when, settlers used to call it pulling 'a Boston' whenever they did something tough. No idea why. But those mountains are a real pain in the ass to climb, so I guess the name stuck."

"Huh," I said, struck by the coincidence. "I guess that makes sense."

"You get all sorts of stuff like that out here. You've got towns like Cuba and Lebanon back east. Then there's the Salem Plateau up in the St. Francois Mountains. But I'm sure you heard that already from Agent Jeffries. That was the worst of the lot if you ask me."

"Oh, aye, the Salem Plateau," I echoed, pretending I had at least some idea what he was talking about. Max shot me a look over the deputy's head, trying to communicate something with his eyes. When I could only shrug in response, however, the brujo addressed Holt directly.

"Could you remind us what happened there, Deputy?" Max asked.

"Didn't Jeffries fax over the crime scene photos?"

"He did," Max replied, hurriedly, "but it would be better coming from someone who was there."

Holt was already shaking his head. "Happened before I got on the case. It's some three hours east of us, way outside our jurisdiction. Far as I know, that was the first. The others have all been out here."

Max fell silent, for which I was grateful; we needed information, but the more questions we asked the less it sounded like we knew. Worse, Holt struck me as a clever guy. Cops like him weren't easy to fool to begin with.

"Looks like it's just Agent Jeffries up ahead," Holt remarked, squinting up at a dark smudge atop a flat crest some thirty yards away. "Sheriff won't like that. Come on."

As we drew closer, that smudge became a trim, middle-aged Hispanic man dressed in a polo and moleskin trousers with a windbreaker curled over one forearm. Special Agent Leo Jeffries stared down at a notebook, tapping his lips with a pen, looking older than I remembered; his hair was more silver than black, now, and the lines of his face were carved that much deeper.

"Hello there, Deputy," Leo called, still scribbling. "Who's that you've got with you?"

"It's us, Leo!" I shouted back, hoping to prevent the agent from outing us on the spot by saying the wrong thing.

Leo jerked as though he'd been slapped, looking downright stunned as he turned to us. "Quinn? Is that really you?"

"Aye, we came, just like ye asked us to," I replied evenly, willing him to play along. "Sorry I didn't call ahead. We made better time than we expected. Anyway, Deputy Holt here was kind enough to escort us and fill us in on *our* case."

Leo blinked at me in surprise but recovered far more quickly than most would have given the circumstances; he slipped the notepad into the pocket of his windbreaker and slung it back over one arm. "That so? Well, I'm glad you made it here so fast."

"Agent Jeffries," Holt interjected. "Where's Sam? He was supposed to be keeping an eye on things until the Sheriff got here."

"An eye on me, you mean," Leo replied, his eyes twinkling with something between amusement and anger. The question was uncharacteristically blunt, but then the federal agent had a unique talent for parsing out lies from truth. A magical talent, in fact, which probably made it hard to put up with the territorial disputes and bureaucratic bullshit that came with the job.

"It's nothing personal," Holt insisted.

"I can tell you mean that, but I am not so sure the same would hold true for your Sheriff."

"Terry's had a tough time of things lately. He isn't usually so..." Holt waved a hand about as if searching for the right word but gave up. "Anyway, he's not usually like this."

"I am sorry to hear that," Leo replied, looking thoughtful. "Officer Nelson and Agent Collins are in the valley, checking for tracks. Doubt they'll find any, but your Sheriff will want proof."

"He will. And he'll want to know what these two civilians are doing here, so you might want to come up with something a bit more plausible than what she did." Holt jerked a thumb at me as he strode past the federal agent. "I'm going to go see if Sam needs help."

"Shit," I muttered under my breath so Holt wouldn't hear me. "Busted."

"What makes you think Miss MacKenna was lying, Deputy?" Leo called after the man, ignoring me.

Holt halted, glancing back at me before ultimately addressing Leo. "Just a hunch. Maybe I'm wrong, but if these two aren't who they say they are, it would be best if they were gone before I get back."

"Why lead them here, if you weren't sure?"

"I don't give a rat's ass how the job gets done so long as the bodies stop falling, but I'm not in charge. I don't make the rules. Doesn't mean I can't bend them from time to time, though."

"Appreciate the honesty, Deputy," Leo replied.

"Don't mention it."

Leo waited until the deputy was well out of earshot before wheeling on me, his expression oscillating between amazement and outrage. "What the hell did you tell him, MacKenna?"

I opened my mouth to explain but didn't get a chance before I felt the agent's arms wrap around me in a hug so fierce that it drove the breath from my lungs. It also put the man's face uncomfortably close to my breasts. Of course, as short as Leo was, that was bound to happen; the man's head barely crested my chin on a good day, which meant I could smell the minty shampoo he'd used that morning. I coughed out a nervous laugh and patted his back. "Missed ye, too, Leo."

Leo pulled away, shaking his head. "We looked for you for over a year, chasing down any leads we could find. We thought you were dead, Quinn. We really did."

"I'm sorry, Leo," I said before drawing him in for another, less awkward hug. "I never intended to be gone for so long."

"Do I get one of those, too?" a voice called.

I glanced past Leo to find a man staring at me from a half dozen yards down the ridge.

"Well," I said, breathily, "if it isn't Jimmy Collins."

CHAPTER 18

J immy was so unchanged, he might as well have stepped directly out of my memories. Imposingly tall and built like a cross between a basketball player and an NFL linebacker, the former detective was arguably one of the most beautiful humans I'd ever met. For most men, that boiled down to great bone structure and the lustrous, ageless skin that keep dermatologists up at night. But there was also something in the eyes, in the tilt of the mouth, which set Jimmy apart from the rest—a confidence that bordered on swagger.

Frankly, if it weren't for the gold band wrapped around his ring finger, I'd never have known a year and a half had passed since we last saw each other. If Jimmy noticed me eyeing his newfound bling, however, he gave no sign. Instead, the man stood looking still as the grave and chiseled as a tombstone, hiding behind a placid, pleasant expression that might have fooled someone who knew him less intimately than I did.

Of course, I wasn't behaving much better. I found myself smiling down at my childhood friend with a degree of warmth I wasn't certain I felt. It was one thing to hear he'd gotten married, but another thing entirely to see proof. My mind began plaguing me with questions I wasn't sure I wanted answers to. Half-formed queries such as *what's she like?* or *where did you honeymoon?* or, most troubling of all, *would I have been invited to the wedding?*

Leo—perhaps picking up on the tension between us—disentangled himself and stepped aside in an obvious attempt to give Jimmy and me some privacy. Unfortunately, he also took that opportunity to introduce himself to Max—presumably so he could interrogate the brujo under the pretense of small talk. And I refused to let that happen.

"He's a friend," I warned Leo, feeling way too much like a girl bringing a boy home to meet her father for comfort. "Be nice."

"I'm always nice," Leo replied as he extended his hand. "Hello there, sir. I'm Special Agent in Charge, Leonardo Jeffries. And you are?"

"Maximiliano Velez," Max replied, though he made no move to shake.

"Something wrong with my hand, Mr. Velez?"

"*Sí*, it is attached to a hedge witch."

Leo froze, the trademark smile he used to charm women and disarm bad guys locked into a grotesque caricature of itself. At that precise moment, Jimmy reached the top of the ridge, looming over us all like somebody from the goon squad. Or maybe that was just the way he was dressed; between his tight black t-shirt and seam-popping jeans, Jimmy could have had any security job he wanted.

"Everything alright, Leo?" he asked.

"That depends on Mr. Velez, here."

Max studied both men with a cool gaze, though I could tell Jimmy's height had thrown him. That's the thing about being abnormally tall, though: you get so used to being as big or bigger than everyone else that you forget what it's like to feel small. Not that Max had much to worry about in that department; what the brujo lacked in inches he more than made up for in mass.

"What seems to be the issue, Mr. Velez?" Jimmy asked.

"You are behaving like I have insulted you, Agent Jeffries," Max said, ignoring Jimmy's question. "But where I come from, it is a sign of respect to fear another practitioner."

"Is it, now?" Leo relaxed so visibly that Jimmy extended both arms to catch him. "I had no idea that was customary."

"Is it not the same where you come from?"

Leo shrugged. "Might be. Might not. I learned most of what I know from my grandmother, but she passed when I was ten and my dad didn't possess the gift."

Max ducked his head. "*Lo siento.*"

"*De nada.*" Leo waved that away, smiling. "Funny thing is, some members of my family called her a hedge witch, though never to her face. I thought it was some sort of joke, or a snide comment. Like calling someone a hermit. I take it I was wrong?"

Max gave me a look.

"Go ahead," I suggested. "Ye know a lot more about this than I do."

"You were not wrong, no," Max said in answer to the agent's question. "It can be an insult, depending on one's heritage. Broadly speaking, hedge witches are what you might call general practitioners. They do not specialize in any one thing, and most exhibit only minor powers. Some are not even aware of what they are. You see them from time to time selling healing crystals and reading auras. It is very sad. There are a few, however, who display a great deal of untapped potential, or those who have inherited a powerful curse. Like you."

"Did Quinn tell you that?" Leo asked, stiffening.

"No. Quinn told me very little about any of you, in fact," Max replied, radiating displeasure.

"Then what makes you think I'm cursed?"

"I can see it. It is there, in your ears and on your tongue. I cannot tell what manner of curse it is, not without casting my own spells. But I have seen others like it among the old families, especially in the Southwest."

Leo's eyebrows climbed at that.

"What is it?" I asked.

"I'm from Arizona, and my mother's maiden name was Vasquez.

My uncles always swore we were descended from Coronado, himself. Illegitimately, of course."

"So does that make you a witch, too, Mr. Velez?" Jimmy asked, tilting his nose up as if scenting the air.

"A brujo," Max corrected. "We have more in common with shamans than we do witches. Some might even call us witchdoctors. But the appropriate term is brujo, or bruja for a woman."

"Yeah, you don't smell like a witch," Jimmy remarked, his voice sounding gruffer than a moment ago. "But then you don't smell human, either."

The two men locked eyes. I briefly considered butting in—if only so I could get this proverbial show on the road—but opted to let this run its course. So far, the boys had managed to talk without challenging each other to an arm wrestling competition; I could wait a little longer. Fortunately, Leo appeared as eager to wrap this up as I was.

"Let's table this for later," he said. "Jimmy, did you or Officer Nelson find anything down there?"

"Not a thing," he replied, turning his attention to the older man. "Whatever or whoever did this one, they left no tracks. No scents, either. If I didn't know better, I'd say this guy was dropped out of the sky."

"This one?" I asked, struck by the curious way he'd phrased it. "D'ye t'ink there's more than one killer?"

The two federal agents exchanged looks before turning to me as one wearing identical expressions—the kind all cops wear when they're about to interrogate you. The only question was who would be playing bad cop.

"Leo," Jimmy drawled, "why do I get the feeling this isn't a social visit on Quinn's part?"

"Because you aren't stupid, that's why."

"Oy, that's not fair!"

"Definitely not a social visit," Jimmy quipped.

"Look here—" I began.

Before I could defend myself, however, I was interrupted by the belligerent shouts of another man hiking up the ridge from the same side we had. From that distance, all I could really make out was a pale face beneath a mop of dark hair—and the fact that he was pissed. His words were largely lost to the wind, and yet I caught enough to know two things: this man was the notorious Sheriff, and we were all in serious trouble.

CHAPTER 19

I stood over a mangled body not some fifteen minutes later, wondering what karmically fucked up thing I'd done lately to deserve to see that while Leo and Sheriff Terry Watt went at it behind me. Everyone else—including a baby-faced Officer Nelson—loitered at the top of the ridge, waiting for us to return with a verdict. Was it an unfortunate accident, or a horrific murder? Personally, I was on the fence. But then, my vote didn't count anyway.

The valley in which we stood was surprisingly barren of trees, dominated instead by rocks and brush; I'd had to surreptitiously alter my footwear to avoid twisting an ankle on our descent. Worse, between the sun overhead and the white rocks baking below, I'd had to tie my jacket around my waist by its sleeves to keep from sweating all over the crime scene.

"I'll say it again, Jeffries, this was an animal attack," the sheriff was insisting. "They're rare as hell, but they do happen. Why can't you just admit you're grasping at straws? We both know they're bound to call you and your people back home any day, now."

"It's Special Agent Jeffries, Sheriff. Though you're right about one thing. I am grasping at straws. It's been weeks since the last killing. And most cops would be happy about that because it means they got close enough to spook their suspect, or that their killer got caught doing something else. But for us, all that means is waiting for another body to fall somewhere else and starting all over again. Because the job doesn't end for us until our suspect is dealt with."

"What's your point, *Agent* Jeffries?"

"My point is, we have a dead body with almost no forensics. And I'm not going to overlook that inconvenient fact just because you say it's an animal attack."

The body—which I'd taken one good look at before pretending I was anywhere but here—was a meat puzzle held together by bits of stringy ligament and bony protrusions. The result was a mutilated, malodorous mess shrouded in black cloth. At first, I'd assumed someone had tried to cover it up, but a second stolen glance suggested he'd been garbed from head to toe in black—possibly robed, even.

"Hikers come up here all the damn time," Watt argued. "Shit, two of them found the body. It's obvious a bear or a cougar got a piece of him and the vultures did the rest."

"Please," I said, snorting. "He wasn't hikin'."

"What was that?" Watt barked.

I pointed to the tattered clothes while trying not to think about the remains of the person beneath. "No one goes out for a hike in all that black. It gets too damn hot. Hell, it's not even 9 o'clock yet and I'm startin' to sweat. Also, I get the pants, but why the long sleeves? Why the robe?"

"Tick season," Watts supplied, though I could hear a kernel of doubt in his voice. "Or maybe he was up here at night. It gets cold at night."

"Okay, sure, but then where's the flashlight? What about a water bottle? A backpack? Also, why is there no blood trail? Even if he were attacked, wouldn't he have tried to run away, or at least gotten dragged?"

"I thought you said this woman works for Homeland," Watt said to Leo.

That felonious falsehood, surprisingly, had been Leo's brilliant idea. Apparently, the Department of Homeland Security was one of those sprawling federal agencies with more fingers than there were pies, which made the claim tough for anyone to immediately disprove. Especially once Leo started dropping phrases like *it's above your pay grade* and *you'd have to be read in* and so on. In the end, the Special Agent in Charge had made a strong enough case to let me stay that Watt had insisted I weigh in on cause of death. Unfortunately, while hiding my identity from the deputy had lent some credence to the whole thing, it hadn't earned me any points with the locals; Watt watched me like a dog he couldn't wait to kick, while Holt had actually looked a little hurt to discover how big a lie I'd fed him.

If only he knew.

"That is what I said," Leo replied, smoothly.

"Then how come she's talking to me like she's Nancy fucking Drew?"

I whirled on the man only to find Leo's hand on my shoulder, his expression telling me not to let the sheriff get to me. What Leo hadn't expected was to see me smiling. I patted his hand, reassuringly. There was a time, perhaps, when I'd have launched into a tirade and gotten in Watt's face—badge or no badge. But now? Now, I just wanted to know why a cop who was sworn to protect and serve was working so damn hard to ignore the evidence sitting right in front of him.

"What's the matter with him?" I asked Leo in a hushed voice.

"The fuck did she just say?"

"Nothing important," Leo replied, though I could tell from his expression that he agreed with me, and that there *was* something wrong with Watt. "Sheriff, why don't we take a breath and—"

"No, I want to know what the bitch said."

"I'll have ye know I'm a very nice lady," I remarked, nonplussed.

"That's what all you cunts say."

"Watt!" Leo was suddenly in the sheriff's face, his right hand making a chopping motion as he berated the other man. "You talk to any of my people like that again, and I'll have your badge if it's the last thing I do!"

"Fat fucking chance, Jeffries. You don't have the authority."

"I can pull every case you've ever worked and have it under review by sundown. How many infractions have you had, Watt? How many complaints?"

"None," Watt spat.

"Well, I'll still find something, Watt. Something you don't want me to. I'll talk to your neighbors. Your family. I'll—"

"You'll stay the hell away from my family!" Watt bellowed; his face contorted with blind rage. I took a step forward in alarm, but it was too late; Watt had already drawn back to sock Leo in the jaw. The blow caught Leo square on the chin with a sickening clap of teeth, and the federal agent collapsed to the ground in an unconscious heap.

And then Watt pounced on him.

CHAPTER 20

A dark-skinned doctor in her late thirties shone a light in both of Leo's eyes, one after the other. A tense moment of silence ensued until at last she made a satisfied sound in the back of her throat. She scribbled a note on his chart, walked to the end of his hospital bed, and hung it over the edge before addressing the room.

"Agent Jeffries suffered a concussion, according to the CT scan we performed, but the MRI showed no sustained damage. We would like to keep him overnight for observation, but I expect a full recovery."

"Hear that?" Leo asked, too full of painkillers to mind his busted lip and swollen jaw. "The doctor says I'm right as rain."

The temperature in the room dipped fractionally, sending goosebumps up my forearms. A stunningly muscular blonde leaned over the side of the hospital bed, her expression obscured by a curtain of the finest, palest hair I'd ever seen. But I didn't need to see her face to imagine the look Agent Hilde Thorsdottir was giving her immediate superior and mortal lover.

It wasn't a friendly one.

"Rain isn't right," she said, her voice low and menacing. "It's wet. And cold. And if you ever get into another situation like that again,

Leonardo Jeffries, I swear on Odin's missing eye that I will drop you into a storm cloud so you can see that for yourself."

Leo coughed out what sounded a lot like an apology—proving that he had a brain. After all, Hilde's threat wasn't an idle one. As a full-fledged Valkyrie, she could sprout wings and fly whenever her heart desired. She could also convert her clothes into armor with a thought and pull weapons out of thin air on a whim—none of which I'd mastered, yet.

And yes, I was jealous.

"Ahem." The doctor waved a hand, awkwardly. "I hate to interrupt, but which one of you two was it who broke Terry's arm? When I heard it was a woman who did it, I have to admit I was surprised. But, no offense, I could honestly imagine either of you pulling it off."

I started to prevaricate, but the two agents gave the game away immediately by pointing at me in unison. Great, I thought. Now I was going to get a lecture on snapping poor, defenseless bones. To my surprise, however, the doctor clapped her hands together like a child, grinning at me from ear to ear.

"So it's true!" she exclaimed. "That's just...awesome."

"Hilde," Leo whispered, his eyes almost comically wide, "I think we should ask for a new doctor. This one's broken."

"Oh, you must think I'm terrible! Please, let me explain. Terry is my former brother-in-law. People say he's a good cop. A great guy, even. But he was a crappy husband, and he's made my sister's life a living hell since they divorced. Anyway, what I meant was that he had it coming. So, thank you."

"Anytime," I replied, too amused by the Midwestern tendency to overshare to say much else. Fortunately, it seemed to do the trick; the doctor flashed me another dazzling smile before turning her attention elsewhere.

"That reminds me. Agent Jeffries?"

"Yes, Doctor?" Leo's gaze was much sharper, now. Which meant either the drugs had worn off, or his doctor's little confession had piqued his interest. Knowing Leo, I was betting on the latter.

"Make sure you have someone nearby to monitor you, just in case. And don't be afraid to report unexpected visitors to the nurses."

"Not to the guard on duty, the one whose office is on the first floor?" Hilde asked.

"Greg?" The doctor shook her head, her smile dimming considerably. "He and Terry's little brother went to school together, and Greg wants to be a cop. A good word from the sheriff could go a long way."

"Should we be expectin' trouble?" I asked, struck by the implications of what she was telling us.

"Just a precaution," she assured me, patting the edge of the bed as she left the room, though not before shutting the door firmly behind her.

"Watt must have more pull around here than I gave him credit for if he's got hospital staff looking the other way," Leo said after a moment of silence.

"We know he's not involved with the killings, though," Hilde interjected, gripping the rail of his hospital bed hard enough to make the metal creak. "You tested him and his people as soon as we arrived. So why would he be threatening us?"

"I wish I knew. It's entirely possible this murder had nothing to do with the others, and that he's somehow involved. There's no way to be sure without asking, and he won't talk to me."

"Or me," I chimed in.

"Or you." Leo shook his head in bewilderment. "I still can't believe you broke his arm."

"He was goin' to hit ye again." I shrugged as if that was all that needed to be said. But, in my mind, I watched Watt launch himself at Leo in slow motion. He'd already cocked one arm back as though planning to deliver a second blow to Leo's defenseless face. I could tell from Watt's face that it wasn't the heat of the moment or a bad judgment call. He'd wanted Leo out of the way—for good. "Ye were already knocked out, so ye couldn't defend yourself, and everyone else was too far away to step in. So I took care of it."

"By shattering his arm in three places."

"I wasn't goin' to let him hit ye, again, Leo."

The senior agent actually looked embarrassed, as though my stepping in on his behalf was something shameful. It was a guy thing, of course. Some macho pride thing. But that was alright, because the fierce approval on his partner's face was more than enough thanks, under the circumstances. In any case, the moment passed before I had to say anything else.

"Quinn," Leo began after clearing his throat, "you should know that we are all extremely glad to find out you're alive. But—"

"Ye want to know why I'm here," I finished for him.

"He is worried it has something to do with this case," Hilde interjected. "If that is why you're here, it would complicate things for us."

"Oh, no. I'm not here about your case."

They both relaxed.

"I'm actually here for Hilde."

"For me?" Hilde asked, her glacial blue eyes narrowed to slits. "Why?"

"The short answer? Freya sent me."

Before Hilde could freak out or start asking me all sorts of questions, I proceeded to give them both an extremely truncated summary of the events which had led me to Fólkvangr. Then, in much greater detail, I described what happened while I was there— including the deal I'd made to find and return Freya's wayward Valkyrie. Of course, I may have left out one or two potentially prickly details that I thought might unfairly prejudice Brynhildr's daughter. When I was finally done, however, I held out both hands in supplication.

"Please, Hilde, I need ye to come with me. Once Freya hears what happened to ye from your own lips, she'll have to honor her promise. After that, I can go back to Boston without this hangin' over me head."

"I refuse," Hilde replied, her tone so chilly it made me want to hug myself for warmth.

"Ye what?" I blinked owlishly at the Valkyrie, unable to process her outright dismissal. "What the hell d'ye mean, ye refuse?"

"I mean I will not go to Asgard with you."

"But, if ye don't..." I left the rest unspoken.

"You made a foolish promise, Quinn MacKenna. There are things you do not know. Reasons why I am here, why I left her service, that I cannot share." Hilde slid around her side of the bed, her expression implacable and unyielding. "We have a case to solve. With Leo in the hospital, that means I am in charge. You should go home and be with your friends with the time you have left. I'll leave you to say your goodbyes."

And, with that, the key to my freedom stormed out of the room.

CHAPTER 21

I found myself staring at the hospital room walls. They were two-toned; white as bone on top, the bottom a maddening shade of butterscotch that was clearly meant to compliment the mustard yellow curtains and lemon-tinted pillowcases. The furniture was a collection of those functional Scandinavian pieces which never ceased to remind me of a dentist's office. A clock on the wall told me it was a little past two in the afternoon, which meant the Hex Moon was now eight nights away. If we left now, I thought, Max could get a good five or six hours of sleep in the backseat before taking over.

"You could have called," Leo suggested, shattering the fraught silence Hilde had left behind. "It might have given Hilde a chance to think about it, or at least saved you some time."

"I didn't have your number," I explained. "I only found out where ye were from a mutual acquaintance of Jimmy's who doesn't like me much. I don't even have me own phone. Or an apartment. Oh, and I'm flat broke until me bank says otherwise."

"Huh...want some Jell-O?" Leo asked. He snatched up a cup of cherry red gelatin from the nightstand and held it out to me. "They took the spoon, but I'm sure you know how to slurp it down."

"It's like ridin' a bike," I muttered, accepting the cup graciously before slumping into the visitor's chair, feeling so defeated I hardly noticed how the plastic upholstery clung to my thighs and back. "I really thought Hilde had gotten tricked by someone pretendin' to be Odin, Leo. I was sure she'd want to go back, to clear t'ings up and find out who it was."

"I don't know about any of that," Leo confessed, clearly pitying me. "Hilde doesn't talk about her past. It upsets her, which is probably why she reacted as strongly as she did. Did you say this person you made a deal with was a goddess?"

"Freya, aye. She's Odin's wife."

"Could she have been lying to you?"

Unfortunately, I'd already considered that. More than once, in fact, given the fact that her blessing hadn't sheltered me from the worst Niflheim had to offer—not to mention Nevermore's occasional wardrobe malfunctions. Frankly, I could make a case that Freya had failed to honor her side of our bargain. The trouble was, at the time it really had *felt* like she was telling the truth. That she'd *wanted* me to succeed.

"It's possible," I admitted.

"But you don't think so."

I grunted as I peeled off the lid off the plastic cup, my stomach grumbling. "Am I that easy to read?"

"If you are asking whether I can tell if you're lying or not, I can. But that also means I know you didn't come here with the wrong intentions. And knowing that makes a big difference."

"How so?" I asked as I slid one finger around the circumference of the cup's interior to dislodge the gelatin. Standard Jell-O shot procedure. Funnily enough, I couldn't remember the last time I'd actually had a drink. With Charon, maybe? The boatman had been the very definition of a functioning alcoholic.

"Well, if you'd come here solely to save your own ass, then I'd have been hard pressed to talk to Hilde on your behalf. As things stand, however, I should at least be able to get her read on what this Freya is really after."

"Really? Ye would do that?" I stopped with the cup halfway to my lips, almost afraid to nurture the flicker of hope he'd just offered me.

"If she says she won't go," Leo warned, "she won't go. But, at her core, Hilde is a fiercely loyal person. You saved Lakota from the Carol Killer after she was taken. Then you went to Moscow with us to save her, putting yourself at great personal risk in the process. And you protected me, today, which I never properly thanked you for."

Suddenly it was my turn to look away in embarrassment. "It's what friends do."

"Precisely my point. You've done right by us, and Hilde knows that. Which means, if you ask for her help, there is no doubt in my mind she'll do what she can."

"Amen to that," came a voice from the doorway.

Thinking one of Watt's people had come to finish what he'd started, I sat up so quickly the chair groaned in protest. Thankfully, I needn't have worried; the speaker was clearly no friend of the sheriffs. Unfortunately, it took me several breaths longer than I'd have liked to figure out how I knew that for sure.

"Hiya, Quinn. Heard you broke Watt and nearly got us kicked off this case. And all before lunch. Where *do* you find the energy?"

"Lakota?!"

Under normal circumstances, I'd have taken the federal agent's teasing in stride, even fired off a rib-tickler or two to make light of the situation. Something about beating cops for breakfast, probably. But, at that precise moment, I was too busy trying to scrape my jaw off the floor to crack a smile, let alone a joke.

"In the flesh," she replied, her snide little smirk an exact replica of the one she'd worn the very first day we met. But that's where the similarities ended. Because everything else—from the frisky cut of her chin-length hair to the swell of her chest and hips—was different. Gone was the androgynous, baby-faced youth hiding beneath an illfitting suit, supplanted by a woman whose primary identifier would forever be *exotic*.

"I'll say." I made a sweeping gesture towards her whole body. "I almost didn't recognize ye."

Lakota shrugged in reply, baring a thin line of tanned midriff above a pair of black leather pants that might as well have been painted on. Not that her outfit was salacious. It wasn't because Lakota wasn't. If anything, the Native American woman exuded a hands-off-or-else vibe.

"What did you find out?" Leo asked, clearly eager to move the conversation to other waters.

"Hilde says I should let you rest," Lakota replied. "I just came by to make sure you weren't going to give up the ghost."

Leo cursed under his breath.

"Of course, if you *ordered* me to tell you as my boss, I'd have no choice." Lakota pulled both hands from her jacket pockets and threw them wide with a dramatic flourish. "Bureaucracy and all that."

"Oh, good point. Tell me what you found, and that's an order."

"Gladly," Lakota said, grinning. "So, still no word on the victim. Not that I expected Watt's people to share intel. They've gone on record with the animal attack, so it'll be on us to prove otherwise. Assuming we can be bothered."

"Not unless the evidence falls into our lap," Leo confirmed. "I'm not going to waste resources looking for a killer who can drop bodies out of thin air. If it happens again, we'll call in the Academy. Have their Justices sort it out."

"Heard."

"Well?" Leo cocked one eyebrow. "Is that all? Or did you actually have some good news to run by me, for once?"

"Please. You thought I'd show up to your hospital room without a Get-Well gift?"

"Go on, then."

"We caught a break with ATF. Seems like all our crime scenes line up with a route they found on an old bootlegger map."

"You're joking."

"Nope. Looks like there's an improvised road that runs all the way through the Ozarks. Most of it is overland, but it's got some underground sections we'd never have known about. Tunnels and what not."

Leo buried his head in his hands and groaned. "Jimmy is never going to let me hear the end of this one, is he?"

"Maybe next time you won't doubt him so much," Lakota chastised, shaking her head at the senior agent. "If you'd have trusted his nose like you trust your ears, we might have figured this out sooner."

"He said he smelled strong alcohol, not booze. I assumed that meant a cleaning agent. Sue me."

"It probably won't come to that," Lakota teased. "Just buy him a beer when this is all over. Anyway, I'm still waiting for you to ask me about the good news."

"There's more?"

"Sure is. Guess what's on the outskirts of town, up in the mountains?"

"You know I hate it when you do this."

"Just guess."

"Come on, just tell me. I'm sitting over here with a head injury. I could be dying right this minute."

"You aren't dying." Lakota rolled her eyes. "But fine. How about a whole campsite's worth of alleged bootleggers? ATF says they live in caravans. Been on their radar for a while, now, but no arrests. Quite the coincidence, wouldn't you say?"

"Yeah..." Leo frowned so hard for a moment that I thought he might be having a stroke. "It's not adding up, Lakota. We've got a dozen victims connected to this town, but not to each other. And I don't see any of them having anything to do with bootlegging."

"It's a lead, boss. I seem to remember some geezer telling me more than once that the whole picture only becomes clear once the puzzle is finished, and that the only part we can control is connecting as many pieces as we can."

"Sounds pretty damn smart, your geezer."

"He has his moments."

Leo cracked a smile. "You going to take a run at them, then?"

"That's the plan."

"I want you to take Quinn with you."

"Me?" I asked, surprised. Up until now, the most I'd been able to do was follow their conversation. And even then, there were bits and pieces I couldn't quite figure out.

"Yes, you."

"Are you sure, Leo? No offense, Quinn. I tend to do my best work alone, that's all."

"None taken. I get it."

"I'm sure," Leo insisted. "I don't want you out there alone on this one, not until we know more about what we're dealing with. Hilde is going to want to stay and keep an eye on me, I'm sure. Plus, she and I need to talk. I'd have Jimmy go with you, but he tends to put people around here on edge."

"Uh huh." Lakota's expression soured, her reaction suggesting Midwestern hospitality hadn't lived up to its reputation.

"Yeah, I know," Leo said. "Trust me. But we need something to keep the Bureau from pulling us off this one, and we don't have time to waste. Besides, this way you can fill Quinn in on what's going on. I don't know how long she'll be here, but maybe she'll catch something we missed."

I glanced at the clock a second time. "I can tag along, but I have to be back and in bed before dark."

"A curfew, at your age?" Lakota teased. "Guess that explains the Jell-O."

"It's a long story," I drawled, nonplussed.

"Something to do with that hole in your soul? Or are you trying to get back in time to cuddle up with that *Pejuta Wicasa* in the lobby? Not that I'm judging."

"The hole in me...wait, what was that ye called Max just now?"

"Ah, so that's his name. Jimmy didn't seem to know it. Before we leave, remind me to send the two of them to get you a room in our hotel."

I felt my eyes threatening to fall out of their sockets at the thought of Jimmy and Max spending time together. What would they talk about? Shit, nevermind that, *who* would they talk about?

Lakota took one look at my face and started laughing uproariously. "Come on, we'll snag a coffee on the way. My treat."

CHAPTER 22

I'd never seen a campsite full of caravans before. I'd seen a couple trailer parks over the years, mostly during business trips which required visiting the more remote regions of the country in search of some obscure relic. But ultimately, most parks mirrored your typical suburban subdivision; provided you substituted the single-family homes and two-car garages for camper vans and gravel driveways. Hell, Staten Island had one with nicer trailers than most people had homes—including tire to ceiling windows and water-resistant siding.

This was nothing like that. Whereas trailers tended to hug the road in designated intervals, the bootlegger caravans—ranging all the way from stainless steel Airstreams to motorbikes with teardrop trailers in tow—formed a complete circle around the circumference of the campsite, making it all but impossible for anyone to enter unannounced. Which was presumably why Lakota and I remained in her rental car, watching the caravan owners from the relative seclusion of an overgrown side road.

"We goin' down there?" I asked, voice hushed.

"We're not in a library, and they can't hear us," Lakota remarked. "And that depends."

"On?"

"Here, Leo texted me as I was leaving the hotel to say you might be needing these," Lakota said, ignoring my question. She reached past me, opened the glovebox, and fished out a lanyard and a black leather wallet. "Don't go flashing them unless someone asks, but they should hold up whenever you're with us."

"What are they?"

"This is a CAC card," Lakota replied, pronouncing the acronym like I would say *sack*. "Don't ask me what it stands for. I honestly have no idea."

She tossed the lanyard at me, and I discovered it had a thick plastic case attached at the end. Inside was a chip ID with my face printed on it, complete with my name below and a very official-looking *Department of Homeland Security* above. The wallet landed in my lap a moment later. Inside was a badge with DHS splashed across the front and what appeared to be a valid serial number at its base. For a moment, I could only stare at them.

"Is this badge real?" I asked, stunned.

"No idea. Never seen a DHS badge. And neither has anyone else, which is sort of the point. You can thank Leo for thinking ahead and getting these made. After Moscow, he thought it might be a good idea to make sure you had better credentials. Honestly, I had no idea he'd hung onto them this long, though. Guess he knew something we didn't."

"After Moscow..." I drifted off, reminded of yet another friend I'd neglected since returning. Othello. These had to be her handiwork; they were too damn good to be run-of-the-mill forgeries. In fact, knowing her, the cover identity would probably stand up to a ridiculous amount of scrutiny before anyone was the wiser.

"Everything alright?" Lakota asked, eyeing me.

"Aye, just feelin' like an ass is all."

"I wouldn't worry about it too much. Othello will be too glad you're alive to throw a fit."

I shot her a look of surprise.

"I'm a Seer, remember?"

"I remember," I replied, cautiously. The truth was, Lakota's ability —far more so than any of the others'—bothered me. It was like, when she looked at you, she could see things you didn't even know about yourself. Like the "hole" in my soul, for example. What the hell had she meant by that? And what about Max? She'd called him something in another language. But what?

"Relax, Quinn, or your head is going to explode." Lakota tapped her temple, and that's when I noticed a rose gold band encircling her ring finger.

I opened my mouth to remark on it but was interrupted by the rap of knuckles on my passenger window.

"Shit!" I cursed, nearly jumping out of my skin, my heart hammering against my ribcage. A man's face leered at me through the window. Behind him, I could make out the chests and shoulders of at least two others.

"You lost?" the man shouted, his eyes glinting with something darker than amusement. He was an ugly sort with a missing eyetooth and more patches in his scraggly facial hair than anyone I'd ever seen.

"That was fast," Lakota muttered. "They must have lookouts in the woods."

"Ye knew they would find us?" I hissed.

"I figured as much, yeah. They probably smelled us coming a mile away."

"Smelled us?"

Another rap on the window interrupted whatever response Lakota might have offered. It was harder this time, though. So hard, in fact, that I worried for the integrity of my window. I turned a glare on the bastard, but he merely smiled.

"I said, are you ladies lost?"

"No, we know exactly where we are," I snapped. "Now back the fuck away from me door before I tear it off its hinges and beat ye to death with it."

The smile dimmed, replaced by something uncertain and vulnerable that reminded me of a kicked dog. The man backed away, both hands held out to show he'd meant no harm. And maybe he hadn't. Still, a girl can never be too careful.

"Now, Quinn, be nice to the poor werewolf flunky," Lakota admonished, grinning. "Come on, let's go track down their Alpha and say hi."

CHAPTER 23

The caravan owners emerged from their homes to form a ring around us the moment we stepped onto the muddy campground, their arrival accompanied by the sound of swinging screen doors, barking dogs, and the raucous laughter of playing children. A peculiar odor rode the wind, growing stronger with each step until the air was a heady blend of charcoal and acetone—enough to make you feel lightheaded and faintly nauseous. Thankfully, the sensation passed by the time we reached the epicenter of the campsite.

We were met there by two people. The first was a short, stout man covered in so much hair I wasn't entirely convinced he'd come back from his last lunar transformation; it coated the tops of his bare, thickly calloused feet like moss, curled in ringlets from beneath his overalls, and ran up his neck to join a beard so bushy it could have doubled as steel wool. The second was a thin woman with carrot-colored hair and a face that would have looked right at home in a nun's habit.

"You young ladies lost?" the man said, his tone as gruff and gravelly as he was, his Ozarkian accent so thick it turned every word into a redneck battle cry.

"Is that some sort of hillbilly catchphrase?" I muttered, low enough only Lakota could hear. Or so I thought, anyway; the moment I said it, damn near every camper bristled and turned to glare at me. Apparently, it wasn't only their noses that were sensitive. Whoops.

Lakota patted my arm and took the lead, holding her badge high for the whole pack to see. "Agent Lakota Collins, FBI. I'm here to ask you some questions."

I froze like a startled deer, struck both dumb and mute by the surname she'd so casually dropped.

"Ezekiel Brown," the man replied, shoving both thumbs into the curve of his overalls, just below his nipples. "But you can call me Zeke, same as everybody. Say now, who's your friend? Ain't she gonna introduce herself?"

Lakota glanced over her shoulder at me, which gave me enough time at least to pick my metaphorical jaw up off the ground and begin dusting it off. Sadly, that's as far as I got in the recovery process before Lakota took stock of whatever expression I wore on my face. Her eyes went extremely wide for a moment, then soft with what I could only assume was pity.

She thought I'd known.

"This is Quinn MacKenna," Lakota replied, all business by the time she turned back around. "She's with me."

"Would that be Miss MacKenna?" Zeke asked, gazing up at me from beneath the bushiest damn eyebrows I'd ever seen. "Ain't often we see someone pretty as you around. Always liked me a tall woman."

"Zeke, stop talking with your pecker," the woman behind him barked, her attention focused squarely on Lakota. "What's the FBI want with us? We ain't done nothing."

"I never said you did, Miss..."

"Missus. Mrs. Pauline Brown. This idiot here's my husband. Though, I'll tell you what, honey..." Pauline shifted her raptorial gaze to me, "if you want his sorry ass, he's all yours."

"Now, Pauline, don't be like that—"

"Stuff it, Zeke. I done told you what'll happen. 'Sides, even a deaf bat could see the girl has her own problems without you pawing at her."

For some reason, that seemed to sober the man up; Zeke studied me with a much shrewder expression than I'd have given him credit for a minute ago. He took a deep breath, his belly swelling against the seams of his overalls, and let it out slowly.

"Sorry, sweet pea. I reckon you're right."

Pauline responded with a satisfied humph. "I'm always right. Now, Agent...what was it, again?"

"Call me Lakota," the Seer replied, quickly.

"Whatever flogs your log, sweetheart. But if you ain't here to accuse us of nothing, what is it you want?"

"I'm looking for answers."

"This ain't no church," Pauline sassed, drawing a series of titillated giggles from the gathered crowd.

Lakota, clearly unamused, waited for the laughter to die down before trying again. "I'm here about the bloodless cadavers left to rot up and down your bootlegging route. Does your little...congregation happen to know anything about that?"

Every adult in the whole camp stilled as one. That is until Zeke began howling with laughter. Within seconds, the crowd joined in like baying dogs, their snaggle-toothed grins raised to the sky as dozens of terrified birds abandoned the surrounding trees.

"Don't be ridiculous, Miss FBI," Zeke said once the cacophony finally died away, his bumbling manner usurped by something much more menacing. "We're just a bunch of like-minded folks trying to get by in a cruel and unforgiving world. But, seeing as how we have a permit to be here, and ain't done nothing to earn any federal attention as far as I know..."

Lakota shook her head in response to his unasked question, confirming his supposition.

"Well, then," he continued, "I think it'd be mighty kind if you and your friend here were on your way."

To my surprise, Lakota nodded. "We'll do that. Mind if I ask one last question before we go?"

"So long as you don't mind leaving without an answer."

"Fair enough." Lakota turned a slow circle, her voice raised. "Earlier today, the sheriff's people found a body a couple miles east of here. I was wondering if anyone in your pack was missing?"

The crowd stirred at her use of the word *pack*, and I noticed Zeke's hands had balled into meaty fists at his sides. The instant Pauline put her hand on his hairy shoulder, however, he relaxed. Lakota, meanwhile, continued to scan the faces gathered around us as though waiting for someone to come forward, or at least speak up.

No one did.

"Sorry to disappoint, Miss FBI," Zeke drawled.

"That's alright. It was a longshot, anyway. Here's my card in case you or any of your people think of anything else."

Pauline snatched the card from Lakota's outstretched hand and pocketed it, staring daggers at us both. "Go on, then."

We left the way we came, though I couldn't resist the urge to glance back at the motley collection of faces, wondering what could have possibly driven this assortment of supernatural beings to live the way they did. Was it the freedom? The threat of discovery? Whatever the reason, I couldn't wrap my head around it. But then, who was I to throw stones?

I couldn't even *rent* a glass house.

"I'm really sorry about before," Lakota whispered as soon as we were well out of even a werewolf's earshot. "Jimmy said he thought you already knew."

"I guess I did, sort of," I confessed, my stomach knotting with the anxiety of having to hold this particular conversation, especially after having worked so hard to not think about it. "I mean, his old partner told me Jimmy had gotten married."

"But not to whom," Lakota supplied, groaning. "Dammit. I should have known the instant I saw you. No one is that Zen. I just assumed, what with how long you'd been gone, and the fact that you came with another man...I really am sorry."

"God, stop," I snapped. I halted and took a deep, bracing breath. "Stop apologizin', please. It was an honest mistake."

Lakota didn't reply. Indeed, for perhaps the first time since we'd met, the Seer refused to look me in the eye. Which is what made me realize she wasn't simply apologizing for the shitty way I'd found out that my ex had married someone I'd considered a child when we last parted ways. No, she was apologizing because she felt guilty—the same guilt any decent person would feel when dating a friend's ex without at least their tacit permission.

Unfortunately, part of me thought she *should* feel guilty.

Which made saying what needed to be said that much harder.

"I'm not jealous," I began, though I had to hold up a hand to keep Lakota from responding. "I'm not even surprised, really. I could tell ye two were close back in Moscow. Hell, ye had him carryin' your bags for cryin' out loud."

Lakota snickered at that.

"What I mean to say," I continued, pasting a smile on my face, "is that I'm happy for ye both. I truly am. Will it take some gettin' used to? Probably. But ye don't have to take me into account. Which means if I notice either of ye tiptoein' around me out of pity or in an attempt to spare me feelin's, ye should know I'll have no choice but to beat ye both to death."

"With a door you've ripped off its hinges," Lakota added, bastardizing my ridiculous threat from earlier.

"Please. We're friends. I'd use me bare hands."

Lakota chuckled and resumed our march to the car, shaking her head as she went. I fell in behind her, my steps considerably lighter now than they'd been before our talk. Of course, there was no way it was going to be that simple—and we both knew it. Seeing Lakota and Jimmy together was going to be flat out tough, especially at first. Not because I had any right to be upset, but because feelings were feelings; if people could turn them off at will, they'd have done so already.

But hey, maybe I was exempt from that rule?

Divinity had to come with *some* perks, after all.

"Oy," I began as we climbed, "when ye said that bit about the hole in me soul, what exactly—"

"Shhhh," Lakota hissed, her whole body suddenly on alert. "Someone's waiting for us at the car."

"Who is it?"

Lakota relaxed. "Oh, good. It's that kid."

"Kid? What kid?"

"The one who ran off when I asked if someone from the pack was missing. Come on."

The kid turned out to be one of the three who'd led us to the campsite. I recognized his checkered flannel shirt the instant we cleared the embankment and found him lounging on the hood of Lakota's rental. Though, honestly, I thought "kid" was a bit of a stretch; he may have had the gangly, pimply look of a teenager who'd shot up six inches and only just learned to shave, but everything else about him screamed jaded.

"Get your ass off my car," Lakota barked.

"Damn, lady!" The teenager hopped up so fast I thought he'd been bitten by something. He thrust a finger to his lips, his eyes pleading. "Keep your voice down, alright? If Pauline finds out I was talking to you, I'm toast."

"Pauline, huh? Not Zeke?"

The teen rolled his eyes. "Zeke would kick my ass, but he'd pour me a drink and we'd laugh about it, after. The guy talks tough, but he has a heart. Pauline's more likely to cut me open and to pour that drink over my freaking wounds."

"Sounds unpleasant," Lakota noted. "So, why risk it?"

The teen clammed up for a moment, his gaze flicking back and forth as though trying to decide which of us was going to try to steal his lunch money. "How do I know I can trust you?"

"What makes you think you can't?" Lakota countered.

"I've never met a Fed before, but I've met plenty of cops, and the honest ones don't talk like you."

Lakota raised an eyebrow. "That's pretty perceptive, actually. Where are you from, kid?"

"It's Leon," he replied, bristling. "And I'm from Atlanta."

"And what brought you here, Leon?"

"To the Ozarks? Or to your car?"

"Both."

Leon sniffed. "Same thing, I guess. It's my brother. He heard about Zeke and his crew from a friend. He was in deep with some dirty cops, and things started going sideways, so we came out here. Fresh start, you know?"

"Yeah, I know."

"Anyway, this body you found...what did it look like?"

"I can't tell you that, Leon," Lakota said, regretfully. "I wish I could, but I can't."

Leon licked his lips and looked away, his body language stiff. "Did it have a robe on?"

Lakota managed to keep a straight face, somehow, but it didn't fool Leon; he hunkered down into himself so hard that I instantly understood why Lakota had called him a kid. It wasn't his age she'd been referring to, or what he'd survived. It was his heart—a child's heart.

"Leon," Lakota began, "why don't you come with us, and we can—"

"No!" Leon snapped, wiping at his cheeks. "No, I'm good. I need to get back before they notice I'm gone. I've got a good thing going, here. I don't want to screw it up."

"I get that. But I want you to take my card. Hide it if you want, just take it." Lakota thrust it into his trembling hands. "If things here don't turn out the way you hoped, I want you to call me, okay?"

Leon nodded, though I could tell his heart wasn't in it. The shock of realizing he'd never see his brother again was just setting in. Lakota, sensing the same thing, retrieved the card and slipped it into his pocket, instead.

"If it was Mike you found," Leon said, his eyes staring at nothing, "then you should check out the Fairy Court. It's this new show on the Strip. Mike wouldn't tell me why, but that's where he went yesterday. I remember because he was wearing that robe, and I thought it was weird. I mean, the hell was he wearing that for, anyway?"

Lakota started to say something, but Leon had already started trudging down the hill. Within seconds, he was loping towards the campsite, moving with the eerie grace of a shapeshifter.

CHAPTER 24

T hat night I dreamt of fire.

It began how the most disturbing dreams so often do: with me waking up in the place I'd fallen asleep. The hotel room was dark, the blinds closed, and the curtains drawn. I'd stuffed one of the complimentary towels into the crack below the door to dampen any noise from the hall outside before downing Circe's potion an hour before dusk, anticipating a full night of uninterrupted sleep. If all went according to plan, Max would check on me come morning. He'd booked the adjoining room next door.

The moment the thought crossed my mind, I realized I was in that other room. The differences were minor: there was no towel at the door and the curtains weren't shut. There was, however, *something* lying in the center of the bed. I stepped closer, squinting until I could make out a glowing heart, its light winking in and out of existence like the strobe of a firefly. It suddenly felt so alive that I was half-convinced it would leap off the bed at any moment.

And that's exactly what it did.

The organ shot up into the air like a bird, and I found myself chasing after that electric heartbeat as it passed through one wall after another, then from one realm to the next. We raced through worlds trapped in ice and swallowed by darkness. Worlds without water, or life. This went on for so long, in fact, that my muscles began to ache, and my every breath was accompanied by a stabbing, rending pain in my side. I slowed, unable to fight through it any longer, and watched the glowing heart continue on without me.

I fell to my knees, reached down, and discovered Areadbhar lodged between my ribs, the tip of her blade kissing my heart. Hands brushed my shoulders and back, and I was suddenly surrounded by kneeling, faceless figures whose names were as familiar to me as my own.

Cernunnos, the Horned One.

Aengus, the Lover.

Ecne, the Wise.

Goibniu, the Smith.

Cliodhna, Queen of Banshees.

As I thought these names and more, the respective gods and goddesses rose and joined what sounded like a battle at my back. By the time I was done, the clamor was deafening—the high, piteous wails of lost children intermingled with the cries of dying men and women. Unable to resist, I twisted around to see what horror could break such spirits and orphan so many.

A figure stalked a darkened landscape, her skin ablaze with an unquenchable flame that consumed everything and everyone it touched. She held no weapon and wore no armor. Instead, she reached for man after man, woman after woman, clutching them to her naked breast until their screams died away and they turned to ash in her arms while their children watched. In her wake, the gods and goddesses crawled like whipped dogs, bound to each other by iron chains. I called out to them, screaming their names, but it wasn't their attention I received.

It was hers.

The infernal creature dropped her latest victim and reached for me; a relentless need etched across her face. No, not *her* face.

My face.

The sole remaining faceless god—whose name I hadn't dared

utter even in my own head—yanked me backwards, drawing me into her arms with the strength of creation itself. Once in her embrace, the pain at my side faded to little more than a dull ache and all suddenly felt right in the world. When at last she spoke, however, it was with a voice that could crack the world in two.

"This is what you become. Not who you are."

CHAPTER 25

I was sitting in the shower when I heard Max's voice outside the bathroom door asking me if everything was alright. According to him, everyone was downstairs in the lobby snagging their complimentary breakfast and wondering where I was—which at least partially explained why the brujo had used magic to break into my room when I hadn't answered my door.

I certainly hadn't given him a key.

I hugged my legs tighter to my chest and raised my head, blinking past the merciless droplets which ricocheted off my knees and into my face, until I could see the door through a gap in the curtain. Max began banging on it so hard it rattled, shouting my name. I didn't want to talk to him—or anyone, for that matter. Between the worsening side effects of Circe's potion and last night's unsettling dreams, all I really wanted was a few hours to myself to shake off the general malaise. On the other hand, if I stayed silent, he was bound to come barging in and make a fuss.

"I'll be out in a minute!" I called.

Climbing to my feet was a struggle; my legs had nearly fallen asleep, my tailbone throbbed where it had been pressed against the porcelain tub, and my skin was that mottled shade of pink that generally means you've spent far too long in the hot water. Indeed, the reflection in the mirror after I'd wiped it clear of condensation revealed a pair of glassy green eyes surrounded by a puffy, freckled ruddiness.

I looked, and even felt, feverish.

Deep down, I suspected it had more to do with Circe's potion than the dream. She'd warned me it was a temporary fix to a long-term problem—no being with that much power could be held at bay by something so simple forever. Still, I would have thought I had more than a couple days to find a better solution before it affected me during my waking hours.

I came out wrapped in a towel with a second coiled around my head, the residual steam spilling out into the bedroom like I'd hired a freaking fog machine. The clock by the bed read a quarter past ten, which meant I'd been in the shower for nearly an hour and had missed out on breakfast. Of course, what I really needed was—

"I got you coffee. It's on the dresser with cream and a couple packets of sugar." Max had his back turned to me so that he faced the door. "Your friends told me to make sure you hurry. They want to leave by eleven."

I had the paper cup nestled between my hands and held posses-sively to my chest before I could even begin processing the second half of what he'd said. In fact, it wasn't until I'd mixed in the cream and sugar that I remembered what he and I had agreed to the day before.

"The Fairy Court," I said, feeling foolish for having lost track of time. "The Branson show Leo wanted us to go see with him and Lakota. I almost forgot."

"Sí. I must tell you, the blonde Señorita did not seem happy about us going."

"That's Hilde, the one I was supposed to find. And I'm not surprised. She t'inks it's a wild goose chase and a waste of time, which she made very clear yesterday."

"Is she upset with you?"

I took a sip of the coffee while I considered how to answer that.

The truth was, I had no idea. In light of what Lakota and I had found, she and I hadn't spoken again about my deal with Freya. If anything, she'd acted like I didn't exist—addressing Lakota or Leo, but never me. Jimmy hadn't been around for that conversation, nor was he supposed to join us at the show. Apparently, he was looking into the possibility of a feud between the local werewolves and any other supernatural groups in the area.

"I'm not sure. Right now, I plan on doin' everythin' I can to solve this case. If she doesn't warm back up to me by then, well..." I shrugged, unwilling to consider what that might mean.

"Any idea how long that could take?"

The way he said that made me set down my coffee. "Why, is somethin' wrong?"

"No, not wrong. It is Camila." Max shrugged so hard his shoulder muscles bunched beneath his t-shirt. "She still will not tell me what she is planning to do. She says it is a work in progress, and that she will explain it all when everything is in place."

"But you're worried."

"It is not like her to be so...daring. Or, I should say, it is unfamiliar. When we were young, she was like this. But after Victor..." Max shook his head. "I worry she is risking too much, too soon."

"I get that."

"Then can you promise me that you will have this case solved before the Hex Moon?"

"No, I can't," I said, truthfully. "But if Hilde and I haven't made any progress in a few days, we can talk about leaving. And, if you need to go, I'll understand. Speakin' of which...I t'ink ye should step out while I get dressed.

"I turned around," Max replied, sounding faintly amused.

"Aye, and that's an easy t'ing to do a second time. So go on, before I call down to the front desk and report ye for breakin' into me room."

"Very well," Max said before pulling open the door and stepping halfway through it. "But if you need help with any zippers or clasps, I will be right outside."

"What about chainmail?" I muttered once the door was shut,

eyeing the discarded pieces of armor strewn across the floor on my side of the bed—all of which, apparently, I'd removed in my sleep. The digital readout on the clock ticked forward another minute, giving me under half an hour to dry my hair, sort out my defective armor, fix whatever was going on with my face, and meet everyone in the lobby downstairs...and people liked to say Hercules had it rough with those weak ass labors.

Greek, please.

CHAPTER 26

The Branson Strip on Highway 76 stretched out in front of us like a kindergartener's caricature of Las Vegas. Soft serve ice cream shops, flea markets masquerading as antique stores, motels, and a hodgepodge assortment of roadside attractions competed for space along either side of the street in an absurd clash of colors and eras. So far, we'd passed a yellow biplane mounted in mid-dive, one half of the Titanic, a three-story Mount Rushmore featuring the likes of John Wayne and Elvis Presley, a hundred and fifty foot Ferris wheel, and a go-kart race track with more levels than most parking garages.

"Hillbilly Heaven," Lakota commented, having caught my befuddled expression from the backseat. "What you don't see is the nationally-ranked amusement park, the wildlife safari, Table Rock Lake, and Dolly Parton's Stampede."

"Her what, now?"

Lakota laughed. "It's hard to describe. If you end up sticking around at all, you should check it out."

"We've been on this case for weeks," Leo explained as he merged into the right lane. "I encouraged everyone to take a day or two off to get their heads right. I didn't realize they'd use it to ride rollercoasters and eat funnel cakes."

"Says the man who went white water rafting with his subordinate," Lakota chimed in, grinning.

Leo flushed, but I could tell he enjoyed the ribbing. They all did, come to think of it. Maybe that was how they dealt with the job; murder and mayhem had to take its toll, especially when you were the last line of defense between the oblivious masses and the things that went bump in the night.

"D'ye come up with any new leads after I left last night?" I asked, out of curiosity.

"No," Leo admitted. "Finding out we had a pack of werewolves in town was a break in some ways, but it still doesn't account for the victims or the way they were killed."

"Lakota said they were exsanguinated."

"That's right. Not an ounce of blood in their bodies. And yes, I know what you're thinking. Vampires. But we looked into that, already."

"And?"

"And the Sanguine Council representative we spoke to said Branson is a Masterless city. Something about all the silver they used to mine here making it hard for them to tolerate. Not to mention the Bible thumpers."

"They have a museum for that, too," Lakota noted.

"For vampires?"

"No, for Bibles."

"Right. So...you're sayin' it's no country for old vampires?"

Max, who'd remained silent up to this point, sniggered. "Nice."

"T'anks."

"I think that's it," Leo said, pointedly ignoring my superbly timed reference as we rounded a bend in the road. "The place on the right past the barn with the giant cock."

"What?" Max grabbed the back of my seat and pulled himself forward, peering over my shoulder with eyes as wide as saucer plates.

"He meant a giant rooster," Lakota said, swatting her superior's arm.

Leo cackled until he found a parking space, infecting us all with his good humor. But then, that was the sort of guy Leo was when he wasn't arresting bad guys or going toe to toe with monsters. In another life, we might very well have been drinking buddies or next-door neighbors who hosted joint barbecues. Instead, I helped him catch—and occasionally execute—bad guys.

What a world.

Outside, the noonday heat had climbed high enough that I regretted having turned my pauldrons into a lightweight bomber jacket. Unfortunately, there wasn't much I could do about it except hope the theater was air conditioned. It'd been difficult enough getting the *seitr* magic to stick without worrying about the weather; I'd had to cast the spells several times to make sure it didn't look like I'd been dressed by a colorblind orangutan. If Hilde ever warmed up to me again, I'd have to ask her about that.

"This place is drenched in magic," Max said as we approached the entrance to what looked like a miniature medieval castle from some Russian fairytale, complete with onion domes and hedges trimmed to resemble towering trees.

Frankly, it should have looked silly—or like something only a child would appreciate, at the very least. Instead, the closer we got, the more majestic the castle became. The colors were vibrant, the palette sophisticated enough to earn admiring looks from the adults as they corralled their rambunctious children and shepherded them towards the double doors.

"Not just any magic, either," Lakota added, her eyes dancing from one architectural marvel to the next as though following the flight of a hummingbird. "There's something very strange about it."

"What do you mean, strange?" Leo asked as we joined the crowd.

"It's...wild."

"It is *magia de Hadas*," Max said, squinting. "Fae magic."

"Fae magic?" I asked, wheeling. "Are ye sure?"

"*Sí*. Look, there, what does that remind you of?"

I followed the trajectory of the brujo's outstretched finger and saw the turrets bathed in the warm glow of the golden hour. Except that was impossible because it wasn't quite yet noon. Indeed, now that I knew what to look for, I saw all manner of impossibilities, including a nonexistent breeze which kept the flags flying unabated.

"It's like the alley, in Boston," I remarked. "It's glamour and gram-marie combined, probably to make the place more appealing to tourists if I had to guess."

"Not tourists," Lakota countered. "Or not just tourists. This place is calling to me. I can feel it."

Now that she mentioned it, I could sense the same thing; there was a wistful yearning in my gut that tugged at me, promising a life-affirming experience on the other side of those open gates. Looking at my companions' faces, I realized we all felt it to some degree.

"So, I'm startin' to t'ink Leon's tip is goin' to pay off. But does anyone else have a bad feelin' about this?"

As one, the others nodded.

"Good. So long as I'm not the only one."

CHAPTER 27

W e sat in the back of a darkened theater staring down at an empty stage, waiting for something strange to happen. At first, however, it was everything you'd expect from a crowded venue: children squealing, parents shushing, and the general hubbub of casual conversation. Feeling oddly anxious, I reached into my pocket to hold the Spear Stone, as I'd come to call it. The rock throbbed once in response to my touch, warming incrementally as the overhead lights dimmed, leaving us immersed in utter darkness.

A figure stepped out onto the stage.

Dressed in a gossamer gown garlanded with gilded water lilies beneath which lay arguably the loveliest silhouette I'd ever beheld; the actress was an ethereal creature with white blonde hair and skin that seemed never to have seen the sun. For the space of a single breath, she stood stock still, staring at us all like a startled deer. Then, with an abruptness that quite literally stole my breath away, she smiled.

The actress began skipping from one side of the stage to the other, a basket of blackberries tucked into the curve of her arm swinging to and fro at her side. As she moved, she was trailed by motes of light that mimicked fairy dust, and with every footfall came the subtlest chime of distant bells.

So enchanting were her movements, in fact, that I almost didn't notice the shadowy figures appearing in the wings until she reached that end of the stage and turned to us, her expression terrified. She bounded to the other side, only to come upon the second mass of dark shapes. The basket went flying, sending berries everywhere as she raced to stand in the center of the stage, her breath coming so fast her pale chest heaved against the bodice of her gown, her bare feet smeared with pulp and juices.

And that's when the lights went out.

I pressed a hand to my own heart, suddenly very aware of how horribly fast it was racing. Sweat pricked my brow, and movement to my right and left suggested my companions were experiencing the same sensation. Fear, of course, but not just any fear. This was the terror of being hunted. Of being preyed upon.

I heard a child's muffled cry from below.

A woman's sob to my right.

Then a light shone on the stage, which was now empty except for the stains smeared across the hardwood—evidence that the actress had been taken away by force. A father in the audience gasped, no doubt wondering exactly what sort of show he'd brought his children to see.

"My fellow subjects," a voice called, its shaky tenor reverberating above our heads in a desperate plea, "our beloved sovereign has been taken, abducted by the Maker Children, who know she will have no choice but to grant their every wish."

Anguish hit me like a physical blow.

"Soon, the mortal sun will set on the Sithen, and our people will leave this realm forever. Thus does the hour of her return grow short."

Panic clawed at my throat.

"And so I have come to you, the Fairy Court, to seek a champion. One who will rise up and reclaim our Queen."

The panic receded almost immediately following this declaration, and the anguish with it. In its place, a burgeoning sense of duty took hold of my heart—a sense that I owed my life to our beloved Queen.

"One who is noble and strong."

Righteousness flooded through me.

"One whose power will no doubt strike fear into the cruel hearts of the Maker Children."

I started to shift in my seat, preparing to stand and declare myself the Queen's champion, when a hand snatched me by the wrist, pinning it to the plastic arm of my seat. I froze, startled by the contact.

"Quinn," Lakota whispered, "it's some sort of crazy strong spell. We have to fight it. I've got you and Leo, but you have to take Max's hand."

Provoked by the urgency in her voice, I snatched up the brujo's hand just as he was about to climb to his feet. He stilled, turning to me with an anesthetized look in his eyes which likely mirrored my own.

"Ah, our champion rises!"

Genuine panic surged through me as I swung around to see which of the other two had succumbed to the power of the spell. But it wasn't Lakota, or Leo. It was a young, blonde guy several rows down. An overhead light tracked him as he worked his way towards the aisle, which should have been awkward, but wasn't. Perhaps it was the graceful way he moved, or the awed faces of those he passed. Either way, by the time he reached the stage, he'd proven himself more than worthy in all our eyes.

Here was our champion.

"What is your name, champion?"

"Bredon," the young man replied, one arm thrown across his eyes to shield them from the glare of the stage lights, which inadvertently cast the rest of his face in shadow and dispelled any suspicion that he'd been planted among the audience. After all, any actor worth their salt would surely know how to avoid such things.

"And will you rescue our Queen, Bredon?" The voice asked. "Even if it means risking eternal death?"

"If it would serve the Fae, then I would gladly give my life."

The voice hesitated, and for the briefest instant it was as if I could see the insidious spell hovering on the peripheries of my vision. But that sensation passed as quickly as it came, supplanted by a feeling of overwhelming gratitude.

"Then go forth, noble Bredon, and prepare thyself for the coming battle!"

The young man dropped his arm as lights along the stage guided him towards an empty wing. Just before stepping through, however, he looked back as if scanning the crowd—presumably looking for whomever he'd come with. Then, between one heartbeat and the next, he was gone.

CHAPTER 28

The second half of the show was nowhere near as compelling as the first, though there was significantly more spectacle by comparison. Executed in a series of intricately choreographed dances, an armored knight meant to be Bredon—though far broader through the chest and shoulders than the young man had been—fought to win back the Fairy Queen from malevolent figures in dark cloaks who refused to speak and yet still managed to send shivers up my spine.

The final scene featured the Queen bound to a painted wall by iron chains, her beautiful gown torn at the hem and shoulder, her hair tousled and full of twigs and leaves. And yet, even as the knight rushed to slay her captors and break her chains, you got the sense that her spirit had never been, and would never be, broken. The effect was admittedly rather rousing—though, frankly, it was difficult to tell how much of the show's achievements hinged on the emotional cues the audience received, courtesy of the spell.

In any case, by the time the Fairy Queen was at last safe in the arms of her champion, the audience was cheering and clapping like they'd seen the greatest show of all time. Indeed, that feeling lasted until well after the curtain fell and the lights came back on. Everyone but us began moving towards the exit, the children tittering with excitement, the adults showering the production with praise.

"That was unbelievably brutal," Lakota said, her face haggard with exhaustion. "I tried to fight it, but it was like trying to hold my breath. Eventually I had no choice but to give in."

"I have never encountered magic like that before," Max agreed. "It was subtle, but also completely irresistible."

"We need to find out who cast it, and why." Leo rose and beckoned us to do the same. "Come on, let's go take a peek behind that curtain."

"Good idea, Dorothy," I replied in an attempt to lighten the mood. Unfortunately, the joke fell flat. It seemed none of us were there yet, and that included me.

We waited for the aisles to clear before marching single file towards the stage. Leo took point while the rest of us remained on high alert, aware that the spellcaster could—in theory at least—hit us again at any moment. I, for one, had no desire to find out what a targeted assault looked like.

"Don't rush backstage," Leo whispered over his shoulder, perhaps thinking the same thing. "Once we get up there, look for any evidence of the spell. And keep an eye out for traps."

Thankfully, we made it all the way to the stage without being molested, though I couldn't imagine the creak of the floorboards beneath our feet would go unnoticed for long. With that in mind, I took a chance and left the others to investigate the stage while I crept to the far end where the curtain met the wall, took hold of its heavy material, and opened a gap large enough to spy through.

At first, all I could make out were stage props and costumes shoved into the wings, a ladder leaning against the far wall, and an array of ropes attached to a pulley system. The lights were dimmed, which meant the actors had likely retired elsewhere. In fact, I was about to say as much to Leo and the others when I spotted a furtive gesture beyond a rack of cloaks.

It was the Fairy Queen—or at least the actress who had played her—speaking adamantly to a curly-haired man with his back turned towards me. At first, it appeared they were arguing. But then the man lunged forward and planted a deep, spine-bowing kiss upon his fair-haired companion. She melted into him, her damaged dress falling open at the bust, and for a second, I seriously considered closing the curtain to give them some privacy.

Thankfully, I didn't.

Because it was at that precise moment the actress tugged at the man's mane of hair and pried him from her lips, revealing his face to the light. Her lover barked a laugh that gave me chills, his uncommonly large eyes shining with mirth, the tips of his ears poking out further from the curls of his hair than should have been humanly possible.

But then, Liam the Gancanagh wasn't human.

Before I could even begin to wonder what he was doing here of all places—let alone decide whether or not to confront him—the Faeling said something to the actress and backed away impishly, his hands held out in surrender, only to disappear so thoroughly into the shadowed recesses of the theater it was as if he'd never been there at all.

"Quinn?"

A hand settled on my shoulder, causing me to jerk and curse. I whirled to find Max holding up both hands, inadvertently mirroring Liam's body language from a moment ago. He shuffled backwards, likely startled by whatever it was he saw on my face.

"Liam was here," I whispered, gesturing backstage. "Just now."

"Are you sure?"

Unfortunately, I didn't get a chance to answer before the actress called out from backstage in a heavy Slavic accent.

"Who is there?" she asked. "The show is over. You should not be here."

Alarmed by the sound of her bare feet approaching, I scrambled to rise while the others peeled themselves away from whatever they'd been investigating. In seconds, we were all standing rather casually in front of the seam between the two curtains, angled so that Leo could present his badge the moment the actress poked her head out.

"Agent Jeffries, ma'am. FBI." Leo practically beamed at her, apparently hoping to charm his way out of the situation. "I was wondering if you wouldn't mind answering some questions."

The blonde barely glanced at the badge before coolly sizing up the rest of us. I realized in that moment that the actress I'd mistaken for a classic ingenue—essentially an impressionable young lady with unprecedented talent and outrageous good looks—was in fact a self-assured woman in her mid-thirties, her face coated in so many layers of stage makeup that I couldn't decide where the cosmetics ended and her face began.

"As a matter of fact," she replied, "I would mind."

"Oh? And why's that, Miss..."

"My name is none of your business. Neither is what goes on in theater. So, unless you wish to buy tickets to tomorrow's show, I do not see reason for you or your companions to be here."

"Well, I'm afraid I have to disagree with you, there." Leo slapped the wallet shut and slipped it into the back pocket of his jeans. "See, I have good reason to suspect a crime was committed somewhere in this establishment. So, I'd appreciate it if you could point me to someone in charge. The stage manager, for example. Or whoever owns this theater."

"You wish to speak to owner?" The actress slipped between the curtain to join us on the stage. This close, I could tell the juice stains and the tears on her dress had been strategically placed, and that the body beneath it was corded with lean muscle. "Well? I am listening."

"You own this theater *and* star in the production?"

"It cuts down on cost of running show," she replied, acerbically. "Now, what is business about a crime?"

"I'll get to that in a moment," Leo said, switching tactics. "But first, I'd like to ask you about those robes your dancers were wearing."

"What about them?"

"Would it be fair to say they are all accounted for?"

"I would have to check with costume designer to know for sure."

"But she would be able to tell if you were short one? And would she know whose robe it was, if so?"

"I do not see why not. We keep good records here."

"I'm glad to hear that. Is your costume designer in the building, by chance?"

"No, she will not be back until tomorrow morning. Why do you ask this?"

"Because we have a corpse in the morgue who was, I believe, wrapped up in one of your performer's robes when he died."

"One of our robes? Forgive me, I do not understand..." The actress shook her head and opened her mouth to say more but was cut off by the slam of a door being thrown open and a familiar voice bellowing above the din.

"Angelika! What are you doing talking to these people?"

A plainclothes Sheriff Watt came puffing down the aisle, his good arm held out for balance as he rushed the stage. The other was in a sling and a soft cast, and seeing it reminded me how lucky I'd been that Deputy Holt had talked his boss out of pressing charges. Unfortunately, by the time the sorry bastard reached us the woman he'd called Angelika had recovered both her composure and her haughty attitude.

"I was telling them to come back with warrant if they wish to know more about our costumes," Angelika said, crossing both arms in defiance.

"Does that mean you're certain the body isn't one of your performers?" Leo asked. "Because if it was one of my people who got hurt, I'd want to know."

Angelika's eyes widened as though that possibility hadn't occurred to her.

"Don't tell them anything, Angelika," Watt snarled. "They're a bunch of fucking snakes who shouldn't even be here."

"Sheriff Watt!" Angelika snapped. "Do I come to your office and tell you how to do job? No, I did not think so."

To all of our surprise, Watt muttered an apology.

"Thank you. Now, perhaps you could show these people the door? Then you can come back and tell me what *you* are doing here."

"That's alright," Lakota chimed in, pulling at Leo's elbow. "We'll see ourselves out."

Leo started to protest, but one look at Lakota's face was all it took to convince him to stand down; the Seer flicked crazy eyes in Angelika's direction, mouthing a word that only I and he could see. A word that raised a whole hell of a lot of questions.

And that word was...witch.

CHAPTER 29

To my surprise, Max was the first to speak once we made it to the relative safety of the parking lot. The brujo leaned over the top of the car to address the group, his voice so hushed we had to crowd in to hear him over the sounds of vehicles whizzing past. Fortunately, ours was the only car in the lot aside from Watt's cruiser, which meant our discussion about being emotionally violated by magic wasn't likely to be overheard by passersby.

"I know you have no reason to listen to what I have to say," he began, haltingly. "But I believe I know what magic was being cast back there, and how it may be tied to the case you are investigating. What I cannot say is for what purpose any of it was done."

Leo and Lakota shared a look.

"I picked up a few things in there," the Seer said, shrugging, "but nothing that gets us any closer to solving this case."

"Yeah, well, that's more than I've got," Leo confessed. "I can't stand watching live theater. Too many lies masquerading as truths. It's like watching television with the volume on the fritz. Anyway, we're all ears, Señor."

"*Gracias.*" Max dipped his chiseled chin in gratitude. "First, the spell cast on the audience. I believe glamour was heavily involved, and that it was responsible for manipulating our emotions. I would not have thought it possible, but Quinn and I have felt something very similar before, and recently. And we have reason to believe that is no coincidence."

"Aye," I chimed in, picking up on the brujo's cue. "When I snuck a look backstage, I saw a Faelin' we know makin' out with the owner. His name is Liam, and he's a Gancanagh."

"A what?" Leo asked.

"He is a creature of Fae," Max answered. "A love-talker, or seducer."

"Like a succubus? Or would that be an incubus?" I can never seem to keep them straight." Leo looked to Lakota for clarity, but the Seer simply shrugged in response.

"*Querido Dios*, no." Max shuddered. "The Gancanagh is no dream-walker, though his glamour is unusually strong. Far more powerful, in fact, than I would have thought possible."

"The witch was the same," Lakota said. "I couldn't tell how strong she was at first, but when she blew up at Watt she lit up like the Fourth of July. You think it had something to do with the ritual they were performing? I mean, using all that magic to sell tickets...somehow, I doubt it. Maybe if this was Vegas."

"*Sí*, it makes very little sense. But, if you think about it, I do not believe the ritual was designed to take anything from the audience. You saw them after. They left feeling energized and happy."

"I wasn't energized, or happy," Lakota countered, glancing at each of us in turn. "How about you all?"

"No," Max agreed, "but that is because we fought it. If we had not, I do not think the spell would have caused us such distress. In fact, I believe it was what we call white magic."

"Hold on," I cut in, "are ye sayin' ye t'ink whatever's goin' on in there is innocent?"

"Not entirely," Max replied. "White magic is neither good, nor bad. Just as black magic can be used for good or evil, so too can white magic. The difference between the two is not ethics, but whether natural or unnatural energy is being channeled."

"You mean like scrying versus divination," Leo said, his expression thoughtful. "My grandmother explained the difference between them to me, once. She said scrying was like searching for a tune on the radio, whereas divination was like calling up a station and demanding they play your song."

Max barked a laugh. "I think I would have liked your *abuela*, Señor Jeffries. And yes, it is a good example."

"Fair enough," I acknowledged. "But then what makes that spell white magic, as opposed to black?"

"It used the natural energy in the room," Max explained. "Our fear, our excitement. It may have amplified them, but that is all. Except that brings us back to the earlier question. What is the point? If money is not their goal, and neither is fame, then why bother with the ritual at all?"

The rest of us exchanged uncertain glances.

"It gives them a willing victim," Max explained. "And not just any victim, either. Remember when the spell called on us to rise? How hard it was to resist? Do you think most people would be able to stay in their seats if the same were happening to them?"

"Freaks," Lakota said, snapping her fingers. "That's why the castle was so alluring to us! The ritual isn't designed to siphon power, it's designed to identify it."

"And not only power," Max added. "But nobility. Purity. A willingness to sacrifice oneself for the good of others. Which just so happens to be the ideal traits you look for in a human sacrifice."

That shut us all up.

"And what would you know about sacrificing people, Mr. Velez?" Leo asked after several heartbeats, his tone downright menacing.

"I used to work for someone who dabbled in such things," Max admitted, refusing to meet the elder man's gaze. "It was not by choice."

"And is your former employer still killing people?"

"No, he is dead and cannot hurt anyone else." Max shot me a grateful look. "Thanks to Quinn."

"Oh?" Leo swung all that negative energy my way. "Do you have something to tell me?"

I glared at Max with the same look you'd level at a friend for outing you to your parents for having a party in their house while they were out of town. "Well, Leo, that depends."

"On?"

"On whether the FBI's jurisdiction extends to Atlantis?" I said, turning it into a question.

Leo opened his mouth, closed it, then opened it again before rubbing his forehead like he had a headache. "Only person alive...crazy ass life..." I thought I heard him mutter under his breath. "Fucking Atlantis...give me a freaking break..."

"Wait, Leo," Lakota said as she reached out to grab his arm. "He said they could be using human sacrifices. What if that's how this Liam guy and the witches are channeling so much power?"

"Witches, plural?" I interjected.

Lakota nodded. "Every one of those performers had the witches' mark on their souls. But then, that would have to mean every one of our victims was a closet Freak, and we've found no proof of that, so far."

"I am only telling you what I think is happening," Max replied. "I said before that I do not know the reason why. Perhaps it is to gain power as you say, but I do not think it is that simple."

"Why not?"

"Because taking lives that way leaves a stain. It taints our spells. If power were their only goal, they should never be able to cast anything like what they did today. Again, it makes no sense."

"Either way," Lakota replied, perhaps picking up on the brujo's mounting frustration, "you've helped us out a lot with all this. It gives us something to look into."

"It is not enough. I could see how it worked, but not why. For that, you would need someone with more experience. Someone who has studied Fae magic."

"Ye t'ink we could ask one of the refugees?" I asked, attempting to be helpful. "I don't know if they'd be able to tell us much, but we could at least find out why Liam is here, of all places."

"That we must do, anyway. It may throw a wrench into Camila's plans. But no, I do not believe the Fae can help us with this. Their understanding of magic is too simplistic. To them, using glamour is as easy as breathing. What we need is a witch willing to help who has been around long enough to have dealings with the Fae."

"I take it you have someone in mind?" Leo asked.

"I do." Max looked directly at me as though I should know who he was referring to, but frankly I had no clue who he meant, at least not until he said the name out loud. "She's an enchantress, and her name is Morgan le Fay."

Oh, right.

Her.

CHAPTER 30

I paced the hotel lobby some thirty minutes later, fretting over whether or not to bring Morgan le Fay on board. The Sickos—sans Jimmy, who had not yet returned—had largely been for it, Leo especially. But then he would accept the assistance of anyone who could help him close this case, even if that meant divulging sensitive information to a mythical figure from Arthurian legend. What he didn't know, of course, was that the infamous enchantress had once known my father, intimately. Or that she'd tried to kill Max, once before. Or that she'd used me to hunt down rogue witches from her own coven. Or that she'd offered to train me to use magic I no longer possessed—an offer, by the way, which I'd neglected to take her up on before vanishing for a year and a half.

"What makes ye t'ink she'll even help us, anyway?" I asked Max now that we were alone.

The brujo stood watching me with the patient expression a parent uses on a child who won't listen to reason. "She will help us."

"But how can ye know that, for sure? She has her own agenda. Always has. Which means she can't be trusted."

"I never said anything about trust. I said she can help us, and she can. She knows things we do not. Does that mean she will give her knowledge free of charge? I doubt it. But, if we can afford whatever price she charges, it will be worth it."

"And what if we can't afford it?"

"I do not think she will ask for anything we cannot give her. She is a shrewd negotiator."

"And how would ye know that?" I asked, head cocked. "Ye were mostly passed out when I dealt with her."

"I know because she has been working with us for some time now. Who do you think Maria learned her magic from?"

"From Camila, I assumed."

"My sister is a bruja. She cannot conjure illusions as Maria did to fool you. That is the power of an enchantress. It is a rare gift, practiced by very few. When Maria finally realized this was where her talents lay, she sought out the best to train her."

"And Morgan actually agreed to that?"

"I do not believe Maria gave her much choice," Max replied, grinning. "She is a very stubborn woman."

"Stubborn is one word for it," I muttered, then sighed. "I don't like this."

"I can see that, but I do not understand why."

I grunted, finding it inexplicably difficult to articulate what it was about Morgan le Fay that bothered me so much. Deep down, I had to admit it wasn't for any of the reasons I'd already considered; in none of those cases had the enchantress behaved spitefully or caused more collateral damage than was absolutely necessary. If anything, she struck me as an exceptionally practical person—a trait I traditionally valued in others.

No, what unsettled me most about Morgan le Fay wasn't her temperament or what she'd done to and for us in the past, but the secrets she'd kept. What she'd known, and yet refused to share. At the time, she'd seemed wise, her words profound. But, in hindsight, it was easy to see how she'd hoped to manipulate me into becoming her protégé. How she'd plotted to put a feather in her cap by claiming Merlin's daughter as her apprentice. Not because she was malevolent or power hungry, but because she was the type of person who simply *had* to be in the thick of things to feel worthwhile.

Basically, she was an immortal busybody.

"Look," I said, at last, "it's a personality issue, that's all. You're right, if Morgan le Fay is willin' to help, then we should invite her to join us. It's a no brainer. Just don't expect me to be happy about it."

"I would not dare," Max teased.

"Uh huh." I rolled my eyes. "Anyway, what did Camila have to say about Liam. Anything?"

"She is looking into it, now, but sounded as surprised as we were to hear he was out here. Whatever Liam is up to, and why he targeted you, is still a mystery."

"Great. Just great." I stopped pacing and shoved both hands into my jacket pockets. "So, what, are we supposed to prick our fingers and paint the wall with blood to summon Morgan? Say her name three times in front of the mirror?"

Max flashed a look at me that suggested I was a crazy person, took his phone out, hit a couple buttons, and held it to his ear. "Hello, Señorita le Fay? It is Max. Maria's friend. *Sí*, that one." A deep throated chuckle escaped his lips. "The former, I am afraid."

Max held up a finger at me and walked to a secluded corner of the lobby, presumably so he could explain our current situation without being overheard. I, meanwhile, was left to wonder what that ageless hussy could possibly have said to earn that laugh. Probably something about the call being about business, or *pleasure*.

"Ye do remember the time she sliced ye up, right?" I grumbled as the brujo returned with the phone at his side. "Ye know, after she sent her people to abduct ye from your store and nearly got Camila blown up?"

To my surprise, Max's smile merely widened. "It is not the worst thing that could have happened."

"How d'ye figure?"

"Well, I was eventually rescued. By a very beautiful woman, no less."

I scowled at the brujo. "Ye t'ink you're so smooth, but I see right through you, Velez."

"Do not be mad at me because you cannot take a compliment." Max pocketed his phone, looking bemused. "I see right through *you*, too, you know."

Well, he had a point, there.

Dammit.

"Whatever," I replied, huffing. "Anyway, when does she t'ink she'll be here, by? D'ye tell her we were on a clock, of sorts?"

"*Sí*, I stressed that part." Max pointed over my shoulder to the hotel's electronic doors so that I turned just in time to see them whisk open to admit a stunning, raven-haired woman in a pair of wedge boots and a bust-hugging bell-sleeve dress that left her shapely legs bare to mid-thigh. "Once she heard you were here, she said she would rush right over."

"Perfect," I drawled. "Just perfect."

CHAPTER 31

Morgan le Fay and I sat across from one another in the deserted hotel bar while Max did the rounds and gathered everyone to join us. She'd ordered a mojito and sat sipping it, occasionally swirling the mint leaves to pass the time. I hadn't ordered anything. Partly because it was hardly two o'clock, partly because I was broke, and partly because the only identification I had on me was a forgery that might get me past caution tape but sure as hell wouldn't get me past a bouncer.

But mainly because I was broke.

"Max should be back any minute," I said to fill the silence.

"Oh, I doubt that," Morgan replied. "I asked that lovely young man you've practically enslaved to give us some privacy once I saw the state you were in."

"Ye did what, now?" I asked, scooting back in my chair.

"Don't worry, he'll be along in twenty minutes or so. Please, relax. I simply wanted to see how you were holding up. Have you been sleeping? You seem...tired."

I glared at the enchantress, both annoyed and impressed by her perceptiveness. Of course, it was entirely possible Max had mentioned it to her during their phone call. He'd been kind enough not to mention my little episode that morning, but the brujo wasn't stupid. He had to realize there was something fishy going on.

"If I tell ye the truth, it'll sound like I'm crazy," I replied, looking away. "Besides, I don't trust ye."

"That hurts." Morgan lay a perfectly manicured hand over her heart, her kohled eyes glinting with amusement. "I am only trying to help. Besides, why invite me to meet your friends if you don't trust me?"

"First of all, I didn't invite ye. Max did. And that's only because ye know t'ings that can help solve a murder case. Or at least we hope ye do."

"A murder case?" Morgan leaned forward onto her elbow, cradling her chin with that hand. "Max didn't say anything about that."

"What did he say?"

"That there was a coven in this area practicing magic and passing it off as performance art, and that the Fae may be involved."

"He didn't say anythin' about the murders?"

"Oh, he mentioned that. Something about human sacrifices, if memory serves? But just now you made it sound like something the mortal police might investigate. The Regular authorities, I mean."

"They are," I replied, wishing Max were here so I could ask him what the hell he'd spent damn near ten minutes on the phone talking to her about if it wasn't the case...and then strangle him. "That's why we're here, actually."

"You're working with a Regulars to solve murders caused by *magic*? My, my, how times have changed."

"They aren't Regulars. But they do work for the FBI. Ye know who the FBI are, don't ye?"

"Of course," Morgan replied with a chuckle. "I don't live under a rock. I even have a blog. And an Instagram. In fact, I'll let you in on a little secret. You can never have too many followers. Your father taught me that."

"And what's that supposed to mean?"

"It means, my dear, that he knew better than to pick fights with people whose help he might one day require. Connections. Networking. Relationships." With each word, Morgan tapped the tabletop with her fingernail. "You say you don't trust me, but I'm beginning to think that merely lumps me in with everyone else you know."

That stung a little, though not as much as it would have if it were entirely true. The trouble was, I could count the people I trusted implicitly on one hand and still have fingers left over. If Christoff were here, for example, I'd have told him everything. Even the bit about the dreams. Hell, if I ever got the chance, I'd tell him all about Ryan's last moments and hold nothing back. He'd earned that by being there for me in the past, and by proving he could handle himself in a crisis. Everyone else...well, let's just say the bar was high and leave it at that.

"Ye may be right about that," I admitted after taking a moment to cool down. "But I am entitled to keep me own secrets, and that isn't goin' to change just because ye t'ink I should feel guilty."

Morgan picked up her glass, only to find it empty. She waved it at the bartender, then gestured back and forth between herself and me. "Make it two, dear!"

"I don't—" I began.

"Don't be a pain in the ass. If you're going to insist I treat you like an equal, then we will have to drink like equals."

"Ye sound like Charon," I muttered as the hotel bartender set two glasses down and walked away without asking for my ID or my room number.

"The Boatman?" Morgan asked, arching a shapely eyebrow. "He's still around? Where on Earth did you run into him?"

"On the way to see Hades," I replied as I stirred the contents of my own drink to keep from replaying too much of that frankly chilling experience. "Then again after Atlantis. And once more when I left Circe's island. Strange guy. But his homebrew was somethin' else."

When I looked up, I found Morgan le Fay gazing at me with such complete and utter shock that—for some reason—all I could do was laugh. I mean, how often does the mind of someone whose been around longer than Christianity get blown? Fortunately, the enchantress recovered in time to greet Max and the others as they sauntered into the bar.

"Hello there," she said, rising to shake hands and exchange nods. "It's a pleasure to meet you all."

"Sorry to keep you waiting," Leo said, eyeing our drinks. "Looks like you got started without us."

"Oh my!" Morgan exclaimed, leaning forward to ogle the senior agent the way a child might thrust its face against the glass of a zoological exhibit. "You're a Demagogue!"

"Excuse me?"

"And a Valkyrie! And you, look at you!"

"Who, me?" Lakota asked, her eyes narrowed in suspicion. "What about me?"

Morgan opened her mouth to say something, then shut it and shook her head. "No, it's too soon for that. Much too soon. You wouldn't be the first vessel that crafty creature left empty, after all. Oh, Quinn, you never told me you kept such marvelous company! I take back what I said before. You've made some truly worthwhile connections."

"Umm...t'anks?"

"Now then, to business," the enchantress continued as she resumed her seat and invited the others to join her. "I've been told you all solve murders that defy mortal comprehension. How fascinating. Please, tell me everything."

CHAPTER 32

L eo did most of the talking, though Max was glad to offer
clarifications whenever metaphysics got involved. Morgan
was the perfect audience member throughout—oohing and
ahhing and nodding along like some beautifully crafted bobblehead.
Still, I had to admit the few questions she did ask were more perceptive than anything I'd have come up with.

By the time the senior agent was done, we all had drinks in our
hands. Nothing so strong as to turn the debriefing into a true happy
hour, of course, but enough to at least enliven the conversation. Or it
would have been if the other two agents present had been more interested in chatting than scrutinizing the beguiling enchantress' every
move. But then, I couldn't exactly blame them for that.

Some witches simply couldn't be trusted.

"My," she said at last, clapping her hands together, "what a
thrilling few days you all have had. I must say, I am very impressed. I
had no idea there were people like you all out there, doing the Academy's job for them. It's very admirable."

"We appreciate that," Lakota replied, speaking up for the first
time in nearly a half hour. "But we're more interested in results than
praise."

"Oh, but of course. Your kind always are, dear."

"My...kind?"

"Self-sacrificing individuals," Morgan elaborated airily. "People like you have been the backbone of every notable civilization throughout history. The plebeians of Rome, the Viking thralls, the serfs of Russian, and so on."

"You mean slaves?"

"No, dear. I mean those who buy into the social contract and strictly adhere to it. You believe you are doing a service to your fellow man that only you can provide. It's a noble cause. One that inspired the legend I am associated with. In my time, they'd have called you all knights."

Lakota blinked at the enchantress as though uncertain whether to take offense or say thank you. In the end, she hoisted her beer in a mock toast. "May all our tables be round."

"*That* nonsense again," Morgan replied, rolling her eyes. "Anyway, back to business. It sounds to me like you have stumbled onto a rather old ritual that went out of fashion quite a few centuries ago. It's no surprise you haven't come across anything quite like it before."

"What is the ritual?" Max asked.

"Actually, it's more of an event. I'm not sure the Fae consider anything they do ritualistic, though that is precisely what it is. But, back in the day, we called it a Sithen Dance. That was when there were far more entrances to Fae, before the industrial revolution and the dawn of empirical science. It seems like this coven and your Gancanagh have recreated the practice."

"To what end, though?" Leo asked, apparently hoping to avoid any more off-topic discussions.

"Well, traditionally the Fae would lure unsuspecting mortals for a night of feasting and dancing before sending them home with tales to spread. In some cases, however, they'd find a powerful mortal who piqued their interest and would keep him or her for a much longer span. So long, in most cases, that the mortal could never return, or had become so changed that they came back as something other than what they were. There are many legends associated with these people, even in American folklore."

"I still don't see the connection between that and our victims," Leo admitted.

"That's because there isn't one. Not an obvious one, anyway. The Sithen Dance is a largely benign experience. Even those who were taken were rarely harmed. It violated Fae hospitality to do otherwise. What you need to find out is—"

"There you all are," an all-too-familiar voice declared, cutting off whatever else the enchantress had been about to say.

"Sheriff Watt," Leo said, rising halfway out of his seat, "to what do we owe the pleasure?"

"Sit back down, Jeffries," Watt barked, scanning our faces while his deputy loomed like a shadow at his back. "Having a drink, huh? Why am I not surprised? Deputy, call Nelson in here. We're going to take them all in."

"And who is this incredibly rude human?" Morgan asked, her face screwed up in puzzlement. The sight of the gorgeous creature in our midst momentarily stunned the sheriff into silence, at least until her insult registered.

"I'm the officer arresting your friends, lady. Now stand up, step away, and shut up, unless you want to join them in a cell."

"On what charges, you lunatic?" Leo demanded.

"I'm glad you asked. You and your people are going down for interfering in a police investigation, tampering with evidence, and witness intimidation. Oh, and I've already got your man Collins behind bars, so don't even think about trying to get your damned stories straight. Now, get your asses up and put your hands in the air before I add resisting arrest to the charges."

CHAPTER 33

Deputy Holt came for Max at Watt's insistence. The brujo rose and slid both hands behind his back without complaint, though the tension in his neck and shoulders suggested he was anything but happy. Officer Nelson stood awkwardly, watching the whole scene take place with the sheepish look people often get when standing idly by while wrongs are committed.

"You petty son of a bitch," Leo snarled, only Hilde's hand on his arm keeping him from lunging at the sheriff. "What the hell do you think is going to come of this?"

"Oh, plenty," Watt retorted. "I think I'll have *your* badge, for one thing. Maybe your people's, too. Depends whether they knew what you were up to. If not, I'll cut them a deal."

"What are you talking about?"

"Don't play dumb with me, Jeffries. The owner of the Fairy Court told us how you threatened her business after she came forward to testify about our victim in the woods. Now that I know how you solve all your cases; I can see it's no wonder you're so highly regarded in the Bureau."

"Look, Watt, I don't know what that woman told you, but she—"

"Imagine," the sheriff interjected as he unclipped the cover of his hip holster to rest his good hand on the butt of his pistol. "A federal agent who goes around committing the murders he eventually solves. Well, not you, per say. That's what you have Collins for."

"Leo…" Lakota growled, her face contorted by more hate than I'd ever thought to see on it. "If he says one more word about my husband, I'm going to feed him his gun."

"Nelson, cuff that mouthy bitch. We'll add threatening a police officer to her rap sheet."

"Sheriff…"

"Now, Nelson!"

The officer jumped and started edging towards the Seer with an apologetic look on his face. Holt, meanwhile, gaped at his boss over Max's shoulder. If I had to guess, I'd have said this was the first time Watt had voiced these accusations in front of his men. So, the real question was whether Watt was insane, or just that damned vindictive.

"Agent Jeffries, may I call you Leo?" Morgan chimed in, startling us all with her cheery tone. "Would you mind terribly if I stepped in? Before things get any less civil, that is."

"I told you to get lost, dammit!" Watt snapped.

Surprisingly, it was Hilde who answered the enchantress.

"Please, do it."

The enchantress smiled brightly, nodded, and waved a hand just as Watt drew his gun. The room's occupants stilled so suddenly that I could have sworn I was looking at statues—as opposed to living, breathing human beings. At first, I thought she'd frozen time much the way I had been able to not so very long ago. That is until an ice cube in my glass got caught in an updraft of soda bubbles and rose to the surface, tinkling along the way.

"Huh, that's a neat trick," I said, waving a hand in front of Holt's glassy eyes.

Morgan—who'd risen to inspect the sheriff—spun round, groping at her chest. "Holy Grail in a Temple, you scared me half to death! Why aren't you asleep like the others?"

"They're sleepin'? But their eyes are open."

"It's an expression," she hissed. "This is a spell that dull people's minds and makes them too sluggish to move. Quit doing that!"

I jerked my hand away from Holt's face. "Fine, sheesh! Ye don't have to yell."

"You're right," Morgan replied, visibly regaining her composure as she ran her hands down the length of her dress, smoothing nonexistent wrinkles. "Well, since it did not seem to affect you the way it should have, maybe you can help me."

"Help ye, how?"

"Come stand over here and tell me what you see when you look at this Regular."

"Why, what's wrong with him?"

"I can't say for certain, that's why I wanted you to take a look," Morgan replied, rolling her eyes in exasperation. "Must you always be this difficult?"

"It's probably hereditary," I quipped, though I did as she asked and sidled past the others to stand in front of Watt. He held his gun pointed at the floor, though I could tell the strain of holding it upright was causing his forearm to twitch. That's something most people don't realize about guns; you can't hold them long in the shooting position before your shoulder burns and your hand cramps up. Rather than risk him dropping it and a shot going off, I pried it out of his hand, wiped it down, and set it on a nearby chair.

"You aren't looking at him," Morgan chided.

"What's to see?" I asked, scanning the rest of him. He'd changed into his uniform since last I saw him, though it was wrinkled and stained under the armpits, suggesting he'd meant to clean it, first. So, he'd been in a hurry. I mentioned that to Morgan.

"What in the name of Camelot are you talking about? I'm asking you to look at him. Really *look*."

And, just like that, I knew what the enchantress wanted. I closed my eyes and opened myself up at the same time, allowing my senses to flourish as I had with Gretel and later Max. Admittedly, I'd never thought to try it on an ordinary person. For some reason, I'd assumed there would be no point. But that wasn't the case, at all. Albeit fainter, perhaps, Watt gave off the sickly-sweet aroma of cooked meats and felt of slick tarp beneath my fingertips. Of course, Morgan had insisted I *look*, which meant staring at the odious man with all my senses dialed up as high as they could go.

Ugh.

"What's that on his face?" I exclaimed as soon as I opened my eyes.

"So, you see it, too," Morgan replied. "Interesting. And what does it look like to you?"

"A handprint?" I held up my own for good measure, marveling at the way the phantom mark glowed across the sheriff's ugly mug like paint beneath a black light. "Aye, definitely a handprint."

"Really?"

"Why, what's it look like to ye?"

"It's more of a smudge, really. But then my third eye has always been a little nearsighted. I wonder why your Seer friend didn't catch it. Her second sight is rather remarkable, perhaps the best I've ever seen. Excluding your father's, of course. But then his was primarily prophetic. Hard to compete with that."

"Second sight? Is that what ye call this?" I motioned at my face and nose, deliberately avoiding talk of my father. "Circe didn't have a word for it."

"It is a name for it, yes. The Greeks reputedly thought of it far differently than we do. Anyone who had the gift was a pythoness. A descendant of Pythia. They regularly mistook seers for prophets, which I believe led to some rather unfortunate and gruesome deaths."

"And what made ye t'ink I had it?"

"Between your mother and your father, I assumed it was inevitable. In any case, at least now I have some idea of what happened to this man to make him so disagreeable."

"Pretty sure that's just who he is," I replied, unable to resist eyeing my handiwork.

"Oh? That's a shame. But in this instance, I would have to say his actions are not entirely his own. I'll explain in depth once we've woken your friends, though. I'd hate to go over it twice. Come on, you can start with your lover."

"Whoa, there," I said, waving both hands in denial. "Max isn't me lover."

"Really?" Morgan cocked an eyebrow. "But if that's true, then...No, there isn't time. We'll have to discuss that, later. For now, go pinch his nose shut. It should shock him awake. I'll do the others."

I went to do as she asked, though part of me desperately wanted to know what she'd been about to say. Of course, I shouldn't have been surprised; that was how the enchantress operated. She'd offer a tiny morsel of information to whet your appetite, then invite you to dine under her roof—which meant you were a guest in her house, forced to play by her rules.

"Max," I called once I was close enough for him to hear me. "Oy, are ye in there? Hello?"

Once I was certain he was unresponsive, I grunted, grinned, and reached up to clamp the brujo's nostrils together between my knuckles. He came to like a dog startled from a nap by its own bark, panting, his eyes panicked. In fact, he jerked away from me so violently he damn near knocked Holt to the ground

"Easy there, Cujo," I teased, patting his beefy arm. "Ye were under Morgan's spell for a few minutes, that's all. Shake it off, you'll be alright."

"I will be once you get these things off me," Max hissed, making a show of his handcuffed wrists.

"I don't know," I drawled, waggling my eyebrows in an effort to remove some of the sting. "I t'ink ye look pretty good in handcuffs."

"Not funny."

I shrugged. "A little funny."

Several minutes later, all six of us were gathered around Watt while Holt, Nelson, and the poor hotel bartender continued to stare into the void. Though it seemed unlikely anyone would stumble in this early in the day, we'd already shut and locked the doors that led to the bar; if anyone wanted in, they'd have to knock, first. Once it was clear everyone had fully recovered and I'd removed Max's cuffs, Morgan gestured to Watt's face and the mark that lay upon it.

"Can any of you make out what's there?" she asked.

"I can."

"*Sí.*"

Lakota and Max spoke at the exact same time, only to exchange that look—the one that says *okay, I see you*. Depending on the personalities involved, that look could result in anything from a friendly wager to a knockout, dragout brawl. Which was why, when Max bowed out with a smile, I was so impressed. It wasn't often a man could admit he was beat without having to take the beating.

"It's a Cleric's Mark, right?" Lakota asked. "I saw something like it down in New Orleans, once."

"Oh, very good," Morgan replied, clapping her hands together. "Do you also happen to know what it represents?"

"Afraid not. The supernatural community there was very hush hush, though I got the sense it was a blessing of some kind. Something the Vodun priests did to honor the spirits." Lakota eyed Watt, distastefully, and shook her head. "I noticed the mark when he walked in but couldn't figure out what it was doing there, so I kept quiet about it. Besides, I couldn't risk spooking the other two by pointing it out. Not with Watt losing his shit enough for all of us."

"Ah, that explains it. Very sensible. Unfortunately, the Cleric's Mark is no blessing. If anything, I'd call it a curse. Whoever bears that mark, you see, has been tasked to undertake a cause of some sort. Usually, that cause is rooted in dogma, or religious doctrine. They were quite the rage during the Crusades, as I'm sure you can imagine."

"Yeah." Lakota looked troubled. "I mean, no. I'd rather not."

"In any event," Morgan continued, "it is my experience that only true fanatics are capable of placing them. The recipient, sadly, need not be a believer."

"You're saying Watt may be under someone else's influence?" Lakota asked.

"I'm saying it's possible. In order to find out for sure, however, you all will have a decision to make." Morgan said, glancing at each of us in turn as though measuring our resolve. "I can remove the mark and free this troubled man from its influence with little difficulty. Or I can wake him up as he is. Albeit restrained, of course."

"I don't see how that helps us," Leo confessed. "If I understand you correctly, even if we tie him up, the mark will force him to keep coming after us."

"That's true. What's more, it could cause a great deal of damage to his psyche to remain in such a state for too long without being able to do what he came to."

"Then I say remove it."

"And I shall, but removing the mark means wiping this man's mind of the events leading up to and immediately after the time it was placed. Which means whoever it was will likely get away with it."

"We know who it was," Leo declared, matter-of-factly. "It has to be that witch, Angelika. She's the only person he could have met with before rushing to change into his uniform, arresting Jimmy, and coming here. Plus, he had to get that witness intimidation bit from somewhere, and I doubt he'd have gone there on his own."

Leo had a point. If Watt wanted to lock us all up on false charges, he could have gone about it in a half-dozen ways that made it damn near impossible to refute. Relying on the testimony of a civilian, on the other hand, was asking for trouble. What if she changed her story when forced to give a statement? What if her story didn't line up with Watt's?

It made no sense.

"You intend to stick with your original decision, then?" Morgan clarified. "Very well. Give me a moment, and I'll have it right off."

"Wait," Max interjected. "A minute ago, you told us we would have a choice to make. But it seems like the choice was painfully obvious. You said it yourself, the sheriff would be in no condition to answer questions if we woke him up as he is. So why bring it up?"

The enchantress ducked her head. "While it is true that, under normal circumstances, this man would rant and rave until he was no longer lucid, you have Leo."

"Me? I can only tell if he's lying or telling the truth," Leo said. "That won't help us if he's nuts."

Morgan chuckled, though her laughter ended abruptly once it became clear no one else was joining in. She made a disbelieving sound and stalked towards the senior agent, forcing Hilde to wedge herself between them. Not that the enchantress noticed.

"Is this true?" she asked. "You truly believe that's all you're capable of?"

"Of course. Why would I lie?"

Morgan barked a laugh. "Why, indeed. And what if I told you that you possess the ability to do a great deal more than that? That you, a Demagogue, have the capacity to not only gauge what is true, but to compel honesty from everyone around you?"

"I'd say no thank you," Leo replied, immediately. "It's one thing to know when people are lying to me. That still leaves a lot of grey area. But forcing everyone around me to tell the truth? That would be so much worse."

"How incredibly wise of you," Morgan said, practically purring with approval. "Indeed, that is precisely why your power is so often considered a curse. Although, the fact that you do not currently suffer from such a fate suggests you have already overcome the curse, despite having no idea how. You must be extremely gifted, Special Agent Leo Jeffries."

"I do what I can."

"Oh?" Morgan licked her lips in anticipation. "And is that a throwaway phrase, or do you truly mean that?"

"I hope this isn't you flirting," Hilde growled, stepping into the enchantress so that the line of their bodies nearly touched. "Because that would be a mistake."

"Flirting? Not at all! It's merely a question. Does he, or does he not do what he can in any given situation? Is he the kind of man who would run into the burning building if he heard a child's cry, or who would push a stranger out of the way of a moving car?"

For a moment, no one spoke.

Of course, that was probably because the answer was so painfully obvious.

"Why do I feel like I'm not going to like where this is going?" Leo asked.

"Because you're no fool. Though, if I'm being honest, that's what makes this so intriguing."

"Stop wasting our time," Hilde snapped. "Say what you have to say, already."

For some reason, that sobered the enchantress up.

"Quite right," Morgan admitted. "The truth is, I would love to see your gift in action. What's more, if you allow me to help you, you could successfully interrogate this man before his mind gives out. Given the sheer probabilities involved, I believe it's likely he knows or perhaps overheard something that might, dare I say it, crack your case wide open. The question is whether it's worth the risk."

Everyone stood silent at the end of Morgan's spiel, staring anywhere but in Leo's direction. It was a tough call, and none of us envied him the decision, though I suspected we'd all take his place if we could—even Max, who knew him the least. After all, that's the kind of guy Leo was. You couldn't help but love him, at least a little.

"Oh, and no pressure," Morgan whispered, her voice wafting through the tension building in the air. "But you have about five minutes before the other two wake up on their own. So, you should probably—"

"I'll do it," Leo said. "If you can promise me you'll help me put the genie back in the bottle once we're done."

"Oh, that goes without saying, dear! Don't be ridiculous."

"Why not swear it on your power, just to be on the safe side?" I suggested, helpfully. "Consider it spell insurance."

The enchantress shot me a scathing look.

"What? Afraid to put your magic where your mouth is?"

"The only thing that frightens me, dear, is how poor your manners have become," Morgan replied, airily. "But if it will make you happy, then yes, I swear it on my power."

"See? Now, was that so hard?"

CHAPTER 34

Watt woke up screaming, thrashing so hard he nearly overturned the table we'd handcuffed him to. Fortunately, Hilde and Max were there in an instant, pinning it down with their combined weight and strength so that it wouldn't budge no matter how violently Watt reacted. A few feet away, Leo sat in a chair with his eyes closed while Morgan chanted away behind him, her hands circling his face in sweeping motions.

Hilde watched them like a hawk, her distress mounting to the point that the table had already begun to splinter beneath her hands. She alone had tried to convince Leo that he should avoid the risk and question Watt the old-fashioned way. Then, when that hadn't worked, she'd pointed out the fact that he could always use his fully manifested powers as a last resort. Sadly, as Morgan had already noted, doing so came with its own drawbacks—like losing out on potentially vital information.

So, here we were.

"Get these damn handcuffs off me, you sons of bitches!" Watt shrieked, spittle flying from his lips. "I mean it! You're all going to prison for this! And you! You're mine, you hear me?!"

Distantly, I realized the sheriff was barking at me. Rather than feed into his psychosis, I turned away. Which, of course, only seemed to piss him off more; the sheriff lunged at me so suddenly I heard his shoulder come out of its socket with a sickening pop. The sorry bastard wailed in agony, writhing on the floor with his utterly useless appendages flopping along for the ride.

"He's begun to go mad," Morgan said, her voice carrying over the screams. She'd removed her hands from Leo's ears, though the senior agent's eyes remained shut. "If you do not make him see the truth soon, Leo, he will harm himself even further."

In response, Leo leaned forward so that his elbows rested on his knees, his fingers interlocked, and gazed upon Watt with cold, dispassionate eyes. When at last he spoke, however, it was with a voice laden with heat and power.

"Sheriff Watt."

Watt's next scream died in his throat. He rolled onto his side to stare up at Leo, his face slack with awe. For a moment, I wondered what it was like for him to be under Leo's spell—then decided I'd rather not know.

"Why are you here, Sheriff?"

Watt stayed silent.

"It's too complicated a question," Morgan said in a hushed voice. "That's like asking him for what purpose he was born. You've got such a tight grip on him right now that he can't understand nuance. You have to ease up a bit. Perhaps try a few yes or no questions, first, until you get the hang of it."

Leo dipped his chin and tried again. "Did you come here to arrest us?"

"Yes."

"Did someone ask you to do that?"

"No."

Leo frowned. "Did someone *tell* you to do that?"

"Yes."

"And who was that person?"

"Angelika Novak."

"Do you know why she wanted us taken into custody?"

"No...but I have my suspicions," Watt replied, his face becoming more expressive by the moment.

"Which are?"

"I think she wanted you all out of the way for a while so that you wouldn't interfere with her plans. I warned her it would cause problems for my career, but she didn't care. She did something to me." Watt shuddered, fear flitting across his face. "She's done it to me before, back when I first began poking around her theater."

"Poking around? What did you suspect her of?"

"Being an illegal. We get a couple undocumented performers every year, especially the circus folk from Eastern Europe. When I heard that's where she was from, I thought I'd either deport her, or blackmail her. You'd be shocked how much money these people make to send home to their families. Paid off my mortgage last month."

Leo hissed between his teeth.

"Focus," Morgan advised. "Don't get distracted. Remember, if you let your emotions get the best of you, the power will spread and then you'd have us all under your spell. And you wouldn't care for that. Believe me. Though maybe I was wrong about loosening your hold on him. I didn't realize how repulsive this man was."

"This plan of Angelika's," Leo began again, forced to visibly swallow his anger. "What was it?"

"I do not know."

"What *do* you know about it?"

"I know it has something to do with the supermoon and the Ozark Caverns," Watt replied in a monotone voice. "She called it something else, but I don't know what else she could have been talking about. And I know about the caverns because she had me meet her there, several times. Also, before she sent me here, she mentioned something about visitors coming from out of town. She called it a ceremony."

"Right. Is there anything else you can tell me? Did you find out anything about this Angelika woman when you looked into her?"

"I did. You wouldn't guess it to look at her, but she's in her forties.

She rents a place in Lucia Ridge and lives alone with two cats. And she hates werewolves."

"Werewolves?" Leo's eyes widened, his stunned expression mirroring my own. "Did she say why?"

"She claims they terrorized her village when she was growing up and one day slaughtered her whole family, and that was why she came to this country. When I accused her of lying, she...did what she did to me."

"And what did she do to you, Watt?"

"She...made me do things I didn't want to do. Whenever she called, I came and took the bodies. I left them where she told me to. And then I forgot about it. But...how could I have forgotten about that?" Watt's bloodshot eyes began scanning the faces in the room, frantically. "What did that bitch do to me?"

"You're drawing out his subconscious mind, Leo," Morgan warned. "You have to pull back."

"And what happens if I don't?"

The way Leo said it, so feral and hate-filled, made the hair on the back of my neck stand up.

"Then he'll be forced to relive everything he's ever repressed," Morgan explained, calmly and without judgment. "You'll strip his mind of all its defenses, and he will experience what is known as psychic death."

"So it would kill him?"

"In and of itself? No. Though suicide is a likely outcome. Few have what it takes to face who and what they truly are, much less who they've hurt and been hurt by."

"Leo..." Hilde said, speaking up for the first time since he'd vetoed her concerns. "This is cruel, and you are not a cruel man."

"How would you know?" Leo asked, shifting the full weight of his attention to the Valkyrie before Morgan could warn him not to. Between one heartbeat and the next, Hilde's face slackened until almost nothing remained of her previous expression.

"I know, because I could never have fallen in love with a cruel man."

"Hilde..." Leo drifted off as though startled by the confession. Or maybe it was the fact that she'd said it in front of all of us; Hilde never had been the warm and fuzzy, sharing-is-caring type. The senior agent cursed, sat back, and pinched his eyes shut. "Get that mark off the sheriff, Miss le Fay, then help me reign this in, please. Before I do something I'll regret."

As if on cue, Watt slumped, his head striking the floor with a dull thud, having no idea how close he'd come to being psychically eviscerated for being a shit human being.

Pity, that.

CHAPTER 35

Roughly thirty minutes later, we sat and watched two EMTs load Watt into the back of an ambulance. The sheriff had already been sedated and restrained so as not to further impair his absurdly damaged arms, which perhaps explained the goofy grin on his face—not to mention the drool spilling down his weak chin.

"I had no idea the sheriff was having such a hard time," Holt mentioned as the scene unfolded. "He had some trouble after his wife left him. Anger issues. Hit the bottle a little too hard and a little too often. And after what he pulled with you and Agent Jeffries, maybe I should have suspected it was something worse...but still, a psychotic break?"

That was the official story we'd come up with. It wasn't a hard sell; by the time Holt and Nelson came to their senses, we'd staged it to look like Watt had drawn his gun and aimed it at himself. Of course, it helped that even after Morgan removed the mark, the sheriff couldn't stop muttering all manner of demented nonsense. Talk of killer werewolves and dead bodies, mostly.

"He's gettin' off easy, if ye ask me," I muttered.

"Oh, hey now. Look, I know he wasn't exactly on his best behavior, but that don't—"

"D'ye know why I came down here, Deputy?" I interjected, speaking low enough not to be overheard by any of the guests who'd wandered out from their rooms to watch the show. "It's because I heard a nasty little rumor that your sheriff was blackmailin' undocumented immigrants. D'ye know anythin' about that?"

Holt's eyebrows climbed so high I thought they might actually touch his receding hairline. "Watt? No way, not a chance. His ex-wife's family was from Cuba, for Christ's sake. Hell, I've never heard one person have a bad thing to..."

"Somethin' cross your mind just then, Deputy?"

"No...I mean, yes. It was something Watt's former sister-in-law said the other day, that's all. A story about how he met his wife." Holt shook his head. "No, I still can't believe it. This is all his ex-wife trying to get back at him, I bet, for getting the house in the divorce."

"Interestin' to hear ye say that, Deputy. Any chance ye can explain how a recently divorced Sheriff Watt managed to pay off his mortgage in full last month on a cop's salary?"

"He did what?"

"Aye. And we have the bank records to prove it," I lied. "So, do me a favor next time ye chat with your alcoholic boss with the anger management issues? Let him know that we hope he gets well sooner rather than later, because we have a prison sentence with his name on it."

"I don't—"

"Hey, Holt!" Nelson called to the older man after conferring with Lakota and Hilde on the other side of the street. "Those two want to come get the guy Watt took into custody."

"Son of a bitch." Holt spared me a sidelong glance before shouting his response. "Tell them to hold on a minute and we'll join them! Speed things up."

"Really? You sure you wouldn't rather go with the sheriff, boss?"

"Yes, dammit, I'm sure! We'll deal with him, later. First let's focus on cleaning up his mess." Then, in the same tone of voice but much quieter, he said to me, "If what you're saying is true, I'll find out."

"And?"

"And what?"

"And what will ye do?"

"If I find out he hid behind his badge while exploiting hard-working people for money? Oh, trust me, prison will be the least of his problems."

Funnily enough, I believed him.

Holt sauntered off a few seconds later with a muttered farewell. Together, he and Nelson hopped into their cruisers and waited for Lakota and Hilde to pull out so they could all head to the station. From there, the two women intended to fetch Jimmy and go back to the caravan, hoping to unearth whatever tenuous connection linked their pack to Angelika's coven. Leo and Max, meanwhile, were taking it easy at the bar while Leo recovered from bottling up all that power. Which was why when a raspy, feminine voice purred over my shoulder, I knew it had to be Morgan.

"Nicely done! Remind me never to play poker with you."

"Who said I was bluffin'? Didn't ye hear?" I held up the badge I'd palmed in case Holt had pushed back harder or, worse, been complicit in Watt's blackmailing schemes. "You're talkin' to Special Agent Quinn MacKenna, Department of Homeland Security."

"My, what a lovely forgery! May I see it?"

I handed it over without comment.

"Superb craftsmanship. Simply marvelous. Here you are, dear, you can have it back."

"Is there somethin' I can do for ye, Morgan?"

"On the contrary. I believe there is something I can do for you." Morgan slid an arm through mine and began escorting me away from the crowd of gawking onlookers. "I thought you and I might have a chat, and perhaps do a little sightseeing while we're at it."

"Ye seriously want a tour of Branson? Now?"

"Oh, absolutely not. I find this city repulsive. Nothing but squeal-

ing, misbehaved children as far as the eye can see. And all that dreadfully kitschy decor, don't even get me started."

"Then where d'ye have in mind?"

"Why, here, of course."

Morgan yanked me abruptly around the corner of the hotel and
out of sight. Expecting to step onto the flat, paved surface of a sidewalk, I whipped around to ask the enchantress what the hell she
thought she was doing. Instead, it appeared I'd stumbled onto the
overgrown floor of a dense forest; I went flying, my left foot caught on
a tree root. Luckily, Morgan was there to break my fall.

The enchantress shrieked as we tumbled to the ground, then
again after I mounted her hips and pinned her wrists to the dirt. She
squirmed and bucked, reflexively, but had nowhere near the experience she needed to shake loose someone who'd fought as much as
I had.

"Get off!"

"Not until ye tell me where we are!"

"First let go of me, you thankless heathen child!"

"D'ye use a Gateway?" I glanced in both directions, searching
among the trees for any sign of those magical rifts that allowed
exceptionally gifted practitioners to bypass customs—not to mention
defy the laws of physics. Unfortunately, there were none. Wherever
we'd ended up, we were stuck here until she decided otherwise.
"Take us back, right now!"

"I will do no such thing," Morgan snapped, her eyes dancing with
irritation. "I brought you all the way out here so we could talk in
private, and so we might investigate those caverns that odious
Regular mentioned. Because I'm *nice* like that. Now, kindly get off of
me before you ruin this dress more than you already have, and I am
forced to turn you into a toad."

"Swear ye mean me no harm, and I'll let you up," I insisted,
warily.

"You have my word."

I slid off her, slowly, and sat with my back pressed against the thin
trunk of a young tree. A quick scan suggested Morgan was telling the

truth. The forest mirrored what I'd seen of the Ozarks thus far— nothing but viridescent trees and rock clusters everywhere the eye could see. We were at the base of a downhill slope leading to a hilltop backlit by a setting sun.

"This better come out," Morgan muttered as she rose and inspected the back of her dress. "I didn't exactly pack a second outfit."

"Well, what the hell d'ye expect? Ye should have just told me what ye were goin' to do."

"I wanted it to be a surprise," she huffed. "You were looking a little sad and pathetic, so I thought we might go do something useful to lift your spirits."

"I appreciate the sentiment," I admitted, grudgingly. "But we need to go back. I can't be out after dark, it isn't safe."

"Nonsense, there are several hours' worth of daylight left. Besides, that's one of the things I needed to talk to you about."

"Come again?"

"Max tells me you're taking sleeping potions to keep your latent power at bay? And something about a goddess trying to take you over? Why don't you fill me in. Perhaps I can help."

I sighed, shoulders slumping with the realization that this would be the third time in as many days I'd had to recap what had happened to me over the course of the last year and a half. Still, the enchantress was right. She'd been around for centuries, if not millennia, and had an intimate knowledge of Celtic lore. If anyone was qualified to offer advice, it was her. Rather than go into the whole spiel, however, I painted the tale in broad strokes until I got to my time on Aeaea and Circe's tutelage. And, to Morgan's credit, she didn't interrupt me once—not even when I detailed my first nocturnal ascension.

"So," I concluded, my throat a little dry from all the talking, "that's what happened. I got back from the Underworld, and Circe brewed the potion to help keep me from terrorizin' this realm and drawin' unwanted attention to meself."

"Oh, she was quite right to do that, dear," Morgan acknowledged. "The gods may run amok far more often than mortals think, but any deity worth their supernatural salt knows how to cover their tracks and keep collateral damage to a minimum."

"Aye, and I don't."

"Yes, and we'll get to that. But first, do you happen to know what she used? In her potion, I mean?"

"She didn't say."

"Hmm...by any chance, could she have had any petals from that lotus flower left over?"

I scowled at that.

"The reason I ask," Morgan continued, "is that I can't think what else it could possibly be. Gods do not sleep in the traditional sense. They simply go elsewhere. And if ambrosia is their catnip, then the lotus flower is their peyote."

"What's your point?" I asked, a shiver running up my spine at her ominous tone.

"My point is, where have you been going when you lay down at night?"

"Nowhere. I dream, that's all. They're just dreams." I glared at the enchantress, willing her to disagree with me. "They aren't real. They can't be."

"Maybe they are nothing more than dreams," she allowed. "But downing a potion night after night is dangerous and will come back to haunt you in the end. Fortunately, I came prepared."

Morgan reached into the air like she'd pluck a fruit from the bough of a tree, only to have the lower third of her arm disappear into a miniature Gateway. She rummaged about, grinned, and withdrew her hand with a flourish. Wrapped around her fist was a silver bracelet with familiar patterns decorating its surface. From it hung a single silver charm: a feather.

"A woman commissioned one of these, some thirty years ago or so," Morgan explained as she passed it over. "And it worked so well that I made a few extra, with some improvements of course. It should do what your potion was meant to. It's designed to shield you from your own power, so long as you don't take it off."

I stared at the accessory, turning it over in my hands until the feather dangled. "The woman who requested ye make this...did she ask for one with crows on it?"

"You know, I think she did! Why do you...wait, how could you have known that? You weren't even born."

"I expect I was about to be," I replied, thinking back to the first time I'd seen a bracelet like this one—an accessory designed to blunt my burgeoning abilities before exposing me to the powers that be. Was it, I wondered, that her legendary foresight had included even this?

"Oh, that infuriating creature!" Morgan exclaimed, having apparently come to the same conclusion. "If she weren't already dead, I'd kill her. I know Nemain was your mother, but I swear—"

"Nemain?" I interrupted.

"Your mother. That was her name."

"I t'ink I'd know me mother's name," I drawled. "I'm tellin' ye she went by Morrigan."

"Oh right, the *geas*! It's been so long I'd actually forgotten. The truth is, your mother put a rather potent spell on her name to keep it from being spoken aloud by anyone, centuries ago. I don't know why. As far as I know, no one did. Of course, your mother refused to be called the Nameless One or anything ridiculous like that, which is why everyone began addressing her by her title. Morrigan. Originally, however, her name was Nemain."

"Nemain..." I echoed, experiencing a strange wistfulness at the sound of it. Like I'd heard it before, somewhere. I shook my head, secured the bracelet around my wrist, and held it up to catch the light. "T'anks for this, Morgan. If it works, I will genuinely owe ye."

Morgan lowered her arms, looking sheepish for the first time since I'd met her. "There's no need for all that. Consider it a gift from your Godmother."

"From me what, now?"

"Your Godmother," she repeated. "The way I see it, that woman who raised you was your mother's choice. I can't fault her for that. Nemain and I weren't exactly close."

"Given what I just heard, I'd say that's an understatement," I teased.

"Yes, well, sorry about that. It's just that your *father*, on the other hand, would most definitely have chosen me for the job. And, if he'd had any say in the matter, it's just as likely that you would have been raised by me, instead."

For some reason, I found myself charmed by the notion that Morgan le Fay, enchantress extraordinaire, envied my Aunt Dez in any capacity. Of course, hers was a ridiculous sentiment; she'd have turned me into a toad for real the second I hit puberty. But it made me think better of her, all the same, to know she'd fantasized about it.

"So, should I call ye me Fairy Godmother, then?"

"If you must," Morgan replied, her face screwed up in distaste. "But I'd prefer you didn't."

"Fair enough," I said, chuckling.

"In any case, as your paternal Godmother, I'd like to offer you some exceptionally sound advice."

"Oh? And what's that?"

"Sleep with that obscenely sexy brujo. Please. Do it soon, and do it often, for all our sakes."

I gaped at the enchantress, too stunned by her bold pronouncement to speak.

"Listen," she continued, "your heart is your business. But if I have to spend another minute in a room with you two, I think I may have to bespell you both and get it over with. And I mean that. It's like watching a lit match hover over a candlewick for hours on end. My nerves can't handle it."

"I have no idea what you're talkin' about," I mumbled, blushing. "We flirt, sure. And he's attractive. Alright, extremely attractive. But this t'ing between us..."

"That's what I mean!" Morgan exclaimed. "The untapped metaphysical potential between you two defies logic. For someone like me, it's like standing in a magnetic field wearing a suit of armor. Can you imagine what you two could do with all that power?"

"No, I really can't."

Morgan opened her mouth to say more but hesitated when she saw my face. "Did I say something wrong?"

"No." I hung my head. "It's nothin'. I appreciate the advice, but I'm not interested in bindin' Max any closer to me than I have, already. He may not be an ordinary man. Hell, he may not even be mortal, thanks to me. But until I get this goddess t'ing under control, I can't risk it."

"Ah...I see, now. Your heart isn't the problem. You're worried the closer he gets to your flame, the more likely he'll get burned." Morgan made a show of shrugging. "That's sensible. Or it would be if you weren't so colossally wrong."

"Come again?"

"I never met Circe, you know," Morgan went on, switching gears so quickly it nearly gave me whiplash. "By all accounts, however, she was one of the very best of her age. Of any age. Sadly, where you are concerned, she has one glaring deficiency. She's Greek. And you, dear, are not."

"What's that got to do with Max?"

"Given what you told me, it has everything to do with him. Thanks to Circe's incompetence, or shall we say her ignorance, you mistakenly believe your godhood is linked to a celestial principle. To the night, or to the moon. Which is, and please forgive the pun, pure lunacy."

"What? Why?"

"Because the moon is up there as we speak!" Morgan exclaimed, pointing overhead. "Night is occurring across half the planet! What sort of deity could possibly be expected to endure such ridiculous constraints? Oh, yes, I can think of one pantheon...the Greeks!"

"Surely they aren't the only ones—"

"Of course they aren't. But your people? The Tuatha Dé Danann? Not one was bound in such a way. Even your mother and her sisters, who were divided into three separate aspects so they wouldn't reshape the world with a sneeze, managed to wield their power freely. What makes you think you're so different?"

At this point, I was starting to get angry.

"I don't know," I snapped. "Maybe it's the fact that it's happened like clockwork everywhere I've been? Even in Valhalla, for cryin' out loud. The moon came up, and she took over."

"Or," Morgan countered, "the moon came up, and you gave in!"

"Really? Semantics?"

"Don't be daft, I know you're brighter than this. Think! On Circe's island, you were given access to untold power. Enough juice to turn you into a totally unrecognizable person with completely different priorities."

"So what?"

"So, you did what you've always done. You compartmentalized. You shoved all that power into a box, slapped a label on it, and put a timer on the lock. The wild side, that Otherworld persona, what do you think those are if not coping mechanisms?"

"Copin' with what, trauma?" I asked, surging to my feet to loom over the enchantress. "Fine, let's say that's true. Let's say all the voices were just in me own head. Let's—"

"Stop and listen to yourself, Quinn," Morgan interjected, calmly. "What you just said is the problem. You are a *goddess*. Coping mechanisms and trauma are human concepts, tied to their psychology. But that's to be expected. Because you were raised among them, you don't *know* any better. Isn't it possible you're trying to apply human solutions to a goddess' problems?"

"Meanin' what, exactly?"

"Meaning it *is* all in your head. Meaning you put the restrictions in place because you didn't *want* to be someone else, because you feared who you'd become. Not an alternate version of yourself. Just you. You're immortal, Quinn, and immensely powerful. You would simply rather hamstring yourself than admit it."

I fumed in silence, replaying Morgan's arguments over and over in my head, trying to find fault with her logic. Not because I refused to believe she was right, but because—if she was—it meant I was somehow to blame not only for my current circumstances, but also for my past failures. How many times had I lamented my own weakness since Aeaea? What might I have done differently, done better, if

I'd had access to all that power? Because the way she made it sound, it was—and always had been—a choice.

I opened my mouth to say as much, but a booming laugh from somewhere north of us cut me off before I could. Within seconds, voices began calling to one another, and soon the air was filled with the sounds of people traipsing through the forest, none of whom had been there only a moment ago. Suddenly, a figure in a dark robe materialized at the top of the hill, passing through the trees like a wraith. Two more followed. Then five. Morgan and I exchanged baffled glances, then ducked out of sight to avoid being spotted.

"Where are those caverns we were supposed to investigate?" I whispered, pressing my cheek to the trunk of the tree I hid behind.

"Over that hill, in the same direction they're walking. And no, I cannot imagine that's a coincidence."

"Of course it isn't," I hissed. "Shit. Come on, let's follow 'em. I want to see what's goin' on."

"As do I. One of those voices actually sounded familiar. In any case, we can table this discussion for another time."

"Aye, let's do that."

I started to emerge from my hiding spot and ascend the hill, only to have Morgan drag me back by my sleeve. She pulled me down beside her and stared at me like I'd lost my mind, forcing me to yank my arm out from under her hand.

"What?" I asked, exasperated.

"What do you mean, what? Look at you! You're in jeans and wearing a red jacket for Camelot's sake. You'll stand out like a sore thumb, and I'm guessing those are witches up there. They won't hesitate to cast a spell on you if they catch you following them."

Unfortunately, she had a point.

"You're right," I admitted. "D'ye get a good look at those robes?"

"Yes. They were dark red velvet. Hooded, obviously. Late Renaissance. Actually, they may have been High—"

I held up a hand, cutting the enchantress off before she could go on one of her tangents. After all, past a certain point, specificity didn't help. What I needed was a red velvet robe with a hood. How fancy it turned out to be was, honestly, up to Nevermore. Or it would have been, had she been so inclined. Instead, I was left making futile gestures and tapping myself like I had some sort of tic.

"My, is that *seitr* magic?" Morgan asked, sounding impressed. "I haven't seen anything like that since the Battle of Clontarf, the day Brian Boru fell."

"D'ye say Boru?" I asked, struck by the familiar ring of that name as I vainly flicked my hands about.

"Hmm? Oh, yes. Why?"

"It's nothin', nevermind. Thought I recognized the name, that's all." After a few more tries, I threw my hands into the air in frustration. "Dammit! It's not workin'."

Morgan began laughing so hard her shoulders shook.

"Well, what were ye goin' to do?" I snapped, grumpily. "At least I was dressed like I could be out for a walk. Ye look ready for a night on the town."

"You really think so?" Morgan asked, brightening.

"Well, minus all the dirt. That bit makes it look like ye already had a night out on the town. But I wouldn't worry about that. It's very walk-of-shame chic."

"Is that so?" Morgan's eyes narrowed to slits. She snapped her fingers, muttered a word, and suddenly we both had on the exact same livery as the figures we'd seen above. Indeed, with our hoods up and on such uneven ground, there was a chance we'd have a tough time telling each other apart. "After you, Goddaughter, dearest."

"Is this where I say age before beauty?"

"Not unless you want me to push you off a cliff," Morgan muttered as she shoved me back out into the open, her expression wry.

"Guess it's a good t'ing I can fly," I lied, smirking. "Come on then, old lady. I'll race ye to the top."

CHAPTER 36

A crowd of scarlet cloaks had already gathered at the mouth of the cave by the time we arrived. Fortunately, the atmosphere was a lively one, which meant we were about to straggle in without drawing too much attention to ourselves. Morgan and I moved in tandem, joining the fringes of the mob just as those in front spilled into the cavernous aperture. Within seconds, the whole crowd surged forward, their casual conversations dying out one by one until all I could make out were whispered snippets that ended the moment we crossed the threshold—an experience not unlike walking into church.

The caverns, admittedly, were worthy of reverence. The walls looked like melted flesh turned to stone—pooling to create layer after bulbous layer or joining the ceiling to the floor to form misshapen columns. Everywhere we looked, conical structures rose in clusters and descended from above like the teeth of some ravenous monster. Indeed, only the path we walked—as wide as a two-lane road and lit by a warm, amber glow that pervaded the entire cave—was worn smooth.

We shuffled on in silence for several minutes, accompanied only by the sound of dripping water and the swish of our robes along the stone. Morgan and I tried to exchange meaningful glances as we went, but there was little point; until we reached our destination, or until everyone started talking again, there was no way to communicate our thoughts. Fortunately, we didn't have to wait long for either.

The pace gradually slowed until we were all but standing still, waiting at the end of what appeared to be some sort of queue. Up ahead, I could make out trills of laughter as the general hubbub of conversation resumed. Directly in front of us, a slim, hooded figure nudged their neighbor.

"I hear Angelika is going to put on a real show, this time," a woman said, her voice carrying just enough to be overheard.

"That would explain all these people," the man beside her replied. "I've never seen it so crowded."

"Rumor has it she's going to summon a god," the woman said, giggling at the absurdity. "I guess it would be like her to try, though, wouldn't it?"

The man grunted.

"Were you here for her last performance piece? I missed it, but I heard it was spectacular."

"It was something," he replied, sounding nonplussed. "I wish I knew where she's channeling all this power from. On our best day, our coven can maybe manage a weather spell. And even then, it's iffy. We ended up turning poor Kelly's wedding into the hottest day of the year by trying to make sure it wouldn't rain. She was miserable."

"Serves you right, playing with nature like that."

"That's what I mean. The last few months, I've seen Angelika and her troupe cast spells that should have taken years to prepare. Two weeks ago, I watched them clear every cloud in the sky simply by linking hands."

"You think she's made a deal with something?"

"Maybe. There's plenty of minor devils up north in Kansas City, from what I hear. The White Rose saw to that."

"St. Louis is worse," the woman insisted. "We have to cross over into Illinois if we want to do any major casting. Otherwise we risk our spells going haywire or catching the attention of that damned wizard and his flunkies."

"Yeah, I hear you. The wife and I are thinking about taking the kids and moving west. Feels like the thing to do, before those morons go and start another war and get us all pulled into their mess."

"Oh, I don't know. I kind of enjoy it. Keeps life interesting, at least."

"Says the Millennial."

"Okay, Boomer."

The man coughed a laugh, then gestured. "Looks like we're about to go through. You got your costume and mask ready?"

"Sure do! This is going to be great. I've never been to a masquerade ball before."

"Me either. The wife will be pissed she missed this. She's always telling me I don't take her anywhere fancy, anymore."

I bit back a curse as I lagged behind, the rest of their conversation lost to the dull roar of conversation up ahead. A masquerade ball? Seriously? A glance showed that we were being funneled through a narrow opening, beyond which I swore I could hear a swing band and the clink of champagne glasses. By my estimation, I had a couple minutes at most to change into something suitable—including fashioning a mask out of thin air.

"Everything alright?" Morgan asked, craning forward so she could see into my hood. The enchantress wore an artfully crafted half-mask with silver filigree and freaking emeralds.

"Overachiever," I muttered.

"Oh, this old thing?" Morgan touched the mask absentmindedly, and I realized her nails were painted the same shade of green. "The perks of being an old lady. You tend to be prepared for any situation. How's yours coming along?"

I flashed her a go-fuck-yourself smile and began blindly fiddling with the clothes beneath my robe, praying that Nevermore would cooperate, and whatever she became would suffice. Unfortunately, there was no way to check on the result without flashing everyone and drawing a different sort of attention to myself. Still, I could tell *something* was going on beneath my robe; the fabric molded to something lighter and yet somehow more constricting, clinging tightly to my waist in particular.

"See you on the other side, dear," Morgan said, her voice thick with repressed laughter at the panic I'm sure she saw on my face.

"Uh huh," I replied, too distracted to hit her with something snarky. I pictured a basic mask and made the corresponding gesture just as the press of bodies at my back forced me into the narrow gap. I turned sideways and shuffled forward, the echo of my own breath loud in my ears.

Then, so suddenly I nearly stumbled into the person in front of me, I was through and standing in an absurdly wide canyon that should not have been geographically possible. Overhead, I could make out intermittent wisps of clouds against a purpling sky. Upbeat music drifted through the air.

"First time here, ma'am?" Next to me, a masked man held out his arm, his smile both servile and gracious at the same time. "Don't worry, I won't tell anyone. Please, let me take your robe, and enjoy the evening."

I swallowed, nervously, before undoing the clasp at my throat and passing the robe over. The man ducked his head in appreciation, only to stop and stare at me with eyes so wide they dominated the slits in his mask. Alarmed at his reaction, I prepared to snatch the robe back as I glanced down at myself.

"Forgive me," the man apologized, a blush spread across what little of his cheeks could be seen. "That's just quite the outfit, Miss."

"Oh, my..." Morgan slithered up next to me in a green satin ball gown that hugged her in all the right places—and she had a lot of those. "He isn't kidding. You clean up rather well, dear."

"Will ye excuse us?" I asked, speaking as sweetly as I could manage under the circumstances. Then, once out of his earshot, I demanded the enchantress do something about my clothes.

"Why would I do that?" Morgan asked, looking genuinely puzzled.

"Because this!" I exclaimed, showcasing the sequined flapper dress and tights that had drawn so much attention only a moment ago. "It's—"

"Sexy."

The voice belonged to a man in a very expensive looking three-piece suit. His half-mask, like the suit itself, was a shade of grey so dark it could have passed for black were it not for the silver cufflinks and tiepin. He came swaggering forward, head tilted so that his perfect jawline and the pout of his sensual lips were on full display. Of course, the man's raw sex appeal was never going to do anything for me.

I knew him too well.

"Dorian? Dorian Gray?"

The immortal playboy froze in midstep. Even with the mask on, I could tell he looked guilty. He rocked back on his heels, coughed into a gloved hand, and adjusted his necktie. "Ah, yes. You must forgive me for misplacing your name. There are of course so many names to remember. It does tax the mind, I'll admit. Though, to be quite candid, I cannot imagine forgetting a vision as radiant as yourself. Perhaps a refresher is in order, before this night gets too far under-way? Your lovely friend may join us, of course."

"How charming you are." Morgan barked a laugh. "But I must decline, for your sake.

"For my sake?" Dorian replied, hand held over his heart in mock surprise.

"Yes. I'm afraid I'd haunt your dreams, dear."

"Oooh, such confidence. I love it. And you, my red-headed vision? Will you haunt my waking hours, as well?"

"Not a chance," I replied, glaring at the decadent fop. "But, if ye say one more flirtatious word, I'll make sure to have *Live by the Whore, Die by the Whore* engraved on your tombstone. How's that?"

"Oh, Quinn MacKenna, it's you!" Dorian brightened, throwing his arms wide. "Someone told me you were dead. Come here and give us a grope!"

CHAPTER 37

W e spent the next twenty or so minutes catching up with Dorian Gray, an acquaintance of mine I hadn't seen in years. Funnily enough, we'd only met twice before this —once when he was trying to make a high production value snuff film starring yours truly, and again on a gay cruise run by his on-again-off-again lover, Narcissus. Finding him here of all places should have been quite the surprise. And yet, I couldn't think of anything more Dorian Gray than a masquerade ball hosted by performance art witches in a canyon that shouldn't exist.

"I heard about it from a girlfriend of a boyfriend back in Kansas City," Dorian explained as we meandered towards the sound of swing music, his hips gyrating to the beat in perfect synchrony. "Very hush hush. On atmosphere alone, I'd say it was worth the trip. I mean, look at that rooftop view. So gorgeous. But I must say, I'm glad you two showed up. I was in very real danger of becoming dreadfully bored."

"So, ye don't know whoever's runnin' this show, or what tonight is all about?" I asked.

"Only rumors. Gossip. The usual." Dorian arched an eyebrow that could have been drawn by God himself. "Why, what do you know?"

For a moment, I debated whether or not to say anything. On the one hand, I knew the immortal could be counted on, provided something was in it for him. On the other, I had no idea how deep the conspiracy went. Was it possible Dorian really had come here on a whim? Absolutely. Was it also possible he was involved, and this seemingly innocuous conversation was in fact him testing the waters? Of course it was.

"We heard someone is going to summon a god," Morgan replied, offhandedly.

"A god?" Dorian made a face. "Why would anyone want to do that?"

Morgan shrugged like it made no difference to her. "Just repeating what I heard, dear."

"Well, *I* heard the local coven is going to put on a once-in-a-lifetime show as soon as the sun sets. Though, speaking as someone who's lived more than a few lifetimes, I'd say that bar is damn near stratospheric." Dorian waved that away. "Whatever, as long as it isn't another orgy, you won't hear me complain."

"You wouldn't want to participate in an orgy?" Morgan asked, sounding surprised.

"I mean, I wouldn't say no...but this would be my third this month, and no matter how 'magical' they turn out to be, I always wake up sore the next day." Dorian did a quick survey of the crowd. "You didn't happen to see any centaurs when you came in, did you? I've decided to give them up for Lent."

"You practice Lent?"

"Practice is exactly the word I'd use, yes."

"Isn't Lent almost over?" I asked.

"Yes. It. Is." Dorian's eyes lit up and he began rubbing his hands together so that his gloves made a slithering noise. "Fat Tuesday...it's gonna be big."

I'd only just opened my mouth to crush Dorian's hopes and dreams by explaining Fat Tuesday was the day before Lent *began*, not the day after it ended, when the music died. By this point, we were near the front of the crowd gathered around to see the band, which meant it didn't take long to clear the way and discover the musicians packing it up for the day and thereby ceding the floor to a couple of minstrels and their lutes.

Though masked and wearing identical finery, the two musicians were almost comically different from one another. Whereas the first was short and so perfectly proportioned he might as well have come out of a box—complete with a jaw that could cut glass and hair kinkier than Adam putting the moves on his own rib—the second was about my height and looked like the ideal spokesmodel for a travel brochure targeting the modern WASP. To be honest, all they had in common in my opinion was that neither looked like they belonged here.

And yet, the moment they began to play, their nimble fingers flying up and down the necks of their respective instruments to a tune both lively and sinister, I could feel the magic in the air. Magic so heavy and so ripe that it felt like an oppressive weight against my skin. Sensing something awful was about to happen, I tried to turn and warn Morgan to run and get help. Unfortunately, I was too late...because our hosts had finally arrived.

And it seemed the real show was about to begin.

CHAPTER 38

Compelled by the magic, the crowd parted with the efficiency of a marching band, making way for a cavalcade of hooded figures. The tune slowed to a dirge as they came forth, the solemn procession not terribly unlike what you'd find at a Catholic Mass. Indeed, the atmosphere was permeated with that same sense of cultish mysticism—the cultivated ambience which made it possible to let a sexually repressed man put a silver dollar sized piece of flesh in your mouth.

At the tail end of the procession walked three individuals who were not like the rest. The first I recognized instantly as Angelika. The witch was covered head to toe in silver from the feathered crown of her gaudy half-mask to the tips of her bedazzled stilettos. The second wore checkered gold, his Harlequin mask riddled with tapered ribbons and tinkling bells, its upturned lips painted black to match the kohl around the wearer's eyes. Of course, no matter how elaborate the getup, there was no hiding Liam's helmet of curls, or those pointed ears.

The third came last and plodded forward like some automaton who grasped the theory of walking, but not the practice. Unlike the other two, there was no way to know this person's identity; the mask was a full-length Volto that obscured everything but the eyes and a crop of reddish blonde hair, its leather surface was dyed the same shade of virginal white as the tunic and breeches below.

I nudged Morgan as the hooded figures filed past, my voice so low it was barely audible over the music. "Can ye get word to the others? Somethin' is happenin' here, I can feel it."

Morgan continued to stare straight ahead as though I hadn't spoken, her gaze fixed on the eerie parade.

"Morgan, d'ye hear me?" I asked, louder this time. "Morgan le Fay? Hello?"

I turned to Dorian, expecting him to have some sort of insight into what was going on—or at least a critique of their showmanship. But the immortal had eyes only for our hosts as they cruised past us and mounted a stage carved into the side of the canyon. Indeed, it seemed everyone was similarly fixated. The crowd filled the gap they left behind in silence; their faces turned up in awe.

"Good evening, everyone!" Angelika stood front and center, presenting herself like a showgirl. "And welcome to our final show!"

Cheers erupted from every corner, including whistles and chants. Beside me, Dorian raised a fist in the air and pumped it, while Morgan put both hands to her mouth and screamed for joy. Then, as abruptly as they'd begun, everyone simply stopped—their mouths clamped shut, hands loose at their sides.

"Many of you know me," Angelika began as she paced the stage, a rousing melody playing gently in the background. "You know us. We are entertainers! We are artists! And we are, of course, witches."

The members of Angelika's coven took a step forward and began revealing their faces one at a time. Each was a variation on a Slavic theme, making it nearly impossible to tell who was from which part of a nation that had once spanned much of the known world. Without exception, however—whether round or square jawed, thick or thin-lipped, fair-haired or dark—every individual among the thirteen men and women had dried blood smeared across their foreheads.

"And yet, for all we have done to make it better place, this world suffers! So many wage war, starve, get sick, and die. And why? Because they say magic is not solution."

Boos and other disapproving noises rose from her audience as surely as if someone had held up the requisite sign during a live studio recording.

"They say magic is secret thing! Is like having tool others do not. Is to be controlled. Mastered. Regulated." Angelika waggled her finger at the crowd. "They tell us that world is not ready for magic. But world *is* magic. And once, we knew this was true fact. Once, we were more than artists. More than entertainers. More than witches. We were the chosen of the gods!"

Angelika held out a hand to silence the crowd before it could get rowdy once more. Then, with the other, she beckoned Liam and his companion to join her. He did so with little fanfare, dragging their third by the arm like a teddy bear.

"And so, to save world, we shall be this again!"

As if on cue, Liam thrust the all-white figure forward to land on all fours at Angelika's feet. The witch glared at the Gancanagh, bent down, and raised the man's chin so that he stared up at her through his mask. Whatever she said to him was gentle, perhaps even loving. In any case, he rocked back on his heels so that—when she began untying the ribbon of his mask—his face was nestled in the folds of her skirt.

Which was likely why it took me a few seconds longer to recognize him than it should have. Still, by the time Angelika turned his face towards the crowd, I knew exactly who I'd see.

Bredon.

Beneath the light of the overhead moon and the torches scattered throughout the canyon, I could see that he'd been beaten. He had a black eye, a busted lip, and a bruise covering so much of one cheek that I wondered if his jaw was broken. And yet, when he saw us all standing there, he smiled—revealing missing and shattered teeth.

"Together, we beseech you!" Angelika shouted, throwing both arms wide as her fellow witches joined hands and closed their eyes. "We call you from past!"

A true wind began to pick up this time, whipping at everyone's attire until all manner of accessories went flying about.

"We call you with power!"

The air became so thick with humidity that it coated our skin and soaked our clothes.

"We call you with blood!"

Lightning arced overhead, its forked tongues racing across the sky in a flash so blinding I nearly missed the silver blade that appeared in Angelika's outstretched hand and was forced to stare through spots as she plunged it deep into Bredon's chest. I screamed and lunged forward in an effort to reach the wounded man, but my cry was drowned out by the howling wind and my arms held fast by my two companions.

"There!" Angelika cried as the gales died down, pointing to the heavens with a hand covered in blood. "There it is! We have called Hex Moon, days early!"

Sure enough, above us hung the largest, brightest moon I'd ever seen outside of Fae. Compelled by Angelika's words, the other witches opened their eyes. They began shouting and jumping with excitement, reveling even as the sacrifice who'd made it possible bled out at her feet.

Feeling more and more helpless by the second, I struggled against Morgan and Dorian's grips. Unfortunately, they were both strong enough that the only way to break free was to hurt them, and I wasn't willing to go that far, yet. Besides, Bredon was surely dead by now. I couldn't save him. What I could do, however, was put a stop to the second act of their mad play. After all, from what I'd been told, the Hex Moon only had one purpose: to amplify spells. Which meant they'd called it early for a reason.

"Everyone back into position!" Angelika called to her coven, grinning. "This was only first obstacle."

The others did as she said.

"Now, we join hands, brothers and sisters!" Angelika drew a mark on her forehead with Bredon's blood which mirrored those on her fellow witches. "Tonight, we use the power of Hex Moon and last drop of blood from thirteen evildoers to call to you, Belobog, Lord of Light and Saviour of all—"

"Actually, go ahead and let me stop you right there."

Liam's voice cut through the ritual like a snapped string in the middle of a guitar solo. And yet, no one in the crowd so much as stirred. Instead, they looked on with glassy-eyed stares as the Gancanagh strolled across the stage radiating so much power it leaked out the eyes of his mask like gold dust.

"Liam, what is this you are doing? Do not be a fool."

"Guilty as charged," Liam replied merrily, flicking one of his many bells for emphasis.

"I am serious. Get off stage while we summon Belobog."

"I'm afraid that's not possible. The summoning part, that is. I could get off the stage. I won't. But I could."

A disgusted look crossed Angelika's face. "What is this madness you speak?"

"The truth *can* be a little maddening," Liam replied, nodding sagely. The Gancanagh spun on his heel to face the audience, arms folded behind his back, his chest puffed up. "But would you all like to hear it, anyway?"

"YES!"

I flinched, startled by the crowd's collective response.

"Know your audience," Liam said as he turned to Angelika. He snapped his fingers, and all the other witches fell to their knees with cries of alarm. He snapped them again, and they went down onto all fours. In a matter of seconds, fountains of blood began pouring from their eyes and mouths—far more than any ordinary person could afford losing and live.

"Stop this! What are you doing?!" Angelika raced to aid the nearest witch.

"I am returning things to the way they used to be. Isn't that what you said you wanted? To bring back magic? To bring back the gods?" This time, Liam waggled his finger at her. "You were never chosen, you delusional creature. You were slaves. You were *created* to serve. Having magic simply made you better at it."

"Stop killing them, please!" Angelika crouched beside a twitching body, the hem of her dress stained crimson. "Let them go!"

"My lovely Angelika...you know I can't do that. Not after all the effort I went through to convince you this was the only way to get what you so desperately wanted. And certainly not after you murdered all those poor, innocent people thinking they were werewolves."

"You said—"

"Oh, no. I let you do all the talking tonight. It's my turn, now. And what I want to talk about is..." Liam drifted off; his masked face turned towards the moon. "Hmm...someone's gone and done something they shouldn't have."

Angelika's head shot up, her cheeks stained with tears and runny mascara. Perhaps sensing an opening, the witch bared her teeth, gathered up the voluminous mounds of her bloody skirt, and launched herself at the Gancanagh with all the athleticism she'd cultivated over the decades. Liam backhanded the dancer as one might a fly, sending her careening across the floor like a skipped rock.

"I really hate leaving the party before it's over," the Gancanagh muttered to himself. He walked to the center of the stage, stepping over the shattered body of his lover so casually she might as well have been a crack in the pavement in the process. "Oh well, I suppose it can't be helped. Maybe I'll double back. See what a mess he makes of you all."

Realizing now was my best chance to end this gruesome blood-bath once and for all, I doubled down on my efforts to free my arms —using whatever means I could think of short of breaking their hands. If I could only awaken Areadbhar, I thought, I was sure I could stop the demented bastard with one well-timed throw. I yanked Dorian forward and began prying his fingers off with my teeth one at a time, but it seemed I was too late.

"Chernobog!" Liam shouted; his hands held to the heavens as though he planned to pluck the moon from the sky. "Lord of Darkness and Devourer of Souls, I give you the souls of thirteen...oh, make that fourteen, can't believe I almost forgot Angelika...witches bathed in the blood of the innocent! By the power of the Hex Moon you are called! Awaken, and feast!"

At first, all I sensed was an abrupt release of pressure as that horde of metaphysical energy dispersed into the night. Then a bestial roar, louder and more primal than a clash of thunder, split the night. Even more ominous, however, was the feeling of pervasive dread that seemed to accompany the horrendous sound.

"Ah, there he is," Liam said, sounding quite satisfied with himself. "Should be along any minute now. Probably best I be on my way."

With a flourish, the Gancanagh swiveled and bowed farewell to his audience—and yet it felt an awful lot like his blazing eyes were locked solely on mine. Was it possible Liam knew I was here? Was that how the other two had known to restrain me so I wouldn't interrupt? As if on cue, Dorian and Morgan released me simultaneously, their faces so slack and unwitting that their mouths hung partially open. The Gancanagh came out of the bow and retreated into a portal of his own making, waving cheerfully until the portal closed, leaving nothing behind but his final words.

"Die well, everyone!"

And that's when the screaming started.

CHAPTER 39

The screams were those of startled women, mostly, though a few men joined in with shouts of shock and disgust at waking from Liam's spell to find a stage covered in corpses. Not that I could blame them. Frankly, I couldn't remember ever having seen so much blood in one place; it oozed outwards by the pint, spilling over the stage to form puddles which lapped at the feet of those in front. Unsurprisingly, those were the people screaming loudest.

And yet, I had a feeling the nightmarish scene was nothing compared to what awaited us.

"What's going on?" Morgan asked, grabbing my arm for the second time in as many hours, her gaze sliding from the stage to the sky. "What happened here? Is that the Hex Moon?"

"Are those people dead? Because they look dead to me," Dorian chimed in before I could answer.

"Ye don't remember any of this? Neither of ye?"

They both gave me blank looks.

I opened my mouth to explain as best I could, only to be cut off by a second barrage of screams. Except these weren't squeals of dismay. They were cries of genuine horror. I spun round to find the lifeless corpses spasming so violently that a few had even rolled to their backs, their arms and legs flopping bonelessly about like those of the inflatable tube men that haunt automotive dealerships. Within seconds, a foul wind whipped about the canyon, blowing out the few remaining torches like candles on a birthday cake, and something huge began to rise up from the center of the stage—a bulbous, amorphous shape covered in a bloody sheet. No, I realized, covered in a sheet *made* of blood. The more the colossal figure swelled and expanded, the more liquid was pulled into its wake.

Moments later, all that blood rose into the air, floating above our heads like some sort of possessed blanket. As we watched, however, shapes began bulging at the edges. Here, a hand. There, a leg. A hideously emaciated arm emerged from one side, only to be yanked back down by a thicker, more muscular limb. This continued for several heartbeats until, without warning, the whole mess came dribbling down like juice from a freshly squeezed fruit.

And, where it landed, a god began to take shape.

Aside from what had been insinuated during the ritual, I couldn't tell you exactly how I knew he was a god except to say that the energy which roiled off him was unlike anything of this world. Indeed, it was unlike anything I had ever encountered before. Whereas I'd met a fair number of gods, many of whom had the potential to level whole civilizations on a whim, this creature—the one Liam called Chernobog—struck me as an odious and contemptible being capable only of laying waste to everything he touched. Which meant, by the time the abomination rose to his full height, his ebony black skin slick and dripping with gore, I knew we were all in serious trouble.

And so, too, did everyone else.

Those in the back of the crowd surged towards the exit, their terrified shrieks inciting even more panic than there would have been otherwise until the rest of the mob joined them in a mad dash to freedom. Except the only way out was that narrow gap, which meant the vast majority of us were more or less trapped.

"What is that thing?" Dorian asked, forced to shout to be heard over the clamor. "And what is it doing, now?"

The god had raised both arms like a conductor about to put on the symphony of a lifetime. His eyes blazed with the same infernal fire that poured from his mouth in great gouts as he spoke in a tongue so vile it made me nauseous to hear it. And yet, I knew what he was saying as surely as though he were speaking English.

Rise, my children.

As though snatched up and held aloft by the collars of their robes, the corpses rose to hover several inches off the ground, their heads hanging limp on their chests, their blood-caked faces mercifully hidden from sight.

Tear them to pieces.

As one, the possessed launched themselves dozens of feet into the air and began descending on those gathered at the exit. Where they landed, blood sprayed, and bodies fell. Those in the immediate vicinity scattered, trampling their neighbors in a mad rush to escape. Unable to look elsewhere, I watched in mute horror as one of the possessed quite literally tore the head off someone as they tried to rise. Indeed, I was so fixated that it wasn't until I felt something tugging at my wrist that I realized Morgan was dragging me in the opposite direction, Dorian hot on our heels.

"This is so not the party I had in mind," he said.

"Me either," Morgan hissed. "This is bad. I can't create a Gateway. Whatever that thing is, it doesn't want any of us to escape."

"Chernobog," I said, repeating the name Liam had used. "I t'ink he's a god. A nasty one."

"*That's* Chernobog? That's impossible. He was one of the very first to go into exile, and for good reason!"

"Aye, well, it took a whole lot of killin' to make it happen," I replied. Once we'd ducked into the relative shelter of an alcove, I gave them the briefest possible summary of what they'd missed, sticking mainly to what seemed relevant to our current situation. The rest—how the victims and werewolves fit into everything, not to mention the role Liam had played in it all—I kept to myself. One problem at a time.

"So, any chance either of ye have any idea what to do, next?" I asked as I removed the mask I'd been wearing and wiped away the sweat on my brow.

The two exchanged glances.

"Run."

"Definitely run," Dorian agreed.

"Aye," I grimaced, recognizing the merit of that response. After all, we were outnumbered and metaphorically outgunned. Even if I removed the bracelet Morgan had given me and embraced everything I was, I doubted I'd stand a chance against a god with Chernobog's experience. It'd be like walking into a prize fight as a promising first-degree black belt going up against a seasoned operative who killed people with his bare hands for a living.

And yet...

I glanced over to the mayhem taking place near the exit. Already, small clusters had veered off from the main group, trying their best to avoid Chernobog's murderous pets. A few, to my surprise, appeared to be mounting a resistance. Unfortunately, that only served to delay the inevitable. At this point, we were trapped like rats in a cage. Only...this wasn't exactly a cage, was it?

Because cages had lids.

"Morgan, what's the biggest enchantment ye can do?"

"What?"

"Your magic. What's the most it's capable of?"

"In terms of what?"

"Remember when ye made that cloak for me, before? I knew it was an illusion, but it felt so real I actually got hot in it while we were walking. So I guess what I'm asking is how real an illusion can you cast?"

Morgan thought about it and shrugged. "Depends. With illusions, the more you have to draw from, the less work is required. But to make something out of nothing and then breathe life into it like I did with that cloak? It can be taxing."

"So, if I said I wanted ye to create a ladder..."

"Ah. I see what you're getting at, dear, but the walls of that canyon are a good hundred and fifty feet high. There's no way I could fashion anything tall enough *and* real enough to get us out of here."

"Not just us," I corrected. "Everyone."

"Them either," she drawled.

"And what if ye had help?"

"Help from whom?"

I shook my head and pointed. "Not whom. What."

"Oh, that's right," Morgan replied, her eyes tracking my finger all the way to the enormous Hex Moon overhead. "That's *right*! Oh, you clever girl."

"Could ye do it?"

"I think I could, yes. Not a ladder, of course. That would present its own difficulties. But perhaps a ramp...yes, that would work. Especially if I use the stone that's already there as a foundation."

"Excellent! Now, Dorian, I want ye—"

"Whoa there," Dorian said, cutting me off before I could finish. "Slow down, and let's be clear about this. You and I both know this is not my time to shine. Unless you want me to try and seduce tall, dark, and loathsome over there. Though, if I'm being honest...not my type."

"Dorian," I repeated, grabbing the immortal by both shoulders, and staring into his eyes, "I want ye to lead everyone up the ramp. Get 'em out while I distract the corpses."

"And what if it's not just the corpses you have to distract?" Dorian asked, eyeing Chernobog.

"Then I'll put on me freakin' black belt and take it like a girl."

"Huh?"

"Listen, it won't matter," I replied, shaking him a little for emphasis. "You'll be long gone by then, and so will a lot of other people who would have died down here, otherwise. I'm not askin' ye to be a hero, Dorian. I'm askin' ye to let all these people ogle your fine ass while ye run away as fast as ye can."

"Oh, well, when you put it like that..." Dorian grinned rakishly, glancing down at his own rear with an appraising eye. "It is rather fine, isn't it?"

I chuckled despite myself, only distantly aware of how ludicrous my life had become that these were the sorts of conversations I had in a crisis. But then again, maybe that's what separated people like us from those poor saps getting violently torn to shreds. Survivor 101: don't you dare cry about it unless you need the lubricant.

"Alright then, here's what we're goin' to do..."

CHAPTER 40

I took my position at Morgan's back while she prepared the spell, chanting in a language that sounded like some guttural rendition of Gaelic. Dorian, meanwhile, had already begun his job; the immortal jogged past the survivors, waving at them like one of those perky aerobics instructors from an 80s dance video. Still, whether it was his charisma or the fact that he was the only person who looked anything other than terrified, it worked. Within a couple minutes, he'd orchestrated an exodus.

"They're comin' this way," I warned Morgan.

I felt her nod.

Realizing that meant I, too, was on the clock, I placed a fist over my heart and spread my fingers wide—the *seitr* sign that amounted to pulling the fire alarm. At first, nothing happened, and I began to seriously worry that Nevermore would refuse to change for me. But then, almost grudgingly, the hem of my frisky flapper dress became the tail end of a chainmail shirt. My bodice became a breastplate, the shoulder straps pauldrons, the open neckline a gorget. The rest materialized quickly, and I finally stood in all my armored glory holding a fearsome looking helm that had once been a mask and a pitch-black stone that was about to become a flaming spear.

"Areadbhar, it's time."

The stone pulsed in my hand. I flung it into the air and watched in fascination as the rock exploded in a shower of sparks to reveal the first Jewel of the Tuatha Dé Danann. I thrust out my hand, and she came to it singing with bloodlust.

"Soon," I whispered, lovingly.

"Now!" Morgan shouted. Behind me, the canyon wall split apart with a thunderous crack. I turned in time to see slabs of stone spill onto the canyon floor, skidding towards us with so much momentum I began to worry we were seconds away from being crushed beneath the rubble. But I needn't have worried; the very last pebble came skittering to a stop a mere inch from Morgan's feet.

The enchantress held both hands out wide and began bringing them together like she was squeezing an invisible accordion. The stones began to shift, some even leaping atop their fellows before settling in place. Within seconds, the landslide became a ramp.

Do you think that will stop me?

Hellish flames spewed from Chernobog's mouth as he spoke, but the god remained rooted to the stage as Dorian came jogging up to us. The immortal winked at Morgan and me as he cruised past, his skin glistening with the lightest sheen of sweat I'd ever seen on a human being. Then, after literally cheering everyone on, the immortal charged the ramp, trailed by several dozen miserable people in evening attire. I watched him go, marveling at the fact that our plan had actually worked.

"It is a very nice ass," Morgan remarked.

And yes, that, too.

"They're right behind us!" a portly man yelled, huffing as he scrambled onto the ramp in his dress shoes.

As he'd indicated, I turned to find at least six of the possessed witches coming for Morgan and me—their legs churning at speeds no human could possibly match. Unfortunately, the enchantress was far too exhausted to put up any sort of fight. Not that I was surprised; she had warned me before we enacted our plan. Which meant it was up to me...and Nevermore...and Areadbhar.

"It's good to have friends ye can rely on," I said as I donned my helmet, found my center, and swung Areadbhar around so her blade was pointed skyward. Then, I waited, bouncing lightly from one foot to the other, refamiliarizing myself with the raw physical enhancements the Valkyrie armor provided in conjunction with her damn near impregnable shielding.

The first witch came at me howling wordlessly, her mouth so impossibly wide it made me wonder whether she'd unhinged her jaw during her seizure. In that moment, I realized I might have pitied this woman before I'd discovered how she'd gotten that black mark crusted on her forehead—how she and her coven had obtained all that immense power. A spiteful part of me wished I could ask her if it had been worth it. The rest of me simply didn't care.

I planted the butt of my spear between two stones, crouched, and swiveled in one smooth movement so that Areadbhar took the witch right between the teeth. As I'd anticipated, the witch's momentum carried her onto the blade and halfway down the shaft, effectively bisecting her face. Hoping to shake her loose and deal with her companions in a similar manner, I started to pull Areadbhar free. But then a hand latched onto my wrist, squeezing with enough force to pulverize bone. I glanced down to find the witch's blood-rimmed, hate-filled eyes staring up at me from a face that had once belonged to a living, breathing human being with hopes and dreams and people who might actually miss her when she didn't make it home tonight.

Alright, so maybe I did pity her, a bit.

"Areadbhar."

The spear responded to my unspoken command with relish, her shaft suddenly ablaze with unquenchable flames that began to lick at that woman's face, leaving it charred and flaking. At first, the grip around my wrist tightened, and I began to worry we were dealing with literal zombies—the kind that have to be chopped into pieces to stop them completely. Fortunately, as soon as the cursed mark on her forehead went up in flames, her hand fell away.

Which explained how Chernobog was controlling them.

Good to know.

"Quinn, look out!"

I'd only just flung the witch's remains to the ground when I heard Morgan's warning. Expecting one of the other witches to have covered the distance while I was distracted, I quickly brought Areadbhar to bear. What I hadn't anticipated, however, was a coordinated strike; from above, two of the remaining twelve witches had leapt into the sky in defiance of gravity, while a second pair came at me from either side like those goddamned velociraptors from *Jurassic Park*.

At this point, I could see that over half the surviving guests had started up the ramp, which meant I only had to hold my ground for a few more minutes to be certain the majority escaped. Unfortunately, I wasn't sure I could guarantee them that much time; I could take one of the witches head on, maybe even two, but fending off more than that at once was bound to be a defensive battle I was sure to lose.

Unless, of course, I was willing to up the ante.

I'd already wrapped a hand around my bracelet, prepared to yank it off and let the chips fall where they may, when a lone howl split the night. A moment later, dozens more joined in. The witches coming at me from below very unexpectedly stalled not fifteen feet out before immediately breaking off their assault. At my back, Morgan made a startled noise.

"Well, you don't see that every day."

I wheeled round to find at least thirty pairs of glowing amber eyes staring down at us from the lip of the canyon. Eyes which belonged to wolves the size of horses—some shaggy and barrel-chested, others impossibly sleek and lean. One, however, stood well above the rest. Half-human, half-wolf, it was she who held out her arm and pointed at us with one absurdly long claw.

On their Alpha's command, the wolves galloped down the ramp, weaving as they went so as not to knock the remaining survivors over the side. Before I could decide whether they'd come to fight with or against us, however, a winged figure came soaring across the sky to meet the airborne witches. Special Agent Hilde Thorsdottir, her armor gleaming in the moonlight, rammed the first hard enough with her shield to send him plummeting to the ground in a shattered heap. The second she dealt with by lopping off a hand, then an arm, and finally a head. Having apparently caught sight of me watching from below, the Valkyrie saluted with her sword.

"I said it before, Morgan, and I'll say it again...it's good to have friends ye can rely on!"

Morgan laughed, weakly, before slumping against me. I caught and lowered her, only then realizing how much her not so little spell had cost her. The werewolves reached the canyon floor, several peeling off to form a protective circle around the two of us. A single wolf, burlier and more savage looking than the others, trotted forward with his tongue lolling halfway out his mouth. Somehow, I felt I recognized the creature's leering grin—or maybe it was the look in his eyes.

"Zeke?" I asked, tentatively.

The wolf barked in response.

"I'll take that as a yes."

Another bark.

"Are ye here to help?"

Zeke spun in a quick circle, plopped down, and howled at the moon. An emphatic yes, that time. Good to know.

"Can a couple of ye keep an eye on Morgan here? She's a wee bit tuckered out."

Zeke swung his shaggy head around to scent the air, then rose and took a step forward as if to sniff the enchantress directly. His tongue was all the way out by this point, and he was drooling.

"Step one paw closer, dog," Morgan warned, "and I'll turn you into a squirrel and watch your closest friends hunt you down and swallow you whole."

Zeke froze, his hackles raised.

"I'd do as she says, Zeke. See that freakin' ramp? She did that. I wouldn't press your luck."

The werewolf shuffled back the way he'd come, turned, and yowled at his canine companions. Three remained behind while the others tore off after their fellows, most of whom were engaged with the witches.

Which reminded me.

"Zeke, ye have to tell your pack that the creatures they're fightin' can be stopped by destroyin' the marks on their foreheads."

The werewolf barked an acknowledgment, spun on his hind legs, and went loping off into the night, braying his freaking head off for all to hear. In the relative peace and quiet Zeke left behind, I craned my neck to study the one piece in this chess match who had yet to make a move.

Chernobog stood in the center of the stage, arms folded across his naked chest, watching it all unfold with a fucking grin on his nightmarish face. He was enjoying this. The slaughter, the mayhem, even the loss of his so-called children—I could sense it. To a god of destruction, such struggles were entertaining, but ultimately pointless. And why? Because there wasn't a game he could lose once he smashed the board to bits and lit the pieces on fire.

"Where do you think you're going, Goddaughter?" Morgan asked, rapping a knuckle against my breastplate.

"Who says I'm goin' anywhere?"

"Don't play dumb with me, dear. I can see you're planning to do something stupid."

Rather than reply, I scanned the canyon floor until I found Hilde; the Valkyrie was helping the stragglers and the wounded navigate the battle so they could reach the base of the ramp, which meant she'd be coming to me next. Perfect.

"I mean it, Quinn," Morgan insisted, sitting up so she could grab my shoulder and turn me to face her. "What are you going to do?"

I considered lying, for her sake. I could tell her I wanted to help Hilde with the survivors or take out the last of the possessed witches. Either would mollify the enchantress. But, frankly, Morgan le Fay was not my Godmother. If anyone deserved that title, it was my Aunt Desdemona. Now *her* I would definitely have lied to. No question. Because she could have stopped me.

"I'm goin' to find out how it feels to kill a god."

"You can't be serious." Morgan gaped at me. "You can't go after Chernobog on your own. Not as you are. He'll cut you out of that armor piece by piece."

"Don't ye worry," I insisted, patting the enchantress' arm in reassurance. "I won't be alone."

"That's not what—"

"Oy! Hilde!" I called, a hand perched on the side of my mouth.

The Valkyrie finished handing off a poor old lady who could have been somebody's grandmother—her tattered gown stained with someone else's blood, her flabby arms covered in more bruises than a ripe banana—to the care of one of the werewolves before replying to me.

"What is it?" she asked, her whole body practically humming with pent up rage.

"Want to go kill a god?"

A grin so wolfish it would have sent Zeke and his pack running for the hills with their tails between their legs spread across the Valkyrie's face.

"You're damn right, I do."

CHAPTER 41

Hilde brandished her sword, swinging it in swift, chopping motions while we discussed strategy. For a brief moment, I considered doing something similar with Areadbhar—twirl her around a bit, turn it into a fire show midway through for kicks. Unfortunately, I had far more important things to worry about than competing with Hilde. Like staying alive...and killing a god.

"We should do a fly by, to start," the Valkyrie said as she eyed Chernobog. The god had yet to step into the fray, but there was no doubt in either of our minds that his patience was wearing thinner by the second. "We don't yet know what he's capable of, so we'll start with a feint. In and out. How he reacts should give us at least some idea what we're dealing with."

Though it pained me to do it, I coughed a muffled sentence into my gauntleted hand.

"Sorry, what was that?"

"I said I can't fly," I admitted, shoulders slumped.

"Ah. Yes, well, it takes even a Valkyrie years to master. There's no shame in it. I'm sure we can come up with an alternative strategy."

"No, ye don't understand. I can't *fly*. As in, I lack the capacity, not the capability." I jerked a thumb over my shoulder for emphasis. "Wings weren't included with this model. It's sort of a prototype. I guess you could say it's *the* prototype. The Valkyrie who wore it before me was Odin's first champion, ye see, and...are ye alright?"

Hilde's face had lost all its color.

"Look. I was goin' to tell ye, I swear!" I insisted. "It just didn't seem like the right time to mention it at the hospital, and afterwards ye refused to speak a civil word to me. Which I still don't entirely understand, mind ye, but—"

"Take it off, Quinn."

"What?" I froze, alarmed by the Valkyrie's unexpected tone. Frankly, I'd assumed she would be pissed, or maybe even distraught. Either of those were reactions I could empathize with. What I couldn't understand, however, was why she sounded like a hostage negotiator telling me to remove the bomb vest. "Why should I?"

"Because that armor is cursed."

I sighed in relief. "Aye, Freya told me about all that. Somethin' about Ragnarök and the end of days. Honestly, it all sounds a bit dramatic."

"It has nothing to do with that tired old prophecy," Hilde insisted, heat leaking into her voice at last. "I can't believe Freya never thought to warn you. Listen, Quinn, my mother's armor was cursed to come alive and kill whoever possesses it the instant their heart is broken. She placed that curse on it the day she killed herself. The day after I was born."

I suddenly felt very hot. At first, I assumed that was my body's reaction to the news that I'd made an even more one-sided deal than I thought—and also that I might one day be strangled by my own clothes in the middle of a breakup. But then I realized the whole werewolf pack was either whining or snarling, and that the heat had a source.

"Shit, look," I said, pointing.

It seemed Chernobog had stepped off the stage, at last; the god paced the canyon floor, moving like a bull about to gore his opponent at the first flash of red. More disconcerting, however, was the thick film of crude oil which bubbled up from deep below the earth's surface, pooling at the god's feet so that it lapped at his toes. As we watched, Chernobog bent to scoop up a handful of that black tar and began lathering it all over himself. Scariest of all, however, was the fact that he seemed to grow larger in stature with each application.

"Quinn, about the armor—"

"Maybe not the best time," I interjected as I showcased our opponent. "In case ye hadn't noticed, we could all very well die right here and now, and then your mother's curse won't matter to anyone. No offense."

"No, you're right. We can talk about this, later." Hilde shook herself and rolled her neck. "Alright...I want you to stay low and watch him to see how he reacts when I fly at him. Look for openings. Weaknesses. In actuality, killing a god is practically impossible. But we might be able to hurt him, and hopefully chase him off before he can hurt us or anyone else. That's our play. Sound good to you?"

"Aye, I can live with that," I confessed, though deep down a part of me knew that wasn't true. Whether it happened now or some indeterminate time in the future, Chernobog had to die. And the longer it took to make that a reality, the more devastation he'd cause—and something told me he wouldn't hold back the way other gods might.

Hilde dropped into a staggered squat, her sword and shield at the ready. From her shoulder blades, a pair of metallic wings unfurled. Seeing their slender, aerodynamic shape, I was reminded of what another Valkyrie had said about Hilde's particular specialty—her midair maneuverability. It also made me wonder how she'd become a Valkyrie in the first place. Had she inherited the title from her mother? Had she been raised as a Valkyrie? What kind of childhood could that have possibly been?

Hilde sprinted forward and took off, the gusts from her wings whipping at my hair and reminding me this was no time to get distracted. Thinking to find a better vantage point, I jogged in the same direction, keeping an eye on Chernobog the whole time. The god had packed on even more mass, though he'd lost his proportions in the process; what awaited Hilde was a vaguely man-shaped creature, the size of a townhouse, covered in tar.

The Valkyrie went low to start, flying around one of Chernobog's legs to see how he'd react. The god treated her like a buzzing insect, swinging at her like one might swat a fly. Fortunately, he was far too slow to do any harm. Hilde adjusted in midair, rising up between the god's legs to hover a few feet from his exposed back. It was an absurd opening. A chance to possibly end this fight before it really began. I saw Hilde realize the same thing, watched as she decided to abandon the plan and strike, and knew it was a mistake.

Because, beneath all that oil, Chernobog was still grinning.

"Hilde, don't!" I shouted.

But it was too late.

A third appendage emerged from Chernobog's back with a wrenching, popping sound just as Hilde raised her sword to plunge it into his spine. A fist of black tar struck the Valkyrie like a battering ram, though she did manage to somehow get her shield up in time for it to take at least a portion of the damage. Worse, Chernobog wasn't done; the second his blow hit, crude oil splashed across Hilde's chest and arms, hardening so swiftly it kept her pinned in place as surely as if he'd snatched her from the sky.

Surprisingly, Hilde didn't struggle. Instead, she brought her sword down at an angle as if she might saw through the whole damned wrist. It was a bold move, and one I respected. Unfortunately, her blade got stuck the instant it bit at his arm. And that's when Hilde started to thrash.

Realizing it was all over for the Valkyrie if she couldn't break free, I changed directions, forced to hold Areadbhar angled so that her tip nearly grazed the stone floor. Wolves, watching the skirmish but not wanting to get directly involved, scrambled out of my way as I reached the base of the ramp. Having no time to explain, I ignored Morgan's cry as I sprinted past, only distantly aware that I was covering more ground in less time than I ever had before. Finally, three-quarters of the way up, I took all that momentum and used it.

I couldn't fly, that much was true.

But I could fall...with style.

I leapt from the top of the ramp, clearing an absurd distance in a bid to strike unexpectedly from above. Which might have worked...if I'd had even the remotest idea what I was doing.

I came down intending to plunge Areadbhar into Chernobog's arm with all the force I could muster. Granted, even that wasn't a fool-proof plan; Hilde's blade hadn't fared so well in a similar exchange. But Areadbhar was no ordinary weapon. Hell, she made even extraordinary weapons pale by comparison.

Sadly, what I hadn't accounted for was how difficult it was to maneuver in midair. Which was probably why, when I finally did come down, I did so staring up at the moon—wondering how badly this was going to hurt and whether I'd die now or a few minutes from now.

When I landed, however, I did so on something soft but not entirely yielding. Someone shrieked in pain—quite possibly me. Eventually, though, whatever it was snapped beneath my weight, effectively breaking my fall so that—when I hit the ground—the worst I experienced was a brutal loss of breath. Once I got that back, I groaned and sat up.

And found the bottom third of Chernobog's arm lying beside me. I stared at it in shock until the sound of Hilde prying herself loose from the god's dismembered hand, the oil no longer solidified, got my attention. Overhead, it seemed Chernobog was trying to reach his wounded appendage with his good arms, his howls so loud I could have mistaken them for thunder. Of course, that still meant there was a distinct possibility of getting stepped on.

"Hilde, we need to move!" I scrambled to my feet and ran to her side, grabbing her by the arm that didn't look broken.

"That was the craziest stunt I've ever seen in my whole life, you know that? And I'm a *Valkyrie*." Hilde spat out a gob of black gunk. "I mean, using your whole body to take out his arm? Seriously? How did you know that would even work?"

I debated telling her the truth but ultimately decided that would only make me seem *more* reckless, not less. So instead, I offered her a blithe, noncommittal reply and hooked the Valkyrie's good arm over my shoulders. Together, we began trudging forward, not content to stop until we were well out of the god's reach.

Unfortunately, Chernobog had other plans.

"Look out!" Hilde cried, shoving us aside just in time to avoid being stomped on.

I skidded to a knee and glared up at the grisly bastard as he raised his foot for another strike. Hilde, meanwhile, was struggling to rise. I cursed, knowing she was in too bad shape to move and that Chernobog had no intention of missing a second time. So, rather than try to drag her out of harm's way, I made my stand.

I ducked the Valkyrie's arm and lunged in the same motion, driving Areadbhar point blank into the fucker's heel. At first, there was so much give it felt like I'd shoved her into a foam mattress. Thankfully, that changed the instant the god drove his foot downward; the blade broke through the mucky exterior and—at last—pierced skin.

"Areadbhar!" I bellowed, my muscles screaming with the effort it took to hold her steady against the weight of his foot.

A smoldering light appeared as her flames reached the god's flesh, only to grow and spread like wildfire the instant they reached his oily exterior. Within seconds, Chernobog's entire foot was aflame, and he was dancing away on the other like a child who'd stepped on a fire ant nest.

Forced to withdraw Areadbhar or risk getting dragged about and possibly trampled, I quickly gathered Hilde up and made a break for it. At this point, however, my own exhaustion was beginning to take its toll; the enhanced strength and speed were as excellent as advertised, but the suit could do nothing for my stamina. It seemed running at a full out pace, leaping from a hundred feet up, amputating a god's arm with my sweet backside, and lighting said god's foot on fire was my limit.

Who knew?

We both collapsed at the base of the ramp, our chests heaving, surrounded by pitiful-looking wolves. Zeke, I noticed, was no longer grinning. In fact, they all looked like they wanted to cut and run. Not that I blamed them.

"Well, are you satisfied?" Morgan asked as she strolled up to us, her face stern with disapproval. "You went up against a god and gave him a case of hot foot. Very commendable. Now, shouldn't we be going?"

A tall, bipedal creature rose from amidst the pack, her body covered in a short brindle coat that made her look more jungle cat than werewolf. Still, there was no mistaking she was the one in charge; the other wolves prostrated themselves the instant she stood, their muzzles flat against their paws.

"How 'bout it? Y'all plan to keep fighting?" Pauline asked, her Ozarkian accent garbled in the mouth of a wolf. Too many teeth, I figured. Not to mention the elongated tongue.

"Of course they aren't!" Morgan snapped. "It would be suicide. Look, he's already recovering!"

As she said, Chernobog seemed to have dealt with the flames before they got too far along. Which was a shame, because his burning corpse would have made for one hell of a bonfire. As things stood, he'd already begun reapplying oil to his injured foot.

"What d'ye want to do?" I asked as I exchanged looks with Hilde, who simply shrugged her uninjured shoulder.

"I would prefer to get my sword back," she said, grinning through blackened teeth.

"Aye, one should never leave one's sword behind," I acknowledged, sagely. "Pretty sure Jesus said that."

"I should've known," Pauline replied with a yip of laughter. She gestured at her packmates while Morgan sputtered and spat. "Way I see it, this thing was gonna come for us all, eventually. To him, we're all just prey. Which means there ain't no sense in running away and letting y'all do this by your lonesomes. Besides, we owe you one for looking after Leon."

"Leon?" I asked, surprised.

"That's where Jimmy and Lakota went instead of coming here," Hilde explained. "They found out he'd gone to that theater to investigate what happened to his brother."

"He's a good kid," Pauline said. "Shame what happened to Mike. But we'll make that right when the time comes."

"Ye won't have to," I replied, pointing to the stage, then to the bodies of the fallen witches they'd hunted down and torn apart. "Everyone who had anythin' to do with that is dead and gone. All that's left is dealin' with the ugly mess they created."

Of course, that wasn't entirely true.

Sadly, I couldn't reveal the fact that there had been a mastermind behind this whole gruesome affair. Because Liam was mine, and I wasn't interested in sharing.

"Well then, I think it's about time we help y'all with the mop up," Pauline snarled. "Isn't that right, folks!"

Howls greeted the Alpha's challenge.

"You will all die," Morgan insisted the moment they died down, sounding more exasperated than upset. She began pointing to each of us in turn. "Your wolves won't be able to lay a single scratch on him. You can't even lift your arm, let alone challenge a god. And you nearly got yourself killed *without* his help."

When none of us backed down or hung our heads in shame, however, the enchantress simply threw up her hands.

"Hopeless! Suicidal and hopeless! Why do I even bother with you people?" Morgan demanded. But then, so suddenly it put us all on edge, she froze. The enchantress slid her gaze to the left and actually smiled. "Oh Quinn, dear, it looks like you are about to have some company! Be sure to play nice."

I frowned at her delighted tone until I saw what she was looking at: the not-so-distant outline of a Gateway being formed, its edges wreathed in scarlet flames, radiating an absurd amount of heat. A leg appeared, first, then an arm—as if whoever had created it had no idea how a Gateway worked. Of course, by the time the man poked his head out and spotted us, I already knew exactly who had arrived to crash our little mixer.

"Well, if it isn't Mad Max!" I called, waving. "What took ye so long?!"

CHAPTER 42

Thus far, it was safe to say we'd brought the fight to Chernobog, and that we'd done so in a big way, all things considered. We'd killed his possessed slaves, gone on the offensive, and even managed to wound the miserable bastard for our trouble. But we'd also been incredibly lucky. Had Chernobog given us less time to strategize and come after us all sooner, or simply smothered Hilde rather than trying to crush her...well, there was no telling how many ways things could have gone even more sideways. That said, we really should have been better prepared for Chernobog to bring the fight to us.

Because, when he did, none of us were ready.

Fresh from climbing out of his brand-new Gateway, Max had nearly reached us when a gob of piping hot tar came crashing down into our midst. It landed with a splash, its contents showering several werewolves. Almost instantly, the air was rank with the stink of burning fur and melted flesh, accompanied by agonized screams that no dog could possibly have imitated.

A second gob joined the first, further back this time. The wolves began to scatter, some even tearing up the ramp—their over-whelming instinct to flee overcoming all others. Within seconds, pandemonium had broken out as everyone sought cover from Chernobog's long ranged assault. The god was laughing, flames spurting from his maw in bursts as he chucked handful after handful of searing hot pitch at us.

Hilde, Morgan, and I hid behind a shelf of stone that the enchantress had created by picking at her enchantment. I felt helpless and more than a little foolish for thinking I could so easily take down a god. Everywhere I looked, I saw the fallen victims of Chernobog's attacks, their bodies caked in steaming black resin. Some still lived, though their movements were so feeble it was hard to tell how long that would be the case. Pauline was nowhere in sight, and the same was true for Max—though I'd seen both scramble for shelter when the assault began.

"We have to stop this." Hilde hugged her injured side like it ached, but you wouldn't have known it to look at her face. "If I can get out there and fly, he'll start aiming for me. I'm sure of it."

"You're too hurt for that," I insisted. "I should go. I'm not an easy target, either. Ye need to get everyone out of here. Morgan was right. Better to run and live to fight another day."

"As much as I love hearing you say that," Morgan said, "and I do, truly...I think we may have another alternative."

"Aye, but..." I glanced down at the bracelet, feeling its weight like a manacle around my wrist. Only an hour before, I'd have removed it in a heartbeat if it meant saving those who couldn't save themselves. I told myself then that I could bear the consequences. That—even if Morgan turned out to be right and I'd been placing limitations on myself this whole time—I could afford to lose myself if it meant finding out who I was meant to be. Only...what if the goddess I was meant to become was no different than Chernobog? What if, at my very core, I was destined to give into my darkest impulses?

"Oh, no, not that," Morgan said, patting my arm. "I was actually thinking more about the other thing we talked about. The sex thing."

"You want her to have sex with that monster?!" Hilde exclaimed, utterly aghast.

"I mean, he's pretty big, but I wouldn't call Max a monster."

Morgan replied, cocking an eyebrow. "Of course, we all have different tastes."

"She thought ye meant Chernobog," I explained. "Not that it matters. I won't be jumpin' Max's bones right now, either."

"Too classy?" Morgan drawled.

"Too messy," I replied, showcasing the canyon floor and its patchwork of sizzling puddles. "*And* too classy."

"Shame, I'd have paid good money to see that. But honestly, I don't think sex is a must for you two. To channel your combined power, that is. I still say if you don't get that out of your system soon, you're going to implode."

"You haven't slept with the man you brought?" Hilde asked, only slightly less appalled than she'd been when she thought Morgan had proposed I seduce the sick bastard trying to actively murder us all.

"No, why?"

"Oh, no reason. I would have lost that bet, that's all."

"I know, right?" Morgan said, going all bug-eyed.

"Ye two are just two gossipin' old ladies, aren't ye? Come on, we don't have time to waste. What were ye sayin' about channelin' power?"

Morgan had only just opened her mouth to explain herself when the barrage ended. The three of us, surprised, craned our ears, waiting for a renewal of that horrifically repetitious splat and tell-tale hiss. When it didn't happen, we poked our heads out to see what had changed.

At first, all I could make out was the silhouette of a shirtless man approaching the god, his muscular arms bare and held out to either side, palms up like some sort of saint. Fire danced along his naked back—tongues of flame that arced and twirled in a hypnotic pattern. Chernobog, for his part, seemed unusually wary; the god had taken several steps backwards and raised both arms, defensively. Something about the brujo's heat, his elemental power, had done what we could not: frightened a god.

"What's he doing?" Hilde asked, her voice laced with something like awe.

I didn't wait to hear an answer. Instead, I raced after the brujo. Frankly, it didn't matter to me; whatever Max hoped to achieve, I couldn't let him do it alone. I owed him that much, at the very least.

"Max! Wait up!"

The brujo hesitated and turned to see who was calling him, his eyes glowing scarlet with power. Relieved that he'd stopped, I waved with the hand not holding the spear, perhaps only thirty seconds or so away from closing the gap between us. Max waved back with the same eagerness, clearly mimicking me.

And that's when Chernobog chose to make his move.

The god snatched up a wad of that murky black tar the instant Max was distracted, hurling it with hardly a sound so that only I knew it was coming. Realizing the brujo was in danger, I flung out a hand in warning. But it was already too late; there was no way Max could move out of the way before it struck.

"Max, look out!" I yelled in vain, tormented by the thought of him suffering the same awful fate as those who lay wounded or dead behind us.

In response, the brujo raised his own hand—almost as though bidding farewell, as if he understood what was about to happen. Except that hand was not aimed at me, but at Chernobog. Before I could figure out why, however, a brutal surge of heat sent me skidding to a stop, forcing me to reflexively shield my eyes. The blast of hot air that accompanied the tar when it hit its target, I realized. I felt something in my chest give way in that moment, a sob caught in my throat.

I didn't want to look.

But I knew I had to.

I lowered my arms, prepared for the worst, only to discover the heat I'd felt had an altogether different source: Max himself. From the brujo's outstretched palm spewed a raging tornado of flame that had taken Chernobog in the center of his chest. The tar the god had chucked at Max was nowhere to be seen—likely consumed by the gyrating inferno the brujo had seemingly conjured up from nowhere.

You cannot kill me, Salamander! Your kind never could.

Chernobog's voice rang in my head like a gong, his rage tempered by a perverse sort of glee. Worse, it seemed he was right. The column of fire continued to burn so hot that sweat dripped down my face from beneath my helmet simply from being near it. And yet, though Chernobog couldn't do much to stop it, he did withstand it.

"You begged, and I came."

Having closed as much of the distance as I dared while that fire raged, I found myself standing near enough that—when the strange, slithering voice spilled from Max's lips—I could hear every word. It took me a few awkward seconds, however, before I realized the statement was directed at me.

"Are ye the Salamander?" I asked, on a hunch. "The spirit coiled around Max's heart, I mean? The one keepin' him alive?"

"Fire is life. And fire is death."

Oh good, I thought, because nothing makes a person feel saner than holding a philosophical conversation with a creature who'd recently immigrated from an abstract plane of existence only to hijack the mouth of its host like some he was some sort of sexy flesh puppet. Out loud, however, I said, "And what does that mean, exactly?"

"It means you must choose."

"Choose? Choose what?"

"Life...or death."

"Look, I'm not sure what ye want from me, but—"

Max dismissed the inferno, reached back, and caught my wrist in one smooth motion before I could finish my sentence—sending a jolt of so much power up my arm in the process that I nearly dropped Areadbhar. And yet, for some reason, I didn't mind.

In fact, I found myself staring down at that hand in fascination, mesmerized by the patterns that swirled across his knuckles and up his forearm. Somehow, I knew in that moment that they were, in fact, meant to be camouflage. That every Salamander's skin could mimic such flames, which was all that saved them from being discovered by those who once exploited and abused them.

Namely, the gods.

On the heels of that alien thought, a series of images flooded my brain. Horrific scenes of Salamanders being thrown in cages that could only have been crafted by the cruelest of creators. Except, according to the visions, it wasn't just Salamanders they'd collected. There were other spirits, too, locked away in cages designed to trap their respective elements and eat away at their essence. The Sylphs. The Undine. The Gnomes. All had suffered. Few had survived.

"I'm sorry," I whispered, filled with unexpected sorrow at the loss of so many. "I didn't know."

"You begged, and I came," the Salamander replied, commandeering Max's mouth once more. For a moment, I assumed the elemental was merely repeating the phrase, until it added another to the mix. "You were the first. The only one who ever begged for our help. And now, you must choose."

That again.

"Aye, between life or death ye said...but I'm still not sure what that means."

"Fire is life."

As he spoke the words, I saw in my mind's eye all those who'd been hurt and left to die. I could sense their hearts beating, could feel the dwindling heat of their bodies, and knew I could use the Salamander's power to save them.

"Fire is death."

This time, I saw Chernobog. He stood probing at the exposed meat of his chest, his fingertips grazing the smoking hole the Salamander's opening salvo had left behind. I realized I could sense his heart, too, pumping so slowly it was a wonder he needed one, at all. Of course, he really wouldn't—not if we poured our combined power into him.

Suddenly, I understood.

"Ye have the power to grant life, as well as end it."

"Yes."

"But I have to choose?"

"Yes."

"Why me?"

"Because you are the one who begged, and I am the one who came."

"Meanin' ye make the rules, is that it?"

To that, the elemental had nothing to say.

So, it seemed the responsibility fell to me, and to me alone. I could either choose to use the Salamander's power to save perhaps the half dozen wounded who remained, or to kill the god who'd hurt them and so many others. For some people, it might have been a tough choice. One of those needs of the many, needs of the few scenarios that ordinary people seem to obsess over.

Frankly, I thought it was a no-brainer.

"Fire is life," I said, yanking my wrist free and pushing past the elemental. "Go ahead and take care of 'em. *I'll* be death."

What happened next was one of those crystalline moments in life you replay over and over again in your mind, unable to explain *how* you did what you did—only knowing that you did it. For some, it's an athletic memory. A full court shot at the buzzer to win a high school game, or a state qualifying time that you never got close to again. For others, it's academic. That time you aced a test you forgot to study for, or the two-week assignment you knocked out the night before.

In my case, it was a memory of driving home from a summer job after a hot shift in the sun, practically dozing as I cruised along all-too-familiar streets with my window down. After the long day I'd had, I was essentially on autopilot, my mind occupied by thoughts of concerts and my senior year and boys. And yet, when the driver directly in front of me slammed on his brakes for no discernible reason, I remember executing a flawless lane transition in under two seconds, pulling in neatly between two other cars and avoiding an accident by the narrowest of margins.

I still couldn't explain how I'd done it, exactly; it had all happened so fast. But I had, and—as a result—I'd pulled off something relatively extraordinary without ever considering the improbabilities.

This was just like that.

I reared back, hastily judged the distance to the target, and launched Areadbhar into the air with every ounce of strength I had.

The spear flew from my hand, the devourer in her blade leaving a trail of darkness in her wake as her slender form raced towards Chernobog. The god, hunched over to collect more of his precious oil to patch the hole in his chest, looked up just as she began her descent. He roared with amusement, rose, and flung out one hand to deflect the spear and thereby end this desultory attempt on his life.

Unfortunately for him, in this particular instance, Areadbhar wasn't a spear.

She was a heat-seeking missile.

The legendary weapon swerved in midair, ducking under his careless swipe and descending upon that circle of exposed flesh like a ravenous bird of prey. Between one breath and the next, her blade burrowed deep into the meat of his chest, driving inexorably forward in search of his foul black heart.

The god collapsed to one knee, coughing up billowing plumes of smoke as he reached for the shaft—likely hoping to draw her out so his immortal flesh could recover. Of course, there was no way in hell I was going to let that happen.

I held out my hand, beckoning the first Jewel of the Tuatha Dé Danann to come back the way she went. And come back she did; the mess she made of the god's chest on her way out, though, was easily twice as bad as what she'd made going in. So much so, in fact, that by the time I held her once more, Chernobog had collapsed with a satisfying thud, the spark that had once occupied his eyes reflected in the nebulous facets of my devourer.

CHAPTER 43

I couldn't be sure how long I sat on the lip of the stage staring at the rotting flesh of a god, waiting for his corpse to rise up and torment us once again. Could have been five minutes, could have been an hour. Either way, by the time I was certain I'd never have to see that odious son of a bitch again outside my nightmares and turned away, I found the elemental had upheld its end of the bargain. On the far side of the canyon, four-legged figures drenched in black pitch rose and shook themselves dry like dogs after a bath. The pack—smaller now, but still formidable—gathered around them, prancing and howling like some sort of miracle had been performed.

And maybe it had.

For the moment, it seemed everyone else was keeping their distance, perhaps anticipating I'd need some time alone. Hell, maybe they were avoiding me. I mean, I *had* killed a god after all. The thought made me want to laugh. Frankly, I was far too numb to weigh that burden against my conscience just yet. Too much had happened in too short a span to worry about the implications, or the fallout.

Besides, now that it wasn't the source of all my problems, I realized there was a supermoon to appreciate.

I gazed up at that celestial orb in abject awe until something—a sound, perhaps, or a furtive movement caught out of the corner of my eye—brought me back to earth. I twisted about to scan the stage behind me, surprised to find it so empty. After everything that had happened here, the fact that it was no longer covered in blood and corpses seemed almost perverse, in a way. Like visiting a concentration camp decades after the fact.

Except...that wasn't right.

Because—even if you counted all thirteen of the possessed—that left two of the primary players unaccounted for.

I swung my legs around, clambered to my feet, and began investigating by moonlight. Almost immediately, I found what I was looking for: a blood trail that led me to the shadowed recesses of the canyon wall. I came upon a figure sitting in the dark, propped up against the stone. When I was unable to tell whom, however, I whispered Areadbhar's name. Flames licked the edges of her blade, acting like a torch for me to see by.

Angelika squinted but didn't turn away from that light. Probably because she couldn't; her right leg was bent at an unnatural angle, her left side misshapen, and her dress was no longer silver at all, but crimson. When I stepped closer to inspect her wounds, I nearly stumbled over the other body I'd expected to find. Bredon's corpse was curled up in a ball with his head in her lap, his face mercifully turned away.

"I saw what you did," Angelika rasped, her strangled voice emerging from a throat patinated with bruises. "To Chernobog."

I turned to look back at the god's body. It had begun to crumble under its own weight, going grey like charcoal after it's been used up. Soon, there would be nothing left but stains and ash. "Aye, I killed the bastard."

Angelika's smile was mocking. "You took his soul."

"So what if I did?" I gestured vaguely at the dead man laying across her body. "It's not like I murdered innocent people for access to power."

"Not power." Angelika licked dry, chapped lips. "Justice."

For some reason, I believed her. Not that it excused what she'd done; killing people in cold blood and dumping their bodies wasn't justice, it was psychotic. "Aye, well...from where I stand, it seems like you're gettin' a taste of that, yourself. I hope it's as bitter as it looks."

"His lies..." Angelika coughed until her chin was flecked with blood. "Sweet. Thought I was doing...right thing."

"Liam, aye..." I drifted off, momentarily overwhelmed by a righteous sense of rage I hadn't felt in a long time. "Don't ye worry about Liam. He'll get his, and soon. I know where that fucker lives."

The witch grunted what sounded like an attempt at a laugh, her eyes drawn to a symbol she'd painted on the floor from her own blood. It was eerily similar to the mark that had been painted on the foreheads of her companions but *felt* different. If I'd had to quantify that, I'd have said it was like looking at the symbol of a cross turned right side up after only having seen it upside down.

"I kept him safe...and stopped Chernobog...from leaving for as long...as I could. I am sorry I could...not do...more. I...am so..."

I'd already opened my mouth to ask her to speak up, when I realized there was no point. Angelika was already dead. It wasn't until I reached out to close her sightless eyes, however, that I wondered at the improbability that she'd ended up here of all places, given her injuries. And with Bredon's body in tow, no less? It must have taken incredible reserves. And what had that bit about stopping Chernobog been about? Was it possible *she* was somehow responsible for keeping Chernobog rooted to the stage?

If so, she might just have saved all our lives.

"Still doesn't make us even," I grumbled as I squatted over Bredon, wondering if I should try and bring his body back with us. Surely he had family who would want to bury him. I laid a hand on his cold, lifeless shoulder.

And that's when the corpse lifted his head, groaning.

"Whoa!" I scrambled backwards, pointing Areadbhar directly at the freshly risen zombie, my heart hammering away in my chest.

"Huh?" Bredon turned to look up at me with bleary eyes, rubbing at his mane of reddish blonde hair. "Who are you?"

I lowered my spear, incrementally.

"Where am I?" Bredon asked, scanning first the horizon, then the sky, and finally me. He eyed my armor especially, squinting up at the rune emblazoned across my breastplate. "Is this Jutland? No, too humid. Frisia? Wait, wrong century. Hold on, I'll get it in a minute."

"Are ye alright?" I asked, worried the poor fellow must have some sort of brain damage to go along with having, you know, died.

"I don't know." Bredon ran his hands down his face, inspecting it, then down his chest, until at last he found the bloodstained hole in his tunic where he'd been stabbed through the heart. Miraculously, there was no wound. And yet, for some reason, the instant his fingers touched bare flesh, he threw his head back and groaned.

"What is it?" I asked, alarmed. "Are ye hurt?"

"Dammit!" Bredon bellowed. "Did I really die, *again*?"

I gaped at the bizarre young man, finding myself at a total loss for words. Fortunately, a pair of distraught figures hollered for me before I had to puzzle out a response. I turned to find a half-naked brujo and maskless enchantress frantically searching the stage. Concerned, I asked Bredon to hold that thought and called them over, waving my impromptu torch for good measure.

"Over here!"

"It is Camila!" Max exclaimed the second he reached me, sparing hardly a glance for the fallen witch or the once-dead man. "She is not answering my calls."

"We think she and Maria went ahead with their plan," Morgan added as she joined us, her expression clouded with genuine concern. "Only I just learned who it was they were going up against! We should go to them, now!"

"Wait!" I insisted, holding up a hand to calm them both. "Who are they goin' up against? And what plan? D'ye mean the one involvin' the Hex Moon?"

"*Sí*, Morgan told me everything," Max replied, hastily. "My sister laid a trap at an old iron mine using bait guaranteed to lure all the Fae in the area. Then Maria found Petal and her people a charm that would protect them from its effects. It was their job to rescue Robin, while Camila and Maria kept the Fae busy."

"It was an ingenious plan, really," Morgan added, her tone implying she'd had a great deal to do with it. "The spell I crafted for them was designed to keep the Fae trapped until the caster set them free. That way, all they had to do was extract the proper oaths before releasing them all."

"But..." I said, waving her along.

"But then Max told me who'd taken over! Maria never mentioned her name, or I'd have never let them go through with it."

"Wait, ye mean Catha?" I asked, perplexed.

"Yes!"

"Why? What's she got to do with it?"

"She isn't Fae, obviously!" Morgan replied, rolling her eyes at me like I was being obtuse on purpose. "The trap won't work on her, and neither will the spell!"

"How d'ye know that? D'ye know who she is?"

"Of course I do! And so do you, you silly thing! Catha. *Babd* Catha. The Battle Crow. *Your* blasted aunt!"

CHAPTER 44

After promising to check on him later, I left poor Bredon with Hilde and the rest of those staying behind to lick their wounds, which meant only Max, Morgan, and myself were preparing to go through the Gateway. The Valkyrie had wanted to come, of course, but I wasn't willing to risk her hurting herself any further on my account. Besides, this was Boston business.

Strike that, family business.

I wasn't sure what to think about the infamous Catha being my Aunt Babd. On the one hand, it made perfect sense; both Petal and Gretel had certainly implied something to that effect, though I couldn't figure out for the life of me why they hadn't just come out and told me. On the other, it raised a whole mess of pertinent questions. Like why, for example, was she looking for me? Why bring the slaugh along with her from Fae? What was her connection to Liam and all that had happened here?

Determined to ask her directly, I checked myself over for the third time, gearing up for the most tiresome, maddening square on life's BINGO card: the family reunion.

"She is almost ready," Max said, eyeing me from his peripheral vision before returning his attention to the enchantress. After tapping into so much magic earlier, she'd needed a few minutes longer to prepare. Which was good because it had given Max a chance to find his shirt.

"And how are ye?" I asked, realizing we hadn't yet spoken about his alter ego's hostile takeover.

"I am fine," Max sighed. "It is not unpleasant, when the creature stirs. I am not in control, but I am aware of what it wants. What it thinks. It was very pleased when you chose to use its power the way you did. And very scared when you attacked the god, alone. We both were."

"It sort of just happened," I confessed, shrugging hard enough that my armor clanked when it settled. "I saw an opening, and I took it."

"And if you had failed?"

"Then I'd probably be dead."

"That does not bother you?"

"Death? No, not really. Life is the scary part."

"So, you saw your chance, and you took it."

"Pretty much—"

Max was suddenly there before I could finish, pulling off my helmet and pressing my armored body against his with enough force that I ended up on my toes. I was so surprised I actually squeaked, releasing Areadbhar so that my hands were pressed against his chest as though I planned to push him away—which, for a moment, I seriously considered. When I didn't, however, he brought his lips to hover over mine, his dark eyes searching for the slightest hint of a yes. I slid my hand up his chest, past his neck, and traced that perfect jawline until I reached his dimpled chin and pulled.

The kiss was...not nearly enough.

The second his lips met mine, our tongues twining, our bodies mimicking with clothes on what we'd have much preferred to do with them off; it was like I could no longer ignore all the pent-up sexual tension between us. What had once simply hummed in the background had become an operatic seduction worthy of a Baz Luhrman film. Worse, it seemed we both knew it.

Max pulled away, first. "No time."

"Later," I said, breathily. "I mean definitely sooner rather than later. But later."

"Well, whatever you decide, do be sure to take pictures for posterity," Morgan chimed in, grinning like the cat who ate the chimera. The enchantress beckoned us, flapping her hand madly back and forth as though we were the ones holding everything up. "Come along, love birds! We haven't got all night. Apparently."

Max handed me back my helmet while I retrieved my spear, the two of us blushing so hard I thought I might have a face to match my hair. A few seconds later, we fell in at her back, physically aware of each other in ways we hadn't been only a few minutes before. The enchantress, meanwhile, pointed two fingers and waved them in ever-widening circles until a ring of sparks formed in the air. It expanded, growing wider and wider until I could make out a moonlit landscape not terribly unlike our own. A quarry, perhaps? I remembered Morgan saying something about an iron mine, which meant we were at least several miles north of the city.

"I'll go first," I said as soon as the Gateway was large enough to pass through. I slipped by the enchantress holding Areadbhar at the ready.

"Be careful," Morgan warned, sounding worried. "We have no idea what we can expect once we're over there."

I'd only just turned to say something cavalier and reassuring, however, when both she and Max lunged forward, simultaneously. I had about half a second to wonder what on earth they were doing when a sinuous arm snaked around my waist and yanked me backwards so hard I actually dropped Areadbhar. The owner of that appendage raised me high and flung me to the ground like a rag doll. A blinding light and the acrid stench of burning ozone immediately followed, accompanied by a scream that sounded like Morgan's.

"Quinn!" Max yelled. "Quinn, come—"

The rest of what the brujo had to say was lost, however, swallowed up the instant the Gateway snapped shut. Another voice, so familiar it raised unbidden memories of the goddess it belonged to, filled the chilling silence that followed.

"If anyone else tries to interrupt, kill 'em."

CHAPTER 45

I lay flat on my back with the wind knocked out of me, staring up at a dark-haired figure dressed in so much black leather that her pale skin seemed luminescent by comparison. Or maybe that was the moonlight itself; the Hex Moon shone brighter here than it had in the mountains of the Ozarks, for some reason. Next to her stood a moor troll—larger and swarthier than their bridge troll cousins, his kind were notorious for guiding those wayward travelers who wandered lost among the fog, primarily to their deaths. Rumor had it they were meaner, too. I'd never met one before, myself.

"Get her up," Babd commanded.

The same arm that had taken me and the others by surprise a moment ago came down like the trunk of some enormous elephant to wind across my chest and yank me, quite violently, to my feet. The arm retreated as quickly as it had come, like a turtle's head, into the furry mass of a Faeling creature even I thought was made up.

"That's enough, Fachan, ye can go."

The Fachan bared its razor-sharp teeth, blinked its singular eye, turned on its heel, and hopped away on its one and only leg. All of which should have been odd, at worst. And yet, having stared into that baleful creature's eye, I felt infinitely better the moment it left.

"Where d'ye find that one?" I asked, offhandedly.

"Shut her up."

The moor troll backhanded me so hard it sent my helmet flying and created a ringing in my ears. I blinked through spots in my vision, the right side of my face stinging with pain. I spat, tasting blood.

"Is that any way to talk to family?" I rasped.

"What part of shut her up didn't ye understand?" Babd snapped as though she hadn't heard me, planting her fists on her hips for emphasis.

The moor troll raised his hand again, preparing to slap me once more, open palmed this time. Unfortunately, I'd already given the flunky his freebie for the evening. This time, he was going to have to pay the toll.

I waited until the troll's hand descended and went up under the intended blow, effectively trapping his arm while I threw all my weight into his shoulder and rode his sorry ass to the ground. From there, all I typically had to do was lean back and apply pressure on the shoulder joint to make my opponent tap out. Sadly, nothing about this scenario was typical. One, because this wasn't a sparring match. And two, because my opponent outweighed me by a couple hundred pounds.

Which was why I had no choice but to pop his arm out of its socket.

I flipped over the troll's back, keeping hold of his wrist, and essentially worked it like you might a water pump—using all my weight to force the limb in a direction it wasn't meant to go. The joint snapped loose with a wet pop, and the moor troll began to squeal like a stuck pig. I released the wrist, straightened, and turned just in time to find myself held three feet off the ground by my throat.

"Who do ye t'ink ye are, hurting me people without me permission?" Babd demanded, shaking me for emphasis.

"You're tellin' me ye don't even recognize your favorite niece?" Thanks to the gorget around my neck, I spoke without any strain. "That's almost hurtful, Auntie Babd. It's me, Quinn."

"Quinn..." Babd lowered me until my feet hit the ground. "Aye, I've been lookin' for Quinn...d'ye know where she is?"

"What? Don't be ridiculous, I'm right here." I took hold of her wrist, squeezed, and pried her hand from my throat. "Look at me, Babd. It's Quinn. Morr—Nemain's daughter."

"Nemain...Macha!" Babd snatched both my arms, her expression ravaged by some wretched emotion. "We have to save Macha! Before it's too late!"

"Easy there," I soothed, realizing for the first time that I might be dealing with someone who wasn't simply violent, but quite possibly mad. "What's happened to Aunt Macha?"

"You!"

Over Babd's shoulder, four figures approached. The two in the middle I recognized immediately, though they'd been smacked around so much their faces were puffy and mottled with bruises. Still, the eyes of the two Hispanic women remained defiant even as their captors tugged them forward by the ropes that bound their hands. The captors themselves I clocked only a few seconds later. The first was Albi, standing tall and menacing like some nightmarish version of the Easter Bunny. The second, and the Faeling who'd spoken, was Liam.

"How did you get here?" Liam demanded. The Gancanagh passed Maria's rope over to the Pooka dismissively and came marching up to the two of us, his humor from earlier supplanted by a seething rage. "You should be dead."

"Why? Because ye sicced a god on me?" I shook myself loose from Babd's grip and faced the soon-to-be-dead Faeling. "You'll have to do better than that, ye two-faced fuck."

"Did you escape, then? I knew I shouldn't have come back here until I was sure. Still, I'd have thought he'd make short work of you and your friends. Maybe he slept too long?" Liam waved that away. "Oh well, I'm sure he'll shake off the rust, soon enough."

"Oh, he tried." I shrugged, insinuating Chernobog's attempts to murder us all had been less than impressive. "Also, and I hate to be the one to tell ye, I t'ink it's hard to shake off the rust if you're dead."

"You killed him?" Liam asked, shock writ large across his face. Then, to my surprise, he cracked a wide smile that turned into gut-busting laughter. "All that work, and *you* killed him? Tonight is just getting better and better!"

"Liam? Liam, what is this?" Babd asked, sounding eerily like a lost child. "What's happenin'?"

Like he'd flicked some sort of switch, the Gancanagh's whole manner changed in an instant. He reached out, taking my aunt to his breast like a lover, and patted her head. "It's alright, m'lady. Everything is fine. The slaugh await your word to hunt down the traitors. We have captured the mortal witches who planned to expose you. All that's left is to deal with this wretched creature that came here to kill you."

Liam turned my own aunt to look at me, pointing. His skin had already begun to shimmer. Indeed, by the time he looked up at me I could hardly gaze at his face without feeling the urge to touch it. Babd, of course, did just that—pulling him into a kiss that left her glowing with her own power.

"That's pretty impressive," Albi remarked, his voice as bland as I'd ever heard it. "Using your power on a goddess, and in the midst of all this iron, no less..."

I tracked the Pooka's gaze, realizing he was right: we were surrounded by iron. Not ore deposits, of course, otherwise it wouldn't have been abandoned. Instead, the limestone vista was littered with rusted iron beams—the kind that were used as train tracks before the newer, higher quality rails were invented. They sat piled atop each other in sad bundles, maybe six to a stack.

"Mind your own business, Albi," Liam snarled, though I noticed the loving expression he bestowed on Babd never so much as flickered.

"I'm only pointing out we could have gotten these two talking a lot sooner if you'd have taken the lead," Albi replied, scratching idly at his cheek, his furry hand matted with his captives' blood. "I mean, it's nearly midnight...on the night of the Hex Moon."

"I said keep your thoughts to yourself," Liam snapped. "If you're so concerned about the time, why don't you go send the slaugh after their prey."

"They listen to her, not me," Albi replied.

"Babd," Liam whispered lovingly, "will you send the slaugh? For me?"

"Of course, Liam," the goddess replied, petting his cheek. "Ye have but to name your prey, and the slaugh will hunt the poor, unfortunate souls to the ends of this realm."

"And will you fight this one?" Liam released my aunt, giving her a light shove in my general direction. "She wanted to sneak in here and challenge you. She believes you are no match for her. And look at what she's already done to your favorite troll!"

The moor troll sat cradling his wounded arm, looking nowhere near as fierce as he had when I first laid eyes on him.

"She wants to fight me?" Babd glared at me, her momentary indecision replaced by the promise of violence. She took a threatening step forward, tiny arcs of electricity dancing along her fingertips. "Surely no one is that stupid. I am Babd Catha, goddess of battle."

"Yes, you are, my love," Liam replied, already turning his back on us as Babd began stripping off her bulkier, more cumbersome leathers. "Enjoy nesting her to death."

"Wait!" I yelled, hoping to stall while I came up with a plan that didn't involve going toe to toe with my batshit crazy aunt. I caught Albi looking at me, his sickly yellow eyes flicking to the sky and back like he was trying to tell me something. Wait...what had he said before, about it being before midnight? And the Hex Moon...

"Don't bother trying to get out of this by talking," Liam warned, cheerily. "When she's like this, you either have to knock her out, or kill her. Otherwise, you'll be dead."

"What, ye refuse to fight me, yourself? Are ye a coward? Or are ye that disloyal? Because, if ye ask me, those who are *loyal* to someone should always serve that person's best interests, whatever they may be."

Albi merely blinked at me, his expression sour.

"What a charming sentiment," Liam replied. "To tell you the

truth, I'm actually rooting for you. I'd never have wasted all that time in the Ozarks if I'd known there was a local ringer who could take this one down. Good luck!"

The Gancanagh beckoned Albi to follow him, presumably so he could tell the slaugh to hunt down Petal and the others who'd gone to rescue Robin. But the Pooka declined.

"I want to watch this," Albi explained. "I mean, how many battles between the Tuatha Dé will we ever get to see?"

"What did you say?" Liam froze, his whole body tensed.

Albi repeated himself.

"She's one of the Tuatha Dé Danann?" the Gancanagh asked, gesturing at me. "You're sure?"

Albi shrugged. "Rumor has it."

"I don't deal in rumors, Pooka. I deal in facts." Liam marched back to where he'd stood a moment ago. "Show me, then, or I'll have Babd stomp on your pretty little head until I could spread your brains like jam on toast."

"That's just gross," I remarked, thinking furiously. Frankly, I wasn't sure how I was supposed to prove anything to the Gancanagh. Hell, I couldn't say with any certainty that I *was* one of the Tuatha Dé. Though, of course, there was always *that* option...

"That's it," Liam said, his impatience clear. "Babd, get in there and end this."

"Hold on!" I shouted, taking hold of the bracelet Morgan had given me, and holding it up the way someone might produce a grenade as a negotiating tactic. "Are ye sure ye want to find out what I'm capable of? Ye may regret it."

As soon as I said it, I realized I might as well have been talking to myself. *Was* I ready to know what I could do? More importantly, at this point, did I even have a choice? With Areadbhar and my friends left behind, my chances of survival here were slim, at best. And I knew I couldn't count on backup, either. Judging by the lack of reinforcements, I could only assume Morgan had taken a hit, which meant there would be no more Gateways unless Max learned to master his in the next few minutes.

Except...was I really that desperate to survive? I'd meant it when I told Max I wasn't scared to die. Death I could wrap my head around. But becoming something, becoming someone, else just to keep it at bay? That was the part that I struggled with.

Or, at least, that's what I kept telling myself.

But...what if that wasn't all there was to it? What if—instead of giving it different names and characteristics, different manifestations and limitations—I opened myself up to all that power and somehow stayed me?

In that moment, I realized *that* scared me even more; not the fact that I might change, but that I might not. Because, if it *was* me, then there'd be no one and nothing else to blame when I failed to live up to my own expectations.

"Was that a rhetorical question, or..." Liam drawled, snapping me out of my moment of clarity.

"In a way," I replied, grinning like a madwoman.

"Why is your face doing that?"

Why? Because, I thought to myself, now that I knew what I was *truly* afraid of, my hesitance seemed rather silly. So what if I failed as a goddess? I'd failed plenty as a human being, especially over the last few years. That didn't make me a failure. It just meant I had room to grow. And, as a goddess, I'd have all the time in all the worlds to do that.

"Because I know somethin' ye don't."

"You're stalling," Liam said, sounding disappointed. "That's it, I'm—"

A wet gurgle spilled from Liam's mouth just as I began fiddling with the clasp of the bracelet. I hesitated, startled by the sound, and looked up to find the point of a rusted iron rail spike jutting from the Gancanagh's throat. I couldn't be sure if I'd ever seen someone look so shocked. Liam tried to turn his head and see who could have dared, a murderous gleam in his eyes.

Maria, freed from her ropes, refused to let him. Instead, she shoved harder, wedging the impromptu weapon deeper until it threatened to split his neck in two. The Gancanagh began to shine, calling his power in defiance of what should have been a mortal wound and reaching for Babd. The goddess was staring off into space, however, waiting like a trained dog for her lover's command. Except her lover couldn't speak.

And what good was a love-talker who couldn't talk?

Liam, realizing how powerless he was without his voice, panicked. He tried to grab hold of the spike and force it back out. But, with his hands slick from his own blood and the spike being forged from iron, the best he could do was stop Maria from pushing it in further. After a few seconds more of hushed, violent struggle, the Faeling collapsed to his knees, the sound of which at last alerted my aunt to the situation.

"Liam! No!"

Before Babd could say or do anything else, however, Camila arrived. The bruja came running at full bore, using all her momentum and strength to swing the flat head of an unwieldy sledgehammer into the side of the Gancanagh's skull. The strike caved in two-thirds of his head, spraying gore and grey matter everywhere. Liam's shine flickered and dimmed.

He was dead before he hit the ground.

CHAPTER 46

Babd lashed out immediately. The moment her lover's needy headless corpse collapsed, the goddess raised a hand to the heavens, her face a mask of rage and grief, and shrieked at the top of her inhuman lungs. The sound was horrifying—a blend of long, drawn out caws, like a thousand crows speaking out at once. We all covered our ears, and I could have sworn I saw blood trickling down Camila's neck. The instant the screaming ended, a blinding bolt of lightning descended from the cloudless sky, hitting Babd's outstretched fingertips and spiraling down her arm like a writhing snake.

"I will make ye pay!" Babd declared, whipping her arm up and bringing it back down so that the lightning became a braided cord of hair-raising, body-bowing energy. With a savage cry, she drew back to strike at the bruja, who could do nothing but cower from the blow.

"No!" I shouted, racing to intercept the goddess before she did any permanent damage.

I didn't make it in time.

Babd whipped her arm around like a pitcher throwing a slider, and a coil of lightning went racing towards the bruja. I tried to turn, to put myself between Camila and the blow, only to end up slipping and falling to one knee, forced to watch in horror as it sped towards her fragile mortal body.

But then a dark figure stepped in the way.

Albi took the blow on his sleeve, his face a grimace of pain that made him snarl and bare his teeth. But the Pooka didn't buckle, or even twitch, as the electricity coursed through his body. Instead, he locked gazes with Babd, waiting until the last of her power was gone before throwing his suit jacket over that arm.

"That's enough of that, I think," he said, nonplussed.

"Get out of the way, ye fool! I'll kill her! I'll kill 'em both!"

"And will you kill me, too, for freeing them?"

Babd hesitated. Not because she was unwilling to kill Albi, necessarily, but more likely because his question forced her to think past her grief. She blinked rapidly, shaking her head. "Why would ye free 'em?"

"Because it was in your niece's best interest. And I made a deal." Albi flicked his eyes to me. "Apologies for not mentioning your aunt's true identity earlier, by the way. She used a *geas* to keep anyone affiliated with the Chancery from divulging her secret."

"Her secret?"

"Her being here, I believe. There was something about overstepping. Reprisals. Drawing the ire of the other gods."

"I don't understand," Babd interjected, her expression so tormented it seemed as though Liam's death had shattered something inside her. "How did this happen?"

"Aunt Babd..." I started, reaching for her.

"Aunt?" Babd looked up sharply, perplexed. "Have ye seen me niece? I have to find her. Me sister...she has to help me...I came to find..."

"Came to find who, Aunt Babd?"

The goddess shook her head, violently.

"It's Liam's glamour," Albi explained. "He's warped her mind, somehow. I honestly didn't realize how much control he had over her until tonight's disaster."

"What were we supposed to do?" Camila asked. "The Hex Moon came early. The whole plan hinges on it."

"You could have sent someone ahead to warn me. Then I might have distracted Catha long enough for your plan to work without you getting captured or interrogated."

Camila looked away. "You still did not have to beat us."

"It was the only way to convince Liam the information I gave him was genuine."

"Well, you did not have to enjoy it so much."

The Pooka grinned. "Had things turned out differently, I would have paid far more dearly for my deception than a few scrapes and bruises. You'll get no sympathy from me."

"What are ye lot talkin' about?" Babd asked, looking so genuinely wretched that it made all of us uncomfortable. "What is happenin' to me?"

"It will be alright, m'lady," Albi declared. He gestured to the moor troll I'd injured, who climbed to his feet without saying a word. "Let's return to the manor house. Perhaps there we can see about unraveling all this glamour."

"You're going to let her go?" Maria hissed, speaking up for the first time. "After everything we did to stop her?"

"Yes, I am. The more I think about it, the more I am beginning to remember. I'm starting to believe that the one who orchestrated this whole mess is already dead. You two saw to that. And besides...look at her."

We all did as he suggested.

Babd hugged herself, rubbing at her naked arms, her leather jacket and vest laying in a pile at her feet. I couldn't remember ever having seen someone look so lost. It reminded me of the way elderly people sit and stare at nothing, sometimes—like their mind is taking a trip to see where their soul is meant to be.

"Fine," Maria snapped, though I could see her heart wasn't in it. "But if she turns around and comes after us, it'll be on you."

"Very well. I will take responsibility for her, for tonight at least. Tomorrow, perhaps she might receive a visit from her niece?" Albi gazed at me, meaningfully. "I'm sure they would have much to discuss."

I nodded, though part of me was already dreading the prospect.

"Good. Here's the address." He fetched a card from the lining of his jacket. "As for you, Camila, shouldn't you be running along? I believe there's a recently emancipated Redcap who could use your tender loving care."

"Robin." Camila's eyes lit up, immediately, his name uttered like an answered prayer. "Wait, my care? Is he alright? He is not hurt, is he?"

"That I don't know," Albi admitted. "I wasn't allowed to see him."

"Maria, we should go." Camila paused, turning to me. "How is my brother?"

"Alive and well, last time I saw him," I replied.

"Good. *Gracias*, for coming. Without you..."

"You'd have managed, I'm sure." I waved that off, preferring not to think how badly things could have gone for them if Liam had gotten his way. Of course, thanks to them, Liam would never be getting his way, again. "Tell Robin hello for me, would ye? Oh, and t'anks for killin' that piece of trash, by the way. Especially what ye did, Maria. Stabbin' him in the throat? That was bloody brilliant."

"You're welcome..." Maria looked suspicious of my compliment but didn't pick at it. "Let's go."

The two women left, chattering amongst themselves in Spanish as they descended the slope which led to what looked like a parking lot.

"Well, now that we've dealt with that, I believe it's time to get going." Albi made a move towards Babd but hesitated when he caught me staring. "What is it?"

"You're a lot smarter than I gave ye credit for."

"Most of the Fae are, I expect." Albi shrugged. "I've been alive a long, long time. Once, I wouldn't have noticed or cared about that. But this world, it works on our minds. It changes us. Forces us to decide to be something, to play a role, if only to feel like we're part of things."

"Aye, I'm beginnin' to notice the same t'ing," I replied, twisting the bracelet absentmindedly. "What would ye want to be, then, if ye had the choice?"

"I wouldn't want to *be* anything. That's the point. We were never meant to think the way Manlings think. We were meant to live on our own terms. To *be*, without *being*."

To that, I could say nothing. Mostly because, in his own way, Albi was making the same argument Morgan had. And maybe they were both right—maybe growing up in this world had done to my mind what Liam had done to Babd's, making me believe in something that wasn't real.

The question was, would I ever break free of its spell?

CHAPTER 47

I was standing alone, looking up at the moon and wondering whether or not I was going to have to hoof it back to civilization, when I saw a slim, dark shape dart across the sky. I squinted, laughed, and began waving both arms like an air traffic controller. Not that I needed to; Areadbhar had made it this far without my help, she obviously didn't have any trouble tracking me down.

The spear skidded to a stop perhaps a foot away, bobbing up and down with what I could only assume was joy. I'd already reached for her, planning to pull her in for an awkward but necessary hug, when she drifted back and lowered her blade to dangle an object in front of my face.

It was the gaudiest, most bedazzled cell phone I'd ever seen, expertly tied to her shaft by a series of complicated knots that took several minutes to unravel. When I finished, Areadbhar rose into the air and promptly turned into a stone. I caught her, amused.

"Guess ye were pretty exhausted, huh? Don't ye worry, I'll carry ye around for a while."

I performed a little *seitr* magic and slipped the stone into the pocket of my embroidered jean jacket before turning my attention to the phone. I flipped it open—yes, it was one of those—and found only one number programmed under the name CALL ME.

So, I did.

"Quinn? Quinn, is that you?"

"Jimmy?" I held the phone away from my ear for a moment, then put it to my mouth. "What the hell d'ye t'ink you're doin' sendin' me this totally ridiculous phone?"

"Oh, thank God!" Jimmy said, laughing. When he spoke again, his voice was distant and hard to make out. "She sounds fine...I'll ask her...oh yeah, she hated it...so great."

"Jimmy, is everythin' alright?" I asked, wishing I could see who he was talking to. "Is anyone hurt? What about Morgan, is she okay?"

"What? Oh, yeah. Everyone here is fine. The enchantress, charming lady by the way, is resting in your room at the hotel. She's a little out of it, but she'll be fine. Hilde is on the mend, already. She keeps saying she needs to talk to you about Asgard, but that's all she'll say because she *doesn't trust people!*" Jimmy shouted the last bit, then chuckled. "What's that?"

I thought I could hear a woman's voice in the background.

"Oh, right. Hilde says to come back as soon as you can. What the hell happened to you? Your *man* filled us in on most of it. He says hello, by the way. What? Oh, excuse me. *Hello, beautiful.* He says hello, beautiful."

I laughed, only moderately discomfited by the idea of my married ex and my whatever-Max-was passing along love notes. Of course, three could play at that game. "Tell him I said 'soon,' would ye?"

"Soon? She says *soon.*" Jimmy made a sound that I recognized from high school, so familiar I could practically picture the stunned look on his face. "Did you know your man could light up like that? I mean, like literally light up."

"Aye," I replied, repressing the urge to giggle. "Anyway, how's everyone else? How's Leo and Lakota? And what about the guy I left with Hilde? Bredon."

"Oh, right. Him. He's a strange one. You know, he's the one who suggested we let your weapon go? Took one look at it trying to fly away and told us we'd better set her free so she could find you. Even called it a she."

"No kiddin'," I replied, my mind suddenly occupied with all sorts of questions about the man who refused to die, questions that Jimmy couldn't answer.

"Anyway, the phone was my idea. Well, technically I guess it was Leo's. Apparently, you told him you didn't have a phone, so he sent me to buy one earlier this morning. You know me, I'm not exactly an impulse buyer. But all it took was one look and knew it was the phone for you."

"Is that when Watt arrested ye?"

"Not long after, yeah. Why?"

"Because," I replied, scathingly, "that's what I like to call karma."

Jimmy barked a laugh. "Maybe you're right. Still, it worked out for us. If I hadn't gotten locked up, I'd never have gotten the tip about that kid's brother."

"D'ye mean Leon? Is he alright?"

"Actually, I meant the older one. Mike. And yeah, the kid seemed a little shaken up, but their Alpha tells me he'll be fine. Intense lady, even for a werewolf."

"Pauline? I'll say. So, what happened with Leon, anyway?"

"Seems like he put two and two together and realized his brother was looking at the Fairy Court for all the bodies that kept showing up on their route. Sounds to me like Leon's brother was their rum runner. Anyway, Leon got caught doing the same, and whoever it was put him in a cage. That's where we found him. What I don't get is why the coven dumped Mike's body like they did, though."

"Maybe it wasn't the witches," I said, thinking out loud. "Maybe it was the one pullin' the strings. Maybe he worried if Angelika found out the people she was killin' weren't werewolves, it would throw a wrench in his plans."

"Yeah, about that. This..." Jimmy hesitated, probably looking over a pad filled with meticulous notes, knowing him. "Liam. What do you know about him? Right now, he's the only one we haven't accounted for, and the Academy Justices want to take a look at everything we've got. The summoning of a god on their watch has them in a tizzy. Anyway, I was hoping you might know more about him than we do."

"I wouldn't worry about Liam," I insisted. "And ye can pass that along to the Academy."

"And why shouldn't we be worried?"

"Because I was lookin' down at his corpse not twenty minutes ago."

"You what? Wait...don't tell me you killed him?"

"Oh, no, not me. It was actually Maria who did the honors, if ye can believe it."

"Maria? *My* Maria? Maria Machado?"

"She's a very vicious person, Jimmy," I replied, stifling a snicker. "I've been tellin' ye that for years. In fact, ye may want to watch your back, because she's pretty pissed at ye for gettin' married. I'd hate to see ye die with a knife in your face."

"Hah. Right. About that..." Jimmy cleared his throat. "I'm sorry I didn't tell you about Lakota and me. I genuinely thought you knew, and that you would bring it up if—"

"Jimmy Collins, ye don't owe me an explanation," I chastised, though I was relieved to find that I meant it. "I was a bit thrown; I'll admit. And, when I first heard, I might even have been a bit jealous. Or maybe not jealous, so much as upset I missed it. Hard to tell. But when I found out it was Lakota...listen, I'm just happy for ye both. Truly."

"I..." Jimmy hesitated to say whatever he intended to say next, before eventually sighing in relief. "Thanks, Quinn."

"But ye should know that if either of ye hurt the other, I'll have no choice but to kill ye both. Machado-style."

"Sounds painful," Jimmy remarked, his voice light with suppressed laughter.

"A rail spike to the throat? Oh, ye better believe it will be."

"Jesus! Really? What happened over there?"

"A family reunion gone wrong, I guess ye might say? I'll fill ye in on all of it when I get back, hopefully in a day or two. Tell Hilde for me? She and I have some unfinished business to take care of, preferably sooner rather than later. Oh, and when Morgan wakes up, do me a favor and see if she'll pop on over and give me a lift?"

"Can do. Oh, and speaking of, do you need me to call someone? Have them pick you up? Morgan told me where you were, and I still know a few good cops out that way who owe me favors."

"Actually, that would be great," I admitted, relieved to find I wouldn't have to walk back, after all. "I really appreciate it, Jimmy."

"You bet. What was it that your Aunt Dez used to say? That little friendship rhyme. The one about the boats."

"There are good ships and there are wood ships, ships that sail the sea. But the best ships are friendships, may they always be," I replied, imitating the sing-songy quality she'd always infused it with.

"Well, there you have it," Jimmy said, laughing.

"Aye, there ye have it."

CHAPTER 48

W hen the patrol car pulled into the parking lot a good hour later, I supposed I should have been surprised to find Officer O'Malley in the driver's seat. And yet, for some reason, I really wasn't. In fact, it felt right that he should be the one—implausible though it was. Stranger still, I could tell from O'Malley's placid expression that he thought the same.

"Miss MacKenna, I take it?" he asked, leaning his head out the window. He looked for a moment as if he might comment on the coincidence of running into me again or ask me what I was doing so far off the beaten path—alone, at night. But either he could tell I wasn't in the mood to explain, or he knew it would all be a bunch of lies, because he didn't bother with either. "Go ahead and hop in."

I slid into the passenger side, careful to avoid hitting the dash with my long legs. "T'anks for the ride."

"Sure thing. Buckle up."

Several minutes passed in total silence after that as O'Malley cruised in Boston's general direction. Fortunately, it was the companionable sort, utterly devoid of tension or nervousness. In fact, it wasn't until we reached the city's outer limits that he bothered asking the obvious question.

"You know where we're going?"

I did, and I told him.

"Oh yeah, I know where that's at. I grew up not too far from there."

"Really?" I asked, though again I wasn't the least bit surprised.

O'Malley nodded, and the silence resumed. I settled back, refusing to think about tomorrow or the days to come. What I needed was a chance to breathe. To, as Albi put it, *be*. And so I watched the city pass by in chunks as we worked our way through the districts, basking in the familiar glow of my hometown. Indeed, at night, with the lights shining gold and soft beyond the windshield, I realized that—contrary to what I'd concluded upon arrival—Boston hadn't actually changed that much.

But I had.

CHAPTER 49

I watched O'Malley's squad car turn the corner of the residential street, creeping the way cops always do when cruising around a quiet neighborhood. As a teenager, I remembered I used to hate that. Especially when they seemed to tail me and my friends as if looking for an excuse to stop and ask us what we were up to. Of course, that's because we were usually up to something.

Back then, Aunt Dez used to joke that I'd end up married to a cop. That then I'd have to find a better use of my time than staying out until the wee hours doing the Lord knew what. She'd always called it that—the Lord knew what. Like she couldn't imagine what kind of trouble I routinely got into. Unfortunately, I couldn't exactly argue with her; half the boys in our neighborhood were being groomed to wear the badge, including damn near all the ones I had crushes on.

Funny, I thought, how so many of our tastes can change, and how so many can remain the same. It made growing up feel like a game of inches—like if you watched your feet the whole time you were walking you'd feel like you were going nowhere, but if you stared straight ahead and looked down only every so often, you'd see you were miles from where you started.

At least that was how it felt to me, now.

Resolved to stop looking at my metaphorical feet, I took a deep breath, turned, and looked up. And there, standing just how I'd left it after her funeral, was Aunt Dez's house. My house, I corrected. Unlike my apartment, the mortgage had been paid in full decades ago. And, as for upkeep, I'd set aside a separate fund to cover the expenses, which accounted for the orderly state of the front yard and exterior despite my absence.

Not that I had ever intended to come back here.

A year and a half. Eighteen whole months surviving one fresh hell after another. Was that how long it took to recover from the death of a loved one, I wondered? Or was that simply as much time as it took to properly grieve? I couldn't say; I hadn't recovered, and I was still grieving.

But maybe that was okay.

Maybe that's what made me...me.

"Aunt Dez," I said, speaking to the dark, empty house and all the life that once filled it, "I'm back from doin' the Lord knows what."

I unlatched the front gate.

And went home.

∽

Quinn MacKenna will return...

∽

DON'T FORGET! VIP's get early access to all sorts of Temple-
Verse goodies, including signed copies, private giveaways, and
advance notice of future projects. AND A FREE NOVELLA!
Click the image or join here: *www.shaynesilvers.com/l/38599*

Turn the page to read a sample of **OBSIDIAN SON** *- Nate Temple Book 1 -
or* **BUY ONLINE (It's FREE with a Kindle Unlimited subscription)**. *Nate
Temple is a billionaire wizard from St. Louis. He rides a bloodthirsty
unicorn and drinks with the Four Horsemen. He even cow-tipped the
Minotaur. Once...*

TRY: OBSIDIAN SON (NATE TEMPLE #1)

There was no room for emotion in a hate crime. I had to be cold. Heartless. This was just another victim. Nothing more. No face, no name.

Frosted blades of grass crunched under my feet, sounding to my ears like the symbolic glass that one would shatter under a napkin at a Jewish wedding. The noise would have threatened to give away my stealthy advance as I stalked through the moonlit field, but I was no novice and had planned accordingly. Being a wizard, I was able to muffle all sensory evidence with a fine cloud of magic—no sounds, and no smells. Nifty. But if I made the spell much stronger, the anomaly would be too obvious to my prey.

I knew the consequences for my dark deed tonight. If caught, jail time or possibly even a gruesome, painful death. But if I succeeded, the look of fear and surprise in my victim's eyes before his world collapsed around him, it was well worth the risk. I simply couldn't help myself; I had to take him down.

I knew the cops had been keeping tabs on my car, but I was confident that they hadn't followed me. I hadn't seen a tail on my way here but seeing as how they frowned on this kind of thing, I had taken a circuitous route just in case. I was safe. I hoped.

Then my phone chirped at me as I received a text.

I practically jumped out of my skin, hissing instinctively. "Motherf —" I cut off abruptly, remembering the whole stealth aspect of my mission. I was off to a stellar start. I had forgotten to silence the damned phone. *Stupid, stupid, stupid!*

My heart felt like it was on the verge of exploding inside my chest with such thunderous violence that I briefly envisioned a mystifying Rorschach blood-blot that would have made coroners and psychologists drool.

My body remained tense as I swept my gaze over the field, fearing that I had been made. Precious seconds ticked by without any change in my surroundings, and my breathing finally began to slow as my pulse returned to normal. Hopefully, my magic had muted the phone and my resulting outburst. I glanced down at the phone to scan the text and then typed back a quick and angry response before I switched the cursed device to vibrate.

Now, where were we?

I continued on, the lining of my coat constricting my breathing. Or maybe it was because I was leaning forward in anticipation. *Breathe*, I chided myself. *He doesn't know you're here.* All this risk for a book. It had better be worth it.

I'm taller than most, and not abnormally handsome, but I knew how to play the genetic cards I had been dealt. I had shaggy, dirty blonde hair—leaning more towards brown with each passing year—and my frame was thick with well-earned muscle, yet I was still lean. I had once been told that my eyes were like twin emeralds pitted against the golden-brown tufts of my hair—a face like a jewelry box. Of course, that was two bottles of wine into a date, so I could have been a little foggy on her quote. Still, I liked to imagine that was how everyone saw me.

But tonight, all that was masked by magic.

I grinned broadly as the outline of the hairy hulk finally came into view. He was blessedly alone—no nearby sentries to give me away. That was always a risk when performing this ancient rite-of-passage. I tried to keep the grin on my face from dissolving into a maniacal cackle.

My skin danced with energy, both natural and unnatural, as I manipulated the threads of magic floating all around me. My victim stood just ahead, oblivious to the world of hurt that I was about to unleash. Even with his millennia of experience, he didn't stand a chance. I had done this so many times that the routine of it was my only enemy. I lost count of how many times I had been told not to do it again; those who knew declared it *cruel, evil, and sadistic.* But what fun wasn't? Regardless, that wasn't enough to stop me from doing it again. And again. And again.

It was an addiction.

The pungent smell of manure filled the air, latching onto my nostril hairs. I took another step, trying to calm my racing pulse. A glint of gold reflected in the silver moonlight, but my victim remained motionless, hopefully unaware or all was lost. I wouldn't make it out alive if he knew I was here. Timing was everything.

I carefully took the last two steps, a lifetime between each, watching the legendary monster's ears, anxious and terrified that I would catch even so much as a twitch in my direction. Seeing nothing, a fierce grin split my unshaven cheeks. My spell had worked! I raised my palms an inch away from their target, firmly planted my feet, and squared my shoulders. I took one silent, calming breath, and then heaved forward with every ounce of physical strength I could muster. As well as a teensy-weensy boost of magic. Enough to goose him good.

"*MOOO!!!*" The sound tore through the cool October night like an unstoppable freight train. *Thud-splat!* The beast collapsed sideways onto the frosted grass; straight into a steaming patty of cow shit, cow dung, or, if you really wanted to church it up, a Meadow Muffin. But to me, shit is, and always will be, shit.

Cow tipping. It doesn't get any better than that in Missouri.

Especially when you're tipping the *Minotaur*. Capital M. I'd tipped plenty of ordinary cows before, but never the legendary variety.

Razor-blade hooves tore at the frozen earth as the beast struggled to stand, his grunts of rage vibrating the air. I raised my arms triumphantly. "Boo-yah! Temple 1, Minotaur 0!" I crowed. Then I very bravely prepared to protect myself. Some people just couldn't take a joke. *Cruel, evil,* and *sadistic* cow tipping may be, but by hell, it was a *rush*. The legendary beast turned his gaze on me after gaining his feet, eyes ablaze as his body...*shifted* from his bull disguise into his notorious, well-known bipedal form. He unfolded to his full height on two tree trunk-thick legs, his hooves having magically transformed into heavily booted feet. The thick, gold ring dangling from his snotty snout quivered as the Minotaur panted, and his dense, corded muscles contracted over his now human-like chest. As I stared up into those brown eyes, I actually felt sorry...for, well, myself.

"I have killed greater men than you for lesser offense," he growled.

His voice sounded like an angry James Earl Jones—like Mufasa talking to Scar.

"You have shit on your shoulder, Asterion." I ignited a roiling ball of fire in my palm in order to see his eyes more clearly. By no means was it a defensive gesture on my part. It was just dark. Under the weight of his glare, I somehow managed to keep my face composed, even though my fraudulent, self-denial had curled up into the fetal position and started whimpering. I hoped using a form of his ancient name would give me brownie points. Or maybe just not-worthy-of-killing points.

The beast grunted, eyes tightening, and I sensed the barest hesitation. "Nate Temple...your name would look splendid on my already long list of slain idiots." Asterion took a threatening step forward, and I thrust out my palm in warning, my roiling flame blue now.

"You lost fair and square, Asterion. Yield or perish." The beast's shoulders sagged slightly. Then he finally nodded to himself in resignation, appraising me with the scrutiny of a worthy adversary. "Your time comes, Temple, but I will grant you this. You've got a pair of stones on you to rival Hercules."

I reflexively glanced in the direction of the myth's own crown jewels before jerking my gaze away. Some things you simply couldn't un-see. "Well, I won't be needing a wheelbarrow any time soon, but overcompensating today keeps future lower-back pain away."

The Minotaur blinked once, and then he bellowed out a deep, contagious, snorting laughter. Realizing I wasn't about to become a murder statistic, I couldn't help but join in. It felt good. It had been a while since I had allowed myself to experience genuine laughter.

In the harsh moonlight, his bulk was even more intimidating as he towered head and shoulders above me. This was the beast that had fed upon human sacrifices for countless years while imprisoned in Daedalus' Labyrinth in Greece. And all that protein had not gone to waste, forming a heavily woven musculature over the beast's body that made even Mr. Olympia look puny.

From the neck up, he was now entirely bull, but the rest of his body more closely resembled a thickly furred man. But, as shown moments ago, he could adapt his form to his environment, never appearing fully human, but able to make his entire form appear as a bull when necessary. For instance, how he had looked just before I tipped him. Maybe he had been scouting the field for heifers before I had so efficiently killed the mood.

His bull face was also covered in thick, coarse hair—he even sported a long, wavy beard of sorts, and his eyes were the deepest brown I had ever seen. Cow-shit brown. His snout jutted out, emphasizing the golden ring dangling from his glistening nostrils, and both glinted in the luminous glow of the moon. The metal was at least an inch thick and etched with runes of a language long forgotten. Wide, aged ivory horns sprouted from each temple, long enough to skewer a wizard with little effort. He was nude except for a massive beaded necklace and a pair of worn leather boots that were big enough to stomp a size twenty-five imprint in my face if he felt so inclined.

I hoped our blossoming friendship wouldn't end that way. I really did.

Because friends didn't let friends wear boots naked...

∾

Get your copy of OBSIDIAN SON online today!
http://www.shaynesilvers.com/l/38474

∾

*If you enjoyed the **BLADE** or **UNDERWORLD** movies, turn the page to read a sample of **DEVIL'S DREAM**—the first book in the new **SHADE OF DEVIL** series by Shayne Silvers.*
Or get the book ONLINE! *http://www.shaynesilvers.com/l/738833*

Before the now-infamous Count Dracula ever tasted his first drop of blood, Sorin Ambrogio owned the night. Humanity fearfully called him the Devil...

TRY: DEVIL'S DREAM (SHADE OF DEVIL #1)

God damned me.

He—in his infinite, omnipotent wisdom—declared for all to hear...

Let there be pain...

In the exact center of this poor bastard's soul.

And that merciless smiting woke me from a dead sleep and thrust me into a body devoid of every sensation but blinding agony.

I tried to scream but my throat felt as dry as dust, only permitting me to emit a rasping, whistling hiss that brought on yet *more* pain. My skin burned and throbbed while my bones creaked and groaned with each full-body tremor. My claws sunk into a hard surface beneath me and I was distantly surprised they hadn't simply shattered upon contact.

My memory was an immolated ruin—each fragment of thought merely an elusive fleck of ash or ember that danced through my fog of despair as I struggled to catch one and hold onto it long enough to recall what had brought me to this bleak existence. How I had become this poor, wretched, shell of a man. I couldn't even remember my own *name*; it was all I could do to simply survive this profound horror.

After what seemed an eternity, the initial pain began to slowly ebb, but I quickly realized that it had only triggered a cascade of smaller, more numerous tortures—like ripples caused by a boulder thrown into a pond.

I couldn't find the strength to even attempt to open my crusted eyes, and my abdomen was a solid knot of gnawing hunger so over-whelming that I felt like I was being pulled down into the earth by a lead weight. My fingers tingled and burned so fiercely that I wondered if the skin had been peeled away while I slept. Since they were twitching involuntarily, at least I knew that the muscles and tendons were still attached.

I held onto that sliver of joy, that beacon of hope.

I stubbornly gritted my teeth, but even that slight movement made the skin over my face stretch tight enough to almost tear. I willed myself to relax as I tried to process *why* I was in so much pain, where I was, how I had gotten here, and...*who* I even was? A singular thought finally struck me like an echo of the faintest of whispers, giving me something to latch onto.

Hunger.

I let out a crackling gasp of relief at finally grasping an independent answer of some kind, but I was unable to draw enough moisture onto my tongue to properly swallow. Understanding that I was hungry had seemed to alleviate a fraction of my pain. The answer to at least one question distracted me long enough to allow me to think. And despite my hunger, I felt something tantalizingly delicious slowly coursing down my throat, desperately attempting to alleviate my starvation.

Even though my memory was still enshrouded in fog, I was entirely certain that it was incredibly dangerous for me to feel this hungry. This...*thirsty*. Dangerous for both myself and anyone nearby. I tried to remember why it was so dangerous but the reason eluded me. Instead, an answer to a different question emerged from my mind like a specter from the mist—and I felt myself begin to smile as a modicum of strength slowly took root deep within me.

"Sorin..." I croaked. My voice echoed, letting me know that I was in an enclosed space of some kind. "My name is Sorin Ambrogio. And I need..." I trailed off uncertainly, unable to finish my own thought.

"Blood," a man's deep voice answered from only a few paces away. "You need more blood."

I hissed instinctively, snapping my eyes open for the first time since waking. I had completely forgotten to check my surroundings, too consumed with my own pain to bother with my other senses. I had been asleep so long that even the air seemed to burn my eyes like smoke, forcing me to blink rapidly. No, the air *was* filled with pungent, aromatic smoke, but not like the smoke from the fires in my—

I shuddered involuntarily, blocking out the thought for some unknown reason.

Beneath the pungent smoke, the air was musty and damp. Through it all, I smelled the delicious, coppery scent of hot, powerful blood.

I had been resting atop a raised stone plinth—almost like a table —in a depthless, shadowy cavern. I appreciated the darkness because any light would have likely blinded me in my current state. I couldn't see the man who had spoken, but the area was filled with silhouettes of what appeared to be tables, crates, and other shapes that could easily conceal him. I focused on my hearing and almost instantly noticed a seductively familiar, *beating* sound.

A noise as delightful as a child's first belly-laugh...

A beautiful woman's sigh as she locked eyes with you for the first time.

The gentle crackling of a fireplace on a brisk, snowy night.

Thump-thump.

Thump-thump.

Thump-thump.

The sound became *everything* and my vision slowly began to sharpen, the room brightening into shades of gray. My pain didn't disappear, but it was swiftly muted as I tracked the sound.

I inhaled deeply, my eyes riveting on a far wall as my nostrils flared, pinpointing the source of the savory perfume and the seductive beating sound. I didn't recall sitting up, but I realized that I was suddenly leaning forward and that the room was continuing to brighten into paler shades of gray, burning away the last of the remaining shadows—despite the fact that there was no actual light. And it grew clearer as I focused on the seductive sound.

Until I finally spotted a man leaning against the far wall. *Thump-thump. Thump-thump. Thump-thump...* I licked my lips ravenously, setting my hands on the cool stone table as I prepared to set my feet on the ground.

Food...

The man calmly lifted his hand and a sharp *clicking* sound suddenly echoed from the walls. The room abruptly flooded with light so bright and unexpected that it felt like my eyes had exploded. Worse, what seemed like a trio of radiant stars was not more than a span from my face —so close that I could feel the direct heat from their flare. I recoiled with a snarl, momentarily forgetting all about food as I shielded my eyes with a hand and prepared to defend myself. I leaned away from the bright lights, wondering why I couldn't smell smoke from the flickering flames. I squinted, watching the man's feet for any indication of movement.

Half a minute went by as my vision slowly began to adjust, and the man didn't even shift his weight—almost as if he was granting me time enough to grow accustomed to the sudden light. Which...didn't make any sense. Hadn't it been an attack? I hesitantly lowered my hand from my face, reassessing the situation and my surroundings.

I stared in wonder as I realized that the orbs were not made of flame, but rather what seemed to be pure light affixed to polished metal stands. Looking directly at them hurt, so I studied them sidelong, making sure to also keep the man in my peripheral vision. He had to be a sorcerer of some kind. Who else could wield pure light without fire?

"Easy, Sorin," the man murmured in a calming baritone. "I can't see as well as you in the dark, but it looked like you were about to do something unnecessarily stupid. Let me turn them down a little."

He didn't wait for my reply, but the room slowly dimmed after another clicking sound.

I tried to get a better look at the stranger—wondering where he had come from, where he had taken me, and who he was. One thing was obvious—he knew magic. "Where did you learn this sorcery?" I rasped, gesturing at the orbs of light.

"Um. Hobby Lobby."

"I've never heard of him," I hissed, coughing as a result of my parched throat.

"I'm not even remotely surprised by that," he said dryly. He extended his other hand and I gasped to see an impossibility—a transparent bag as clear as new glass. And it was *flexible*, swinging back and forth like a bulging coin purse or a clear water-skin. My momentary wonder at the magical material evaporated as I recognized the crimson liquid *inside* the bag.

Blood.

He lobbed it at me underhanded without a word of warning. I hissed as I desperately—and with exceeding caution—caught it from the air lest it fall and break open. I gasped as the clear bag of blood settled into my palms and, before I consciously realized it, I tore off the corner with my fangs, pressed it to my lips, and squeezed the bag in one explosive, violent gesture. The ruby fluid gushed into my mouth and over my face, dousing my almost forgotten pain as swiftly as a bucket of water thrown on hot coals.

I felt my eyes roll back into my skull and my body shuddered as I lost my balance and fell from the stone table. I landed on my back but I was too overwhelmed to care as I stretched out my arms and legs. I groaned in rapture, licking at my lips like a wild animal. The ruby nectar was a living serpent of molten oil as it slithered down into my stomach, nurturing and healing me almost instantly. It was the most wonderful sensation I could imagine—almost enough to make me weep.

Like a desert rain, my parched tongue and throat absorbed the blood so quickly and completely that I couldn't even savor the heady flavor. This wasn't a joyful feast; this was survival, a necessity. My body guzzled it, instantly using the liquid to repair the damage, pain, and the cloud of fog that had enshrouded me.

I realized that I was laughing. The sound echoed into the vast stone space like rolling thunder.

Because I had remembered something else.

The world's First Vampire was *back*.

And he was still *very* hungry.

Get the full book ONLINE! *http://www.shaynesilvers.com/l/738833*

Check out Shayne's other books. He's written a few without Cameron helping him. Some of them are marginally decent—easily a 4 out of 10.

MAKE A DIFFERENCE

Reviews are the most powerful tools in our arsenal when it comes to getting attention for our books. Much as we'd like to, we don't have the financial muscle of a New York publisher.

But we do have something much more powerful and effective than that, and it's something that those publishers would kill to get their hands on.

A committed and loyal bunch of readers.

Honest reviews of our books help bring them to the attention of other readers.

If you've enjoyed this book, we would be very grateful if you could spend just five minutes leaving a review on our book's Amazon page.

Thank you very much in advance.

ACKNOWLEDGMENTS

From Cameron:

I'd like to thank Shayne, for paving the way in style. Kori, for an introduction that would change my life. My three wonderful sisters, for showing me what a strong, independent woman looks and sounds like. And, above all, my parents, for—literally—everything.

From Shayne (the self-proclaimed prettiest one):

Team Temple and the Den of Freaks on Facebook have become family to me. I couldn't do it without die-hard readers like them.

I would also like to thank you, the reader. I hope you enjoyed reading *MOONSHINE* as much as we enjoyed writing it. Be sure to check out the two crossover series in the TempleVerse: **The Nate Temple Series** and the **Feathers and Fire Series**.

And last, but definitely not least, I thank my wife, Lexy. Without your support, none of this would have been possible.

ABOUT CAMERON O'CONNELL

Cameron O'Connell is a Jack-of-All-Trades and Master of Some.

He writes The Phantom Queen Diaries, a series in The Temple-Verse, about Quinn MacKenna, a mouthy black magic arms dealer trading favors in Boston. All she wants? A round-trip ticket to the Fae realm...and maybe a drink on the house.

A former member of the United States military, a professional model, and English teacher, Cameron finds time to write in the mornings after his first cup of coffee...and in the evenings after his thirty-seventh. Follow him, and the TempleVerse founder, Shayne Silvers, online for all sorts of insider tips, giveaways, and new release updates!

Get Down with Cameron Online

facebook.com/Cameron-OConnell-788806397985289

amazon.com/author/cameronoconnell

bookbub.com/authors/cameron-o-connell

twitter.com/thecamoconnell

instagram.com/camoconnellauthor

goodreads.com/cameronoconnell

ABOUT SHAYNE SILVERS

Shayne is a man of mystery and power, whose power is exceeded only by his mystery...

He currently writes the Amazon Bestselling **Nate Temple** Series, which features a foul-mouthed wizard from St. Louis. He rides a bloodthirsty unicorn, drinks with Achilles, and is pals with the Four Horsemen.

He also writes the Amazon Bestselling **Feathers and Fire** Series —a second series in the TempleVerse. The story follows a rookie spell-slinger named Callie Penrose who works for the Vatican in Kansas City. Her problem? Hell seems to know more about her past than she does.

He coauthors **The Phantom Queen Diaries**—a third series set in The TempleVerse—with Cameron O'Connell. The story follows Quinn MacKenna, a mouthy black magic arms dealer in Boston. All she wants? A round-trip ticket to the Fae realm...and maybe a drink on the house.

He also writes the **Shade of Devil Series**, which tells the story of Sorin Ambrogio—the world's FIRST vampire. He was put into a magical slumber by a Native American Medicine Man when the Americas were first discovered by Europeans. Sorin wakes up after five-hundred years to learn that his protégé, Dracula, stole his reputation and that no one has ever even heard of Sorin Ambrogio. The streets of New York City will run with blood as Sorin reclaims his legend.

Shayne holds two high-ranking black belts, and can be found writing in a coffee shop, cackling madly into his computer screen while pounding shots of espresso. He's hard at work on the newest books in the TempleVerse—You can find updates on new releases or chronological reading order on the next page, his website, or any of his social media accounts. **Follow him online for all sorts of groovy goodies, giveaways, and new release updates:**

Get Down with Shayne Online
www.shaynesilvers.com
info@shaynesilvers.com

[f] facebook.com/shaynesilversfanpage

[a] amazon.com/author/shaynesilvers

[BB] bookbub.com/profile/shayne-silvers

[O] instagram.com/shaynesilversofficial

[y] twitter.com/shaynesilvers

[g] goodreads.com/ShayneSilvers

BOOKS BY THE AUTHORS

CHRONOLOGY: *All stories in the TempleVerse are shown in chronological order on the following page*

PHANTOM QUEEN DIARIES

(Set in the TempleVerse)

by Cameron O'Connell & Shayne Silvers

COLLINS (Prequel novella #0 in the 'LAST CALL' anthology)

WHISKEY GINGER

COSMOPOLITAN

MOTHERLUCKER (Novella #2.5 in the 'LAST CALL' anthology)

OLD FASHIONED

DARK AND STORMY

MOSCOW MULE

WITCHES BREW

SALTY DOG

SEA BREEZE

HURRICANE

BRIMSTONE KISS

MOONSHINE

NATE TEMPLE SERIES

(Main series in the TempleVerse)

by Shayne Silvers

FAIRY TALE - FREE prequel novella #0 for my subscribers

OBSIDIAN SON

BLOOD DEBTS

GRIMM

SILVER TONGUE

BEAST MASTER

BEERLYMPIAN (Novella #5.5 in the 'LAST CALL' anthology)

TINY GODS

DADDY DUTY (Novella #6.5)

WILD SIDE

WAR HAMMER

NINE SOULS

HORSEMAN

LEGEND

KNIGHTMARE

ASCENSION

CARNAGE

FEATHERS AND FIRE SERIES

(Also set in the TempleVerse)

by Shayne Silvers

UNCHAINED

RAGE

WHISPERS

ANGEL'S ROAR

MOTHERLUCKER (Novella #4.5 in the 'LAST CALL' anthology)

SINNER

BLACK SHEEP

GODLESS

ANGHELLIC

TRINITY (*coming 2020...*)

CHRONOLOGICAL ORDER: TEMPLEVERSE

FAIRY TALE (TEMPLE PREQUEL)

OBSIDIAN SON (TEMPLE 1)

BLOOD DEBTS (TEMPLE 2)

GRIMM (TEMPLE 3)

SILVER TONGUE (TEMPLE 4)

BEAST MASTER (TEMPLE 5)

BEERLYMPIAN (TEMPLE 5.5)

TINY GODS (TEMPLE 6)

DADDY DUTY (TEMPLE NOVELLA 6.5)

UNCHAINED (FEATHERS...1)

RAGE (FEATHERS...2)

WILD SIDE (TEMPLE 7)

WAR HAMMER (TEMPLE 8)

WHISPERS (FEATHERS...3)

COLLINS (PHANTOM 0)

WHISKEY GINGER (PHANTOM...1)

NINE SOULS (TEMPLE 9)

COSMOPOLITAN (PHANTOM...2)

ANGEL'S ROAR (FEATHERS...4)

MOTHERLUCKER (FEATHERS 4.5, PHANTOM 2.5)

OLD FASHIONED (PHANTOM...3)

HORSEMAN (TEMPLE 10)

DARK AND STORMY (PHANTOM...4)

MOSCOW MULE (PHANTOM...5)

SHADE OF DEVIL SERIES

(Not part of the TempleVerse)

by Shayne Silvers

Made in the USA
Coppell, TX
05 April 2022

76002966R00192